Praise for MY LEGENDARY GIRLFRIEND

'Full of belly-laughs and painfully acute observations'
Independent on Sunday

'If you like *Gregory's Girl* . . . then this novel has your name of it'
Sunday Times

'Hilarious debut'
Cosmopolitan

'Comic . . . fizzy. Here comes the male Bridget Jones'
Mirror

'A funny and frank account of a hopeless romantic'
The Times

'Wonderfully contagious, humorous and astute'
The Bookseller

'Can't help but win you over'
Company

'Gayle handles the tale impressively and in the almost-Biblically desolate Will, he has created a character who would cheer Holden Caulfield up'
GQ

'Bridget Jones for the boys'
Observer

'A fresh, funny debut for anyone with their roots in realism, but their souls desperately holding out for a movie life'
Birmingham Evening Post

Praise for MR COMMITMENT

'Something near to mid-period Woody Allan . . . a delicate blend of realism and whimsy . . . funny and clever . . . it's refreshing to find a male writer working in this genre'
Guardian

'*Men Are from Mars, Women Are from Venus* meets *Men Behaving Badly*'
Daily Telegraph

'Funny, sharply observed and right in tune with ageing adolescents clinging desperately to the wreckage of their youth. This is a winner'
Yorkshire Evening Post

'Told in an easy, chatty style . . . the lighter moments in *Mr Commitment* say more about what's wrong with the modern twenty-something male than any amount of earnest introspection ever could'
Express

'Unputdownable . . . coloured with cool, rueful wit'
She

'Would you swap your fridge full of beer and an eclectic record collection for trips to Ikea and a series of dull dinner parties? Would you hell!'
Pick of the Week, *Marie Claire*

'Gayle's book has the ability to touch the parts other books fail to reach . . . the funny bits will make you laugh out loud while the beautiful moments will make you remember all those you've loved before . . . Unmissable'
B Magazine

Praise for TURNING THIRTY

'Not just readable, fresh and witty but sophisticated in execution . . . funny but also poignant'
Independent on Sunday

'A lively take on growing older'
Guardian

'This is a warm, funny romantic comedy'
Daily Mail

'Mike Gayle has carved a whole new literary niche out of the male confessional novel. He's a publishing phenomenon'
Evening Standard

'Delightfully observant nostalgia . . . will strike a chord with both sexes'
She (Book of the Month)

'Mike Gayle manages to weave everything together with such a warm-the-cockles-of-your-heart manner that once you've finished reading *Turning Thirty* you want to turn right back to the beginning and start all over again. It's real life – but better than we know it'
B Magazine

'Funny and endearing . . . chuckle-on-the-bus readable'
Heat

Also by Mike Gayle

Turning Thirty

About the author

Previously an Agony Uncle, Mike Gayle is a freelance journalist who has contributed to a variety of magazines including *FHM*, *Sunday Times Style* and *Cosmopolitan*. He is the bestselling author of *My Legendary Girlfriend*, *Mr Commitment* and *Turning Thirty*.

Mr Commitment

Mike Gayle

HODDER

For Mum and Dad

Acknowledgements

Very, very special thanks for everything as always to Claire. Very special thanks for all their hard work to Phil Pride and all @ Hodder (brilliant job on the cover!), Agent on a Motorcycle, her assistant Euan Thorneycroft and all @ Curtis Brown, and my mate, Jackie Behan. Special thanks for help, advice and general nonsense to Helen Lamont, Fergus and Catherine 'Hello B' McDonnell. Special thanks for nice things said and done to Sid Cannon, Lisa Keogh, Emma Unsworth, Neil O'Sullivan, Sheila Goulding, the girl I spoke to on the Manchester to Birmingham train reading *MLG*, Pip, Lorna, Danuta Kean and Leah Hardy. Last but not least, second verse same as the first thanks to everyone I thanked last time round.

The music sounds better with all of you.

A long-forgotten conversation

Her: (Pause.) Do you love me?

Me: Of course I do.

Her: How much?

Me: I don't know . . . loads. To infinity and then some.

Her: (Contentedly.) Good.

Me: That's that sorted, then.

Her: (Playfully.) So what would you do if I ever split up with you?

Me: Are you going to do that?

Her: No.

Me: Then why are we talking about it?

Her: It's called conversation. People do it all the time.

Me: So let me get this straight, the question is what would I do if you hypothetically dumped me?

Her: Yes.

Me: Hypothetically nothing.

Her: Nothing?

Me: Well, as we're mad about each other it'd take me doing something pretty stupid for you to want to get rid of me. (Pause.) Like if I started biting my own toenails or something. I'd dump me if I started doing that.

Her: Do you always have to be so logical?

Me: (Laughs.) I'd be devastated. Destroyed. Dismantled. And other words beginning with 'D'.

1

Her: But what would you *do*?

Me: Do? (Pause.) I would do everything in my power to get you back.

Her: Like what?

Me: Climbing the highest mountain, crossing scorching deserts, fighting man-eating tigers – that sort of thing. Granted there aren't that many tigers, mountains or deserts in Muswell Hill. But you get my drift.

Her: What if the odds were impossible?

Me: Then I'd die trying.

Her: What if I told you I didn't love you any more?

Me: I wouldn't believe you.

Her: But you wouldn't ever give up trying?

Me: Nah. Some things you can't give up on, can you?

Her: Mr Duffy, you've answered every single question correctly.

Me: Great, so what do I win?

Her: Me.

Let's talk about us

'Have I missed something here?'

It was an ordinary Thursday evening in January – at least I thought so. I was round at my girlfriend Mel's flat and it was to her that I'd aimed my question, as for some unknown reason she'd just turned off the TV even though I'd quite clearly been watching it. What really wound me up, however, was the fact that she'd used the remote control to do it, adding insult to injury. It was an unofficial rule of ours that I looked after all TV channel-changing duties – in the same way that Mel got first grazing rights on the top layer of any box of chocolates that came into our possession. We'd arrived at these and various other rules through a process of trial and error over the course of our four-year relationship. These rules made me happy. I always knew where I stood. But when you abandon rules there's bound to be chaos, and right now what I had on my hands was a serious case of anarchy.

My obviously deranged beloved pursed her perfect full lips together and blew into the end of the remote haughtily as if she'd just battled the TV for my attention and won. *There's no need for you to be quite so pleased with yourself,* I thought. After all, it was only a repeat of *Star Trek* – the episode where Kirk and co. go back in time to earth in early 1920s America and Spock has to wear a woolly hat to cover his pointy ears. A young Joan Collins is in it, and Kirk, surprise, surprise, snogs her. I wasn't a Trekkie but I'd seen this episode a million times before and the more I thought about it the more irritated I became that Mel had curtailed my intergalactic viewing pleasure.

Mel, who had disappeared into her bedroom when I'd arrived at her Clapham flat, only to reappear an hour later and turn off the TV, was now looking at me intently as if studying some unknown creature under a microscope. Her face bore the look not of someone annoyed, or angry but intrigued. Even so, I signalled an internal green alert and continued to feel on edge. She stood up – still holding the remote control – and walked across the room to the table in the corner where a bottle of Chardonnay sat. She poured out two glasses of wine, put them on the coffee table, seated herself on my lap and kissed me.

Watching her carefully I began to wonder if she was trying to seduce me. Being seduced was a nice idea, but she really had no need to go to all this effort. When it came to Mel – who was beautiful in a wonderfully understated kind of way – Easy was indeed my first, last and middle name. *No, this isn't about seduction*, I decided. *This is about me doing something wrong*. There was something about this whole situation that had a suggestion of forgotten anniversary about it, only it wasn't our anniversary. Was it?

'It's not our anniversary,' I said unsteadily, attempting to add a dash of confidence to my voice. 'That's not until June eleventh.'

'The eighteenth actually.'

'Oh.'

She smiled and kissed me again.

'It's not your birthday, either . . . that's not until April sixth.'

'Nearly,' she smiled. 'The fifth.'

'Oh.'

She smiled and kissed me once more.

'It's not my birthday, is it?' I said, grasping at nothing. 'I can't be so crap that I've actually forgotten my own birthday, surely?'

'What are you like?' said Mel, laughing. 'Your birthday isn't until October the seventh.'

All out of commemorative occasions, I continued to rack my brains. Mel loved any excuse for a celebration. It was bound to be something strange like the anniversary of the first time we had a Chinese takeaway, or four years to the day since we first cooked for each other or . . .

'I've got it,' I said victoriously. 'It's the anniversary of the day I first told you I loved you.'

'It is?' said Mel quizzically. 'Are you sure?'

'I dunno,' I sighed and shrugged my shoulders. All I could remember about the day in question was that it had been the Friday Channel Four repeated the very first episode of *Cheers*. I'd been looking forward to the moment all week and then five minutes before it was about to begin, I'd felt a sudden urge to tell Mel about the intense emotional turmoil she was causing within my normally placid frame. Such was the sense of exhilaration caused by my outburst, that we ended up missing *Cheers* altogether. It was worth it though. Well worth it.

After some moments of quiet contemplation attempting to work out why Mel had turned off the TV, was sitting on my lap and acting so strangely, I resorted to basic questioning in order to try and find out what was wrong, carefully avoiding the question I really wanted to ask: 'Why have you turned off *Star Trek?*'

Like a panther of passion stalking her prey, she leaned forward and kissed me again, slowly, carefully and seductively. Maybe she was trying to seduce me after all.

'Can't a woman be nice to her boyfriend once in a while?' she purred.

'No . . . I mean . . . yes.' I looked at the TV forlornly. 'I mean if that's all it is.'

'I do have an agenda,' she replied whilst gaily fondling my ear lobes.

I knew it . . .

'So what is it?' I asked carefully.

'It's us.'

'Us?'

'Us,' she said calmly. 'Let's talk about us.'

I felt my whole frame sink heavily into the sofa. I'd suspected she was up to something and I was right. Mel had invited me round to her flat on a Thursday night under false pretences. I thought we were going to watch TV and order a Chinese takeaway (me: Chicken Kung Po; her: King Prawn Egg Foo Yung) and moan about our days at work because that's what we always did on Thursdays. But it wasn't to be. Now we were in this horrendous situation where she wanted to talk about 'Us' while all I wanted was to watch *Star Trek*.

Us.

There was never a good reason to talk about 'Us'. Talking about 'Us' always ended up as talking about 'me'. Mel would, metaphorically speaking, get out her list entitled 'Things that are wrong with Duffy: Part 1', and go through it item by item. I would of course nod and murmur in the right places and promise to reform, because generally speaking they were usually reasonable requests along the lines of 'Will you pick your clothes up off the floor?, 'How about washing out the bath sometimes?' and 'Why don't you look at me the way you used to when we first met?'

Us.

'Duffy?' Mel asked. 'How long have we been going out . . . together, that is?'

I knew the answer to her question but racked my brains for additional information in case this was a trick. 'Four wonderful years,' I ventured tentatively.

'Exactly,' she replied. Against my will my mind began to drift – right about now Spock would be heading to the hardware store to buy some chicken wire to aid his efforts to construct a primitive communicator out of a radio set. 'Four years is a long time, you know—'

I interrupted, even though it was very bad to interrupt. I didn't like where this was going at all. 'It's not that long. If you were a four-year-old child you wouldn't even have started going to school yet. You wouldn't be able to read or write but you could probably just about tie your shoelaces . . .'

'Duffy, don't drivel on, will you?' She glared at me, exasperated, then removed herself from my lap and rested her bottom on the arm of the sofa instead, with her stockinged feet on the cushion next to me. 'You know what I'm getting at.'

I shrugged silently, turning my whole body into a question mark.

'Do I have to spell it out?'

'No . . . yes . . . maybe.'

'Duffy, do you love me?'

'Is that all this is about?' I asked incredulously. 'You've got no worries there.' I was pleased that was all. Mel quite frequently asked me if I loved her. Sometimes I think she got a bit insecure about 'us' and needed a little reassurance from me which I was always pleased to give. I reached out and held her hand and whispered closely into her ear, 'I love you. I love you. I love you.'

She smiled, leaned forward to kiss me and whispered back, 'Then let's get married.'

My first impulse as the words rocketed around my skull, causing all manner of brain damage, was to run.

My second impulse (a little more subtle) was to hide.

My third impulse (admittedly far less subtle) was to run and hide.

Maybe my crap impulses were due to my being a Libran. I hoped so. A dismal astrological sign was a greater source of comfort than simple cowardice.

In the end I didn't run or hide, because that would've really annoyed her, so I went with the only other option available to me – to curl up into a ball and hope she didn't want to do too much damage.

'You want to get married?'

'I do,' she said, laughing.

'To me?'

'The one and only Ben Duffy.' She stood up from the sofa, and pulled the hem of her skirt up slightly before getting down on one knee on the carpet. 'I'm a modern woman, Duffy. Modern women don't have to wait to be asked any more.' She cleared her throat, knocked back a huge gulp of wine and held my hand. 'Will you Benjamin Dominic Duffy do me the honour of becoming my lawful wedded bloke, to have and to hold till death do us part?'

Till death do us part.

How did that ever get into the wedding ceremony? Prior to this moment it had been my fullest intention to live for as long as possible – where was the incentive now?

Till death do us part.

Why couldn't they have put in something less restrictive, like 'renewable on a four-year basis', or 'until either party gets bored' or, at worst, 'for the foreseeable future'?

Till death do us part.

That is what you call a long time.

'I thought you didn't believe in marriage,' I said, regaining my wits. 'Didn't you once call it "an outmoded concept created by a patriarchal society to keep women in their place"?' I was paraphrasing the contents of one of those late-night debates we'd had somewhere in year one. I always knew remembering that conversation would come in handy one day.

'Well, I changed my mind,' snapped Mel as if she considered this reason enough. 'Duffy, we're both twenty-eight. We aren't kids any more. I want to settle down . . . I don't mean that . . . I want to settle up . . . I want a proper life.'

Those perfect lips of hers were now pressed together once again, this time in confusion. This obviously wasn't the reaction she'd been expecting. I didn't understand where this had come from. I didn't understand at all. I studied her face to see if I could locate the answer there.

'Don't look at me like that,' said Mel sternly.

'Like what?' I protested.

'Like this.' She pulled a face which was both amusing and incredibly accurate. 'Like I'm a tinned food without a label. Like I've just dropped in from another planet. Like I'm acting like a "bloody woman".'

I adjusted my look accordingly.

'I know what I've said in the past about marriage. You don't need to remind me what I've said before. I know it doesn't make sense. But it's what I want, Duffy. You want me to be ashamed of wanting to be with you for the rest of my life, like it's some sort of weakness. I know I can live life on my own,

Duffy. I don't need to prove anything to anyone. But I don't want to live on my own. I want to live with you.'

Whilst carefully maintaining my nonjudgemental facial expression, I studied her face again, hoping for some sign that she was winding me up – that at some point she was practically going to wet herself laughing and say, 'Had you going there, didn't I?' I waited for this moment, but of course it didn't arrive because Mel was as serious as the *Nine o'Clock News*.

'Are you sure?' I asked timidly.

She nodded. 'Yes. Aren't you?'

'Yes,' I said instinctively. And then, 'No.' And then, 'What I mean is . . .'

She took another long sip from her wine and swallowed hard. 'What you mean is you're not sure.'

I hesitated cautiously, hoping to make certain 'not sure' was an acceptable response and not one that could and would be taken down and used as evidence against me. Once again I examined Mel's features for clues. There were none. The inner workings of Mel's mind were a total enigma to me. I'd often tried to get in there, in the attempt better to understand, but I could never bring all the strands together into a consistent book of law, because as far as I could work out she was making this stuff up as she went along.

Eventually I went with the 'not sure' option. 'It's just that . . . well . . . I just know that if we change things somewhere down the line you'll discover just how annoying I really am. This way we keep an air of mystery about ourselves.'

She set her wine glass down on the table in front of me with force and sat on the armchair opposite, with her arms crossed. 'Believe me, Duffy, there is no air of mystery. I've wiped sick off your chin, watched you cut your toenails and seen with my own eyes the animalistic way you devour bacon

10

and egg sandwiches. And I still love you. But that's not the point. The point is, do you love me enough to commit to me for the rest of your life? I want you to be truthful. I really don't want to put any pressure on you, but I have to tell you I can't wait for ever for you to make up your mind.'

Leaning forward on the sofa, with my head resting on my hands and my elbows resting on my knees, I tried desperately to find the words I wanted to use to express how I felt, but there were none. At least none that were anywhere near satisfactory. 'You're all that I want,' I said.

'And . . .'

'And that's it. Why do we have to get married? Can't we just . . .'

'Move in together?' She'd thought this one out. I was running to every escape route I could think of, only to discover she'd got there first. 'We've been together four years and we're not even living under the same roof, Duff. You know I've tried to talk to you about this more times than I care to remember but you've always avoided the issue. I even changed tactics. I stopped mentioning it, hoping that you'd suggest we move in together in your own time. But you never did. Now it's too late for temporary measures. It's too late to dip your toe in and check the water temperature. It's all or nothing. Now or never. So what do you want to do?'

I didn't answer and remained steeped in silence, half worrying about where this was going to end up, and bizarrely half worrying about what was going on with the crew of the *Enterprise.*

Mel stood up and began pacing the room nervously, sniffing back tears. 'You just don't want things to change, do you, Duffy?' she said, trying to remain controlled. 'You want everything to stay the same. Well, it can't.'

I still didn't respond. Instead I wondered whether if I'd

insisted on watching *Star Trek* any of this would be happening now. We would've had a row but nowhere near as destructive as what was going on here. Eventually, that is once the silence had become too uncomfortable even for me and the crew of the *Enterprise*, I said the only thing I could think of which was, 'I love you.' These words had always helped me out in the past, and now more than ever I needed them to work their magic. I needed them to stop this situation from getting out of hand.

'You can say that you love me, but do you mean it? I dare you. I dare you to show me that you love me.' Then she started crying. Or more accurately she started to try not to cry and failed abysmally. Each and every tear was a tear of resentment. She didn't want them shed for me. She didn't want them wasted.

Instinctively I wanted to put my arms around her and tell her everything was going to be all right, but I couldn't, because quite frighteningly, for the first time since we started going out, I wasn't sure everything was. Without looking at me, Mel picked up the remote, switched the TV back on and disappeared to her bedroom. As the closing credits for *Star Trek* gradually appeared on the screen, I sighed and switched it off again.

If only I could

I'd been standing in front of the confectionery counter of the 7–11 on Clapham High Street for over ten minutes trying to make up my mind. A number of people had come and gone purchasing fags, newspapers, condoms and bread, while I'd remained hunched over the counter silently gazing at the various bars of chocolate. My argument with Mel had turned my brain inside out. Nothing was as it should be. Not even chocolate. I knew that I didn't want a Wispa, Turkish Delight, Snickers, Star Bar, Twix, Toffee Crisp, Crunchie, Bounty, Aero, Lion bar, Yorkie, Caramel or KitKat. That was the easy part. The hard part came now that I'd narrowed down the selection to either a pack of Revels or a Mars bar. One was an intriguing collection of handy-sized chocolate coated thingies and the other was packed to the hilt with glucose energy. They satisfied two very different parts of me and together they made my life complete. Never one to resist an extended metaphor when there was one going, I picked up the packet of Revels in my right hand – *this is independence and excitement.* I picked up the Mars bar in my left hand – *this is Mel, the first woman in my life to convince me to fall in love with her.*

'Oi, mate!' bellowed the stocky unshaven youth behind the counter, interrupting my confectionery cogitation. 'Are you gonna buy those?'

'What?' I said, gradually returning to Planet Earth.

'You've been standing there for the last ten minutes staring at that chocolate in your hands,' he said, rapping several gold sovereign ringed fingers on the counter. 'Now are you buying 'em or weighing 'em?'

'I was just trying to work out which one I wanted,' I explained feebly. 'It's a hard decision to make, you know.'

'Not any more it isn't,' he said forcefully. 'Those chocolate bars have been in your hands so long now they'll have melted to mush. No, mate, you're not leaving this shop unless you buy 'em both.'

'If only I could,' I said under my breath. I handed him a pound coin, waited for the change and headed towards the door.

'Oi, mate!' he called after me. 'You've left your chocolate!'

'I know,' I sighed. 'You can keep them. I can't make my mind up, mate. So you know what? I think I'm just going to go home and have some toast instead.'

My journey up the Northern Line from Clapham Common to Highgate flew by, occupied as I was with thoughts about The Proposal. Mel and I had been together so long it was impossible for me to imagine life without her, but that was no excuse to tempt fate – to wave a metaphorical two fingers in the direction of erudition. *Like the saying goes*, I told myself, *'if it ain't broke don't fix it.'* But maybe things were broken and I just didn't see it. Mel had after all brought the subject of our living arrangements up more times than I could remember, and I'd always avoided it, reasoning that if we didn't live together we couldn't discover that we didn't like living together. Because it's usually when people discover they don't like living together that they split up, and

I didn't want us to do that. Granted it was a twisted kind of logic, but it was logic all the same. But maybe now was the time to give it some serious thought.

Most women would've given up on me years ago. I knew this and was under no illusions who this partnership would benefit most. Mel lived on her own in a big flat in a well-spoken part of Clapham, while I shared an all-right-if-you-don't-mind-damp-in-the-kitchen flat in Muswell Hill with my friend Dan. Mel had an excellent career in advertising sales while I'd been temping for what felt like forever while I waited patiently (some might say a little too patiently) for my career as a stand-up comedian to take off.

Sometimes I really felt sorry for Mel – her life would've been so much better if she'd fallen in love with someone normal. Instead she fell in love with me and had been paying for that mistake ever since. Occasionally when feeling my lowest I'd imagine what it was like when she met up with her friends for an after-work drink. They'd all be talking about their partners' promotions, increased salaries and company cars, while Mel's sole contribution would be that I'd once (eight months ago to be exact) been paid forty-two pounds for a sketch I'd written about Richard Branson's beard for a satirical comedy show on Radio 4. At this point I always saw Mel's imaginary friends throwing her pitying glances that said, 'Ah, Mel and her bad luck with men.'

Actually Mel never complained once about any of this. In all the time we'd been together she'd never even hinted about me getting a real job and giving up comedy. In fact in a weird sort of way she was proud of me for sticking it out.

'It's one of the reasons I love you so much,' she once told me after a particularly traumatic gig in Manchester in which a good eighty per cent of my material went over the heads of the audience attending the Crumpsall Pensioners'

Association annual dinner and dance. 'I know one day you're going to make it. I just know it. I have faith in you.' Then she added, grinning, 'And when you do, I want a Ferrari.'

Sometimes it was hard to have that kind of faith in myself. In my head I was about as likely to give Mel a Ferrari as I would be to give her the remote control for the TV. It was never going to happen.

It was crap being bottom of the pile, begging promoters to put me on, watching comedians who I knew weren't anywhere near as talented as me become successful. It was soul destroying. But it was the success stories that kept me hanging on: stand-ups who, after spending fifteen years on the dole, had all their blood, sweat and beers vindicated by winning the Perrier Comedy Award at Edinburgh.

There was another side of the coin of course – the ones who no one ever talked about – the comedians who tried and failed miserably and as time moved on joined the real world and became teachers, accountants, bank clerks and builders. That was my real fear – joining the real world. Me and my flatmate Dan, who was also a stand-up, set ourselves a deadline once, that by the time we were thirty we would either have made it or moved on. Originally it was by the time we were twenty-eight, but as we'd never expected time to move half as fast as it had done, we'd given ourselves an extension. I didn't know about Dan, but I just didn't have it in myself to become an accountant.

In the end it took me nearly an hour to get back from Mel's. Seconds after leaving Goodge Street the Tube driver told everyone on the train that there'd been an incident at Warren Street and that we'd be stuck in a tunnel until he got further information. 'Further information', as it happens, didn't arrive for another twenty minutes, seconds after which, we moved off. What with the delay, my row with Mel and a sudden realisation that thanks to The Proposal I'd missed out on the Thursday night Chinese takeaway, my general antipathy towards the world was at an all-time high.

It was ten past eleven by the time I reached home. The flat was empty. I headed straight for the kitchen where there was a note from Dan on the fridge door saying he'd gone for a drink with someone called Natalie. I made a pint glass of Ribena and grabbed a loaf of bread from the bread bin. It was time to make toast.

I love toast. I really do. Toast is just about the best food there is. You take a slice of humble white bread (never brown) and you put it in a toaster (What is it? It's a toaster! What does it do? It makes toast!) and a few minutes later you have a hot nutritious meal. You can put any foodstuff handy from the fridge on top of it and it will pretty much always taste fan-bloody-tastic. *Toast*, I thought, as two slices popped up, *makes a whole lot more sense than chocolate bars*.

Moving into the lounge with three hot slices of Flora'd toast, so hot the toast sweat build-up on the plate was threatening to dampen the crispness of the whole affair, I pressed play on the answerphone. There was only one message, from my mum, in which she rattled on about how much she hated answerphones, and how she especially hated leaving messages on ours because she didn't know who Robert De Niro was. Puzzled, I played back the outgoing message and sure enough there was Dan's voice telling callers they'd got through to Robert De Niro, and to leave a message after the beep.

Looking at my watch I wondered if it was too late to call my mum. I decided that it was, but I currently felt so sorry for myself that I was in danger of calling Mel, so I phoned Mum anyway.

'Hi, Mum, it's me. Did I wake you up?'

'No, not at all. I was just listening to the radio. How are you, Ben?' My mum was the only person in the world who still called me Ben. 'Are you okay?'

'Fine,' I lied. 'You know.'

'You don't sound fine.'

'I'm fine, Mum, honest.' It was nice to be fussed over like this. To know that there was someone in the world who, no matter whether you were a convicted homicidal maniac, a porn baron or crack addict, would love you unconditionally.

We chatted about her life for a while. Since she'd retired as a 'catering assistant' (or dinner lady as she still called it) at St Mary's RC comprehensive for girls in Leeds, she'd been spending more and more time with my mad aunt Margaret. Since her husband had died Aunt Margaret had discovered a new lease of life and was constantly dragging Mum away on out-of-season holidays to places like Corfu and Ibiza. According to my mum their next jaunt was going to be Lesbos, which Aunt Margaret had described as 'the island where ladies who liked ladies lived'. Quite what my mother and my aunt were going in search of I don't know, but their curiosity was sufficiently piqued for them to book two weeks there in the middle of May.

'You'll have a great time,' I said. 'You could do with a holiday.'

'If anyone could do with a holiday it's you and Mel,' replied Mum sternly. 'You two work too hard. You should try relaxing and enjoying yourself more, otherwise you'll become like all these London types who just work and work and don't do anything else. Take Mel on holiday, Ben – and that's an order.'

My mum thought Mel was the best thing that had ever happened to me and frequently told me so. The first time

18

I introduced them, five months after we'd started going out,
they'd got on so well that I almost got jealous. They had this
thing between them as if they could communicate with each
other by means unknown to me. For the most part it didn't
bother me, but occasionally I felt like I had my flies undone
and that they'd noticed but weren't telling me.

'I don't think we'll be going on holiday,' I said.

'Whyever not?' said Mum. 'If it's the money, I'm sure I can
give you some if you're a little bit short.'

'No, it's not the money,' I began. I suddenly felt the strange
urge to do something I'd not done since I was at secondary
school and was worried about a twenty-question geography
test on the Norwegian leather industry – I wanted to share a
problem with my mum. Actually, not just any problem – *the*
problem.

'Mel wants us to get married,' I found myself saying.
'She proposed to me tonight and it's taken me a bit by
surprise.'

'That's wonderful news!' exclaimed Mum. 'Mel's a lovely
girl. I always said she was the one for you. To tell you the
truth I can't believe it's taken the two of you this long to get
it together.'

'But that's just it,' I said despondently. 'I'm not sure I want
to get married. You're right, Mel is an incredible person, but
I'm only twenty-eight. I'm not sure I'm ready for all that . . .
you know . . . marriage stuff.'

'Don't be so silly,' she responded, gearing up into no-
nonsense maternal mode. 'Of course you're ready. You love
her; she loves you. You've been together four years as it is.
What more do you need to know?'

I stopped and thought for a moment. It was a good question.

What more do I need to know?

'I haven't the faintest clue,' I said after some reflection. 'But whatever it is I can tell you now I don't know it.'

Mum refused to let the subject drop for the rest of the phone call in the hope that somehow I might just give in. Perhaps it hadn't been the best idea telling her about the ins and outs of my love life after all. I gave her five minutes to reprimand me and then I told her I had to go. She rounded things off with a reasonably chirpy, 'I'm not trying to organise your life, Ben. I just want you to be happy,' and we said our goodbyes.

Putting the phone down, I hunted for my toast. It was cold now and had gone soggy from toast sweat. While I munched on a slice I took a moment to consider my mum. She must hold the world record for being the world's most optimistic mother. How could one person be that happy after what she'd been through?

I'd never met my dad. He left us when I was six months old and Vernie was two and a half, and divorced my mum five years later. Mum rarely talked about the reasons why he left, and neither Vernie nor I ever asked because we knew it would upset her. All I'd managed to glean in twenty-eight years was that they hadn't been getting on, and that he left two years and ten months after they'd got married.

You would've thought that my mum of all people would be able to see that marriage was a ridiculous idea at the best of times, but she had gone totally the opposite way. She believed in marriage with a strength and a vigour that I've never seen equalled. When Vernie married her long-term boyfriend Charlie four years ago, Mum was overjoyed. I just didn't get it. My dad had promised to be with her for richer for poorer, in sickness and in health, and he'd still felt able to leave her with no money and two kids to raise. Yet here she was, after all this time, still believing it possible for two people to love each other for ever. Now that is what you call faith.

Cosmopolitan is a Ouija board

'Hi, Mel. It's me, Duffy. I left a message on your answerphone yesterday. And the day before that, and the day before that and the day before that and the day before that. I just wanted to say that I'm sorry. And that I'm stupid, but I suppose you already know that. 'Bye.'

It was now Tuesday and five days had gone by since I'd last seen Mel. She was refusing to acknowledge my existence via any of the methods of communication at her disposal – telephone/fax/mobile/carrier pigeon/e-mail/doorbell. My days at work were now spent moping around the office. I couldn't think straight at all and was so depressed that I was taking a toilet break every half hour, which when combined with fag breaks and the mid-afternoon snack runs I'd started volunteering for, meant I got little or nothing done. Not that anyone noticed of course. I'd been in this particular temping job, inputting data for DAB, a market research company, for over three years now. Admittedly, it was a long time for any one person to temp in any one job, but according to the powers that be, it made more sense financially for the personnel officer at DAB to reserve the right to drop me at a second's notice than to employ me full-time. This arrangement suited me fine because in return I reserved the right to tell them what to do with their ridiculously pointless job the moment I got enough stand-up work to make a decent living. Perfect symbiosis.

Having just left yet another message on Mel's home answerphone, I decided it was time to take a look at The Proposal from a different perspective. Sneaking past Bridget on reception (a woman who thought gossiping to management about the lives of temps was a fundamental human right), I escaped to the lift and descended into the bowels of the building, to the newsagent-cum-sandwich-shop in the basement. Bathed in the harsh white glare of strip lighting, I stood staring at the rows of glossy women's magazines, all with unfeasibly beautiful women on the cover airbrushed to perfection.

Mel read these sorts of magazines religiously. Within their pages was a world of wisdom and advice that was completely alien to me. Mel understood these magazines and they understood her. *I'm fed up with being on the outside looking in,* I thought, scanning the shelves. *I'm tired of not knowing what's going on with my own girlfriend.*

I picked up *New Woman* and flicked through it, and then I picked up *19* and then *Company* and continued plucking titles off the shelves until I'd amassed a pile on the counter that left me with twenty-nine pence change from a twenty-pound note. Sneaking past Checkpoint Bridget (thankfully she was on the phone discussing the previous night's *Coronation Street* so I didn't have to explain my reading material) I returned to my workstation and hid the magazines in the bottom drawer of my desk which I normally reserved for sandwiches, my ball of rubber bands and stapler collection.

As soon as the coast was clear I sneaked out the first of the magazines, *Cosmopolitan*, and began to execute my plan. With my tongue firmly lodged in my cheek I'd managed to convince myself that if I directly asked these magazines the questions that I wanted to know – like a Ouija board only more scary – they would somehow provide me with the answers I so longed for.

Checking the coast was clear of snoopers and eavesdroppers I closed my eyes, spread my palms over the magazine and its free astrological supplement and in a deep ominous voice whispered, 'Oh, mighty *Cosmopolitan*. You speak for young go-getting women the world over. I have some questions for you:

1) Why, after four years, does Mel suddenly want to get married?
2) Why does Mel insist on holding conversations in the middle of my favourite TV programmes?
3) What is this season's hem length going to be?'

I was chuckling so dementedly by the time I got to the third question that Scottish Helen, a fellow temp who sat in the workstation opposite me, stared at me open mouthed as if I'd well and truly lost my mind (which in a way I suppose I had). 'What are you doing?' she asked peering over her computer.

'*Cosmopolitan* is a Ouija board,' I deadpanned, 'and I'm asking it questions about women.'

'Oh, that's nice,' said Helen, who had, in the three months that I had known her, come to accept my erratic behaviour more or less without question. 'Can I borrow it when you're finished?'

'No problem,' I said. 'Just give me a moment.'

That 'moment' lasted an hour and a half. By the time I'd finished looking through it and the other magazines it was time to go home, so I put them on a neat pile on Helen's desk and left. Needless to say I didn't discover the answers to questions one or two, but what I didn't know about the current season's hem length really wasn't worth knowing.

With no answers forthcoming from the world of women's magazines, I decided it was time to get a little sisterly advice on the matter. Vernie was two and a bit years older than me and had always been the bossy one in our family. Growing up in a single-parent family, my sister took up the mantle of the man of the house as soon as she was able. Many a time at primary school, having smart-mouthed the school bully once too often, I'd be suffering painful torture at his hands only to have my sister bound across the playground and pummel my assailant within an inch of his life, earning herself the sobriquet Muhammad Duffy.

Years later little had changed. Vernie might not have physically assaulted anyone in the last two decades, but she could still administer the kind of tongue-lashing most people never forgot. Charlie, her husband, was a much mellower character. He was the Yin to her Yang and together they made each other normal. Charlie really was great. He was laidback in a way that made me envious, and yet wise in a way that wasn't obvious. Like me he enjoyed the simple things in life: the love of a good woman, evenings in the pub talking about nothing in particular, and football. So when Charlie and Vernie moved from Derby to London and ended up in a huge house in nearby Crouch End, it was only a matter of time before he became mine and Dan's top mate, drinking buddy and third musketeer.

'What's wrong?' said Vernie, as soon as she opened her front door. 'You look like a right misery.'

'I dunno,' I said, watching my breath rise up into the cold night sky. 'I know that's a bit lame but I really don't know what's wrong.'

'You'd better come in,' she said, and I followed her into the kitchen where she made a cup of tea and handed me a can of Lilt and a glass filled with ice cubes.

We moved into the lounge, and while she told me about her day at work in great detail (she was a system analyst for a large computing firm in the City), I sucked ice cubes noisily and looked out of the bay window wondering what Mel was doing right now. After some minutes of this, it became obvious to Vernie that I hadn't been listening to a single word she'd been saying.

'Okay, let's talk about you!' she said, throwing an embroidered cushion at my head in mock anger. 'That's what you're here for, isn't it? You're so self-obsessed sometimes it's frightening.' She paused and looked at me. 'It's Mel, isn't it?'

I nodded.

'You've had a row because she's fed up waiting for you to agree to move in together.'

'Nearly, but not quite.'

Vernie raised her eyebrows. 'She asked the big question?'

I nodded again. 'How do you know we've had a row? Have you spoken to her, then?'

'No.' Vernie rolled her eyes, signalling my dense stupidity. 'And I'm not psychic either. Duff, this has been on the cards for a long time.'

'That's what she said as well,' I said, kicking off my shoes.

'You don't sound convinced,' said Vernie.

'I don't get it,' I sighed. 'If even you know, how come it was news to me?'

Vernie shook her head and issued the universal sound for stupidity: 'Doh! It would be news to you, Duffy. And do you know why? Because everything is news to you.' Over the next fifteen minutes she gave me one of her many extended lectures on life, love and the stuff in between. This one was about how men didn't pay attention to the small things in life because they didn't think small things were important, when in truth small things are everything. She concluded her speech with the accusatory flourish: 'You bumble about in your own selfish worlds completely oblivious to the things that really upset us and then wonder what it is you've done wrong.'

I concluded from the length, pace and formidable sense of personal frustration in her speech, that Charlie had done something to wind her up and that her words were meant more for her absent partner than for me. Revealing an impeccable sense of timing, this was exactly the moment Charlie chose to come through the front door after his day working in the town planning department of Westminster Council.

'All right, mate?' he called out as he entered the room, dropping his briefcase on the floor and kicking off his shoes.

'Yeah. Not too bad,' I replied, looking at Vernie, who was in turn glowering at Charlie's recently abandoned shoes.

Charlie immediately picked up on the bad vibes that were issuing forth from his wife like a laser beam, tidied away his shoes and briefcase, walked over to the sofa and attempted to kiss Vernie hello. He failed. She glared at him, put her mug of tea down firmly on the coffee table that she never lets anyone put anything down on without a coaster, and in one smooth movement huffed her way out of the room slamming the door behind her.

Charlie tutted quietly to himself and sat down.

'What've you done?' I asked as Vernie banged her way loudly up the stairs. 'Murdered someone? Forgotten her birthday? Started wearing her underwear again?'

'Long story,' said Charlie, which was coded Charlie-speak

for 'Let's talk about something else.' He took off his suit jacket and slumped on to the sofa with his feet up on the coffee table. 'Just visiting, were you?'

'No,' I said flatly. 'Woman trouble.'

'Oh,' was Charlie's disdainful reply. 'You too. Which kind?'

'The kind where Mel wants to get married.'

'Oh.'

'Oh indeed.' I stopped and mulled over a thought for a minute. Here I was sitting with a married man. Someone from my team who had made The Big Decision and lived to tell the tale. Surely he could give me some advice. 'What was it that made you get married, Charlie?'

He frowned and loosened his tie. 'Hang on a sec.' He disappeared out of the room for a few moments and returned with a can of Coke. 'Where were we?'

'You were telling me why you got married.'

'You want the truth?'

'No,' I said. 'I was after complete and utter lies but the truth will do.'

He ignored my attempt at biting sarcasm and took a sip of his drink. 'I knew she was the one,' he said matter-of-factly, as if love was an equation to which he'd worked out the solution. The scientific edge to his voice I'm sure was for my benefit. 'Yes,' it said, 'we are talking about emotions but in a logical non-soppy way, so it doesn't count.' 'She was the right one for me. Simple as that.' He drained the can in four huge gulps and set it on the table next to Vernie's half drunk tea.

'Is that all it takes?'

'That's all it took for me. But you know. Different strokes and all that.'

'Yeah, I suppose,' I said despondently. 'Thing is . . .' I stopped and attempted to add Charlie's logical tone to my voice. 'Thing is I love Mel. I don't want anyone else. So why is this marriage thing freaking me out so much?'

Charlie shrugged his shoulders. 'Only you know that, mate.' He picked up the TV remote control from the coffee table and started browsing through the channels systematically – thirty seconds and then he'd move on.

'How did you ask Vernie to marry you?' I asked, as BBC2 was turning into ITV. 'Did you do something special or did you just come out with it?'

Charlie just raised his eyebrows warily as if his refusal to answer was down to the Official Secrets Act rather than embarrassment. 'I forget now. It was a long time ago.'

It was actually four years ago and Charlie hadn't forgotten, he just didn't want to tell me. Fortunately, I already knew and was just pulling his plonker for the sheer pleasure of it. The manner of his proposal was meant to be top secret, but I knew because Vernie had told Mel and Mel in turn had told me, saying, 'It's the most beautiful thing ever.' Apparently, Charlie had told Vernie he was taking her away for the weekend as a surprise. She was expecting somewhere like the Lake District at the very best, so she must have been ecstatic when they ended up in New York. On their first day in the Big Apple he took her to the top of the Empire State Building, and as she looked through the twenty-five cents telescope on to Central Park he put a piece of paper at the end of it with the words 'Will you marry me?' on it and she burst into tears and immediately said yes. At the time I was really surprised by this story, because anyone who knew Charlie well knew that big romantic gestures just weren't his thing.

'C'mon, Charlie,' I said smirking. 'I need some tips on what to do. Surely you can remember how you asked my sister to marry you?'

'I know you're trying to wind me up,' said Charlie, laughing, 'and it won't work. I'm not alone in my actions, because when it comes to stuff like this, every man has a poem in his heart.'

'It's a nice thought, but mine's bound to be more of a limerick,' I said, picking up my glass.

'Nah,' said Charlie, and for a moment I could've sworn that I saw a flash of his special brand of wisdom twinkle in his eyes. 'You've got a poem in your heart, mate. You've just got to find it. Okay, you get moments like this,' he glanced up at the ceiling pointedly, from where the sounds of Vernie stomping on the floorboards emanated. 'But you know . . . I wouldn't swap it for the world.'

I am not your mother!

It was late evening by the time I got back to the flat. The first thing I did was check the answerphone – no messages. The heartbreakingly pitiful message I'd left on Mel's answerphone had obviously failed to melt her heart. My flatmate Dan was lying across the sofa silently watching the *Nine o'Clock News*. 'All right mate?' I asked, sitting down in an armchair in the corner of the room.

'Yeah, I suppose,' he said despondently, his face half squashed into a cushion. 'Got something in the post today,' he pointed to an envelope on the floor in the middle of the room.

'What is it?'

'Read it and find out,' he said, his eyes still fixed on the television. 'Weirdness.'

I picked up the envelope. Inside was a wedding invitation on cream paper embossed with gold. I read it aloud. '"Meena Amos and Paul Midford would like to invite Daniel Carter and guest to their wedding . . ."' I stopped as it dawned on me what this all meant. 'Your ex-girlfriend is getting married?'

'Looks like it. I know him too. He was on my drama course at Manchester Uni. I've seen him on *The Bill* and *Casualty* a few times. Talentless git. Never liked him. Wouldn't know Ibsen from his arse, that one.'

'Why is Meena inviting you to her wedding?'

Dan shrugged and changed channels.

'I mean it's not exactly like you finished on anything vaguely like good terms is it?'

'Precisely,' said Dan. 'Like I said before, this is pure weirdness.'

'And anyway, isn't it a bit early to be sending out invitations, it says here she's not getting married until September.'

'I know. She always did like to plan ahead.

Meena was the last woman in Dan's life to have fitted the description of 'Girlfriend'. They'd met at university and up until a year ago had lived together in the flat which I now shared with Dan. Back then Meena used to terrify me every time I met her. She was a complete maniac when her back was up and towards the end of her and Dan's relationship her back was permanently in the arched position, teeth bared, claws out and hissing wildly. I couldn't blame her really. As far as I could work out, since they'd moved in together Dan had begun some sort of mission to see just how far he could push his luck. The day they split up was the day that he found out.

At the time Dan was working part-time as a security guard in between stand-up gigs while Meena worked as a set designer for a theatre in East London. On the day in question I'd been round at their flat with Dan, trying to think up less soul-destroying ways of making money than temp work. What I didn't know was that he'd promised Meena that very morning that he'd tidy up the flat because her parents were coming to stay. So when she came home early from work to discover a sink full of washing-up, me asleep on the sofa and Dan watching *Countdown*, she well and truly lost it.

Now Dan might be a lot of things, but he wasn't so stupid that he couldn't see this coming. Although he never admitted to it, it was my belief that this was his way of forcing the issue and letting Meena know that he didn't want to live with her any more. My guess was that he wanted his old life back and he wanted it back now. I think he was banking on my presence in the flat tempering Meena's outburst, thus making the transition from relationship to non-relationship as trauma free an experience as possible. Best-laid plans of mice and men and all that. It was not to be.

'It's not you, it's me,' explained Dan, after a five-minute dressing down in which Meena not only failed to hold back for fear of embarrassing me, but also revealed some information about Dan's sub-duvet activities that I think both of us wished she'd kept to herself.

'Of course it's you,' said Meena defiantly. 'There's only room for one selfish, self-centred, egotistical, monomaniac, commitment-phobic bath-dodger in this relationship, and that's you.'

'Bath dodger?'

'Bath dodger.'

'Who are you calling a bath-dodger?'

'You, you filthy dirty bath-dodger!'

'I had a bath,' protested Dan.

'When did you have a bath?' She reached into her handbag, took out her pocket diary and read from it. '"Tuesday fourteenth, Dan has not had a bath. Wednesday fifteenth, still no Dan bath." Do I need to carry on?'

'You've been keeping a note of how often I wash?' said Dan incredulously.

'Yes,' she snapped. 'I've also got documentary evidence to the fact that you haven't touched the vacuum cleaner in three months, you've not washed the bathroom sink in weeks and . . .' she checked her diary for this one . . . 'right now you're wearing a pair of boxer shorts that you've had on for two days in a row.'

'Two days?' Dan, much to his shame had no answer to this one. 'Time flies, eh?' And then he said something that took me completely by surprise. 'Listen, Meena,' he said, 'I'm sorry. I can change.'

'Pants or personality?'

'Personality,' he said sheepishly.

This was very un-Dan. Very uncool. He normally had his goodbye speeches down pat, a throwback to his days at drama college. He was wavering. I think he was unsure if he really did want to split up with Meena or whether now he'd finally realised that if he pushed hard enough Meena would eventually push back, he wanted her more than ever. But it was too late and he knew that.

'Dan, you'll never change,' spat Meena furiously. 'You are you and that's all there is to it. You leave everything to me and expect me to run around after you like you're some sort of naughty schoolboy. I am not your mother! We've been together since we left college six years ago. We've been living together for just five months of those six years and it seems to me that as soon as we moved in you gave up on us. You used to be so sweet, Dan, you used to try and impress me . . . you even used to take a shower every day when we first met! What happened? Why did you give up? I'll tell you why. You gave up because you're lazy and selfish and think that I was put on this earth to please you. Well, I wasn't, okay? It's over, Dan. We're finished.'

Dan didn't say a word. It was almost like he was in a trance, trapped in his subconscious weighing up the current situation on his internal scales of justice. On the one side was his pride, and on the other his love for Meena. Whatever the result, in the end he decided to bale out – to try and save what was left of his dignity.

'Hang on,' said Dan regaining his confidence. 'You're leaving me? I'm the one who said, "It's not you, it's me." I'm leaving you, okay?'

'You're damned right you're leaving me,' said Meena. 'I spent months looking for this flat to rent and I want you out of it now!'

'Now?'

'No, yesterday.' She pointed to the door. 'I want you to find yourself a time machine like Michael J. Fox in *Back To The Future*, I want you to climb into it, switch on the controls and erase yourself from my history.'

His newfound confidence began to falter. 'But where will I go?'

'I don't care, but whichever stone you crawl under, you can take that one with you!' She pointed at me. It was the first time Meena had addressed me directly in months. She usually refused to acknowledge my existence in the hope I'd somehow dissipate, like an embarrassing fart from an elderly relative.

'It's not enough that you assassinate my character, now you're having a go at my mates?' said Dan in my defence – although strictly speaking it wasn't in my defence, he was just trying to score points now. 'I thought you said you liked Duffy.'

'Is there no limit to your feeblemindedness?' she said, as if addressing a mischievous five-year-old. 'I can't stand Duffy. He eats our food. Watches our TV. Uses our telephone.' I momentarily contemplated some sort of financial offering to make amends for the phone abuse, but all I had in my pockets was a twenty pence piece and a Blockbusters video card. 'I want you,' she pointed at me again, 'and I want you,' she pointed at him, 'out now!'

'Well, I'm not going.' Dan crossed his arms defiantly. 'This is my flat as much as it is yours. So if you want me out of your life so badly, you'd better start packing.'

That was then. Before I moved in Dan and I were just equally non-achieving mates from the comedy circuit, but after twelve months together we were so similar it was scary. We liked the same films, TV, music and sitcoms. The only thing we differed on was relationships. While I had the steadiest of steady girlfriends, after Meena, Dan became a subscriber to what he called the Doner Kebab Theory of Women – 'A nice idea on a post-pub Friday night but not the sort of thing you want on the pillow when you wake up next day.' I couldn't help but think that it was all an act to stop himself from getting hurt again, but as acts go it was remarkably convincing.

Dan didn't seem to want to talk about Meena for the minute, so leaving the wedding invitation open on top of the bookcase next to my seat I disappeared to the kitchen and emptied the remains of a three-day-old jar of Ragu over a bowl of cold pasta and shoved it into the microwave. I watched impatiently as the bowl rotated in the oven, and thought about the wedding invitation. Meena was clearly rubbing it in – letting him know that she'd moved on and he hadn't. Hell indeed had no fury like a woman scorned.

Scratching his stomach absentmindedly Dan came into the kitchen, opened the fridge door and peered in. 'There's nothing to eat,' he said, rooting about. 'Can I have that cheese you bought last week?'

'No problem.' I threw a packet of cream crackers at him.

'Have these as well.' I returned to staring at the microwave waiting for the ping. 'Does it bother you that Meena's getting married?'

'No,' said Dan a little too quickly and then changed subjects. 'What kind of cheese is this?'

'Dunno,' I said. 'Cheddar I think.' Dan didn't want to talk about Meena and her impending nuptials when there were clearly more pressing topics to discuss like cheese. I didn't blame him. He wasn't made of stone, but it was pointless talking about something that he had no control over. He'd do his grieving in private and if he needed me to accompany him on an evening of Drinking and Forgetting down our local, the Haversham Arms, then accompany him I would.

After what felt like a decade the microwave pinged and I made my way back to the living room with my steaming bowl of pasta. As Dan flicked between the weather report on BBC1 and a documentary on Channel Four about burglars in Leeds, I wondered if I should collect his opinion on The Proposal to add to those of Vernie, Charlie and my mother.

'So that's why you've been moping round the flat like a lovesick teenager,' he said after I filled him in on the details of The Proposal. 'You told me she'd gone on a course for work.'

'Yeah, well, I lied,' I confessed. 'The thing is, what do I do now?'

'I'll tell you what to do,' he said, switching channels with the remote. '*Do* nothing. Take it from me, there's no way she's going to dump you just because you don't want to get married. You've been with her what . . . three years?'

'Four years,' I admitted.

'Four years! You're practically Mr and Mrs anyway. My advice – keep your head down and wait for it all to blow over.'

I liked the sound of that. 'Pretend it didn't happen?'

'Exactly. Head in the sand, mate. It was most likely just one of those moments that's best forgotten. She's probably embarrassed she even mentioned it to you. I bet you that's why she hasn't called.'

I gave his advice the consideration it deserved. Ignoring this whole thing in the hope that it might go away was an extremely attractive proposition – neither of us had to lose face and we could go on with life as it was before.

'Are you sure?' I asked.

'Of course I'm sure,' he said confidently. 'Listen, Duffy, it's like this: Mel's invested three—'

'Four,' I corrected.

'All right, four years of her life with you. She's got you pretty much well trained. Think how long it would take her to get another bloke to your level of obedience.'

'So you're saying she's not going to dump me because she's too lazy to train someone else?'

'Sort of.'

'Thing is . . .' I began.

'Don't tell me that you're actually considering getting married.' Dan shook his head in disbelief. 'Have I taught you nothing? Did I not teach you The Ways of The Bachelor? And now you want to go over to the dark side? I can't believe you. I forgave you for that regular girlfriend thing because, well, it was quaint. But getting married? This is definitely one of your worst ideas. It'll be the end of life as you know it. Everything changes.' He looked over at Meena's invitation on the bookcase. 'Me and Meena would've ended up getting married. Now what kind of mistake would that have been?'

Dan was depressing me beyond belief. 'Cheers, Yoda,' I said curtly. 'I'll sort it out myself.'

I stood up, picked up the remote control from the arm

of the sofa Dan was sitting on, and returned to my seat, flicking through the channels erratically while I shovelled huge forkfuls of my now cold pasta dinner into my mouth.

This was the closest Dan and I had ever come to an argument. He must have felt bad about it too, because he left the room and returned minutes later with a maxi pack of Skips and two cans of Red Stripe as a peace offering. Tearing open the bag he placed it carefully on the carpet between us and handed me a Red Stripe while he searched for the video remote control. 'Forget the crappy pasta and forget Mel for the minute. Eat Skips, drink beer, watch telly and stop thinking,' he said sagely. 'Thinking isn't good for either of us.'

Even Nosferatu seemed to be smiling

It was now nine days since I'd last seen or heard from Mel. The advice of my mum, sister, brother-in-law and flatmate had been rattling around my head for days without having any effect on me other than giving me a headache. I couldn't escape the feeling that at the age of twenty-eight the answer to my predicament really should've come from inside me and not from friends and relatives. Which is why, I decided, that even though I still wasn't sure how I felt about marriage, it was time for Mel and me to talk and come up with a solution that we could both live with.

'Oh, it's you.'

It was Julie who answered the door to Mel's flat. She was the only person in the world who could make 'Oh, it's you' sound like 'Burn in hell, you unfortunate bag of crap.' It was a bad sign that she'd taken over door-answering duties, because it meant without question that she'd been spending every second since The Proposal at Mel's, rubbishing my good name.

Julie – whom I referred to in private as Nosferatu, Princess of Darkness, for no other reason than it made me laugh – was Mel's best friend and my arch enemy. The first time I met her I was incredibly nervous, because Mel had told me that if I could pass the Julie Test, then meeting her parents would be a piece of cake. Over poached oysters with iceberg

43

butter sauce at Julie's house, I watched her mentally ticking off the points against me as I revealed I was a temp (-4), had dropped out of university (-2), was constantly broke (-6), considered amusing people in the back room of a pub was a smart career move (-4) and was doing little to rectify any of my point-minusing situations (-10).

At the end of the evening it was clear to both me and Mel that I'd failed the Julie Test with a record-breakingly bad score. I remember thinking, *If my performance tonight is anything to go by, Mel's parents are really going to hate me*. Julie, however, loved Mel just like Thelma loved Louise, although without the lesbian subtext, and so for her sake she tolerated me as if I was a bad habit – like nailbiting or not washing your hands after you've used the toilet – that Mel just couldn't break.

Julie lived with and was engaged to Mark, who I quite liked but for the fact I was totally intimidated by his success. He made music videos for hideously famous bands, was always travelling to glamorous places, and to top it all was two years younger than me – which galled me immensely. Mark was one of life's doers. While I'd been drinking cider in the park and chasing girls who didn't know better, as a teenager he'd been writing and shooting short films on a Super 8 camera. We had no common ground whatsoever. Occasionally when we all went out together he'd try and draw me into a conversation about high-performance sports cars, trekking holidays in China or his latest music video, and every time without fail I'd just look at him vacantly, desperately hoping that at some point he would ask me what was going on in *EastEnders* so that I'd have something to contribute to the conversation.

Together, Mark and Julie were couple perfection at its Dyson-owning-two-newspapers-on-a-Sunday-his-'n'-hers-

Birkenstocks-three-foreign-holidays-a-year-and-smug-about-it worst. But there was no escaping them because we 'double coupled' all the time, usually at Julie's insistence. I never understood why she stipulated that we did so many things together. It was as if because she and Mark were a couple they were only allowed to socialise with other couples for fear of catching single-people disease.

'All right, Jules?' I said chirpily. Julie loathed being called Jules more than anything. 'Are you going to let me in or what?'

Guardedly Julie opened the door to the communal hallway of the house and let me in, but I could tell she was in two minds about whether to do so. 'What do *you* want?'

'I've just popped round to hear what you think's wrong with me this week.'

'How long have you got?' she snorted, flicking a stray strand of strawberry blonde hair out of her eyes.

'As long as you want,' I said grimacing.

She let me in and we squared up to each other in the hallway like two gunfighters at the OK Corral. As I stared deeply into her defiant pale blue eyes. I was reminded of something I'd read once in a magazine. Apparently when two animals hold each other's direct gaze for longer than a minute, the laws of nature state they will either tear each other to pieces or copulate. The thought of having carnal knowledge of Julie unsettled me so much that I began to smile nervously.

'Well, for starters,' said Julie, ignoring the grin fixed to my face, 'you're a selfish pig. You have no respect for Mel or her feelings.'

'And?'

'You're inconsiderate.'

'And?'

45

'You do that hateful thing where you roll your eyes.'

'And?'

'You put everything else that's in your life before Mel.'

'Errrrrrrrr!' I made the annoying quiz-buzzer-type noise from *Just a Minute* on Radio 4. 'Repetition. I think you'll find putting everything that's in my life before Mel is the same as being selfish.'

Julie scowled threateningly. She was officially angry now, which in an incredibly petty sort of way made me happy. 'You *would* say that you—'

'You don't know anything about me, Julie,' I interrupted. 'You just think you do. I do respect Mel and her feelings, I don't put everything that's in my life before her . . .' I paused briefly. 'But I admit I do occasionally leave the toilet seat up, which might be interpreted as inconsiderate, and I definitely do that thing when I roll my eyes, but that doesn't exactly make me Darth Vader in a pair of Levis, does it?'

Julie screwed up her face angrily like a bulldog chewing a wasp. 'I don't know what she ever saw in you . . .' she began furiously, but then her voice trailed off. *Pants*, I thought nervously. *If she's not going to tear me to pieces maybe she is going to have sex with me after all*. Fortunately I soon discovered what had stopped her outburst so abruptly. It was Mel.

'Oh, please, you two,' sighed Mel. 'Can't you ever just give it a rest?'

Like a petulant child Julie threw a thunderous 'It was all his fault' glance in my direction while I cranked my ever-so-angelic smile up in the hope it would make Julie melt, or combust, or whatever it is that vampires do when they've been defeated.

Mel was wearing her it's-Saturday-therefore-I-shop clothes – jeans, white T-shirt and a long thick woollen hooded top.

She'd had a haircut, too, and it made her face look that little bit more beautiful. I resisted a genuine compulsion to tell her that she looked stunning, because I knew she'd only think I was trying to flatter her. So instead I smiled warmly, hoping that the upward curling of the corners of my lips would somehow convey my keen appreciation. Mel didn't return my smile, though. Her expression revealed neither approval nor disapproval of my appearance in her hallway, although the manner in which she sat wearily on the bottom stair was a strong indicator that I was far from being back in favour.

'How are you?' she said abruptly.

'Okay,' I mumbled. 'How are you?'

Silence.

'How's work?'

Silence.

I hated arguments like this. I wanted her to stop being angry with me. 'I love you, you know,' I said, kneeling down in front of her.

'So you say.' She took off her jacket. 'Is that all you came to tell me?'

I looked into her eyes, trying to find the real her. The Mel sitting in front of me was Hard Mel, an alter ego she sometimes utilised to stop herself from forgiving me when she knew she really shouldn't. It was true that she was too forgiving and perhaps I did deserve the harsh treatment I was receiving, but even so, I thought this was a bit much. The offence of Not Knowing When To Marry Your Long-term Girlfriend was new legislation and I felt quite strongly that the marathon begging, shuffling and scraping I'd done in the past week was more than recompense.

So I waited, saying nothing. The silence was so uncomfortable even Julie felt the need to disappear upstairs to Mel's flat on the pretext of getting a glass of water. The longer I said nothing, the more Hard Mel stared through me like I didn't exist. Soon whatever regret I had about the way I'd treated Mel was swallowed up whole by resentment. What I'd done wrong was no longer the point. It wasn't about apology, making up or explanation. All that counted now was winning.

'This is pointless,' I sighed. 'You're not in the right mood to talk. Okay. I'll come back later.'

1–0

In a single swoop I'd claimed the moral high ground, belittled her feelings and made myself out to be the last remaining reasonable person left on Planet Earth.

'You can't stand being wrong, can you?' retorted Mel. 'You're not man enough to admit when you've made a mistake.'

1–1

The moral high ground that I craved so highly was all Mel's. She'd pinpointed my insecurities and cast slurs upon my masculinity. I was in great danger of looking stupid.

'Whatever,' I sighed exasperatedly, *2–1* argument short-hand for 'I'm pretending that I can't be bothered to argue with you.' *I'm bound to win now*, I thought spitefully, and then Mel started to cry.

Game over.

This wasn't fair at all. 'Whatever' wasn't a phrase worthy of tears. Mel had cheated by using the crying card when I hadn't even provoked it. Most of our big arguments ended with tears. She'd say something horrible. I'd say something equally horrible. She'd cry. And I'd feel guilty. Tears were the secret weapon from which I had no defence. *One day*, I decided, *I'm going to get into an argument with Mel and burst into tears before she does, just so she can see how it feels.*

I hated seeing her cry. Absolutely hated it. I wanted to put my arms around her and tell her I was sorry, but I knew she'd just reject my peace offering. So instead, brushing past Julie – who had returned to watch the intriguing spectacle of two people not talking – I shook my head in her direction in a high-minded 'I pity you' manner, and opened the door.

I was – mentally speaking – already huffing my way down Clapham High Street, moaning to myself about how I was never going to understand women and their strange ways, when Mel shouted out after me, 'What *did* you come round here for anyway, Duffy? Just to show me how much I can't stand you?'

I searched for something equally horrible to say, but the genuine hurt I heard in her voice thankfully brought me to my senses, so that the worst thing I could find in the deep well of regret into which I was currently sinking was, 'I came to tell you, yes, I want to marry you.'

This was actually a bit of a lie.

Well, not a lie, but not exactly the truth.

Kind of ninety-seven per cent truth and three per cent total fabrication.

I did want to marry her – just not now – not yet. The words I'd said instead, however, had sort of leaped from my lips and now they were out I was almost proud of them. I'd never quite understood how people came to make decisions of this magnitude: 'Let's have a baby'; 'Let's get married'; 'Let's commit suicide.' These are all monumental life-changing decisions from which there is no return. I'd always believed it would take a certain type of strength from a certain type of person to say, 'Let's get married,' so I was pleased that even I, a metaphorical seven stone weakling in a world crammed full of emotional heavyweights, had been able to cut it with the big boys.

Hard Mel disappeared instantly, as did my incarnation as

'Stupid Boy'. In their places were the Mel whom I knew and loved so much, and the good old me who thought Mel was the best thing since toast. She raced towards me and wrapped her arms around me tightly, making me feel like more of a man than I'd felt in a long time. As she kissed me fervently again, and again I realised I'd just made all her dreams come true. *If only it was always this easy to make people you love happy*, I thought. Sometimes I felt like my whole reason for being was to fill the lives of those I loved with disappointment – it was a nice change to do the opposite.

I was happy.

Mel was happy.

Even Nosferatu seemed to be smiling.

Everything was going to be all right.

The Six-million-dollar Man

The reactions to the news of my forthcoming nuptials were strange to say the least. My mum burst into tears. 'I'm so happy,' she said through her joy-filled sobs. 'I'm just so happy for the two of you.' She dropped the phone about a million times, and made me tell her the details over and over again as if she couldn't believe it the first time.

I went round to Vernie's to tell her, and her initial comment was a terse, 'About time too,' which made me laugh because I knew deep down her excitement was on a par with my mother's. Charlie congratulated me with a hearty handshake and said he thought my getting married was the best news he'd heard in ages.

Dan, needless to say, thought my getting married was a bad idea but didn't say so because he knew that wasn't what I wanted to hear. So he gave me a kind of backslappy hug, cracked a joke about advertising in *Penthouse* for a new flatmate and promised to arrange a celebratory drink on Friday night. As Mel had arranged a quick 'I'm-engaged-isn't-it-great?' drink on the same night, Dan's plans fitted in perfectly with the weekend schedule Mel and I had prepared for ourselves, now that we'd been upgraded into the serious-couple club.

Sitting in the Haversham on Friday night, Dan and Charlie

decided unanimously that the whole evening's entertainment would be at my expense, despite my having been an engaged man for only six days. For the next few hours I was the butt of their jokes, jibes and mockery, which was actually quite reassuring in its own way – laughter was the perfect antidote to any apprehension I was feeling about marriage. The evening's conversation went a little something like this . . .

8.23 p.m.
'What is it about weddings that women like so much?' asked Dan.
'The dresses?' suggested Charlie.
'You could have a point there,' said Dan. 'What have all weddings got in common apart from the bride and groom?'
'A posh dress!' replied Charlie.
I tried my hardest not to become tainted by the sheer ludicrousness of their conversation but I couldn't help myself. 'You're not seriously trying to tell me that women the world over have been getting married just so they can get a new frock? What about Elizabeth Taylor? Married more times than I can remember and she can afford as many posh frocks as she likes.'
'Ahhh,' exclaimed Dan astutely, 'but the wedding means she's always got somewhere nice to wear it.'

9.28 p.m.
Charlie played question master. 'Why do you think blokes are so scared of commitment?'
'Simple,' answered Dan. 'It's the Daisy Duke principle.' With the utterance of those words Dan had our attention in full. For everyone around the table and probably any member of our generation, Daisy Duke – of *The Dukes*

of Hazard fame – was a byword for truth, beauty and cheek-revealing denim hotpants. 'In our formative years we're exposed to a huge number of amazingly beautiful women,' continued Dan. 'We men become conditioned to seek out perfection and spend our lives in pursuit of the ultimate babe. Of course this search will prove fruitless because perfection doesn't exist. But that won't stop us wandering through life nomadically, refusing to put down roots until our quest is over.'

'We are to be pitied not chided,' chipped in Charlie. 'Ours is a thankless task.'

'When you think about it,' said Dan, 'finding the perfect partner is a bit like a game of pontoon. I mean, you get your cards and you make your decision. Do you stick or twist? Do you play safe and settle for nineteen or do you go all out for twenty-one, even if you might end up bust?'

'On a good day Vernie's a twenty-one,' Charlie laughed. 'Although I reckon she thinks I'm an eighteen. What do you reckon, Dan? Ever had a twenty-one?

'Let's think,' he said, mulling it over. 'There was Cerys in college, she was a fourteen. Then there was Louise after that who was probably a seventeen, but I think the closest I've ever come was with Meena.' He hesitated for a moment and took a sip of his beer. 'She was definitely a twenty, but you know me, just like Kenny Rogers I'm a gambler. I had to go for the twenty-one. Didn't seem right not to.'

'Mel's my twenty-one,' I said, more to my pint than to my assembled friends. 'She is the perfect hand.'

10.05 p.m.

It was Dan's turn to pontificate. 'Your conventional modern action hero doesn't need a full-time woman, because they get in the way and reduce his ability to catch the bad guys and save the world from certain disaster. That's why none of fiction's greatest heroes are happily hitched. Discuss.'

I attempted to think of a betrothed hero and found it more difficult than I'd anticipated. 'James Bond,' I said triumphantly after a few moments of deep thought. 'He was married.'

'*Was* married,' said Dan. 'In *On Her Majesty's Secret Service*, to be exact. He gets married but his wife gets killed near the end of the film by a bullet meant for JB. The subtext is obvious: James Bond cannot save the world and be an icon for young men the world over with a bird in tow. Plus, if you take the meaningless sex with all manner of exotic kung fu/spy/killer beauties out of James Bond, what have you got? Nothing but a middle-aged man acting like a teenager.'

'He's right,' said Charlie. 'Think about it, Duff. *Starsky and Hutch, Magnum PI*, Dean Martin in *Matt Helm, Batman, Shaft*, Han Solo in *Star Wars* . . . Han *Solo*, I ask you.'

'All the guys in *The A Team*,' added Dan.

'*The Six-million-dollar Man*,' I contributed reluctantly.

'Charlie from *Charlie's Angels*,' added Charlie. Simultaneously Dan and I turned to him for an explanation.

'I'm pretty sure he was married,' I said. 'Bosley was single I'll give you that but I reckon Charlie was definitely married.'

'He's right you know,' said Dan. 'Charlie from *Charlie's Angels* is married. I think they even mentioned it in one show.'

Charlie refused to be convinced. 'As the only person here who has a wife let me tell you. Any bloke who employs three of the Eighties hottest women to fight crime isn't going to be married. There's no way his wife would let him get away with it. Could you imagine Vernie letting me go off to weekend conferences with Sabrina, Kris and Kelly. I don't think so!'

'You could have a point there mate,' said Dan. 'It would be asking for trouble. But anyway, we're digressing. All of these heroes – bachelor men the lot of them,' said Dan. 'It has to be the way for real men to exist. No ties. No hassle. Just fighting crime and babes on tap.'

'Okay,' I countered. I'd been racking my brains trying to find married fictional heroes. 'What about Bruce Willis in the *Die Hard* films? He's married.'

'You're kidding,' said Dan, laughing. 'How long's a marriage going to last when your husband keeps getting himself into the kind of scrapes where he loses his shoes and has to run around upstate New York wearing nothing but a vest?'

11.15 p.m. (Time ladies and gentlemen please!)

'I'm a pretty amazing bloke,' said Dan, adopting a pompous tone of voice. 'I'm a big hit with the ladies, I look the business – in short I am the bee's knees. But . . .' he paused thoughtfully . . . 'if you were to look through a selection of photographs of me when I was seventeen you'd say to yourself, "Why upon my life, cool Dan is in fact nothing but a geek! Look at that haircut, his dodgy Iron Maiden T-shirt, his pitiful attempt to grow a moustache!"'

'So what's your point?' I sighed, as if I hadn't already guessed.

'Marriage is a lot like a photograph. The person you get hitched to is a snapshot of who you are at the time. Granted, you might think she's the best thing ever, but think about it . . . imagine if you got married to the first girl you fell in love with.'

'What?' said Charlie.

'Imagine her. There you are seventeen years old. You're in love. You think it's never going to end. But imagine meeting her now with her big hair, marble-washed jeans and her Amnesty International membership card. Would you want to be married to that?'

I tutted despondently. 'You're presuming that she's stayed the same. You don't know that. If you've changed, then she's bound to have changed too.'

'Of course,' said Dan. 'But into what?'

11.31 p.m. Inside the Archway Fish and Chip Bar across the road from the Haversham

'I'll tell you what's wrong with living together,' said Dan as we waited for our chips and curry sauce. 'It's the root of all evil in every relationship: you take each other for granted. You assume she's always going to be there, so you stop putting in the effort. She assumes you're never going to change and you go out of your way to prove her right. You start treating each other like furniture – and what's worse, not even furniture that you actually like.'

The phone was ringing. I looked at the glow-in-the-dark alarm clock Mel had given me for my twenty-sixth birthday, only to discover it was 2.57 a.m. I attempted to go back to sleep, but the beer, chips and curry sauce churning in my stomach, combined with the madperson at the end of the telephone who clearly refused to believe we were asleep, made resting impossible. Eyes half closed I got up and walked along the hallway, throwing a menacing squint in the direction of Dan's bedroom as I passed. *I bet he's unplugged the answerphone so he could use the toaster in the living room again*, I thought, scowling. I was right. There next to the phone was the toaster with a piece of cold toast in it. I picked up the toast, took a bite and answered the phone, still chewing.

'Hello?' I said about to take another bite of my toast.

'Isssh meee,' slurred an unquestionably inebriated Mel.

'What's wrong?' I asked, as if I didn't know the answer.

'Aaaallcoooohol,' she said desperately. 'Too much . . . think am going to die . . . come round please . . . now.'

'But it's three o'clock in the morning,' I protested. 'I'm knackered. I've only been asleep a few hours.'

'Oh, please come, Duff,' she whined. 'I think I'm going to be sick.'

'You're not going to be sick,' I reassured her. 'Just take a couple of paracetamols, go to bed and I'll see you in the morning. Okay?'

'Okay,' she said, repeating my instructions with a childlike innocence. 'Take a couple of paracetamols, go back to bed and . . . bleuuuurghhh!' The sentence ended abruptly with the unmistakable sound of projectile vomit hitting the telephone mouthpiece.

It was a quarter to four in the morning by the time the taxi pulled up outside Mel's. I got out, handed the driver twenty pounds and told him to keep the change. I didn't usually tip but I was grateful that he hadn't made any comment on my Man United football shirt and paisley dressing gown. Too ill to open the door when I rang the buzzer, Mel hurled the front doorkey out of the upstairs bedroom window and I let myself in.

She was lying on the sofa, still dressed in her work clothes, with a washing-up bowl next to her head and a look of sheer biliousness across her features. 'Oh, Duffy!' she said, employing the quiet self-pitying whiny voice of the repentant drunkard. 'I'm going to die, aren't I?'

'Of course not,' I comforted, glancing at the carrot-based contents of the washing-up bowl. I kissed her lightly on the cheek and removed the bowl to the kitchen. I returned with a glass of water, which I made her sip while I stroked her forehead. While I attempted to scrub a spot of sick off the carpet with a dishcloth, she laid her head back on a cushion and made small murmuring noises.

'How did you get like this?' I said, and sat down beside her.

With her eyes closed quite firmly she began her sorry tale. 'It was only going to be a quick one after work. Just to celebrate our engagement . . .' she whimpered. 'And then Julie told me about a new bar in Poland Street and then everyone thought we should go there and so we did and they kept buying me drinks and I couldn't refuse, could I?' She opened her eyes. 'I couldn't, honestly, Duff.'

'I know, babe,' I said nodding. 'What were you drinking?'

'Vuuurkahanoorraaahhh,' she mumbled.

'What?'

'Vodka and orange,' she repeated guiltily.

'Oh, Mel,' I chided gently. 'You should know better.' Everyone has a loopy juice, a lethal alcoholic cocktail that releases the beast within. For me it was Cinzano and lemonade, for Dan it was cider and black, but for Mel it was vodka and orange. At various times in the past under its influence she had ruined a dress from Ghost trying to climb a fence, lost a purse containing at least fifty quid, and told me for the very first time that she loved me. They were an amusing but volatile double act. 'You said never again after last time,' I reminded her. The last time being Dan's birthday six months ago when after a large number of vodka and oranges, she'd got up on a table in the Soho All Bar One and started dancing in a provocative manner to Shirley Bassey's 'Hey Big Spender'.

'I know,' she said. Her voice was even more pitiful than before. 'I'm sorry.'

I kissed her forehead. 'You did have a proper meal before you started drinking didn't you?'

'Dry roasted peanuts,' she said sorrowfully. 'It was all I could find.' I had to laugh. With a stomach packed with nothing more substantial than peanuts, and seven hours' worth of vodka and orange juice, it was a wonder her brain hadn't melted, let alone her stomach regurgitated its contents. 'I think I'm going to be sick again,' she whimpered.

I looked around for the washing-up bowl but I'd left it in the kitchen. 'Are you sure?'

She nodded.

'Can you walk?'

She shook her head.

'Right, I'll have to carry you then.' Picking her up in my arms, I carried her to the bathroom and placed her on the floor. On her knees she crawled to the toilet, lifted up the seat and threw up while I held her hair out of her face, then collapsed in a heap on the floor.

'I feel much better now,' she groaned mournfully and promptly fell asleep.

I carried her to the bedroom, where I undressed her and put her pyjamas on. I tucked her into bed and then fell asleep beside her.

'Duffy, are you awake?'

It was the day after the night before and I'd been awake for some time staring at the ceiling and thinking about nothing in particular. 'What time is it?' I asked.

Mel looked at her bedside clock. 'Just coming up to two

o'clock in the afternoon.' She pulled herself up close to me. 'Duff,' she said quietly, 'you do know I'm sorry about last night, don't you?'

'There's nothing to be sorry about,' I said, rolling over to face her properly.

'But I got you out of bed at three o'clock in the morning and dragged you halfway across London to look after me.' She sat up, pulling me up with her. 'I love you, you know. Not many men would have done what you did.'

I shrugged my shoulders, embarrassed by her gratitude. 'It wasn't that special.' I paused, lost for words. 'Anyway, you'd do the same for me.'

'That's not the point,' she said, looking so deeply into my eyes I thought she was going to cry.

'What is the point?' I asked, more than a little confused by her behaviour.

'The point is this: I don't think that I've ever loved you more than I do right now.' And then she kissed me.

Because if you are I will be forced to kill you while you're asleep and plead diminished responsibility

It was a sunny Sunday afternoon, one of those freak flashes of summer that now often occur in spring, thanks to global warming. I'd been engaged for a month and was still getting used to the idea of marriage, but with the help of Mel it no longer seemed like such a formidable proposition. Mel, Charlie, Vernie and I had all been for lunch at the Haversham, and as we headed for Highgate Woods we all donned our sunglasses with pride – *Reservoir Dogs* let loose in Muswell Hill.

Our plan for the afternoon revolved around us finding a patch of grass to sit on, earnestly reading the various sections of Charlie's Sunday newspaper and then discussing any current events that caught our eye – just like we'd always imagined proper adults did. In reality, however, I knew we wouldn't do any of these things, because it was such a beautiful day and all we really wanted to do was lie down on the warm grass, stare at the sky and drink the bottle of wine we'd brought with us.

Walking through the iron gates of the park, Charlie and Vernie decided to race each other to the benches in the open space in the middle of the woods. Laughing maniacally, they grabbed at each other's clothing as they tried to stop each other from getting ahead. Mel and I, still digesting our pub lunch, opted to follow them at a far gentler pace.

There was a new seriousness about the two of us, as if the people we had been before our engagement were becoming more and more like distant relatives. Family and friends' responses to us had changed almost overnight – suddenly I was an adult; I was respectable. In recent weeks we'd driven to Southampton to see Mel's mum and dad and taken them out for dinner; my mum had come down to London specifically to see us both and had stayed the whole weekend at Mel's; and we'd seen more of Mark and Julie than ever. Without fail everyone would mention our 'wonderful new life together' as if our old life together had been a complete waste of time. It was hard not to feel nostalgic for the old days when we just 'were'.

As we ambled along, we were drawn to the sounds coming from the adventure playground in the middle of the woods. We stood by the wire fence looking in. The climbing frames, swings and slides – in vibrant shades of red, yellow and blue – were a heaving, screaming mass of kids, like ants crawling over lollypop sticks in summer. Their parents watched enthralled at how much fun these small people could have without the aid of artificial stimulants. The noise was incredible, their Lilliputian voices communicating overwhelming joy and on occasion individual sorrow. A small boy in red dungarees tripped over whilst racing his friends to the slide and immediately burst into tears. Like a one man ER his dad scooped him up into his arms and gave him a huge hug. Within seconds the tragedy was over and the boy was back with his friends again racing towards the slide. The whole scene reminded me of when I was small and my mum would take me and Vernie to the park. I'd always insist that Mum play football with me, and to her credit she did. She was terrible of course – it's impossible to be a good goalkeeper in high heels – but at least she tried.

Mel nudged me gently on the shoulder, rousing me from my reminiscences. She took my hand and squeezed it gently. 'Duffy?'

'Yeah,' I said breezily.

'You were somewhere else.'

'I know,' I said and kissed her.

Reaching up she put a warm hand on either side of my face, pulled me towards her and placed her lips firmly on mine. 'We're getting married,' she said excitedly.

'Yeah, we are.' Holding her hand in my own I absentmindedly rotated the engagement ring I'd bought her. It was a white gold band with a single sapphire. It wasn't particularly expensive compared to the meteorite-sized rock arrangement Mark had commissioned for his engagement ring to Julie, but Mel seemed genuinely to love it.

'Do you think we know enough about each other?' she asked wistfully.

'Yeah, of course,' I replied. 'What I don't know about you I could write on the back of a stamp. I'd need very small handwriting, mind you.'

She punched me in the arm playfully. 'Are you saying that just to shut me up?'

'No.'

'Are you sure?'

'Yeah.'

She took a moment to collect her thoughts. 'So we agree on all the important things that future husbands and wives should agree on?'

'What like?' I said, sitting down on a patch of grass and pulling her down after me. 'Who's going to do the cooking? Who's going to do the washing up?'

She shuffled herself round on her bum so that she could rest her head on my lap. 'Yeah, I suppose.'

'I'll do the cooking. You do the washing up. I'm a dab hand with the microwave, as you know. But as for DIY jobs around the flat – I think we'll get a man in.' I looked across to the playground to watch the kids again. A little girl, roughly six years old, was sauntering aimlessly, arms outstretched in front of her with a yellow plastic bucket on her head.

I looked down at Mel under the cover of my sunglasses. An expression of deepest deliberation animated her face. She was waiting for me to ask what was on her mind. I let the silence live a little longer. She sighed heavily to get my attention. I kissed her. 'You've got something on your mind, haven't you?'

'No,' she said, shaking her head playfully. She took off her sunglasses and lay them on the grass next to her.

'Okay, then,' I returned to playground watching. Another little girl wearing what must have been the brightest orange tights that have ever existed was racing around the edge of the playground shouting out how many laps she'd done every time she passed her dad.

Mel sighed again heavily. 'Do you ever think about . . . oh . . . forget it.'

I lifted my sunglasses on top of my head and made eye contact with her briefly. 'What is it that you want me to think about?'

'Come on we're going for a walk,' said Mel, standing up. I stood up and she put her arm through mine and led me on a walk around the playground. 'Duffy, do you ever think about . . . you know . . .'

'Watching TV uninterrupted? I dream about that . . .'

'No.'

'Why I'm marrying a mad woman?'

'Don't push it.'

'What is it that you want me to think about? C'mon, just spit it out. It can't be that bad.'

She came to a halt, her face half hidden by the shade of an oak tree. 'Children,' she said firmly.

'Children?' I repeated needlessly.

'Yes, children. Do you ever think about us having children?'

'No,' I said almost under my breath. Suddenly all the kids in the playground became sinister and creepy – they still had the same bodies, but all the boys looked like me and all the girls like Mel. Little people with big people's heads on. It was very disturbing.

'Don't you ever think about kids?'

I refused to look at her while we were having this conversation. I knew that if I locked eyes with her she'd suck me into yet another debate in which I'd come off worse. 'I think about kids about as often as I think about how nice it would be to set fire to all my savings, scratch my furniture, wear patches of sick on my suits as a fashion statement and invite unemployed psychopathic dwarves to share my life.'

'That's exactly the sort of thing that Charlie said,' replied Mel.

I finally looked at her and smiled. 'You've been talking about having kids with Charlie?'

'No.' Mel said impatiently. 'Vernie and Charlie have been talking about having kids for the past few months. Or rather in the case of Charlie – not talking about having kids.'

'How do you know all this?'

'Vernie told me.'

'How come I don't know this?'

'Because all you and Charlie ever talk about is TV and sport. You never talk about anything that's even vaguely important.'

'Now hang on,' I protested. 'That's not true. Why, over lunch we talked about . . .' I mentally flicked through the list of topics: yesterday's football results, ten reasons why Roger Moore was a better Bond than Sean Connery (we only came up with eight) and the various pros and cons of Dan's new haircut (pro: it made him look younger; con: it made him look stupid). I changed subjects. 'Vernie wants kids? What for?'

'You say "what for" as if children shouldn't exist unless there's a logical reason for it, like . . . I don't know, you needed someone to wash the car for free.'

'I'll grant you that's a reason . . .' I smiled. 'What did Charlie say, then?'

'Vernie keeps bringing up the subject and he continually changes it. He says he's not ready, but I think he's just being really selfish.'

'He's not being selfish,' I said, defending Charlie's integrity. 'He's just thinking things through logically. That's what we men do. We think, we ponder, we mull and then we think and ponder and mull some more and then—'

'They've been together seven years!' interrupted Mel. 'They've been married for four of those . . .'

'Exactly,' I countered. 'So why change a winning formula?'

Right at that moment Mel and I simultaneously turned to the adventure playground and watched as a small boy handed his mother a bunch of dandelions. I wasn't sure, but it looked as though this tiny gesture of love had moved his mother to tears.

Mel was momentarily silent. 'So you don't want kids either.'

A sudden nausea came over me as I put two and two together and made five. 'Are you trying to tell me something?'

'You must be joking!' exclaimed Mel, horrified. 'Of course not.'

'Okay,' I said, breathing a sigh of relief. 'It's not like I don't want kids. It's just that I'm sure they'd be a good idea one day, but not right now.' I squeezed her arm affectionately. 'You've got your career. I've got my stand-up. There's plenty of time for that sort of thing.'

'I wasn't talking about right now,' said Mel emphatically.

'Good,' I replied, hoping to put a full stop to the conversation. I tried to change subjects. 'What do you fancy doing tonight?'

She ignored me. She wasn't going to let it lie. 'So when?'

'When?'

'When.'

'When?'

'Are you just going to keep repeating everything I say? Because if you are I will be forced to kill you while you're asleep and plead diminished responsibility. Twelve months on probation for manslaughter and I'll be a free woman, and you won't be so annoyingly smug.'

'Smug?'

'Go on, say it one more time, I dare you!'

'I dunno,' I said disdainfully. 'Four years? Five years? It's hard to say. It's a big enough step getting . . .' My words trailed off as I realised a little bit too late that finishing my sentence wouldn't be the smartest move in the world. 'Let's drop it, eh?'

'Carry on,' she said indignantly. 'It's a big enough step getting . . .'

'Okay,' I said, no longer able to put up resistance. 'When did you have them in mind?'

Mel wouldn't say at first, but I coaxed her gently to tell me, even though I didn't really want to know. I just wanted us to get on well together. I didn't want to have an argument or talk about children we couldn't afford and that fifty per cent of us weren't in favour of. It was the expression on her face that gave the game away. She looked embarrassed and uncomfortable. Together with her silence this was a bad sign. A terrible sign. The sign of the devil. In Mel's facial lexicon this meant 'I've been thinking about babies for a while and I think I'd like them quite soon but I'm embarrassed because I don't want you to think that I'm behaving like "a woman".'

'Oh, Mel,' I said mournfully.

'Don't you "oh, Mel" me! Since Vernie's been going on about babies morning, noon and night these past months, they've been on my mind. It's not about hormones. It's not about feeling maternal. It's about me and what I want from life. It's not a crime to think about the future, Duffy. I know to you it's the biggest crime in the world, but I've got a news flash for you – real people think about the future every day. I'm thinking about my future and your future – our future, to be exact. I'm not talking about having them right now. I'm just talking about them, okay?'

'What's it called?' I countered.

This time she avoided my gaze. She pretended not to know what I was talking about, but it was my turn not to let it lie. 'Okay,' she said resignedly, 'so I did imagine our baby. That's not a crime either. We called her Ella. After Ella Fitzgerald.'

'Ella's a nice name,' I said. 'We'll have a baby one day. But not yet. And when we do we'll call it Ella. Okay?'

'Okay.'

With this sorted, Mel fell strangely silent, and so I gave her a hug because I think we both saw that this one was a draw, and we made our way to join Charlie and Vernie.

Later, having lain in the sun all afternoon, using the various sections of Sunday newspaper for nothing other than shading our heads, the four of us walked back through the woods. Vernie and Mel peeled off after a few minutes, hastened by the need to go to the loo, leaving me and Charlie to lag behind and talk about the sort of stuff Mel accused us of not talking about.

'Mel says that Vernie wants kids.'

'Oh, yeah, who with?' Charlie laughed. His smile soon evaporated, to be replaced with a kind of philosophical grimace. 'Yeah, it's true,' he shrugged. 'She's been on about it for ages. I don't know how I'm going to get out of this one.'

'You never know,' I said encouragingly, 'you might have a low sperm count.'

'I'd be surprised if any of the little fellas could count,' said Charlie feebly. 'Although they're bound to be reasonably intelligent, if their manufacturer is anything to go by.'

'Mel was asking me about kids too,' I said. 'I don't think she was serious, though. Merely speculating, if you get my meaning. I don't quite understand why me and her have got to talk about babies just because you and Vernie are in discussions.'

'Women like doing things in pairs, don't they?' said Charlie, only half joking. 'Going to the loo in nightclubs, supermarket shopping, buying shoes—'

'No,' I interrupted. 'Mel always buys her shoes on her own. Too many opinions cloud her thought processes apparently. That said, she still buys shoes that are a half a size too small in the hope that she'll be able to squeeze into them, but at least they're always the right colour and style.'

'Well, you get my drift.'

We stopped and stood out of the way while a jogger holding a tangle of dog leads raced past us down the hill followed by three Highland Terriers.

'Do you think you'll give in?' I said, once the last of the dogs had passed.

'I don't know,' said Charlie. 'I mean, it's not like I don't want to have kids: a little girl to play footie with, a little boy to hate me when he's a teenager, but you know . . .' His answer trailed off. I nodded sympathetically. 'Thing is, the minute we have kids that'll be it – everything will change. Nothing will be the same. No more just the two of us. No more throwing a couple of bags into the back of the car and clearing off somewhere for the weekend. No more sitting in the Haversham with you and Dan. No more . . . I don't know . . . no more fun. It'll be nappies and feeding times . . . and breast pumps . . . and bright green baby poo . . . and getting up in the middle of the night . . . and baby seats . . . and my mum and dad coming to see us every other weekend . . . and pushchairs . . . and then one day she'll want another baby because one's never enough.'

'I see what you mean,' I said weakly, still somewhat shaken by the thought of bright green baby poo.

'Do you?' said Charlie sceptically. 'Because I'm not sure I do. I think they're just a big bunch of excuses. I think at the end of the day if I'm truthful I have to say that I'm just absolutely terrified by the thought of being a dad. I'm not ready.'

'I suppose it's a bit like how sometimes I don't feel I'm ready to be a husband,' I added helpfully. I thought about Dan and his denial over Meena and the wedding invitation. 'And not altogether dissimilar to how Dan isn't ready to be a dad, a husband or even a boyfriend.'

'When do you think we'll be ready?' said Charlie.

Simultaneously we looked at each other, shrugged a simple 'Dunno' and ran up the hill to catch up with Mel and Vernie.

For days after my conversation with Charlie I couldn't shake the feeling that he, Dan and I were some sort of metaphor for every malaise that had ever affected the modern male. It would only be a matter of time before the women in our lives swapped our real names for American Indian ones: He-whose-sperm-is-his-own; He-who-must-be-single; and He-who-loves-his-girlfriend-but-is-scared-of-marriage.

It really was only a matter of time.

Nice use of light

It was the following weekend and I was just coming to the end of a fifteen-minute set at the Giggle Club – aka the downstairs bar of the Amber Tavern in Islington. Even though I'd only been the second comedian on that evening, the crowd had liked my regular material enough for me to experiment with some new stuff that I'd written on the way over on the bus that night. *This*, I thought, as I thanked the crowd for being a wonderful audience and walked off stage, *has been a very good night.*

As the compère came on and announced a ten-minute interval I sat down at the back of the room and caught up on the comedy circuit gossip with Steve and Alison, the Giggle Club's promoters, and Craig, Lisa and Jim, the other comedians on tonight's bill. Still buzzing from the response of the audience, I very nobly offered to get a round in for everyone. Big mistake. They all said yes. So I took their orders, tried not to cry at the thought of how much this was all going to cost me and disappeared to the upstairs bar. Just as I was about to order the first drink, someone tapped me lightly on the shoulder.

'Ben Duffy?' I turned around to see a woman standing behind me. 'I just wanted to tell you how much I enjoyed your set. You were brilliant.'

Even at this incredibly low level of comedy, it was possible to get the occasional groupie. Not that I'd ever had one. There was no way, however, even in my wildest dreams, that this woman was a groupie. Behind her black oval spectacles – the type hideously beautiful people wear to tone down the effect their visage has on mere mortals – was a pair of deep brown perfectly proportioned eyes. Her waves of thick black hair were tied back from a face so flawlessly perfect it felt rude not to stare. She was dressed casually in jeans, trainers, a cream skinnyrib polo neck and denim jacket. The whole look made her stand out a mile from the pub's mixture of students and professional Islingtonians. It said, 'I know who I am – I am beautiful.'

'Thanks for the compliment,' I said, offering my hand. 'I'm glad you enjoyed it.'

'I'm Alexa Wells,' she said, as if it was a name I should know. 'I kind of know the music video director, Mark Basset, and his fiancée Julie Watson.'

'Do you really?' I asked, balking at the fact that Mark had become so successful that he'd joined that selective band of people whose job title preceded their name.

'I mentioned to Mark last time I went round to theirs for dinner that the programme I work on was looking for a comedian. He told me about you and gave me a video of your act a couple of weeks ago. I only got round to watching it yesterday but I really loved it. *Really, really* loved it.' She floundered momentarily, embarrassed by her own enthusiasm. 'Erm . . . anyway, when I saw in *Time Out* that you were on the bill here tonight I just grabbed a bunch of the researchers and the assistant producer . . .' she pointed at a group of unfeasibly trendy twenty-somethings, their faces obscured in a haze of Marlboro Light smoke . . . 'and dragged them here to see you. And I have to say it was worth it. You were brilliant tonight. So relaxed and confident.'

'Cheers,' I said diffidently. I could feel my forehead furrowing apprehensively – partly because I always got embarrassed by compliments but mainly because I hadn't the faintest clue how Mark had got hold of a tape of one of my gigs. He had mentioned to me several weeks ago that a friend of his who worked in TV was looking for a comedian. He'd even given me the address to send the tape to. It was still on the kitchen cork noticeboard back at the flat.

'What are you up to now?' asked Alexa, lighting up a cigarette and squinting in an outrageously sexy manner as the smoke got into her eyes. She noticed me staring at her. 'Oh, I'm sorry, did you want one?'

I shook my head nervously. 'Not at the minute.'

Silence.

'So?'

I looked at her, bewildered.

'What are you doing now?'

'Right now?'

She nodded.

What am I doing right now?

'Nothing,' I said a little too late for it not to be totally obvious that I'd been trying to think of an excuse why I couldn't talk to her. 'Why? What do you want to do?'

She laughed loudly, unfazed by my lack of social skills. 'You go find a seat,' she said patiently. 'I'll get us a drink and we'll have a quick chat.'

I chose a seat as far away from the bar as possible. My friends downstairs were so Scrooge-like they were bound to send out a search party for their drinks. With my head hidden behind a large cardboard lunchtime menu, I watched as Alexa hovered in the middle of the room looking for me, seemingly unaware that nearly all the pub's male clientele were watching her every move. I waved cautiously. As I stood up to give her a hand with the drinks, I imagined the whole pub sigh collectively as the same thought occurred to all of them: 'What is *she* doing with *him*?'

'So,' I said sitting down, 'what exactly is it you do? All Mark said was that you work in TV. What are you, a runner, researcher or a producer?'

'None of the above,' said Alexa, laughing knowingly. 'I used to present a cable TV music programme about five months ago, but now I co-present *The Hot Pop Show*.

'I watch that!' I exclaimed a little too excitedly. I wasn't lying either. Since Dan and I had been living together, watching Saturday morning kids' TV had become one of the highlights of our weekend survival ritual. 'I watch it every week. I'm a huge fan.' I paused. 'How come I don't remember seeing you on it?'

'You might be a huge fan,' she smiled and took a sip of her Beck's, 'but you must have been busy for the last few weekends because I'm the show's latest presenter.'

She was right. I had been busy on Saturday mornings lately. Busy doing engaged-couple things with Mel.

'Come to think of it, I might have read something about you,' I said. 'In one of those men's mags that always have about a zillion pages of car and clothing ads.'

She smiled and delved into her shoulder bag on the floor and pulled out a magazine. 'Page fifty-six and fifty-seven,' she said succinctly as she handed it to me.

There in full colour was the woman sitting across the table from me, wearing what could only be described as La Perla-type underwear and a big grin. Across the picture ran the headline: 'TV's Hottest Totty!'

'Nice use of light,' I said, examining the picture carefully.

'Yeah,' she smiled. 'That's what they all say.'

'Do you always show men you've just met pictures of yourself in your underwear?'

She shook her head and smiled. 'Only the nice ones.'

We talked for quite a while. She told me about how she'd finished drama college two years ago, gone travelling in Thailand, come back to England expecting to end up on the dole and instead found herself at an audition for a presenter on a cable TV music programme and got the job. She stayed there for about a year before she was poached to front *The Hot Pop Show*.

'That must be amazing,' I said as she finished her story. 'You have the coolest job on earth. What are you doing talking to me? I'm not worthy.'

Although I was joking, there was a degree of truth to what I'd said. I couldn't help but think, *What does a woman like this want with me?*

'I'm talking to you for two reasons. Firstly, like I said before, we're looking for a comedian for the show. Just to do little sketches and gags and all that. I have to be truthful: the powers that be are auditioning quite a few people, but I'd really love it if you came down and gave it a try. What do you think?'

'Yeah, why not?' I said casually, as if it was every day that I was asked to do a television audition. 'Sounds okay.'

'Right then,' she smiled. 'I'll be in touch.' She looked at her watch – a huge, chunky plastic affair with about eight million buttons. 'It's bedtime for me. I'm shooting a piece about urban rock climbing at six a.m. tomorrow morning.'

I smiled and nodded knowledgeably, as if I well understood the rigours of early morning shoots.

She stood up and we shook hands. 'It was nice to meet you.'

'It was nice to meet you too,' I replied imaginatively.

She handed me a business card. 'It's got my work number on it and my mobile . . . so you can get me when you want to.'

'Cheers,' I said, placing the card in the back pocket of my jeans. 'I'll see you around maybe,' I added, although I was pretty sure that the places we chose to be 'around' weren't exactly going to coincide. I watched as she turned, walked halfway across the room, stopped and came back again.

'I was just wondering . . . are you doing anything tomorrow night?' she said, toying with the mobile phone in her jacket pocket. 'I've got tickets for a preview screening of some new Hollywood blockbuster. Lots of explosions, crashes and bullets – a boys' film basically. Do you fancy coming to see it?'

'With you?'

'Yes.'

'Just the two of us?'

'Uh huh.'

I thought about her invitation very hard in the few seconds allotted to me, and then as casually as I could, which probably wasn't all that casual given that for some reason I was unable to use the personal pronoun I said, 'Can't. Staying in with girlfriend.' And if that wasn't bad enough, I managed to spit the word 'girlfriend' at her like it was a bulb of garlic and she was the Bride of Dracula.

'That's a shame,' she said as if she truly meant it. 'Maybe another time.'

'Just one more thing,' I enquired carefully. 'You said that you were talking to me tonight for two reasons. What was the other one?'

She smiled cryptically and said, 'I'll tell you all about it another time.'

* * *

It's not a big deal.

It's not even a medium-sized deal.

If it's any sort of deal at all, it's a teeny weeny teeny tiny one.

All I'd done was have a drink and a chat with a female kids' TV presenter for half an hour tops. All she'd done was have a drink with me, look fabulous and ask me out to a film preview.

She couldn't have fancied me, I thought as I left the pub.

Women like that don't fancy men like me, I convinced myself on the bus on the way home.

So, if she didn't fancy me, there's no reason to tell Mel about the bit where I thought she fancied me, ran my thought processes through my sleepless night.

Nice try, said my conscience next morning, *but you know as well as I do that you're guilty as a guilty thing.*

I laughed so hard milk came out of my nose

Propelled by guilt I decided it was time to spend more quality time with Mel. So the next evening, a Friday night, as Dan had an overnight gig in Northampton, I invited her round to the flat so that we could spend some time on our own. I tidied up in anticipation of her arrival and actually considered cooking a meal, but thought better of it and sorted out a Chinese takeaway instead.

Together we consumed a couple of bottles of wine, ate king prawns in black bean sauce, watched TV and chatted about nothing in particular. She lay on the sofa with her head on my lap, and as I stroked the hair at the back of her neck with my fingertips I suddenly became aware that this cosy domestic scene might just be a snapshot of the future. *This is nice*, I thought. *It feels . . . comfortable*. Then it occurred to me that although I liked comfortable, I needed to be honest with Mel even more.

Though some twenty-fours hours had passed since my encounter with Alexa, I was still feeling guilty. While there was a slim possibility that if I told Mel what had happened she'd see the whole thing my way, I had to accept that my small deal ran the chance of being a big deal to her. Massive. Gargantuan. Even so, I still I felt the need to confess everything.

Up until this point in my life I'd worked on the basis that what Mel didn't know about couldn't hurt her, and without much trouble I'd managed to gather together a nice collection of so-called skeletons in the cupboard. They didn't rattle too much and gave me absolutely no trouble at all, but since The Proposal Mel had, unbeknownst to me, managed to instil in me something approaching a conscience, and I now couldn't rest. I wondered whether now was the time to get those skeletons out. A few sprang to mind immediately, and just for my own amusement, while Mel dozed, I took them out of store in my head and had another look at them.

The Crossover Skeleton

There was a slight crossover period of two weeks between the end of my last girlfriend and the beginning of Mel. I didn't count this as a particularly big skeleton because its existence was due to the fact that I was terrible at dumping girlfriends. Her name was Amanda. She was a comedian I met at a gig at the Edinburgh festival. As she lived in Manchester we only ever saw each other at weekends, which was handy because although she was fun, she certainly wasn't proper girlfriend material.

When the time came, I tried to tell her it was over between us in the only way I could – I didn't phone, I was sullen and surly whenever she came to London to visit, but she thought I was just being enigmatic. I even told her, 'Look, Amanda, I'm sorry but it's over. I'm going out with someone else,' but in her mind that only served to make me even more alluring in a 'he's a challenge' sort of way.

Eventually I had to call upon Dan's master dumping skills to assist me. Which was of course a bad move. A very bad move. He told her that I was dead. She turned up one day at my old flat in Wood Green, and Dan, after having spotted her out of my living-room window, answered the door with tapwater dripping from his eyes. Employing his very best acting skills he sobbed, 'Amanda! Haven't you heard? Duffy was killed last week in a terrible accident. Workmen were repairing Lambeth Town Hall, and as he was walking past, some loose masonry fell and killed him. Instantly.' She believed him, as you would do (who's going to make up something like that?), and even wanted to come to the funeral, but Dan told her it was for close family only.

It should've been perfect. Immortalised in Amanda's head as the Difficult Dead Boyfriend. She would've forgotten all the bad bits about me, and remembered only the good times. But me being me, I had to go and bump into her three weeks later at a club in Hoxton Square when I was out with Mel. She didn't say a single word to me, but her menacing Mancunian scowl spoke volumes.

Mel noticed Amanda's looks of hatred immediately and asked me who she was, so I told her the first thing that came into my head: 'She's a stalker. Comedians get them sometimes.'

In my defence for the overlap, I didn't count it as cheating on Mel because I really was trying to do The Right Thing.

The Naked Skeleton

Last year I kind of semi-lied to Mel and told her I was going with Dan to the Prince Charles to see a rerun of *Get Carter*, when in fact the two of us went to a topless bar called the Rising Moon in the West End. It was all Dan's idea. He'd become obsessed with an article he'd read in a men's magazine, '101 things you must do before you're thirty. Of the 101, Dan was pleased to discover he'd done ninety-two of them. Of the ones that remained, two were illegal, one he decided was definitely immoral, and with his limited finances he wasn't in a position to do any of the others, with the exception of attending a lapdancing club. We both agreed that lapdancing clubs were both morally reprehensible and ludicrously expensive, so we compromised and settled for a topless bar.

As neither of us had ever been to a place like this before, we weren't entirely sure what to do when we got inside. So taking a table in the darkest corner possible, we sat for ages making the tiniest of small talk, pretending that this whole thing wasn't really happening. Eventually a G-string-clad young woman, profoundly gifted in the chest area, sauntered over to us to take our order. Embarrassed beyond belief, I couldn't bring myself to look at her breasts and was too ashamed to look her in the eyes, so I conducted the entire conversation focusing on her nose. Our topless waitress looked about our age. In fact she reminded me of a girl I went to college with called Karen Braithwaite. She had blonde hair and the same puffy forehead that Karen had, but she had a much nicer body, although technically speaking I'd never seen Karen Braithwaite in a G-string. I thought about asking her if she was Karen, but then it occurred to me that if she was the same person this wasn't really going to be the right moment for us to talk over old times. I ordered two bottled beers and she disappeared, leaving Dan and me to gape around the room.

The bar was full of solitary businessmen, tattooed fat blokes with their tattooed fat bloke mates, and large groups of young men on stag nights. This depressing sight brought me to my senses as I was suddenly struck by three things:

1) it was depressing to discover I had anything in common with these people;

2) I'd never felt more embarrassed in my life;
3) none of this was giving me any pleasure whatsoever.

As Dan and I sipped our beers in silence, I thought about being there and I tried to remember the last time I had thought about anyone but Mel. And I couldn't. It was a key moment for me. Like being handed the meaning of life on a plate. Mel was all that I wanted.

The Artistic Butcher Skeleton

About two and a half years ago Mel and I split up. We just weren't getting on very well. So she called an end to it. Depressed beyond belief I met a girl at a gig who mistook my melancholy for sensitivity. I suppose we had a common cause: we both hated our day jobs (she worked in a butcher's but by night painted abstract images in her Clerkenwell studio) and we'd both been recently dumped. I tried to put her off; I told her about my ex-girlfriend and how wonderful she was, but she said, 'You can't have been that serious if you weren't even living together.' I didn't really have an answer for that one. I told her I didn't want anything to happen and I also told her I certainly didn't want a relationship; we could be mates and nothing more.

One evening, we met up for a drink after work. She tried to kiss me and failed; then later I tried to kiss her and failed too; then some time around midnight we both tried to kiss each other and succeeded and I ended up staying the night at hers. I don't know why I did it. I didn't even like her. I especially don't know why I called her the next day and left a message on her answerphone asking if she wanted to go to the cinema. Guilt, I suppose. I thought I owed her something. But whatever it was I owed her, she obviously didn't want it because she never called back.

Mel and I got back together a week later.

End of skeletons

*   *   *

'Is anybody home?'

At the sound of Mel's voice I shook my head clear of the cobwebs of deep thought. I'd been reflecting so intensely on my skeletons that I hadn't noticed her awaken from her nap. Now she was staring up at me intently and probably had been for quite a while.

'What were you thinking about?' she said, curious.

'Oh nothing,' I said dismissively. 'What's on telly?'

Mel sat up and looped her arm through mine squeezing herself closer to me. 'Don't tell me "nothing", Mr Benjamin Duffy. What were you thinking about? Come on, I can tell when there's something wrong.'

It was true. Mel had an amazing ability to monitor my emotional landscape – evidently even when asleep. My mulling over the skeletons must have alerted her sleeping body to my troubled psyche. Resistance would be futile.

'Tell me,' she demanded finally.

I deliberated over her request and decided against it. We'd been together four years. We were planning to get married. Now wasn't the right time for either of us to start telling The Truth.

'Look it's nothing,' I said testily. 'I'm okay.'

'Tell me,' she cajouled, narrowing her eyes at me.

I reviewed my position. I wasn't really giving her a chance. It was unfair to act like she was a walking bundle of unreasonability waiting for an excuse to explode.

I took a deep breath. 'You know I had a gig last night?'

'You said it went really well.'

'Yeah, it did. It's just that . . . well, afterwards this girl . . . well, woman, I suppose . . . the one who Mark knows, who needed a comedian for her TV show . . . well, she was there. Turns out she's a TV presenter.'

'Oh, yeah?' said Mel inquisitively. 'What did she want?'

'She said she liked my act and invited me to audition for the TV show she works for.'

'And?'

I weighed up Mel's 'and' in my head. It would've been much easier if there hadn't been room for an 'and'. I didn't want this to be one of those situations where five minutes later I'd be wishing I'd chosen the 'LEAVE WELL ALONE' option. But I wanted to be honest. In fact I had a deep-seated need to be honest.

'Well, I don't know if it was just in my head, but I think she might have been flirting with me.'

'Flirting with you?'

'And she asked me out,' I blurted.

'And?'

'And nothing,' I said confidently. I was pleased with myself. I'd come up trumps.

'So why are you telling me all this?'

'No reason.'

'But you never tell me anything like that unless I drag it out of you. What's so special about this woman? Apart from the fact that she's on TV, of course.'

'Nothing,' I said, endeavouring to disguise the worry creeping into my voice as masculine indifference. 'There's nothing special about her. I was just making conversation.'

'Why does she fancy you? She hardly knows you.'

'I don't know.'

'Did you tell her about me?'

'Yes.' I nodded.

'So why did she ask you out?'

'I dunno,' I said, shrugging my innocence.

'Did you make her laugh?'

'No . . . yes . . . a little bit.'

'How many times?'

'I don't remember.'

'Is she pretty?'

I had to be deadly careful here. Too attractive and Mel would be jealous. Too ugly and Mel would think that I was lying to cover up the fact that she was TV's Hottest Totty. 'Average really. She was all right, I suppose, if you like that kind of thing.'

'She can't have been that plain if you're telling me about her. You're feeling guilty, Duffy. So what else are you hiding?'

'Nothing.' I wavered. I was seconds away from confessing to anything just to stop this torture. 'I was only making conversation!' I protested. 'Telling you all the stuff that happens in my life that you say I never tell you. But if you're going to accuse me of things every time I tell you what I've been doing, then we won't get very far, will we?'

Mel started giggling wildly. 'Good grief! I'm only pulling your plonker, Duff! I know all about Alexa. Her card is marked, I can tell you.'

'You know?'

'Everything,' she said, leaning over the side of the sofa and rummaging about in her bag. 'Still, you did leave out one small fact.'

'What?' I said warily.

'That she's TV's Hottest Totty!' she said brandishing the men's magazine Alexa had posed for. 'Apparently she described you as "cute in a little-boy-lost kind of way", but you turned her down because you said you were staying in with me, your girlfriend, which I might add was the right response.'

'How do you know all this?' I said, trying desperately not to show any hint of joy at being described as 'cute' by someone as fabulously gorgeous as Alexa.

Mel pecked me on the cheek and giggled. 'I have eyes everywhere!' she laughed. 'The boring answer is that Alexa called Mark and then Mark called Julie at work and told her and then Julie called me about a millisecond after and probably added a bit more to the story to make it more juicy.'

'So she didn't fancy me?' I said, trying to sound relieved.

'Oh yes she did,' said Mel knowingly. 'Julie wouldn't embellish *that* kind of detail.'

'So if you knew all the time why did you put me through all this?'

'I've been waiting all evening for you to tell me. I thought I was going to explode with excitement.' She stopped talking and carefully examined the two-dimensional Alexa in the magazine. 'Granted she's got a pretty face and a nice pair of bazookas, but her teeth are crooked, her bum's much bigger than mine, and green lingerie really doesn't suit her!' She creased up into a ball of laughter. 'My boyfriend chatted up by TV's Hottest Totty!' she tittered, failing to regain her composure. 'I quite like the idea of having to fight for you. Makes you seem more . . . I don't know . . . interesting!' She kissed me and then added, 'It almost makes you seem sexy.'

'Almost?'

'Nearly,' she purred.

'So you're not annoyed, then?'

'Of course not. I trust you completely.'

I hugged her and kissed her firmly. Staring over her shoulder, once again I began to ponder the other skeletons in my mental cupboard, but decided to save them for some other time.

Later that night, still lying on the sofa with the TV on in the

Mike Gayle

background, I looked down at Mel, who was lying next to me with her eyes closed. I whispered her name quietly to see if she was asleep. She wasn't.

She opened her eyes. 'You can turn over and watch *Frasier*,' she said, yawning.

'That's not what I wanted,' I said quietly. 'I still don't understand. How did Mark come to have a tape of my stand-up to give to Alexa?'

'I gave it to him,' confessed Mel sheepishly. 'I knew you'd never get round to sending it off yourself. I'm sorry, Duff. I'm an interfering old cow.'

'Don't be silly,' I said. 'You're right: I should've got round to sending the tape ages ago. I dunno what's wrong with me sometimes.'

'You just got a little bit scared, that's all.' She kissed me sleepily. 'I want to do everything I can to help you. You think that I take what you do for granted, but I don't. I know you sometimes think that I don't think you're funny, but you are. You make me laugh all the time – although not always intentionally. Just promise me even when we're old and grey that you'll keep making me laugh until milk comes out of my nose.'

I looked at her puzzled.

'You don't remember, do you? Last summer. We were round at my flat and I was feeling really down about work. You were trying your best to cheer me up and it wasn't working because I was being a miserable old bag, and then just as I began drinking a glass of milk you leaped up and down on the sofa like a chimpanzee, singing "New York, New York". I laughed so hard milk came out of my nose.'

'I'll try my best.' I paused. 'Mel, thanks for . . . you know . . . everything you've done.' Words seemed to fail me.

'Don't thank me,' she smiled. 'Just get me that Ferrari!'

This isn't about wardrobes

The alarm clock in Mel's bedroom went off at 7.30 a.m. I took a long hard squint at it before entombing it beneath a large pile of clothes. *It's Saturday morning*, I thought groggily, *no one should be up this early on a Saturday*. Out of the only eye I was willing to open this early in the morning, I observed an already up-and-out-of-bed Mel keenly.

'Time to get up,' she said, coyly beckoning me out of bed. She was wearing a long misshapen Snoopy T-shirt and nothing else. She looked crumpled and yet strangely alluring, so much so that I was half tempted to leap up and chase her around the room Benny Hill style. Unfortunately, given how early it was I lacked the strength of will to execute my plan, so instead, as my libido faded to black I resolved not to reply, closing my eyes instead in a bid to feign sleep. *Maybe now she'll leave me in peace*, I thought, turning over.

She didn't. Instead, her counter measure was to wrench the kingsized duckdown duvet off the bed, exposing my body to the cold of the room, and in a move carefully calculated to wind me up shouted, 'Time to get up!' again in a chirpy singsong voice, whilst dancing coquettishly just out of reach. Without saying another word, I made my way to the bathroom and took a shower.

My rude awakening was based on the fact that it was now March and six weeks had passed since we'd become engaged. It was time for us to plan the wedding. We'd already settled on a date in October the following year and her parents' local parish church. My only suggestion for the big day – that we had a disco for the evening do – was shot down by Mel for being 'tacky above and beyond the call of duty'. I couldn't believe it. As far as I was concerned, a wedding reception without a mobile DJ playing the Commodores' 'Three Times a Lady' and Dexy's Midnight Runners' 'Come On, Eileen' just wasn't a wedding reception. Mel, however, wanted something more tasteful, like a string quartet or a band, and wasn't going to budge. Thus began a minor argument which concluded in a win for her corner, when I gave up after ten minutes of going backwards and forwards having realised *The Simpsons* was on TV and I'd already missed five minutes.

These minor wedding decisions were only the beginning. There were the catering, flower arranging, photographers, wedding video, hotel and honeymoon booking, reception-room scouting *and* booking, car hire and cakemakers all to be organised and paid for. Mel had a thick loose-leaf folder with the words 'Wedding Planner' emblazoned across it in swirling gold lettering – a present from my mum. Weekends – once a time to relax and renew one's batteries after a week of work – were now more toilsome than days in the office. Weekends were now officially Duffy and Mel days – devoted to the pursuit of marital harmony.

'Where are we going today?' I asked Mel sulkily, having showered, shaved and sufficiently warmed up my personality.

'We talked about it last night.'

'We did?' I tried to remember the previous night. All I managed to recall was eating a Chinese and falling asleep in front of the telly.

'Yes. While we were watching the news. I told you we needed to go there to put things on our wedding list and your reply was, "Whatever you want."'

'Oh yeah,' I said, bluffing total recall. 'We're going to . . .'

'IKEA.'

I'd never been inside an IKEA before. I'd been as far as the car park on a couple of occasions, but I'd always pre-ferred to wait in the car as though repelled by an invisible forcefield. I didn't understand the concept of shopping for home furnishings at all. To me a chair was a chair. A table was a table. Curtains were curtains. But to Mel these things took on a mysterious significance which I couldn't begin to comprehend. To her a chair wasn't a chair unless it was a set of six and matched the napkins. A table wasn't a table unless it was large enough to seat six to eight people at a dinner party. Curtains weren't just curtains, they were the critical focal point of a room. 'Make a mistake with your curtains,' she once informed Nosferatu, 'and you might as well give up altogether.'

My heart sank the moment we arrived at IKEA. Such was the allure of home furnishings, that like salmon in search of their spawning ground, teeming multitudes of Proper Couples had felt the mysterious urge to come here. We queued for ten minutes just to get into the car park. After that we had to drive around like buzzards circling wounded antelope in search of the last parking space in the western hemisphere. Still, there were brief moments of satisfaction to be had. I spotted a parking space only seconds before a couple in a Vauxhall Tigra; the race was on but even in Mel's 2CV there was no way they could beat me. As I eased into the space and checked the rearview mirror to gloat, I was just in time to see the male driver of the Vauxhall Tigra being harangued by his other half for not being quick enough off the mark.

'What are we doing here, Mel?' I whined miserably, as we came through the electronic doors and she put one of those huge shapeless yellow bags on her shoulder. I'd meant the question metaphysically rather than literally.

'Shopping, stupid,' joked Mel, choosing to take my words at face value.

This one sentence said more about the gap in understanding between Mel and me than anything else in our lives. This was different. This was innate. Shopping to her wasn't a means to an end – it was an end in itself. She was on a spiritual journey, searching for that elusive something or somethings that would help her to make sense of the world and her place in it. Why she needed me to join her on this journey I failed to understand, but I *was* there, and we *were* getting married so I opted to make the most of it.

Within minutes Mel had a look of post-coital bliss over her face as she glided from sofa to armchair to futon and back again, casually stroking their material as if they were fondly remembered lovers.

'So what do you think?'

She was now pointing to a beige object of roughly the same dimensions as the lifts we had at work. By the look on her face I gathered she'd been in conversation with me about this item of furniture for some time. To have admitted my folly would've been, well, sheer folly. So I bluffed.

'It's nice.'

She gave me The Look.

'What have I said?'

Silence.

'What have I said?'

'You know,' she said barely moving her lips.

'What?'

Silence.

'What?'

'Saying it's "nice" like that. I'm not stupid, Duffy. If you didn't want to come why are you here? Can't you just make the effort this one time?'

'What's wrong with it being a "nice" wardrobe? It is a "nice" wardrobe. It's pleasant, agreeable, congenial and pleasing to the eye.' I stepped forward and ran my fingers along its surface, attempting to empathise. 'Smooth.'

A smile gradually cracked across her face, which eventually manifested itself into a toothy grin. I'd won her back from the edge of an argument, which was no mean feat. I gave myself a pat on the back as if I'd just defused the timer on six tonnes of plastic explosive.

'I think it would look great in our bedroom,' said Mel, still examining the wardrobe. Mel had been talking about 'our' bedroom for a while now. She wanted to hand in her notice on her Clapham flat and move in with me and Dan so we could save up enough money for a deposit on a place of our own. While it was true that my flat was cheaper, it was also true that Mel would hate living with me and Dan. Mel was allergic to slovenliness at the best of times and, well, the flat Dan and I inhabited was pretty much the shelter of the slovenly. She'd be fighting a losing battle that would eventually drive her insane.

I looked at the wardrobe again. In Mel's bedroom it would've looked fine with her antique-pine dressing table, framed Hopper prints and lilac walls. But in my bedroom it would've looked crap because it would never go with my off-white walls, Incredible Hulk poster and bookshelves littered with CDs, records, video console games and my ever-growing collection of comedy videos. I had no concept of what 'our' bedroom would look like, but there was little doubt in my mind it wouldn't look like *my* bedroom. Not if Mel had anything to do with it.

Out of curiosity I read the label on the wardrobe and was horrified. 'We can't buy it anyway. It's a flatpack wardrobe. Remember the flatpack chest of drawers we tried to assemble that one Bank Holiday? It took us three days just to find the screws and another three days to give up and chuck it underneath your bed!'

It was a joke of sorts, although to be truthful neither of us had the time or patience for flatpack furniture. Mel, however, didn't laugh. Instead she fell into the kind of silence you'd imagine fills the air before a volcano erupts. I was scared.

'I'm sorry, babe, it's just that—'

I didn't get the chance to finish my sentence. Mel turned and walked briskly away, and I chased after her berating myself for not choosing the option marked 'LEAVE WELL ALONE.'

IKEA was now overspilling with examples from the entire couple rainbow. Ones in matching jumpers, ones with matching kids, odd ones, young ones, old ones – and they were *all* in my way. I lost sight of Mel whilst trying to get round an Indian couple wheeling their children along in two of IKEA's pushchairs. By the time I'd apologised my way through them she'd disappeared. I raced frantically through Beds, Office Furniture and Storage Units before I caught sight of her in Dining Rooms.

'Mel!' I called out after her but she refused to acknowledge me. 'Mel wait!' I shouted.

A blond man wearing a herringbone jacket and jeans, with a small boy on his shoulders and his heavily pregnant significant other by his side, tapped Mel on the arm and pointed to me. She stood still but the flow of couples was coming too fast for her to remain stationary for long. She stepped out of the couple slipstream wearily and sat down on a dining-room chair that was part of one of the displays. It was a sleek modern-look dining room with a frosted-glass table. A perforated metallic black lampshade hung above it; Swedish novels lined the 'Billy' bookcase; a large sign pointed out the wooden-effect flooring was from the Tundra range at £15.00 a square metre.

I pulled up a chair opposite her. 'Look, I'm sorry,' I whispered – we were now attracting a considerable amount of attention from passing couples. 'It was a stupid thing to say. Of course we can get the wardrobe. Please.'

'This isn't about wardrobes!' said Mel through clenched teeth, her voice increasing in volume and anger with each syllable. 'It's about *you* and *your* attitude. All I want is a bit of support. Some reassurance. Is that too much to ask?'

Out of the corner of my eye, I noticed that a stout couple were watching us as though we were some sort of avant garde amateur dramatic society. This was my idea of hell. I hated rows in public. I hated them more than anything in the world. 'Of course it's not too much to ask,' I apologised. 'You're right. I'm wrong. Let's leave it at that okay?'

Mel's face contorted in outrage. 'You're not listening to me!' she screamed. Angry tears streamed down her face. 'You haven't listened to a single word I've said, have you?' Out of the corner of my eye I noted that the stout couple had been joined by a matching jumpered couple and a short couple in wax coats with their baby. I was now the recipient of an increasing number of sympathetic glances from the men and condemnatory glares from the women, as if Mel and I were the sex war writ large. I tried to remind myself I was twenty-eight and not ten. That I was a man not an errant schoolboy. But I couldn't help feeling small. And wrong.

I tuned back to my dressing down, ignoring the flourishing crowds of people no longer struggling to hear what Mel was saying because she was now 'talking' with such volume that eavesdroppers could've easily swapped their position in the eaves for somewhere more comfortable, like Sweden, and still have heard every word. 'Look, Mel. I understand that you're upset, but do you have to be so loud? Can't you just . . .' I made the mistake of issuing a small shushing noise.

'Are you shushing me?' she retorted.

'No.'

'You are, aren't you?'

'No.'

'Don't you shush me!'

'He is shushing,' spat the woman from the stout couple menacingly. 'I know a shush when I hear one!'

'I'm not shushing!' I exclaimed in her direction.

Mel sighed heavily, and the exhaled air seemed to take her volume with it. 'You're not being fair, Duffy. It's time you grew up and realised you're not a kid any more. You can't keep on acting like you're a teenager.'

'Listen, Mel, I'm sorry. Okay? I'm sorry.'

'It's too late, Duffy. It's over.'

Suddenly the world and everything in it seemed to slow down, as if we'd all been submerged under water. 'What?' I said, rubbing the back of my neck nervously. 'What are you talking about?'

'This isn't working, is it?' she said quietly. She refused to look at me. 'You don't really want to get married, Duff. I know you don't. You want your life to carry on just the same.' She began crying, her teardrops exploding on the glass tabletop like miniature water bombs. 'It's not your fault, it's just the way you are – it's part of the reason I love you. I love you because you are so carefree. I love you because you take things as they come. But I need more. I deserve more and you can't give it to me.'

I could barely believe what I was hearing. It was like Mel was having a conversation with me without my uttering a single word. The world had gone all wrong. Wrong and weird. *I have to make everything all right again.* 'What's going on here, babe? What's brought this on? Everything's fine.' I reached out and held her hand. 'Everything's going to be okay.'

'Duffy, I know everything about you,' she said accusingly.

'What are you talking about?' I protested. 'Things are getting out of hand. Let's just calm down and everything will be all right.'

She looked up at me at last. 'Look me in the eyes and answer this question: do you really, well and truly with your whole heart, want to get married?'

I met her gaze briefly and looked away.

'There's my answer,' she said, sniffing back her tears. 'I'd guessed there was something wrong but I wasn't sure until now.'

I wanted desperately to be able to lie. To say, 'Yes, I do want to get married,' but I couldn't. My newly installed conscience wouldn't let me. I loved her. I wanted to be with her. But I did not want to be married. At least not now. Not yet.

'We'll be all right, Mel,' I said, still holding her hand. 'We're going to be okay.' She didn't speak. We sat in silence while her unspoken reply made its way to my brain. It didn't quite get there. 'We're going to be all right, Mel. We can get over this.'

Silence.

'We don't need to split up,' I said desperately. 'We don't. I can learn.' I was grasping at straws now. 'I'll buy you the wardrobe.'

Still crying, she gently rotated her engagement ring off her finger and pressed it into the palm of my hand and closed my fingers over it. 'It was a nice try, Duffy . . .' she leaned across the table and kissed me softly . . . 'but it wasn't enough.'

'I want to do the right thing,' I said, fighting back the tears. She didn't hear me, though – she'd already stood up and walked away. I tried to follow her but she was too far ahead for me to catch up with her, so I watched as she manoeuvred her way through Bathrooms, Rugs and Flooring towards the checkout where finally she was swallowed up into the crowds of happy couples.

I can change

It was early Sunday morning, the day after the IKEA episode and I was on my way round to Mel's, determined to sort out this whole sorry mess. As far as I was concerned, all that had happened was that we'd had a stupid row which had blown up out of all proportion. All we needed to do was sit down and sort everything out and we'd be back to normal. The ten-minute walk from Clapham Common Tube to Mel's flat flew by as I imagined us realising that our row was nothing more than a silly quarrel brought on by pre-wedding jitters. The important thing was that we loved each other. That was all that mattered.

I pressed the buzzer for Mel's flat. After the fourth or fifth ring I heard footsteps on the stairs and seconds later a blurry Mel-shaped figure appeared through the frosted stained glass and opened the door.

'I'm sorry,' I said, not even giving her the chance to open her mouth to say hello. 'Yesterday was all my fault. I was being stupid. I'm sorry.'

Mel said nothing.

While I hadn't exactly expected a round of applause and a standing ovation, neither had I anticipated the short uncomfortable smile she gave me or the silence that accompanied it. I followed her up the stairs to her flat wondering what was going on.

Her living room was abnormally tidy. As a rule Mel was tidy but not obsessive – today, however, the entire room looked as if it had been cleaned from top to bottom by my mum, a woman for whom a thrice weekly removal of dust had taken on an almost religious significance. The flat's pristine condition didn't surprise me too much. It was Mel's way when she was unhappy to clean – to make sense of her environment by completing tasks that were completable. The room seemed to echo her thoughts: 'If only life were cleanable. If only it was a question of time and effort before life took on some semblance of peace and order.'

'I'm just going to make a cup of tea,' called out Mel from the kitchen. 'Do you want an orange juice?'

'Yeah,' I said, watching her movements through the open kitchen door. 'That would be great.'

I sat down in the armchair that Mel's gran had given her when she'd moved into a nursing home. Under normal circumstances it was my favourite seat in the flat but as soon as I sat there I knew I should've sat on the sofa so that Mel could sit next to me. Now there was this huge physical distance between us as well as the emotional gap we were trying to bridge. Just as I was about to swap seats however she entered the room with the drinks and sat on the sofa opposite. The coffee table lay between us like a latterday Berlin wall. We sat sipping and not speaking, listening carefully to the sort of sounds we normally never heard: the ticking of the clock on the wall; the sound of Cliff Richard on Radio 2 emanating from the house across the road; the sound of two people sipping in silence.

I knew I had to say something but I didn't want to mention anything more about our row. I felt that if we didn't talk about the problem directly then it didn't exist. It was ridiculously optimistic of me, but I couldn't escape the feeling that if I could just drum up enough normal conversation with her, through some miracle of amnesia she'd completely forget that less then twenty-four hours earlier she'd broken off our engagement. But what do you talk about when there really is only one thing to talk about? I looked out of the window for inspiration.

'Looks like it might rain later,' I lied. The sky was perfectly blue and cloudless. Clutching at straws? I was grasping at fresh air.

'Does it?' said Mel, gazing out of the window to join me in my meteorological studies.

Silence.

I looked inside the room for inspiration. 'The flat's really tidy.'

Mel took a sip of her tea. 'Thanks.'

Silence.

'This afternoon's *EastEnders* omnibus looks good.'

More silence.

So much for the weather.

So much for tidy flat observations.

So much for soap operas.

So much for sticking my head in the sand hoping it would all go away.

If I don't say something soon we'll still be here on the sofa having monosyllabic I-spy-with-my-little-eye conversations this time tomorrow, I thought nervously. Taking a deep breath to steel my nerves I decided to come out into the open. 'Are you okay?' I asked tentatively. 'I was worried about you.'

'Yeah, I'm fine,' she said lifelessly.

'I'm sorry. About yesterday. I'm really sorry. I was stupid and selfish and I'm sorry. But that stuff you said about us being . . .' I didn't want to spell it out, but the impassive look on Mel's face was scaring me into it. 'It wasn't true, was it? It was just you getting angry with me, wasn't it?' I smiled. I didn't want it to be an accusation – I wanted it to be light and airy.

Mel shook her head. 'We are over – you must know that, Duff, after yesterday.'

I opened my mouth to say something in my defence but she held her hand up to stop me.

'I know that you're going to tell me that you do love me and that you do want to get married after all, and that's really sweet but it's only half true. You don't want to get married, do you, Duff?' The saucer in her left hand was shaking ever so slightly. 'When I asked you yesterday if you really, truly wanted to get married, you didn't answer me. You confirmed what I knew already but was too scared to admit to myself: you love me but you don't want to get married.'

She put the cup and saucer down on the table and looked out of the window. 'I think I knew you felt that way even on the day that you finally said yes. But I was so happy . . . so relieved, that I put it to the back of my mind. I threw myself into making wedding plans, trying to sort things out, celebrating us being together. Looking back at it now, I can see that all I was doing was trying to block out the thought that you might not feel the same way about us being together as I do. I was hoping that somehow you'd catch me up, that this would excite you as much as it did me.' She hesitated slightly and looked right into my eyes. 'Then yesterday as we argued it struck me, just as if someone had slapped me across the face, that your heart wasn't in it – that you were marrying me because it was what I wanted, not because it was what you wanted. All you wanted to do was the right thing. The thing is, Duffy, I don't want you to think of us spending the rest of our lives together as some sort of sacrifice you've got to make. I don't want you to turn round to me one day and tell me I forced you into it. I'd hate it. Absolutely hate it.'

'That's not true,' I said quietly.

'It is, and you know it. If you want proof I'll give you proof.'

I raised my eyebrows sharply, as if she was about to spring a surprise expert witness on me. Who would it be? My mum? My sister? My conscience?

'It's just the small things really,' she continued. 'Like the last time we went to Mark and Julie's – all night you were miserable and I could see it was because they were talking about the wedding. Or when we chose the engagement ring. The look on your face when the jeweller handed it to you – it was only fleeting but I saw it all the same – it was a look of doubt, a look that said: 'Am I doing the right thing? But the real evidence is us. Four years together and the longest we've spent living under the same roof was three weeks in Goa last summer.'

She paused. 'It isn't right that you've made me wait this long. It's not fair that I've not held back anything from you, and this one thing . . . this one thing you can't give me. Well, I can't wait any longer. I have a life too and I can't afford to waste any more of it on you.'

She was right of course. Right about everything. That was the thing about Mel. She had this uncanny sense of seeing things the way they were instead of the way you'd want them to be, of knowing me better than I knew myself. She could sniff out the truth even if it hurt.

I couldn't think of a single thing to say that would stop what was happening, so instead we sat in silence digesting the magnitude of our conversation. Mel was crushing her thumb into her fist agitatedly, something she only ever did when nervous or angry.

I stared out of the window hoping that one of us would say something that would make this all go away, and while I waited for this miracle to occur I tried to list all the couples we knew in my head. *Beth and Mikey, Chris and Jane, Rekah and Veejay, Richard and Liz, Lara and Irvine, Kathy and Alex, Bella and Ian, Jess and Stuart, Mark and Nga, Fran and Eric . . . Mark and Julie.*

It wasn't an exhaustive list by any means, but it did the job. These couples were exhibit A: the evidence that had slowly but surely condemned Mel and me to a permanent parting. Because compared to them, with their perfect his 'n' hers lifestyles and complete togetherness Mel and I looked, well, sort of crap really. Within ten minutes of meeting up with them for lunch or a drink we'd experience the irrational feeling of envy and ineptitude that comes over insecure couples like me and Mel when they feel as if they're being left behind by their contemporaries. The solution to this problem was of course to try and befriend couples more dysfunctional and less secure than ourselves. But then again maybe that was why we were so popular on the dinner party circuit.

The thought leaked out into the real world.

'It's because we're not Mark and Julie, isn't it?'

'What do you mean?'

'It's because we're not perfect like them. You know, *perfect*.' I made the word sound hard and unpleasant. 'You know, stripping floorboards, installing Victorian fireplaces and all that. I thought we were above all that. You and me against the world type of thing. We were a cool uncouply sort of couple. We could do our own things separately as well as doing our thing together. We had our own space. I don't want us to be Mark and Julie.'

'Mark and Julie love each other, which is why they live together and why they're getting married,' replied Mel. 'It isn't unnatural. People fall in love and move in together all the time.'

'But it never stops there, does it? People move in together and just end up on the couple treadmill. Trying to keep up with the Joneses – or in this case the Mark and Julies.'

Mel shook her head in disagreement. 'You know we wouldn't have done that.'

'Yes we would,' I countered. 'Because everybody else does. Name me a single couple you know who own their own flat or house who haven't got a Victorian fireplace.'

Mel thought hard. 'Rachel and Paul.'

'Not good enough,' I said, shaking my head. 'You're right, Rachel and Paul haven't got a Victorian fireplace. That's because, if you remember, their interior decorator friend told them that Italian marble fireplaces were going to be all the rage.'

Mel shrugged her shoulders as if to say 'So what?'

'Can't you see what I'm saying? All these couples are going round trying desperately to improve everything in their lives because they want to be perfect. They want to have a perfect house, go to perfect restaurants and have the perfect relationship. But nothing's perfect, so they'll never be happy because they're not focusing on what they've got, only on what comes next. I love you, Mel. We'll be all right. We will. I know we're not perfect but we're so much better together than the alternative.'

'We'll have to agree to disagree on this one,' said Mel coolly. 'But nothing you've said changes the fact that *you* don't want to live with *me*. I could wait around for ever hoping that you'll change your mind but I'm not going to. Four years is more than enough. So I need you to go, Duffy. I need you to go right now. It's for the best. Please, please don't try and call me. At least not for a while.'

On the doorstep we kissed briefly. 'It's the saddest thing in the world, Duff,' she said, as tears welled up in her eyes. 'The saddest thing ever, because I know without question that you love me. And that we'd be so good together. But you're terrified of commitment, and whatever it is holding you back, this is something you've got to sort out on your own.'

Anyone see that Lassie film last night?

Outside W.H. Smith, half an hour after I'd left Mel's, walked all the way to Clapham Junction in the rain and caught the train to Waterloo station. I had a copy of *What Hi-Fi?* in one hand (the pages of which I was trying desperately to escape into) and in the other a maxi-pack of Revels (from which I'd already frantically located and eaten all of the orange ones). Refusing to think about, confront or admit to myself what had just happened, I made my way to the Tube and jumped on the Northern Line. I sat flicking through the pages of my magazine, poring over any picture or technical specifications that caught my eye. My plan was simple. I was going to go to one of the many hi-fi shops on Tottenham Court Road, hand over my credit card, point at a picture in *What Hi-Fi?* and say, 'Give me that.' For approximately twenty-six minutes – roughly how long it took me to get to my destination – I was happy again.

Even though it was a rain-sodden Sunday afternoon, Tottenham Court Road was busy with shoppers and tourists. I made my way through the crowds and the drizzle to the doors of the first hi-fi shop I saw, called Now Electronics. Walking into the shop, leaving the rain behind, I immediately felt at home. Dotted around the shopfloor were young men like me, exhilarated to be in a secure environment like this where we could stand and admire the latest and the best, and spend money we knew we couldn't afford because we'd managed to provide ourselves with perfectly structured arguments as to why this purchase was, more so than food, light or shelter, not only necessary but essential to our quality of life.

I stood in front of a pair of speakers that had received a five star rating in *What Hi-Fi?* and gazed at them longingly. A sales assistant, roughly my age, approached me, wearing a crumpled grey suit, ill-fitting shirt and really bad shoes. It was as if he didn't care about how he looked because there were so many other more important things in life than clothes. Like hi-fi equipment.

'Nice speakers,' he said reverentially. 'Really nice speakers.'

The people who run these kinds of shops were no fools. They employed people who thought like me to sell to people like me. This sales assistant knew exactly what to say, which buttons to press. It was like being seduced by the most beautiful woman in the world – with the worst dress sense in history. I was powerless to resist his charms.

'Yeah,' I said, acknowledging his point. 'They are.'

'They came in late yesterday afternoon. We've been so busy I haven't even had a chance to listen to them myself.'

'Really?'

He nodded. 'What system have you got at home?'

I hadn't got a 'system'. What I had was a massive, matt black all-in-one thing that I'd bought off Charlie years ago; I wasn't going to tell him that, though. Instead I lied and said I couldn't remember, and then added casually, as if possessed by the spirit of a high-rolling playboy, 'I might as well get a new CD player and amplifier while I'm here.'

'How much are you looking to spend?' he asked.

I shrugged and gave him a figure off the top of my head that in no way bore any resemblance to anything I could afford.

'Right,' he said, barely able to contain his excitement. 'Hang on a sec, and I'll make sure the listening room is vacant and then I'll wire up the speakers to the perfect CD player and amplifier. You'll love it.' He returned moments later carrying a bundle of wires and beckoned me to the glass-walled room at the back of the shop. It had a large worn brown leather sofa in the middle of it, perfectly positioned to optimise the acoustics of the room (apparently). While he matched up the wires with the sockets he gave me a rundown on the entire system. It was beautiful. There are few things in life more enticing than the sound of men talking hi-fi specifications. It put my world into perspective. The real world was a bad place where crappy things happened to me all the time, but this sales assistant was offering a way out, to a world of perfection, a place where every woofer, tweeter and bass note made sense. We both listened and spoke with awe when talking about the equipment. I didn't know as much as he did, but he wasn't condescending – he just wanted to share. The assumed knowledge. The attention to detail. It all brought us closer.

Once the speakers were wired up he asked me if there was anything in particular I wanted to listen to so that we could really put the speakers through their paces. It was then that I disappointed him. Refusing all manner of dance tracks, classic rock, soul, hiphop, jazz, guitar rock or pop, I handed him a compilation CD from the box on the floor, entitled *For Lovers Only*. It had a black and white picture of a preposterously attractive couple kissing in the rain.

'Track seven,' I said desperately. 'Play track seven.'

He looked at me incredulously. 'Are you sure, mate? I've got some banging techno that will sound brilliant through these.'

'Yes,' I nodded, no longer caring about what he thought of

me. 'I know it's cheesy but it was my . . . it was my . . . a friend of mine wasn't going to have it played at her wedding.'

'You're the boss,' he said, raising his eyebrows. He placed the shiny silver disc carefully in the drawer, pushed it shut and pressed 'Play'. Out of the speakers, crystal clear, as if the legendary ensemble were playing live right in front of me, came the rich vocal tones of the Commodores singing 'Three Times a Lady'.

Trudging through the pouring rain, weighed down by my brand new speakers, amplifier and CD player, I was already losing any sense of wellbeing my purchases had given me. I needed help. I needed my friends. I called Charlie on his mobile. He and Dan were holed up in the Shakespeare in Covent Garden watching the football because the TV in the Haversham had broken down. As I put down the phone, my spirits picked up from their downward spiral. Charlie and Dan were just what I needed. Why? Because they were my people.

People who talked about anything as long as it wasn't serious.

People who weren't constantly asking what I was thinking.

People who followed the rules of logic.

People who didn't talk when the TV was on unless it was to shout imaginative abuse at it.

People who thought red satin underwear looked great on the opposite sex.

'Anyone see that Lassie film last night?' said Charlie, absentmindedly dismantling a beermat. 'I think it was *Lassie Come Home*.'

The match had long since finished, a O–O draw and a typically dull performance from both teams, epitomising just about everything that was wrong with modern football. It had been such a tedious game that instead of discussing the highlights we were reduced to talking about what we'd got up to the night before. Well, as I'd spent Saturday night in my darkened bedroom ruminating on the IKEA episode, I lied and told everyone I'd gone to bed early because I was knackered. Dan announced that he'd spent his evening in the company of Lana, a rather attractive heckler who'd harangued him for most of his set at the Happy House in New Cross; and Charlie, rather bizarrely, had apparently spent his evening watching *Lassie Come Home*.

'They're all the same,' said Dan, dismissing the entire Lassie genre glibly. 'Small kid finds dog. Oh, Dad, can we keep dog? No. Please. No. Please. All right, go on, then. Small kid finds himself in danger. Lassie to the rescue. Happy ending.' He clapped his hands and shrugged like a cross between an East End barrow boy and a New York Jewish intellectual. 'All variations on a theme, mate.'

I didn't join in the banter because something about Charlie's evening activities didn't add up. 'Weren't you supposed to be out with Vernie last night? She said she'd booked you a table at some hideously expensive restaurant in Hampstead.'

'Yeah, she did,' said Charlie dejectedly. From the way he spoke it was obvious that their posh night out had been something of a disaster. 'We had a great time,' he added flatly.

'So how come you got to watch Lassie?' I asked.

'I taped it,' he said defensively. The tone of his voice defying us to mock him, which we of course did anyway.

'Do you know how sad that is, Charlie?' I said, laughing. 'I can't believe you taped a Lassie film. What kind of a depraved pervert does something like that in the privacy of his own home?'

Relaxing visibly, now that the topic of his night out with Vernie had been left behind, he bowed his head in mock shame. 'They were classics of their time,' he protested. 'One day they'll be up there with *The Godfather Part II, Les Enfants du Paradis* and *Digby The Biggest Dog in The World* as the greatest films ever made.' He paused, chuckling into his beer. 'Now, what I was going to say before I was so rudely interrupted? Oh yeah, in all the Lassie films, he always has to save a child from being mauled to death by some sort of vicious cougar-type animal . . .'

'Don't you mean she?' I prompted. 'Lassie was a bird.'

Charlie threw a puzzled glance at me, unsure if I was making this up. 'Lassie was a bloke, wasn't he?'

'Of course Lassie was a she,' chipped in Dan. 'Otherwise they'd be called Laddie films.'

'Good point,' said Charlie, nodding. 'All right, then. Well, in Lassie films *she* always has to save a child from being mauled to death by a cougar or something.' Dan and I nodded, wondering where this was going. 'Well how did they do that? Surely they didn't use real dogs to fight cougars?'

'Yeah,' said Dan. 'I once read in a magazine that they went through about eight stunt Lassies per film trying to get those cougar fights right.'

My mind was obviously somewhere else because I was just about to say how outrageous this was and shouldn't the anti-animal cruelty societies have done something, when Dan nearly choked himself to death with laughter. 'They took the cougar's teeth out,' he said, semi-convulsed. 'I found out all about it on a documentary on the Discovery Channel.'

I loved it – what I was experiencing at that very second. To me it was what life was all about; having a laugh and hanging out with my mates. It was the easy life incarnate. It was the way things were meant to be.

As late afternoon turned into early evening our inanity knew no bounds. Between us there was a degree in Drama and English (Dan's), an MA in Town Planning (Charlie's) and an inordinate amount of 'A' levels (some of which were mine) and yet this was the furthest you could get from intelligent dialogue. But the subjects we spoke about felt important. More important than anything else in our lives. Inspired by Lassie, topics of conversation covered the following, which despite long and often heated arguments boiled down to the following basic questions and answers:

Q: Could Batman beat Spiderman in a straight fight?
A: Not really. Spiderman has superhuman strength whereas Batman is just a bloke in a romper suit with some gadgets.
For the record: Charlie wanted it noted that he thought Batman would win because the likelihood of someone actually being bitten by a radioactive spider in real life was extremely small, whereas the odds of a bloke dressing up as a bat armed with a variety of crimebusting gadgets were slightly more realistic.

Q: Who weighs the most?
A: Me: 13 st. 5, Charlie: 14 st. 2, Dan: 12 st. 4.
For the record: Charlie insisted that it wasn't about weight per se, as about 'muscle to fat ratio'.

Q: Woody Allen's best film is . . . ?
A: *Manhattan* (two votes: Charlie and me), *Shadows and Fog* (one vote: Dan).
For the record: Dan refused to accept the judgement and insisted we institute a points system (ie. three points for our favourite, two for the next one, etc.) and demanded we all voted again.

Overall winner under new system: *Annie Hall*.

I disappeared to the gent's at the back of the pub and as I took a leak, checked my watch. It was eight o'clock. Thanks to our concentrated drinking efforts and the eight million packets of crisps I'd consumed as a replacement for Sunday lunch I was inebriated enough not to try and work out how long it had been since I'd last seen Mel but sober enough not to fall into the urinal.

Returning from the toilet I recalled a good anecdote that would embarrass Dan. It was the story of how he'd once confessed to having a bizarre crush on Elizabeth from *The Waltons*. Walking back to the table, desperately troubled by TV trivia ('Just what was the name of the actress who played Ginger Elizabeth?') I noticed that an extra person was sitting at our table talking to Dan and Charlie. It was only when he turned and waved to me that I realised it was Greg Bennet, a mate of mine and Dan's who was also a stand-up comic.

Greg wasn't really part of our inner circle – he was actually more of an associate, someone to drink with when there wasn't anyone else, and an alternative source of comedy-circuit gossip. The thing was, none of us really liked him. He was the sort of person who would make inflammatory comments in the name of humour – usually about women, but animals, asylum seekers and religious groups were often thrown into the bargain – in the hope that his 'on the edge' wit would impress us. What he failed to realise was that in his case, opposing 'the overbearing arm of political correctness' and just being a git were one and the same thing. He was, however, harmless in an odd sort of way and we tolerated him for this reason and this reason only.

'Guess what?' said Greg to all of us as I reached the table and sat down.

For a laugh we all had a guess at Greg's expense. Mine was, 'You've decided to admit that "high foreheadedness" and "balding" are one and the same thing.'

Charlie's was, 'You've discovered that you're not funny.'

Dan, however, got it right first time: 'You're getting married.'

'Yeah,' said Greg with a perplexed look on his face. 'How did you guess?'

I looked at Dan and could see that the news quite saddened him, as it had me. Dan had been on the same drama course at college with Greg's girlfriend – 'the lovely Anne' as we called her – and had nearly got it together with her, but for one reason or another it never worked out and she'd ended up with Greg. Dan always said she was the kind of woman he could've fallen in love with because she was an incredibly genuine person whose only flaw, it seemed, was that she couldn't see how much of a tosser Greg really was.

'It's like that joke,' Dan replied languidly. 'Why did the monkey fall out of the tree?'

'Dunno,' said Greg.

'Because it was dead.' He paused for a moment, letting the punchline soak in. 'Why did the second monkey fall out of the tree?'

'Dunno,' repeated Greg self-consciously.

'Because he thought it was a new game and didn't want to be left out.'

'And your point is?' said Greg, the only one of us not laughing.

'Well, this one here's already married.' Dan pointed to Charlie. 'This one here's getting married.' He pointed to me. 'It was only going to be a matter of time before another

117

monkey thought it was a good idea, and it's not exactly going to be me, is it?'

'Are you calling me a monkey?' said Greg, working himself up to a point beyond indignation but just outside anger.

'No, Greg. I'm not,' said Dan, deflating a potentially combative situation. He'd drunk too much and Greg's presence was bringing out the more antagonistic side of his nature. He offered his hand in congratulation. 'I'm pleased for you, mate.'

'Cheers,' said Greg, shaking Dan's hand warily.

'Married, eh?' said Charlie, offering Greg a handful of dry-roasted peanuts. 'When did you ask her?'

'Last night,' said Greg, accepting the peanuts. 'I'd been thinking about it for a while now and I just thought why not?' He turned to me. 'How about a double wedding, then? You and me, Anne and Mel. It'll cut costs in half!'

I didn't laugh. I didn't grin. I didn't even shrug my shoulders. I didn't do any of the things I was supposed to do. Instead I cried. Big fat tears by the bucketload. Everybody has a few really embarrassing moments in their lives. Well, I decided to have all mine and somebody else's right there in the pub. I honestly couldn't remember the last time I'd cried. Mel used to joke that I'd had my tear ducts removed, but the truth is, I think I just forgot how to. And now she had reminded me.

No one spoke. Instead they stared emptily into their pints. I think even the jukebox stopped playing, although that could've been my overactive imagination. I'd let myself down. Badly. There was a time and place for emotions and this wasn't either of them. Not here in a bar, with my mates watching me like I was some sort of freak show, and not now over Mel. All my tears did was point out the obvious – that whatever I did to avoid or escape it, real life would ultimately rear its ugly head. Everyone around the table knew real life existed – we also knew that was why after Stone Age man invented the wheel, the very next thing he did was invent the pub.

After some moments of awkward silence so painful that I strongly believe they'll scar me for my duration on this planet I reasoned that perhaps I owed my friends an explanation, which would perhaps make me feel better but would without a doubt only serve to make the situation worse. 'Mel and I have split up,' I confessed. 'She said I wasn't sure about getting married. Which is true. But that doesn't mean that I don't love her . . .' overcome with emotion I failed to finish the sentence. The heavy sense of despair that had been bearing down on my shoulders since this morning finally crushed me. 'My life has turned to arse. Somebody, anybody tell me how to be sure.'

There was a huge silence. A tall, wiry-looking bar man with spiky blond hair came over and collected our empty glasses. I wiped my eyes and attempted to clear the snot from my sinuses. Still no one uttered a single word.

A few moments passed and then as if he'd just woken up Charlie said quietly, 'Vernie's pregnant. She told me yesterday at that restaurant she took me to. I knew something was up. We never go out for posh meals without a reason . . . I thought I was ready . . . I thought I'd get used to the idea but I haven't and now it's happened I . . . I don't want to be a dad.'

Silence.

Dan coughed loudly and we all looked at him. 'You all know about Meena's wedding invitation. Well, last night, as I sat chatting up that girl I met after my gig even though I knew my heart wasn't in it, it dawned on me that I made the biggest mistake of my life splitting up with Meena. I think she was . . . you know . . . The One.'

We all exchanged glances and then stared at our pints and then at our laps and nobody said a word.

After a few minutes of contemplative silence, Greg sniffed nervously, lit up a Silk Cut and offered them round the table. We all took one, waiting to hear whether he too had had a shock revelation that would gain him membership to the inaugural meeting of Emotional Losers Anonymous.

'Right,' he said, settling down in his seat and lighting his cigarette nervously, 'did anyone see that Lassie film last night?'

I am committed to non-commitment.

—Federico Fellini

Exchange emotional CVs

In the beginning there was her and there was me and an awful lot of happiness. We were in love. Totally, utterly and incontrovertibly. People, usually women, would comment on Mel and me at parties saying things like 'I can't believe how well you two get on together,' 'You look so in love,' and my favourite, 'You really are each other's best friend.' Which was true. I'd never met a woman like her in my life. She was beautiful, compassionate and intelligent. She constantly made me laugh, drank like a fish, and like me enjoyed nothing more than shouting words of advice at the TV for the benefit of the characters in *EastEnders*. She was some sort of miracle. Some sort of angel from above. The funny thing is, when I first met her I genuinely didn't think I stood a chance.

I was twenty-four, and back then I'd just started a two month block temping in the administration department of a magazine publishing house just off Leicester Square. I spotted Mel on my first lunch break. She was in front of me in the queue in the Italian sandwich shop around the corner from my office building. I walked slowly behind her as she left the shop to see where she went and was immensely pleased when she disappeared into the rotating doors of the Mentorn House, the building where I worked. My joy continued as we shared a wordless journey in the same lift, and nearly exploded when she got out of the lift on my floor and disappeared in the direction of ad sales.

I stood, open mouthed, watching her, as I attempted to define in my head what it was about this woman that stopped me in my tracks. After a few moments, in which I was told off by a senior member of management for blocking the lift exit, I worked it out. It wasn't her face or body that attracted me – although both were pretty hard to fault – it was her walk. She had the most hypnotic walk I'd even seen. It was strident, sexy, and that rarest of qualities, sassy. A living, breathing, moving version of Chrissie Hynde singing 'Brass in Pocket'.

In the next fortnight I discovered the following facts about my dream woman: her name was Mel Benson, she was twenty-four and had gone to university in Edinburgh. She liked chicken and avocado sandwiches, hated her aerobics teacher, did 'something' in the advertising sales department, wasn't married, and looked brilliant in black. It was a further week, however, before I actually managed to have a conversation with her.

Every Friday lunchtime the ad sales department went to the George, a pub just across the road from the office. Realising this could be a way in, I shamelessly ingratiated myself with Tony, a middle-aged ad executive whose sole reason for living was cricket, and within a week he had invited me to the Friday pub session. I ruthlessly abandoned him at the first opportunity and manoeuvred myself into position next to Mel.

We got chatting almost immediately and I asked her what she did. Her answer 'I'm a media planner' left me none the wiser. When she returned the question I admitted to my temp status but told her I was a stand-up comedian too. The usual response I got when I revealed this information was, 'Tell us a joke,' which I hated, because I wasn't a performing seal. Mel, however, just said, 'It's nice to meet someone with dreams,' and left it at that. I was impressed. In the twenty-seven minutes that remained of lunch I made her laugh a total of twenty-three times. A personal best.

I did the same thing the following week and the week after. It soon got to the stage where on a Monday we'd ask about the quality of each other's weekends and on a Friday we'd ask what each other had planned for our time off. Of all the love crusades I've waged in my life, this was by far my longest and most concerted effort.

On the Friday of the fourth week of my campaign I finally made my move. Mel was standing next to the lift, tapping the pale blue plastic bottle of the water fountain with a biro. 'I'll name that tune in three,' I said smiling.

A huge grin spread across her face, so wide it revealed for the first time her teeth, small, perfect and glistening. 'Why are you always making me laugh?' she asked as if I was part of some sort of conspiracy to make her happy.

'I don't know. Maybe you have a low humour threshold.'

'Could be. But maybe it's because you're a funny guy.'

Not bothering to work out whether she meant 'funny' as in 'ha ha' or 'funny' as in 'Stop following me, you weirdo,' I decided this was it. The opportunity. I didn't need to be told twice. 'Do you fancy going for a drink after work tonight?'

'Are you asking me out?' she said matter-of-factly.

I searched around for the correct answer. I'd tried to make my invitation sound as casual as possible, giving her the option to brush me off without smashing my ego to pieces, but here she was asking me to define one of two things you should never, ever define, not even if threatened with death.

'Er, no . . . well, I suppose . . . yes.'

'I thought so,' she said smiling. 'Thanks very much. I'm flattered but I'm afraid the answer's no.'

I hadn't even included rejection on my list of possible reactions. I know I should've just left it at that and walked away, and on behalf of my mouth I'd like to apologise to my ego for not having done so. Instead, throwing caution to the wind, I asked, 'Why not?' the question any man with a modicum of self-respect would never ask because it's tantamount to begging.

'It's just one of those things, I'm afraid,' she said, wringing her hands nervously. 'You've caught me at the worst possible time.'

I scuttled back to my desk to lick my wounds and throw myself into my work in a manner I'd never done before. My survival plan was simple: I was going to avoid Mel for the rest of my life. With this in mind I skulked around the office, dodging her in the corridors, by the water fountain and in the George. On the last day of my contract, however, fate had it that I should bump into her in the lift as I was on my way home.

'You're avoiding me, aren't you?' she said, as the doors closed and she pressed the button for the ground floor.

Once again I searched around for the correct answer. I'd tried to make my avoidance of her as casual as possible, giving her the option to stay well away from me, but here she was, asking me to define the other thing you should never, ever define, not even if threatened with death. 'No . . . well, I suppose . . . yes.'

'I thought so,' she said smiling. 'I've been hoping I'd bump into you.'

'Why?'

'You've changed my mind,' she said shyly. I noted her curious choice of words but refused to let her say any more. Additional conversation would only confuse the matter. If I could change her mind without knowing it, I could just as easily change it back again by accident. So we descended the fifteen floors to the lobby in silence. When the doors opened she took out a biro from her bag, grabbed my hand, scribbled her phone number across my palm and walked away.

We arranged to meet in a bar called Freud that same evening. Mel arrived at a quarter to nine – fifteen minutes late – an ideal length of time for me to reach the wet-palm stage of nervousness and for her to appear more enigmatic than I thought humanly possible. She was wearing dark blue jeans, trainers, a white T-shirt and a jacket. She'd dressed down, which was good. Dressing down called for the kind of self-confidence I admired in a woman.

'Can we get one thing straight?' she said, sitting down at the table. I looked at her blankly. 'I don't want a . . . you know . . . a relationship.' I put on my Blank Face. 'We'll just be friends.' My Blank Face went into overtime. 'Don't take this personally but relationships are too complicated and I could do with the easy life right now. Don't get me wrong, you're a nice guy, but this is a case of wrong place, wrong time, wrong girl, wrong planet.' She paused as if sensing my disquiet. 'Well, aren't you going to say anything?'

It was at this point in the proceedings that I took a chance, the like of which I'd never taken before or since. I kissed her – contravening not just one but two of the rules of snogging people you don't know very well:

Rule one: always drink too much.
Rule two: always wait for The Moment.

In my hand was a glass of lime cordial and soda water (the cheapest drink in the house), and as for The Moment, I can only assume it was subject to delays due to leaves on the

---

track. It was just as I was contemplating where this impulse might have had its origin when she kissed me back. We came up for air three breathless minutes later, somewhat flushed and distinctly hot under the collar.

'I can't believe I've just done that,' she said, avoiding all eye contact.

'Neither can I,' I replied, looking at my shoes. 'But we have.'

We spent the rest of the evening drinking and talking – totally enthralled with each other. Later, we became hungry and Mel suggested we get something to eat. The last of my money had long since disappeared, forcing me to explain my poverty-stricken situation to her. She didn't seem to mind at all, in fact she thought it was funny, and so at her expense we ate at a nearby Italian restaurant. In the middle of a mouthful of pasta, I noticed she was staring at me not saying anything. She clearly had something on her mind.

'What?' I said, narrowing my eyes suspiciously. 'I've got tomato sauce on my chin, haven't I?' I wiped my hand across my mouth.

'No, it's nothing,' she replied in a manner that clearly meant the complete opposite. I shovelled in another mouthful of pasta just as 'nothing' was metamorphosing into 'something'. 'We've kissed each other. We barely know each other. Don't you think we ought to do that background thing?'

'Exchange emotional CVs?'

Mel smiled winsomely. 'Swap relationship resumés.'

'Yeah,' I said, 'but you first.'

She told me she'd recently split up with a man she'd been with for two years who she thought might be The One. Unfortunately he thought she definitely was The One and wanted her to move in with him, but she didn't feel the same. She took two hours to tell me this information. Her narrative was all over the place and massive amounts of useless information came with it, huge chunks at a time.

I discovered that when she was six years old she fell over and cut her knee and now had a scar that looks like a smile. I discovered that three years ago she'd bought an Ella Fitzgerald album at a car boot sale which she claimed was her most treasured possession. I discovered that she had always wanted a cat but now she was single it seemed a bit of a cliché. It was all utterly endearing but confusing at the same time.

The record of my own romances took all of five minutes to reveal. Reluctant to go into the whole Amanda crossover skeleton thing for obvious reasons, I concluded the ups and many downs of my love life with the one before her, Rebecca, whose last words to me were, 'I'm leaving the country. Don't try and follow me.' I thought that was quite funny but Mel didn't seem to want to laugh.

'Is that it?'

'What?'

'Your love life?'

'Yeah.'

'Where are your details? I need details.'

'I've told you everything.'

'You told me nothing. I told you everything.'

I gave her my Bewildered Face – a slight variation on the Blank Face.

'What is it with men? Why can't they talk? Do you learn this at some strange boy school? Do you have your vocal cords removed at birth?'

'No,' I said. Thankfully she laughed this time. So I told her more about my past even though I felt incredibly uncomfortable doing it. I knew it was a good sign – that she was interested in me – but I couldn't help thinking all this talk of failed relationships was somehow tempting fate.

'I think it's time for us to go,' she said, licking the back of her dessert spoon and looking around the restaurant. When we'd come in the room was full; now it was empty and the waiters were dropping the heaviest of hints that we were the only thing preventing them from going home.

'I enjoyed tonight,' I said, as hand in hand we made our way through the crowds emptying from a nearby theatre on Shaftesbury Avenue. 'It was . . . interesting.'

'Me too,' she said as we quickly crossed into the road, narrowly avoiding being struck down by a homicidal bus driver. 'But you know this isn't going to work out, don't you?'

I stopped and looked at her, unsure whether it was her insecurity speaking or whether she was trying to let me down gently. 'Why?'

'Because.' She took a step closer to me as traffic whizzed by on both sides. 'For one thing, I'm trying to concentrate on my career at the moment . . .'

'And for the other?'

'And for the other . . . I've just come out of a long-term relationship. Which would mean you're the rebound. Which means one of us is going to hurt the other, and I already like you too much for it to be me.'

'So don't.'

'What?'

'Like me. Don't like me. I'm not your perfect partner. I'm not the man of your dreams. I constantly forget important dates – birthdays, anniversaries *and* bank holidays – my intentions towards you are totally dishonourable and I spend too long in the bathroom.'

'How long?'

'Half an hour.'

'Practically makes you an honorary girl.'

'But on the other hand, for as long as it lasts we can have a good time. It'll be a laugh. Like a holiday romance without being on holiday. And I promise no postcards or long-distance phone calls when it's all over.'

'A holiday romance,' she said wistfully. 'I like the sound of that.' We kissed, and as a passing taxi beeped its horn at us, drawing us back to reality, Mel stood on the tips of her toes and whispered into my ear, 'Bring on the sangria!'

That was then.

My favourite dress

It was my mum who took the news of my split with Mel the worst. She was devastated, especially when I told her the reason was all my fault. 'Can't you do anything about the way you feel?' she'd asked me, like it was breaking her heart. I tried to explain to her my way of thinking but she wasn't convinced. Vernie wasn't much happier. In no uncertain terms she told me that I was a fool if I thought there was something out there better than Mel. It was clear that with the exception of Dan and Charlie, my friends and family all thought it was my fault.

The whole of April went by in a blur as in response to such criticism I threw myself into my comedy, travelling to crappily attended gigs in places like Norwich, Chichester and Northampton. I threw myself into an awful lot of alcohol (a strangely romantic feeling, conjuring up the sophistication of *A Lost Weekend* and apparently very surreal turns behind the mic), and such was my state of mind that I even threw myself into my temping job.

The only blip on my fast-track attempt to forget Mel came near the start of April, when I woke up on the fifth and realised it was her twenty-ninth birthday. I'd wanted to call her more than anything in the world. Not just because it was her birthday, but also because I missed her. She hadn't even collected her things. Her designated space in my bedroom chest of drawers still contained a jumper, a bra, two pairs of pants, a box of tampons and a pair of tights. The tattered Nike trainers she used for aerobics were still underneath my bed. The freezer still contained the massive bag of broccoli she'd bought after reading a magazine article that said it helped prevent cancer. *What am I going to do with three tonnes of sodding broccoli?* I'd asked myself when I discovered it behind a box of fish fingers. In the end I chucked it in the bin – it was too painful a reminder. But now a month had gone by since I'd last seen her, and as far as I was concerned I'd respected her wishes by not calling – now it was time for her to respect mine.

In the past, like most people, I'd used the phrase 'Let's be friends' as shorthand for 'Please don't put my photo on a dartboard,' but as I thought about calling Mel I really meant it. Pre-Mel girlfriends had always been functional creatures – designed to fulfil their destiny as 'girlfriends' and little else. But this was different. This was Mel. What we had couldn't be scrapped without some attempt to salvage a friendship from the wreckage.

I called her at work at the beginning of the week. 'Hi, Mel, it's me,' I said brightly.

'How are you?' she said eventually.

'Okay. How are you?'

'Okay. Not too bad.'

'How was your birthday?'

'Good.'

'What did you do?'

'Went for a drink with some friends.'

Silence.

'How's work?'

'Okay. How's the comedy?'

'Okay.'

Yet more silence.

It quickly became apparent that without day-to-day inter-action our smalltalking abilities had wasted away. *This is what time apart does to you,* I thought angrily. *Leaves you unable to talk about the small stuff with your ex-boyfriend.* I attempted to get to the point of my call before the repertoire of our relationship disintegrated any further.

'I know it's over between us, Mel, and I know that you'd rather we didn't see each other, but I want . . . I need us to be friends. I know it would be a lot easier just to get on with our new lives alone, clean breaks, and all that. But I don't want a clean break. I want you and me to be part of each other's lives no matter how difficult it is.'

I'd like to think my big speech was a sign of newfound maturity, and I think that's how Mel interpreted it, because she actually agreed to meet up with me that Thursday. If I'm really truthful, though, I'd have to admit that there was the slightest possibility that it had less to do with maturity than it did with me wanting to hang on to any scrap of my ex-girlfriend that I could get.

It was the day that we'd arranged to meet. I left work ten minutes early, cunningly sneaking past Checkpoint Bridge. Once out of the office I avoided any form of transport that might cause me to be late and instead opted to race through central London on foot to my destination.

At Mel's suggestion we had arranged to meet in the base-ment bar of a vaguely trendy Thai restaurant in Soho. I'd never been there before and to the best of my knowledge she hadn't either. I remember at the time thinking that she'd done this on purpose – selecting somewhere unfamiliar to us both so that it would be free of associations. It was a smart move on her part because the suggestion on the tip of my tongue had been the bar, Freud, where it all began.

Mel had called me briefly at work in the afternoon to remind me that she could only meet me for an hour because she had other plans for later on in the evening. I'd said it wasn't a problem even though it was. My confidence was running high now that she was meeting me, and I'd convinced myself that if I played my cards right, any plans she'd made for the night would be cancelled to make room for a whole bunch of my own.

I arrived at the Paradise out of breath but with plenty of time to spare and so I headed downstairs to the bar, perched myself on a ridiculously high stool, bought a bottle of Michelob and sat staring up at the metal staircase expectantly.

When Mel arrived (fifteen minutes late), it was her legs that I saw first. She was wearing her short black sleeveless dress, my favourite dress, the one I'd always thought made her look perfect.

She greeted me with a kiss and sat down. 'Hi, Duff.'

'Hi,' I said sheepishly, returning her kiss with a peck on the cheek followed by a hug to balance the lack of intimacy of the kiss. These were all delicate manoeuvres that required a deftness of touch I wasn't sure I possessed.

'You look great,' I said warmly.

'Thanks,' she smiled. 'You look a bit sweaty.'

I examined myself in the mirror behind the bar. Mel was right. I couldn't have looked sweatier if I'd been in a sauna. All that running to get here on time had taken its toll on a body as unaccustomed to exercise as mine. I attempted to make myself look a little less flustered while she spoke to the barman. She ordered another beer for me and paused carefully before ordering a vodka and orange for herself.

Our conversation was nowhere near as stilted as it had been on the phone. In fact after a while it was almost possible to forget that we weren't a couple. We updated each other on the small but important details of our lives (I told her about work, recent gigs and last night's *EastEnders*, while she told me about work, her flat and new bars and restaurants she'd been out to).

Mel really was pleased when I told her the news of Vernie's pregnancy, and made me give her all the details that I knew. I told her she should go and see Vernie, but she smiled awkwardly and said she didn't think she'd have the time because of work. It was a real shame that our not being together had to mean that she and Vernie couldn't be friends. She asked me to send her love to Vernie and Charlie and made a note in her diary to send them both a card. She asked me about Dan, too, and I told her he was okay. I considered telling her about the wedding invitation from Meena, but reasoned it was a subject too close to home for us to be comfortable with. In the end, though, it cropped up in the conversation all by itself.

'I had a letter from Meena,' said Mel. 'You know, Dan's ex-girlfriend. You'll never believe this, but she's getting married.'

'I know,' I said warily. 'She sent an invitation to Dan.'

'Oh,' she said ominously. 'I suppose she has her reasons.' She paused. 'Meena sent me an invitation, too, along with the letter. Well, actually it's addressed to you and me. She didn't know about us—'

'I think it must just be for you,' I interjected quickly, stopping her from finishing the sentence. 'Meena was never exactly my biggest fan.'

'No,' she said, handing me the invitation. 'You take it. It's ages since I've seen Meena. I'll just send a present or something in the post.'

I handed the invitation back to her. 'Look, she's inviting

you because she likes you. My name's only on the invitation because she's being polite. Anyway, if Dan's not going – which he isn't – then I don't think I should go either. Why don't you and Julie go or something? You know how you love a good wedding—' I stopped, glaringly aware of my own stupidity. 'I'm sorry . . . you know what I mean.'

'Don't worry,' she said. 'I know what you mean.'

The bar was beginning to fill up with after-work drinkers, so to help create a 'groovy' ambience the barman dropped a tape into the cassette deck behind the bar. I was hoping it would be something inspirational to lift my mood, but instead through the speakers came one of those songs you recognise immediately because it's played every thirty seconds on daytime radio.

'Mel,' I said, as the song reached its annoyingly catchy chorus, 'it really means a lot to me that you could come today. I kept thinking that you must hate me and want me dead and all that. I just want you to know that I still love you – it wasn't anything to do with you. What I mean is . . . it's not that I couldn't marry you. I couldn't marry anyone . . .'

'Thanks,' she said bitterly. I desperately wished I'd left well alone.

'I don't understand. Why are you taking this the wrong way? I want us to be friends. I need us to be friends.'

Mel emptied the contents of her glass in one smooth movement. 'This is so typical of you, Duffy. Sometimes you're so caught up in yourself that you don't see anyone else's needs. What about what I need? What makes you think that I'd want to be friends with you? Every meeting, every phone call a reminder that you'd rather live in . . .' she flicked through her internal phrase book for the perfect putdown . . . 'the kennel of the unkempt with Dan than with me! I waited four years for you and I've got nothing to show for it. This isn't a meeting of equals: it was *you* who didn't want to marry *me*.'

I didn't have a leg to stand on. It didn't take any great insight to see that she was right. If the tables had been turned, there would be no way that I'd be sitting in some poncy bar that played terrible music, listening to Mel give me excuses why, although she loved me, she didn't want to be with me until death did us part.

'I've done this all wrong,' I said.

'Yeah, you've got that right,' she sighed, and ordered another beer for me and another vodka and orange for herself.

I tried to get us back on to safer ground by asking how Mark and Julie were getting on.

'They're fine,' said Mel, sipping her drink slowly. 'Mark's been busy at work as usual. Julie's busy, too, but she's somehow managed to take up pottery classes after work. So far all she's made are ashtrays. Well, they start out as vases and then end up as ashtrays. I've got five of the things!' she laughed, seeming to relax a little. 'Do you want one?'

'A Watson original?' I said laughing. 'I'd love one.' *This is good*, I thought. *This is what we are about*. 'Any other Mark and Julie news?'

She paused, sipped, and thought the question over. 'They've decided that they're definitely moving somewhere bigger next year. Hopefully in time for their wedding.' Mark and Julie were obsessed with moving house. In the time I'd known them they'd bought and renovated three houses. I think the plan was that as soon as prices in their corner of Shepherd's Bush reached critical mass, they'd sell up and finally move to their spiritual homeland, Notting Hill Gate. 'Oh, and they're going to rent a villa in Tuscany at the start of August with a few friends. They've invited me along. I told them I didn't fancy it, but Julie's twisted my arm, so I just might take up the offer after all.'

She checked her watch. 'It's seven o'clock, Duff. I'm going to have to go.'

'Okay,' I said, sliding off the stool. I was disappointed that she hadn't changed her mind, but I was sure it didn't mean that I wasn't in with a chance. The bar was now completely packed. We worked our way across the room and up the stairs, stepping out through the door into early evening sunshine.

'Okay then, Duff,' said Mel abruptly. 'I'll have to say good-bye now.'

'Off anywhere nice?'

'Just out with some friends,' she replied. 'Which way are you going?'

'Leicester Square,' I said, having duly noted that her friends were now nameless.

'Listen,' said Mel, 'I'm sorry I was horrible to you just now, about this being friends thing.'

'No. No, you weren't,' I apologised. 'It was nothing less than I deserved. Really.'

She smiled patiently. 'This is still hard to deal with but I'm glad that you want us to be friends, because we are, aren't we? I don't want us just to drift apart, okay?'

This is it, I thought. *The Moment.*

She kissed me on the cheek and I gave her a hug and returned her kiss briefly. On the lips. It wasn't a peck either. It was a full-on, pressure-filled 'give-me-a-few-more-seconds-and-I'll-be-playing-tennis-with-your-tonsils' snog. It was wrong of me, shallow and contemptible. My title was that of ex-boyfriend, and as such my kissing location was restricted to the cheek. Cheeks were for ex-boyfriends, acquaintances and relatives. Lips were for current boyfriends, close friends and stuffed animals. Those were the rules and I'd broken them.

Mel's glare put me right within seconds. She pulled away awkwardly, opened her mouth about to share her thoughts with me on my behaviour, but obviously thought better of it. Instead, she sighed as if I'd managed to disappoint her more than even she'd thought possible, and walked away.

Burdened with guilt I made my way down Wardour Street towards Leicester Square Tube, but something – you could call it a sixth sense but I prefer to label it my sense of tragedy – made me look back just in time to see a black Saab convertible with the licence plate ROB 1 pull up next to Mel. The car's casually attired driver got out, greeted Mel, put his hands on either side of her waist and kissed her.

On the lips.

He wasn't a close friend, otherwise I'd know him.

And he certainly wasn't a sodding stuffed animal.

So there really was only one option left.

Thinking back on it, as I walked to the Tube with a black hole in the place my heart used to be, it occurred to me that it wasn't so much the kiss that bothered me. It was his hands on her dress. My favourite dress.

You need to get out more

Mel's mysterious, lip-kissing, personal-number-plated new 'friend' completely threw my world off course. If I was the earth, then Rob 1 was a huge meteorite knocking me off my axis, thus heralding in a new ice age.

I'd never have believed Mel would want to find a replace-ment me this soon, only a month after we'd broken up, let alone one so solvent, good looking and upwardly mobile. Whatever happened to grieving periods? *That's the prob-lem with modern women*, I decided. *No bloody sense of decorum*. The thing that really hurt was that it hadn't even occurred to me that I might even need a replacement Mel. *That's how stupid I am.*

I wondered whether it was just me being unreasonable. What did 'real' people consider a decent mourning period following the death of a four-year relationship? I conducted a (fairly) scientific straw poll of family, friends and associates to find out.

Results from the Duffy Institute of Relationship Stat-istics as follows:

Dan: 'For a woman like Mel? Three months minimum. You've obviously made some mistake, mate. This guy's got to be her brother. What, as far as you know she

143

hasn't got a brother? Even better, mate, he's got to be her *long-lost* brother.'

Charlie: 'I have difficulty even recalling the existence of any woman before Vernie but I pretty much agree that for a relationship like yours three months would seem to be the industry standard.'

Greg: 'For women to get over a relationship of that length, anything from six months to never. But for us men pretty much as and when we feel like it – the sooner the better, though. It's not sexist, it's genetics: women want a long term provider while blokes just want to have a good time. It's the way of the world.'

Vernie: 'Even though I'm a pregnant woman and therefore a cauldron of unreasonability, I have to say this: women can do whatever they like when they like because all men are stupid.'

My mum: 'Enough time to heal the hurt but not so much that you drown yourself in depression.'

With the exception of my sister's answer (and needless to say Greg's), I interpreted the results of the survey to conclude that Mel should still have been in mourning. She'd obviously made a mistake in her calculations and was gallivanting around town with her new man when she was still, according to conservative estimates, some six weeks away from recovery.

It's only the beginning of May, woman! You're meant to be in mourning! You're not supposed to get over me until at least August!

Up until this stage of events I'd been coping reasonably well with life without Mel – it was as if she'd gone on holiday and was taking a long time to come back – but seeing her with Rob 1 made everything more real than it needed to be

– and now it hurt more than anything I'd ever experienced in my life. When I'd split up with girlfriends in the past, I'd dropped out of their lives so completely that it was easy to imagine that they'd stopped existing altogether. But with this stupid let's-be-friends thing still at the forefront of my mind, I had to come to terms with the fact that the never-ending ache in my heart was bound to get a lot worse before the passing of time would make it any better.

It made no sense to be the only one of us grieving. But grieve I had to. So I let myself go wild for a while. I called in sick at work, cancelled all my gigs for the coming week and ate bag after bag of Butterkist toffee popcorn whilst watching bad daytime TV. I even adopted the uniform of dressing gown and blue Marks & Spencer pyjamas my mum had bought me for Christmas. I told her at the time that I wouldn't need them because I slept naked, and I remember quite clearly that she said, 'Take them. In case of an emergency.' Now I knew what she meant.

During that week I fell apart. Every few days Dan, Charlie and Vernie would try to drag me out of my melancholy, but I always refused, explaining to them that this was only a temporary measure I needed to go through in order to come out the other side.

Two o'clock Saturday afternoon – approximately eight days since I'd gone into mourning – I did just that. It wasn't like I'd stopped hurting – I still felt the Pain as keenly as ever – I think it was more a case that through my grieving I'd learned to live with it.

I let LadyBic razor and chin meet for the first time in over a week (sweet justice indeed. Mel was forever telling me off for using her leg razors to shave with), I moulted my mourning clothes straight into the washing machine, and naked, strode into the shower where I symbolically washed the sadness from me. It was then, as I rubbed a large handful of Mel's abandoned Laboratoires Garnier frequent-use fortifying shampoo into my scalp, that I made a decision. The decision to change. To become a bachelor boy like Dan – a superstud of seduction, a he-who-will-never-again-come-off-worse-with-the-chicks, a righteous dude committed to anything but commitment.

What I needed to start me off in my new role as a superstud of seduction was a dead cert. Someone to break me in gently. I flicked through my address books looking for past liaisons that might have fallen into that category. A–Z and back again. Twice. None of them had been dead certs when I had met them – and it would have taken an outlandish brand of optimism to make me believe that things had changed that drastically in my four years out of the game.

When I came across Alexa's card with her phone number I thought long and hard about making contact. 'Didn't she describe you as "cute in a little-boy-lost manner"?' said my ego eagerly. 'She's TV's Hottest Totty, you know.' Alexa was precisely what my ego needed to get over the Rob1 blow, but I needed practice, a few jogs around the block before I'd be in any shape to tackle a New York marathon like her.

Over mid-afternoon toast and beer (Dan's idea of a welcome-back-to-the-land-of-the-living feast), we discussed the problem at hand and together arrived at the perfect solution not just to my own predicament but Charlie's and Dan's too. Now all we had to do was persuade Charlie.

'I'm not going to a nightclub!'

It was later that same day and Dan and I were round at Charlie's listening to him reject our master plan. He sat on the edge of their huge sofa looking at me and Dan as if we'd lost our minds on the short journey from Muswell Hill to Crouch End. It was at times like this that the age gap between Charlie and ourselves became most apparent. At thirty-four he felt he'd served his time doing pointless youthful activities, and was one of the few people of his years who took comfort in the idea of middle age.

'Nightclub?' goaded Dan. 'Have you just beamed in from 1962, Grandad? "Nightclubs", as you so quaintly call them, lost their "not daylight" prefix a long time ago. You need to get out more.'

'All right, then,' said Charlie, 'I am not going . . .' he faltered as if the word alone was making him feel nauseous . . . 'clubbing.' He paused to see what effect it'd had on him. 'I can't believe you made me say that. What kind of worthless tosser uses words like "clubbing"? It's like "pubbing". Are you coming pubbing on Saturday? No, I'm afraid I can't. I'm going clubbing. After which I'm doner-kebabbing and then cabbing home. I hate progress. Suddenly every noun has been turned into a verb.'

Dan and I exchanged glances as if Charlie was going off on one.

'Sorry, lads. I'm too old for this. I am. Look at me.' We did. Although Charlie had a youthful face, his body let him down. The contentedness of married life had increased his girth like the passing of time adds rings to a tree trunk. But somewhere deep inside him we were convinced there was a teenager who wanted to party. We just had to find a way to let him out.

'Don't stress it,' reassured Dan. 'We've got everything planned out. A boys' night out will take your mind off the baby, Duffy's mind off the whole Mel saga and, fingers crossed, my mind off Meena and her stupid wedding invitation.'

'A boys' night out,' I said encouragingly. 'It'll be just what the doctor ordered.'

Getting ready for our night out brought back a flood of memories. Memories of before Mel. In fact before the girl before that and the one before her too, right back to when I was seventeen and every Saturday night had the potential to be *the* best Saturday night of my life. The ritual was exactly the same every week:

1) Watch *Blind Date*.
2) During the ad break one of my more organised friends would call with a suggestion of where we could go.
3) Me and Vernie would get into a fight over who was next in the bathroom. I'd lose and have to wait an hour for her to finish, only to discover she'd used all the hot water. While I had a lukewarm bath, another mate would call and leave a message with my mum saying who was going, where and when to meet.
4) A whole gang of us would arrive at the Hollybush – just around the corner from our sixth form college – half an hour later than we'd arranged, wearing clothes we thought made us look eighteen and reeking of Paco Rabane.
5) After a few drinks, loud conversations and several rebuttals from the convent school girls who frequented the pub at the weekend, we'd get the bus into town and head off to a club, knowing full well that three quarters of us wouldn't get in.

That was what Saturday nights were supposed to be about: friendship, dressing up and boundless optimism.

* * *

Dan and I met up with Charlie in the Haversham at 9 p.m. half an hour later than arranged. I could tell by the look on Charlie's face that despite his earlier reluctance he was just as excited as me. Even Dan, whose Saturday nights had never been all that mundane, had something about him that bit sharper tonight. It was as if we'd all agreed to pretend that the last ten years hadn't happened to us. For the next few hours we were seventeen again and up for it. It felt great. Such were our good moods that we even invited Greg, who'd dropped into the Haversham by chance, to join us. He was so enthusiastic about the idea that he took a taxi home, showered, and was back in the pub in under half an hour. All present and correct. We were ready to go.

I love this!

The club, just off Leicester Square, was called in predictably kitsch fashion 'Boogie Nights'. The decision to go Seventies had been unanimous. We'd briefly considered trying to get into one of the capital's trendier clubs, but the feeling amongst the super studs of seduction (i.e. me and Dan) was that the women in clubs like those tended to be of the choosier variety. So, for a night of guaranteed good times with the kind of girls whose expectations were as low as our own, the Seventies night was ideal.

Walking through the double doors into the main room of the club was like stepping straight into 1978. Here was a world where the Bee Gees were groovy, John Travolta was an icon for disaffected youth, and bellbottoms were so hip it hurt. As we strode determinedly across the scarlet carpet to the bar, the strobe lighting making us look like we were walking in slow motion, I just knew the night was going to be one to remember.

'What are you drinking?' bellowed Greg in my direction.

I scrutinised the optics for inspiration and found none. 'I'll have a Stella,' I replied.

'Me too,' said Dan, checking his reflection in the mirror behind the bar.

'I'll join you in that,' said Charlie, edging out of the way of a gang of women dancing a drunken conga. He let out a yelp of surprise as they passed.

'What's wrong?' I asked, turning to Charlie.

'One of them just pinched my bum!' he said incredulously.

Hearing this, Dan turned round and gave Charlie a playful wink. 'What can I say, mate? You, my son, are dynamite!'

Dan went off in search of a fag machine and Charlie disappeared to the toilets, leaving me alone with Greg, who was now unashamedly scanning the room for 'talent'.

'Look at the arse on that,' he said, pointing in the direction of a group of attractive girls who had just walked in. I smiled weakly so that he didn't feel totally stupid, but refused to indulge him any further. While I was all for the appraisal of the feminine form, Greg's tabloid manner lacked any subtlety or grace at all. When Dan and I went on the prowl, we'd never say a single word to each other, we just knew – it was a mixture of Jedi mind tricks combined with a unique sense of timing. Greg's coarseness made me feel as far removed from the purpose of coming out tonight as possible. Now I really did miss Mel.

While Greg disappeared to the toilet, leaving me to stand guard over the four pints of Stella on the bar, I thought about Mel, or more accurately Mel and her new man, Rob1.

They're bound to be together tonight. I can picture them perfectly: Rob1's being really attentive, telling her amusing stories, making her feel special – doing all the things I used to do when I first met her. Mel's looking into his eyes, hanging on to his every word, wallowing in that buzz of excitement that comes from anticipating the unknown.

I stopped thinking and felt lower than ever.

By midnight we'd all run out of steam. Charlie had spent the last hour looking at his watch, moaning that he'd served his time in nightclubs and wanted to be in bed with his wife like any normal thirty-four-year-old married man. Next to him, a very disgruntled Dan sat on the arm of a sofa, occasionally sipping his beer. He'd spent most of the night scowling in the general direction of Greg, who was on the dancefloor in hot pursuit of some helpless girl. The irony wasn't lost on Dan and me that Greg – the only one of us who was engaged – was also the only one to have spoken to a member of the opposite sex all evening. Even Charlie – a married man – had had his bum pinched. So much for the superstuds of seduction.

'I can see it a mile off,' said Dan irritably. 'Greg's going to get off with that girl. It's amazing. Why can't women smell a loser when one whiffs by?'

'Depressing, isn't it?' I said in agreement. 'Here's us, two young, free, single guys, and there's him, not so young, certainly not so good looking, and engaged to be married. I dunno what the lovely Anne sees in him.'

'That's women for you,' pronounced Dan. I could feel one of his this-is-how-the-world-is speeches coming on. 'They believe that inside every heartless bastard is a small boy yearning to be loved. But their theory falls short . . .' he glared over at Greg again . . . 'because what they don't understand is that there are certain types of heartless bastard who if hacked in two would only be found to contain yet more heartless bastard.'

As if taking his cue from Dan, the DJ played Gloria Gaynor's aptly titled 'I Will Survive' and the place erupted in unison. A studenty girl wearing a neon-blue Afro wig approached the sofa of doom, and without saying anything, grabbed my hand and pulled me on to the dancefloor. It was a split-second decision: resist and show a modicum of self-respect or surrender and let everyone know how desperate I was. In the end I surrendered, because desperate or not, in spite of the wig I could tell that she was far from ugly.

She grinned at me dementedly and began gyrating as if her life depended on her performance. She knew all the words to the song and was even clicking her fingers in time to the music. It was as if the concept of embarrassment was completely unknown to her. Her confidence was infectious and within seconds I'd lost all my inhibitions as I strutted, boogied and generally got down with my bad self in time to the music.

'What's your name?' yelled Blue Afro Girl, over the music.

'Duffy!' I shouted back. 'What's yours?'

'Emma!' She held out her hand for me to shake. 'Emma Anderson. Nice to meet you, Duffy!'

As we continued dancing I noticed that not only had she got the most beautiful greeny-grey eyes I'd ever seen, but in addition to this she was using them to draw me into her funky world. I tried desperately to remember what I was supposed to do in this sort of situation. The procedure for pulling a member of the opposite sex was supposed to be like riding a bike – something you never forgot – but somehow I'd managed it.

As the song finished I turned to escape, but she grabbed my shirt sleeve and refused to let go. I looked over despairingly at Dan and Charlie, who were clearly enjoying the floor show. Greg, still dancing with the same girl, smiled smugly over her shoulder as if to say, 'Wa-hey! We've both pulled!'

Just as I was convinced that things could get no worse, the Village People's 'YMCA' came on – my all-time least favourite record. For her tenth birthday, my auntie Kathleen had given Vernie a double compilation album of disco hits called *Boogie's Greatest Hits Vol. 2*. For the next few months my sister constantly played 'YMCA' whilst pretending to be *The Kids From Fame*. Every time, she got to be Coco while I had to be Leeroy or else suffer the harshest of Chinese burns.

It wasn't fair. I knew Coco was a girl, but she was just so much more exciting than bloody Leeroy. This was why I hated the Village People. Looking around the club, I realised I was in a minority. Like a clarion call to the inebriated, the record's opening trumpets drew the merry throngs from the bar, the toilets and the sofas to the dancefloor.

'I love this!' screamed Emma excitedly.

'Me too!' I shrieked back. 'Me too!'

My sweat-soaked shirt was clinging tightly to my armpits and back by the time the song came to a close. Emma dragged me determinedly by the hand to an empty sofa at the edge of the dancefloor, lodging herself as close to me as possible without sitting on my lap. 'It's hot, isn't it?' she said feverishly. She peeled off her Afro wig and ruffled her cropped sandy-brown hair. 'I bet you thought I really had blue hair!' A wide smile lit up her elfin face. 'What kind of a name's Duffy, then?'

'Duffy's my surname,' I admitted timidly. 'My first name's Ben but I don't like it. Sounds too much like the name you'd give a Yorkshire Terrier.' Out of the corner of my eye I spotted Dan surreptitiously walking past. Seeing him brought me to my senses. This just didn't feel right. Sitting here with a strange, slightly mad girl who wasn't Mel. It was time to admit to myself that I was no superstud of seduction.

'Listen,' I explained. 'My friends and I have to go soon.'

'Anywhere interesting?'

I shook my head vigorously. 'Home.' She raised her eyebrows suggestively. 'Work in the morning, you see,' I added quickly, and then for some unknown reason mimed digging actions.

'So you're a labourer?'

'Yes. Amongst other things.'

'What sort of labouring do you do?'

'Oh, you know . . . a bit of moving heavy stuff here, a bit of moving heavy stuff there. The work of a labourer revolves around shifting heavy stuff.'

She licked her lips provocatively and squeezed my right arm tightly. 'Hmmm. That must be where you get this wonderful physique from.'

Realising that I was now officially out of my depth and unable to tread water, I made a move to escape before I drowned. Her hands, however, were firmly gripped around my arm and she was using all her weight to keep me anchored to the sofa. 'I haven't finished with you yet,' she said slyly. 'And you're not going anywhere until I have.'

Surely things haven't changed this much since I last went out on the pull? I told myself. *Surely I was the hunter and she the hunted?* In an attempt to calm myself down I considered my options:

a) I could escape her advances (and no doubt regret it the next day);

b) I could succumb to her advances (and no doubt regret it the next day);

c) I could defer her advances (and work out what to do the next day).

It had to be 'c'.

'I really am going to have to go,' I said firmly, 'but do you fancy meeting up for a drink next week?'

'Yeah, brilliant,' she said, nodding enthusiastically. 'Whereabouts do you live?'

'Muswell Hill,' I replied. I couldn't believe it. My first real live date in four years, without even trying! Maybe I was a superstud of seduction after all. 'How about you?'

'Hornsey,' she replied, stroking the hair on her Afro wig playfully. 'Do you know the Kingfisher in Crouch End? It's nice in there.'

'I don't, but I can find it. Sounds great. How about this Tuesday?'

'No can do,' she said, shaking her head.

'Wednesday?'

She shook her head again. 'And before you say it I can't do Thursday either.'

'Busy with university exams?' I asked, hoping that she hadn't changed her mind about fancying me.

'Not exactly,' she said coyly. 'It's just that my parents will go mental if I start going out on school nights again.'

If it had been possible for the earth to have opened up and swallowed me in my entirety, there would've been nothing that could have made me happier. I'd given this life thing a good try, but this time fate had gone too far; now I was reduced to chatting up a girl for whom Seventies nights weren't just an evening of kitsch fun but a lesson in ancient history.

'I think I . . . I—' I didn't manage to finish my sentence, as a sudden commotion across the dancefloor grabbed our attention. We stood up to get a better look, and I saw that it was Dan and Greg grappling on the floor. I took the opportunity to slip away from Emma and over to Charlie, who was standing, pint in hand, watching events unfold before him.

'I knew tonight would end in trouble,' said Charlie, motioning to Dan and Greg.

'What's going on?' I asked.

Charlie took a long, slow sip of his beer. 'Greg was snogging that girl he was dancing with, Dan went off on one, and there you have it.' He pointed at our two friends on the floor again. 'Like I said, I knew I should've stayed home.'

The club's door staff, eager to justify their existence, were over in seconds and dragged out Greg and Dan with the minimum of fuss. Charlie and I followed them, and while they were forcibly ejected we pooled cloakroom ticket stubs and handed them to the woman behind the counter. As I turned to leave with Greg's coat in my hand I was stopped in my tracks.

'Were you going to leave without saying goodbye?' said a voice from behind me.

I turned around. It was Emma. In the bright fluorescent light of the lobby she was quite obviously a lot younger than she'd first appeared, but that didn't stop her being pretty. In fact she was just the sort of girl that the seventeen-year-old me would've gladly laid down his life for, and now here I was eleven years later turning her down. At the end of the day it seems everything is a matter of timing.

'I'm sorry,' I apologised. 'As you can see, my mates got themselves into a bit of trouble. I'm going to have to go.'

'I suppose going out next week is off too,' she said quietly.

I nodded. 'Yeah, I think so.'

'It's because I'm sixteen, isn't it?'

I nodded again. 'You could say that.'

Reaching up she straightened the collar of my jacket and kissed me gently on the cheek. 'You'd better be going, then.'

'Yeah,' I said, as the sensation of her kiss slowly faded away. 'I suppose I had.'

By the time I got outside Charlie and Dan were nowhere to be seen and Greg was attempting unsuccessfully to hail a black cab. 'Taxi drivers aren't that keen on customers with blood across their shirts,' I said, handing him his coat.

'Cheers,' he said, and snatched the coat from me. 'If you're looking for your mates, they've gone.'

'What was that about, then?' I asked, studying his bloody nose.

'Hadn't you better ask your mate Dan?' He searched through his pockets. 'I was minding my own business when he came over and started spouting off about how I shouldn't be cheating on Anne, like it's any of his business.' He finally located what he was looking for. He pulled out his lighter and lit a cigarette. 'Then it all kicked off. He's a nutter.'

Dan was totally in the wrong having a go at Greg like that, but he did have a point. I was tired of humouring Greg and his outmoded ways but I wasn't about to lecture him on his stupidity – I just wasn't going to bother seeing him any more. I held out my hand. 'Look, I'm sorry for what's happened, okay? Let's shake on it.'

Ignoring me, Greg threw his cigarette on to the floor and climbed into the back of a red Datsun Cherry – quite obviously not a minicab but some dodgy geezer on the make – and was whisked away into the night.

Alone and a little bit cold, I thought about what to do next. I didn't particularly want to go home, because even though the night air had taken the edge off the alcohol, I was still on a high of sorts. I'd achieved my goal. I was seventeen again – chasing girls and getting into scrapes – and it had felt so good that I didn't want to go back to being Mr Twenty-eight, single and boring.

Desperate to keep the night going a little while longer, I decided to drop into the Comedy Cellar, a small club on Long Acre that Dan and I sometimes played. I knew the guys on the door quite well and there was bound to be someone around to kill time with.

Without hesitating I walked briskly through the crowds in Leicester Square and was about to cross Charing Cross Road when my eyes locked on to a man and woman in the middle of the street holding hands, waiting for a break in the traffic.

I looked at the woman and was horrified.

The woman stared right back at me, also horrified.

The man looked at the woman and then looked at me, equally horrified.

I looked back at the man and the woman and outdid their combined looks of horror to the power of ten.

What were the chances of this happening? A million to one. *If only*, I thought, *this kind of luck could be utilised for the forces of good rather than evil*.

'Duffy,' said an obviously shaken Mel, coming to a halt right in front of me.

'Mel,' I said distractedly.

'Just come from a gig?'

'No,' I replied unsteadily. 'Where have you been?'

'Dinner,' she said.

'Anywhere nice?'

'The Ivy,' she muttered so quietly even a deaf lipreader would've had problems understanding her.

'Oh,' I said. It was the one restaurant she'd always wanted to go to. I'd promised her that the first thing I'd do when the comedy took off would be to take her there.

'Where have you been, then?' she asked, agitatedly fiddling with a button on her coat.

In my head I attempted to create an evening of sophistication and witty repartee but failed miserably. 'A Seventies night,' I admitted. I couldn't help but compare the two experiences. Mel had spent an evening at one of London's top restaurants while I'd plebbed about with my mates in a grotty Seventies club. I'd got my wish: I was seventeen again – immature, impoverished and girlfriendless.

'How was it?' Mel could barely conceal her smile.

'Okay,' I said and shrugged my shoulders.

'Where's Dan?'

'He had to go home early,' I explained weakly.

As if he'd just been switched on, Mel's companion – who I'd been hoping was a garish figment of my imagination – finally decided to speak.

'Hi, I'm Rob,' he said, and offered his hand for me to shake. He was tall and handsome in the clean-cut sort of way that you usually associate with male underwear models in Grattan catalogues, and his voice was deep and authoritative like a newsreader's. I shook his hand.

'I'm sorry, I'm so rude,' said Mel, taking control of the situation. 'I haven't introduced you two, have I? Duffy, this is Rob.' She gestured inadvertently to his chest which seemed to be rippling underneath his dark blue, classically cut suit jacket. 'Rob, this is Duffy.' She gestured (hopefully inadvertently) to my stomach which didn't seem to be doing anything underneath my T-shirt.

'Pleased to meet you, Rob.' I nodded.

'Likewise,' he said, nodding back.

Mel was still looking at my T-shirt. 'You've got blood there.'

I looked down at my stomach and attempted a chuckle. 'It's not mine, it's Greg's,' I explained, and then added hurriedly, 'Too long a story to bore you with now.' I looked at my watch as if I had somewhere to go. 'I'd better be off. Don't want to be late.' I paused, unsure what to do next. 'It's been good to see you again, Mel.' Inexplicably I began shaking her hand enthusiastically. She just looked at me as if I was mad. I nodded in Rob1's direction. 'Nice to have met you, Rob.'

''Bye, then,' said Mel, tacking a sad little smile on to the end of her sentence.

'Yeah, see you again soon,' said Rob, the tone of his voice revealing the sort of intense satisfaction that said, 'Before I met you tonight you had *power* over me but now I see I have *nothing* to fear from you because you are *no one*.'

'I hope so,' I replied, my tone of voice revealing the sort of intense woefulness that said, 'You drive a *big* car, you wear *expensive* clothes and you have a bloody firm handshake – you're right, I am *no one*.'

As in joyful

I opened my eyes and looked around, blinking hard. Only seconds earlier Mel had declared passionately, 'Whoever wins this duel, wins my heart.' Reacting swiftly I'd grabbed the nearest weapon to hand (a small uncooked chicken) and brandished it threateningly in Rob1's direction. *Finally*, I'd thought. *Vengeance!* Unfortunately round one of Duffy *vs* Rob1 was all just a dream.

I was still wearing last night's clothes. I sniffed my T-shirt. Beer. Cigarette smoke. Doner kebab chilli sauce. I looked around again. *Where am I?* I wasn't in bed. I was on a floor – the kitchen floor. *Good*, I thought, pleased with myself. *At least I'm home*. I stood up shakily like a newborn Bambi and surveyed the room while my memory booted up. It was the numerous slices of bread scattered around the room that finally nudged my brain into place. *Toast*. It all came back to me. *I'd gone toast hunting*.

Distraught beyond belief at my encounter with Mel and Rob1, I'd made my way to the comedy club and there continued drinking beyond the point of daft smile and wobbly legs right up to 'Which way is up?' At 4 a.m. I was kicked out of the club and escorted to a taxi. The driver had asked me where I wanted to go and I'd told him Muswell Hill – which was fine for the moment, but things got a bit more complicated when we reached there and I couldn't narrow it down any further. After making him drive around the area for twenty minutes, I finally remembered where I lived. Once home, I'd headed straight to the kitchen to make toast, and somewhere in the three minutes it took for the bread to go brown I'd said to myself, 'I'll just rest my eyes for a moment,' and promptly fell asleep. Why I smelt of doner kebab chilli sauce, however, I have no idea.

It being Sunday I spent most of the day in bed trying not to move. During my third nap of the day Vernie came round, rousing me from a very deep and peaceful sleep, in order to have a huge go at me. Apparently Charle had got a cab home with Dan, and somewhere along the way Dan had been sick over him. This, however, was not why Vernie was mad with me.

'He's more depressed about the baby than ever,' she berated more loudly than was necessary to a man of my weak state. 'Thanks to your clueless big night out he's convinced himself that he's become some sort of pipes and slippers old fart. I could've planned a better boys' night out myself!'

Hours later, when I'd fully recovered from my sister's onslaught, I finally emerged from my nest and bumped into Dan in the hallway. Judging by the state of him, hair flying off at right angles to his head, nine o'clock shadow on his chin, and blood still caked around his nose, he, too, it seemed, was rising for the first time that day.

'All right, mate?' I said as we entered the living room. 'Bagsie the sofa,' I added, speeding up so that I could lie down on it.

'Whatever,' said Dan, grumpily heading for the armchair.

'You've still got blood on your nose.'

He wiped his hand across his face in an attempt to get it off, sniffed his hand and licked it. 'It's not blood. It's doner kebab chilli sauce. Dunno how that got there, though. Haven't had a kebab in a few weeks.' He settled into the armchair and flicked through the channels. Realising there was nothing on, he pressed the mute button. 'What time did you get back?' he asked, scratching the back of his head.

'Must've been about half five, I think. It probably would've been earlier but I forgot where we lived.' I paused, and looked around the room. 'I bumped into Mel last night.'

'Bad news?' he added, reading my face.

'The worst kind.'

'What? She wasn't with her new bloke, was she?'

I nodded.

'Sorry, mate. Life's crap like that.'

'Certainly is.'

'What was he like, then?' asked Dan. 'I kind of imagine him to be a slightly apelike medallion man.

'No such luck,' I said stretching out both my arms to the side of me. 'Imagine this hand is me.' I waved my right hand. 'Now imagine that this hand is him.' I waved my left hand. 'Now imagine all the millions of different types of men in the bloke spectrum in between. That's what he's like. Nothing like me at all.'

'Tidy, affluent, career minded, witty . . . that sort of thing?' said Dan.

'Exactly,' I pronounced sadly. 'My point entirely. I think Mel's finally found what she's been looking for.'

Monday morning!
7.00 AM!
Monday morning!
7.00 AM!
Monday morning!

7.00 AM!
Monday morning!
7.00 AM!

My alarm clock went off, wrenching me from the deepest of deep slumbers into a Nurofen nightmare. When I was seventeen the effects of a big Saturday night used to be over by Sunday lunchtime at the latest. When I was twenty-five I'd be feeling nearly human by *Songs of Praise*. But here and now at twenty-eight, with my brain throbbing like it was going to explode, and coat the inside of my head with grey matter and memories, I began strongly to doubt whether I'd actually ever fully recover again.

Showered, shaved and dressed for work, I checked my watch. I was late. I raced through the flat, trying to find my left shoe, watch breakfast TV and eat cereal all at the same time. Shoe located, TV switched off and bloated Rice Krispies abandoned on sideboard, I shot out of the door, down the stairs to the communal hallway, sorted through the morning's post and was gone.

The collection of motley souls who frequented the bus stop at my regular go-to-work time had disappeared, whisked away five minutes earlier by my regular bus, the 7.33 a.m. 136. In their place was a similar bunch of odd-looking strangers who appeared to be as disturbed by my appearance as I was by theirs. I could see them silently taking me in, thinking to themselves anxiously, 'Who's he? He's not a regular! He's not one of us!'

After ten minutes of their silent stares the bus finally arrived. Breathing a sigh of relief I got on, showed the driver my pass and settled into my usual seat upstairs, left-hand side, right at the back – a compulsive authority-avoiding habit formed during the school trips of my youth. As the bus juddered along Archway Road I riffled through my post: an invitation to receive a Barclays credit card; a 'Greetings From Lanzarote' postcard from an old college friend and an envelope in my mum's handwriting.

> Dear Ben,
> This letter came for you on Friday. I thought it might be important so I've sent it on. Hope everything's okay with you. Remember, if you need anything at all I'm always here.
> All my love,
> Mum.

I looked inside the large envelope and fished out a smaller one. It was postmarked London and the address was written in a masculine scrawl. I opened it. Read it. Reread it. Looked out of the window. Stared at it again for a bit longer. Screwed it up into a tight ball and got off the bus.

The office where Mel worked was a hive of activity. Telephones rang every thirty seconds and were answered by teams of people sitting at shiny desks on shiny chairs surrounded by shiny potted palms. It was simply the grooviest office I'd ever been in and exactly the sort of place I'd expect to find the advertising sales arm of a TV company. In the two years Mel had been here she'd managed to smash her way through every glass ceiling they had, to become one of their top account managers.

Standing at the reception I waited patiently for the flame-haired receptionist to finish flicking through her copy of *Hello!* so that I could make my presence known. Just as I'd decided that my being here was an extremely bad idea and that I should go, she looked up from pictures of the Spanish

Mike Gayle

royal family and said serenely, 'It's like a madhouse in here today. How can I help you?'

'I'd like to speak to Ms Benson.'

'Do you have an appointment?'

'No, I'm sorry I haven't.'

'Which company are you from?'

'I'm not from a company.'

She picked up her phone, and looked up at me expectantly. 'Who shall I say is here to see her?'

'Tell her it's the man who used to make milk come out of her nose.'

'You've got exactly one minute.'

I could tell from the second I entered the cool, spacious, aircraft-hangar-sized space that was Mel's office, that she was mad at me for coming to see her at work. I'd never seen her office before. I looked around the room for touches of her personality. There were gerberas on the windowsill (her favourite flower) and a photo of her parents on her desk. There was no picture of me, which saddened me greatly. I knew for a fact that she used to have one because she once told me – it was a picture of the two of us eating ice creams on a beach in Paignton. On the other hand there was no picture of Rob 1 on her desk either, which I reasoned had to be a bonus of some sort.

Hard Mel was back, and as well as looking her usual no-nonsense self, she appeared a little bored too. I wanted her to ask me what was up, but she didn't say anything, and neither did I. She started a countdown: 'Three, two, one.' When she reached zero, she said briskly, 'I'll let you see yourself out,' and started fiddling with the mouse on her computer as if she was going to start working right there in front of me. Without having said a single word, I turned around and walked out.

Standing by the shiny chrome lift waiting to escape from this shiny prison wondering why on earth I'd come here in the first place I heard a door open and turned to see Mel – not Hard Mel but my Mel. It was nice to know that even though we weren't going out any more, she still found it difficult to be mad at me.

'Hold on, Duffy!' she called out. I waited. 'I've got half an hour before my next meeting. Do you want to get a coffee?'

'You know I don't drink coffee,' I replied, and she just smiled.

She took me to a small café around the corner from her office building. I hadn't said very much as we'd walked there, and I could see that for her this was all a bit of an uphill struggle, but to her credit she endeavoured none the less. As it was a warm, bright morning Mel suggested that we sit outside, so while she disappeared into the café for our drinks, I found us a table. A couple of businesswomen were busy in discussion at the table behind me, and at the table to the side of me a young Spanish-looking woman was having a breakfast with a chatty toddler. *No matter what happens*, I thought, concentrating on my reflection in the window of the café, *life carries on as it always has.*

Mel returned with a cappuccino and an orange juice and sat down beside me. 'So what's up?' She lit a cigarette.

She never used to smoke.

'Are we . . . friends?' I asked hesitantly.

'Is that what this is about?'

I nodded. 'Partly.'

She raised her eyebrows and took a sip of her cappuccino. I watched carefully as the froth slowly disappeared from the rim of her cup. 'I don't want to be harsh, Duffy. You must know that I still care about you. But I'm not made of stone. I don't think this friends thing is going to work. I know I said it was what I wanted as well, but I can't see it happening. I can't. Not after all we had.'

I took a deep breath and exhaled slowly. 'I'm not saying it's easy. I'm saying it's what I want. I mean, I think it'll be good for us. I promise I won't interfere in your life. Okay?'

She shrugged noncommittally and took another drag on the cigarette she shouldn't have been smoking. 'We'll have to see how things go, Duff. I can't make any promises.'

We sat in silence while I downed my orange juice in six continuous gulps and Mel sipped her coffee and smoked her cigarette. I watched as the two business women got up and a waitress came out to wipe the table with a cloth. I looked over at Mel again and sensed that she had more to say.

'You're still angry at me, because of the engagement thing.'

'Yes, you're right I am. Why, did you think that I'd just forget that you didn't want to marry me?'

'No,' I said, wincing. 'I don't know how I'm ever going to make this up to you. I don't suppose it's the sort of thing that can be made up for.' I paused. 'Do you think you'll ever stop being angry with me?'

'I don't know,' she replied. She laughed quietly. 'Probably not.'

I attempted to look all doglike, but judging from the reflection of my face in the café's window I didn't have to try too hard. I was getting the hang of this remorse thing. It was coming quite naturally to me now. I sucked on an ice cube, rolled it around my mouth and then dropped it back in the glass. I was trying to find words that said 'I'm sorry' without sounding hollow and empty. I hunted high and low for them but they weren't there.

'That guy,' I said after some moments had passed. 'The one I saw you with on Saturday. New boyfriend?'

She shook her head. 'Not exactly.'

My breathing quickened, I crossed every finger I had and sat bolt upright so quickly that I managed to knock the ashtray off our table. *Please*, I thought, picking it up. *Please let him be just a friend. Or even better, her long-lost brother. Or even better, a stray eunuch she's become maty with. Anything but her boyfriend!*

'Do you remember when I first met you?' began Mel. 'I'd just split up with someone. Well, that someone was . . . Rob.'

I cursed myself inwardly for courting such ridiculously optimistic explanations for her mystery man. *That*, I told myself, *is definitely the last time I look on the bright side of life.*

Rob.

I'd remembered his existence but until now not his name.

Rob.

Though I'm sure she'd told me at the time – I was also quite sure that I jettisoned such information straight away.

Rob.

The names of my girlfriend's previous boyfriends weren't exactly the sort of material I wanted lingering in any of my brain cells.

'You're going back out with *Rob* who you went out with for two years? *Rob* who proposed to you? *Rob* who you said was "crowding" you? *Rob* who you dumped because you didn't want to live with him?' I sighed sarcastically. 'Oh, *that* Rob – yeah, I remember him.'

'Yes, *that* Rob,' said Mel, tolerating my playground wit. 'I bumped into him in Bar Zinc a little while after we'd split up. Anyway, we started talking about old times and exchanged numbers and I thought nothing more of it. He called me at home a few days later and asked me out to dinner. I said no initially, and then I thought, why not? Why should I have to stay in crying myself to sleep every night? Why not just go out and have a good time? And that's what I did. I make no apologies for it, Duffy. None at all.' She paused, calming down her quickened breathing. 'Does that answer all your questions?'

It didn't. Not by a mile. But some things, I reasoned, are best left unknown. I couldn't not ask anything. Her question was a challenge of sorts – defying me to face up to what I'd done. 'Does he make you . . . you know . . . happy?' I found myself asking.

She smiled. 'It's not like you to use euphemisms, Duff.'

Mel thought I was talking about sex, obviously not quite understanding that I would not now, nor would I ever be talking about her and Rob1 having sex. 'No, you've got me all wrong,' I clarified. 'What I meant is exactly what I said: does he make you happy? As in joyful. As in cheery.'

Mel looked puzzled. I don't think she'd been expecting that one. 'Yeah, he does. He makes me happy.'

'That's good,' I said. 'You deserve to be happy.'

Then came another of those long pauses that my life seemed to consist entirely of. It was quite possible that I was becoming addicted to them. 'Just the one pause, okay maybe another one.' How long would it be before I'd be visiting dodgy pubs in pursuit of drug dealers with a side-line in pauses? Pauses – they seemed to be everywhere I went, lurking in the darkness waiting for the right moment to highlight my inadequacies.

'None of this is what you came here to talk about,' said Mel breaking the silence. 'So tell me, what's going on, Duff? What's wrong?'

I looked over to the woman with the toddler; at a half-eaten croissant on a table next to me; at my own reflection in the café window. 'I got a letter this morning,' I began, as I unscrewed the letter I'd received and handed it to Mel. 'It's from my dad.'

'Oh,' said Mel quietly after she'd read it. She pulled her chair closer to me and placed her hands on my hand. 'I'm so sorry, Duff. I really am so sorry.'

This was why I was here. Mel was the only person in the world who would know what I was feeling without my having to explain. In fact she probably knew better than I did. I didn't have a clue what it was I was feeling.

'The letter says he wants to meet up with you.'

'Yeah, I know. Strange, isn't it?'

'Isn't he twenty-eight years too late for that?' Mel's eyes filled with tears as she gently squeezed my hand. Embarrassed by her tears, she wiped them away with the back of her hand. 'I'm sorry I'm getting so upset. It just makes me so angry. Does he really just think he can walk back into your life like this?' She wiped away another tear. 'Are you going to meet him?'

'No.'

'Do you need me to do anything? Do you want me to talk to your mum or Vernie about any of this for you? I want to do something to help, Duff. I really do.'

'I'll be all right,' I said. 'There's nothing more to do really. Like I said, I'm not going. I just needed to talk to someone about it, that's all, and the only person on the planet I could think of was you.'

Mel smiled. 'I'm glad we can still depend on each other.' She paused and looked at her watch.

'Me too.' I replied.

'Will you walk back with me?' she asked.

I nodded.

As we headed towards her shiny office block we chatted avidly, avoiding all the big issues of the day – about hair (she was thinking of having it cut short. I was contemplating growing a goatee); magazine articles (I'd read one that said men would be extinct by the year 2030. She'd read one that said women in America were giving up on men and buying dogs instead); and *EastEnders* (in our separate domains watching the weekend omnibus we'd both been shouting the same advice to the same characters at the same time).

Eventually we reached her office building, glinting in the midday sun, and said our goodbyes.

'Thanks for that stuff you said about . . . well, you know . . . wanting me to be happy.' She reached up and kissed me on the cheek. 'It means a lot to me. I do want us to be friends. I want you to be okay.'

I looked into her eyes and suddenly realised that despite my clumsiness I had a heart crammed full of things that I hadn't said, that I suddenly desperately needed to tell her. I wanted to tell her about my dad and the way my mum had thought he'd love her for ever. I wanted to tell her about Greg and how he'd cheated on his loyal girlfriend. I wanted to tell her about Dan and how he'd taken Meena for granted when they moved in together, and I wanted to tell her about all of the millions of men who'd thought they could do commitment but had ended up walking out on their kids, wives, girlfriends and lovers. I wanted to tell her that I didn't know whether I was like them or like me; whether I really could do commitment or just thought I could, and because of that – the fear that I'd one day do to her what my dad did back then – I could never marry her. And last but not least, I wanted to tell her that despite all this I needed her more than anyone in the world. I didn't say any of this, of course. I just whipped out another one of my interstellar pauses.

'Are you okay?' asked Mel. 'You seem to be somewhere else.'

'Yeah,' I replied ambiguously. 'I think I probably am.'

Cinema, drinking, eating, dancing . . . bowling

A few weeks went by in which I spent a lot of time pretending I wasn't thinking about my dad, before I finally admitted to myself that I was being stupid and that it was time I thought about him in the open. Talking to Vernie about it all helped put things in perspective. Strangely, my dad hadn't been in contact with her, but that didn't bother her in the slightest because if he had, like me, she said she wouldn't have been interested in meeting him at all.

After that, there was nothing more really to say or think, so I did a little rearranging in my mind: I put my dad to the back of it, and the idea that Mel and I might become proper friends to the front. I was just sorting the mess I called my career somewhere into the middle, when something odd came along that completely messed up all my arrangements – I got my audition for *The Hot Pop Show*, and if that wasn't enough, a brief conversation with Alexa just as I was leaving it.

'Is that you, Duffy?' called out Alexa. 'It *is* you!'

I looked up and said hello. I'd actually spotted her in the corridor as soon as I'd come through the double doors of Studio 3, where the auditions had taken place, but I was trying my very best to play it cool. Even though it was five o'clock on a humid Thursday afternoon, when by rights even the most gorgeous of supermodels could be forgiven for looking a bit crumpled, Alexa looked amazing.

'What are you doing here?' she asked, after having done her statutory double-kiss hello.

'I've just had that audition,' I said awkwardly. 'You know, the one for your show.'

'Of course,' she said, a look of recognition illuminating her features. 'I saw your name down on the list, but I completely forgot it was today. How did you get on?'

'I dunno,' I shrugged. I wasn't being modest at all. I really didn't know. I'd felt like I'd been at the audition all day. I'd told them a few jokes from my normal routine, run through a couple of sketch ideas I'd come up with based on the brief they'd given me, and told them my life history. And after all that I was still none the wiser.

'Did it look like they liked you?'

'I suppose so. They didn't appear not to like me. It's hard to say really. They don't exactly give a lot away, do they?'

'No they don't,' she agreed. 'They were exactly the same when I had my audition. I couldn't sleep or eat for days afterwards.' She patted my shoulder in a friendly, reassuring manner. 'I'm sure you'll be fine, Duffy.'

'That's enough about me, anyway' I said. 'How are you? How's the show?'

'It's going really well,' she said enthusiastically. 'I'm just so busy all the time that I feel totally exhausted, but it's a good kind of tired, you know?'

'Yeah,' I lied – the only type of tired I was aware of was the crappy kind.

'And what about you?' She bounced the conversational ball back to me again as if I was a guest on her show. 'Apart from the audition, I mean?'

'Okay,' I said, which was the best answer I could manage in the time allotted.

Fortunately Alexa wasn't fazed for a second by my monosyllabic answer. She came back immediately with an enthusiastic, 'That's good to hear,' and in return I faked a cough while I thought of something clever to say.

'Have you managed to catch the show at all?' she asked when I'd finished spluttering.

I had indeed, and she'd looked mightily impressive. On the last show I'd seen she'd been surrounded by kids whilst interviewing an up-and-coming boy band dressed in matching purple silky tracksuits and baseball caps. Though barely above school leaving age, they'd attempted to flirt with her by making thinly veiled suggestive comments, all of which failed to impress her in the slightest.

'No,' I lied. The last thing I needed was her thinking I was only talking to her because she was TV's Hottest Totty.

'You don't know what you've been missing,' she said, looking directly into my eyes. She paused. 'I was talking to Mark the other day.'

'Oh, yeah,' I replied. 'How is he?'

'He's fine. We had quite a long chat about you, as it happens. He tells me you're a single man now.'

'Yeah,' I said, as if this thought had only just occurred to me, 'I suppose I am.'

Silence.

'Was it a bad break-up?' she replied eventually.

'Aren't all break-ups bad?' I responded, wondering what was happening to her trademark snappy deliveries.

Silence.

Here was a woman who under normal circumstances didn't know the meaning of the word 'pause', and yet in the last few minutes she'd paused for England. Why was she suddenly acting against type? As far as I could see there were three possible answers:

1. She was bored but was too polite to cut the conversation short.
2. She really was lost for words.
3. She was doing the Hinting Thing.

I studied her face. She didn't look bored or speechless, so she had to be doing the Hinting Thing. *One more silence*, I thought, *and then I'll ask her out*.

'I'd better be going, then,' I said looking at my watch.

'It's been good to see you,' she replied.

Silence.

I needed no further encouragement. 'I was wondering whether . . . if you're . . . free at the weekend?'

'Oh!' She sighed theatrically in a way real people never do. 'I can't. I'm in Los Angeles. There's some big film thingy that's coming out or something and I'm interviewing the star, what's his name . . . (she proceeded to name a Hollywood star of the calibre that gets to do his shopping in Harrods when it's closed to the public).' I reminded myself never to try and tackle the Hinting Thing again in this or any other lifetime.

'But I'm free a week on Saturday if you're not busy,' she added. 'I'm sorry it's so hectic at the minute, but I promise I'll be worth the wait.'

Ignoring what had to be the come-on of the century, for fear of no-saliva dry-mouth choking syndrome, I pretended to check my busy social schedule in my pocket diary. 'Yeah,' I said, brightening up. 'I think I can make it.'

I felt great after that meeting. Strong, independent, even

virile. My life was back on track. I had an audition for a job on TV and was going on my first hot date in over four years, with a kids' TV presenter!!!! Now that I felt this good, I could handle talking to Mel again. I promised myself our friendship was going to work or I'd die in the attempt.

Before I could change my mind I called Mel up and we got on great. In fact for the rest of that week either she called me at work or I called her at work, sometimes even two or three times a day. Out went the pauses and the tension and in came pure unadulterated making each other laugh.

In one conversation on the Wednesday of that week, in an uncharacteristic fit of bonhomie I told her that I was glad she and Rob 1 were getting on so well. I think I said it to hear what it sounded like – a tentative step on to a frozen lake, if you will. The minute it was out there, however, my façade as Duffy The Amiable Ex-boyfriend cracked. I was not glad they were getting on well. If she really needed to be with someone else, I wanted her to be with someone a little less perfect for her. So far I'd learned that Rob had a great eye for colour schemes, could cook without the aid of a microwave and, wait for it, loved shopping for soft furnishings.

Mel thought my confession was the most wonderful thing ever – a sign that we were true friends, a sign that I'd matured. To me, however, it was just a sign that I was losing my mind.

It was a key point in our let's-be-friendsness. From that call forward, the content of our cosy chats changed. Whereas before, her conversation had been ten per cent Rob 1, ninety per cent other stuff, very slowly his percentage began to creep up. 'Oh, Rob did this . . .' or 'Rob did that . . .' she'd say, and I'd grimace silently. Then occasionally she'd let slip some detail that would really cut to the bone. It wasn't the obvious stuff, like her staying over at his house or him staying at hers – although needless to say *that* didn't help matters – it was odd things like them going shopping together or even going to Mark and Julie's for dinner. According to Mel, Julie and Rob1 got on like a house on fire. Even Mark, though he apparently missed my 'funny ways', thought he was wonderful. Everybody loved Rob1 except me. Mel was even trying to persuade me on that score. 'You'd really like him,' she said one day. 'He's on your wavelength.'

What was I supposed to reply to that? Great, bring him round? Fabulous, I must go for a drink with him? Brilliant, because if you were sleeping with a man who wasn't on my wavelength I'd be really upset? So in the way you do when you're talking to your mates on the phone at work and your line manager approaches you, I said, '. . . thanks for calling, Mr Harrison, I'll make sure the message is passed on to the relevant department,' and put the phone down.

The night of my date with Alexa came round quickly. An hour before I was supposed to meet her I found myself in the bathroom mirror staring at my reflection.

I gave myself a pep talk: 'The difference between you and the legendary soul singer Barry White in a spiritual sense is nonexistent.'

I wasn't suggesting that I was a big bloke with a gravelly voice. I was saying that what I saw in the mirror was pure sex. I looked so good, felt so confident, that I had to have been possessed by the soul of Barry White – god of love and gettin' on down. Alexa might have been TV's Hottest Totty, but she didn't stand a chance against my charm offensive.

'Where are *you* going smelling like that?' yelled Dan, as I strode past the open living-room door. The aroma of my

Chanel aftershave – a present from Mel – had obviously managed to cut through the smell of Cantonese-style sweet and sour chicken.

Without even pausing for thought, I yelled back, 'I've got a date with destiny,' before adding an alarmingly hopeful, 'Don't wait up,' and walked out of the door.

'Hi, Duffy.' Alexa kissed me on the cheek. Just as I was pulling away she came round to kiss me on the other cheek and I ended up kissing her ear.

Bloody media types and their two-part kisses.

'Good to see you again,' she said sitting down.

'Cheers.' I replied, taking in her total visual effect. She was wearing a white long-sleeved T-shirt, a black knee-length skirt and trainers. She looked so trendy, so absolutely now, that she sort of reminded me of the shop window dummies in women's clothes shops like Kookaï and Karen Millen – only without the ridiculously pert nipples.

'You look . . . great,' I said. 'I didn't realise you were going to dress up, otherwise I'd have . . .' I gestured pitifully to my clothing, lost for words . . . 'a bit more.'

'You look great, Duffy,' she said, and waved to someone she knew across the bar. 'I live in my jeans normally. I just fancied a change.'

I got the drinks in. I ordered a beer and Alexa had a Martini. I gave the barman a tenner and he gave me back my change on a small saucer. *Yeah right*, I thought to myself as I carefully picked up the coins. *Like I'm going to leave you a tip just because you gave me my change on a piece of crockery!*

'Here you go,' I said, placing her Martini in front of her.

She took a small sip. 'Vodka,' she purred. 'How did you know that's the way I liked them?'

'I just guessed,' I replied, as once more my banal conversation compelled Oscar Wilde to rotate 360 degrees in his grave. I took a sip of my beer to fill in some of what was bound to be a long night of pauses. 'It took me ages to find this place. I walked past it four or five times. What is it with these trendy bars? Why don't they put signs with their name on so you can find them?'

'That would be too easy,' said Alexa, wrinkling her nose in the cutest manner possible. 'If it wasn't difficult to find, it wouldn't be a cool place to drink, would it?'

'It's ridiculous. If they really wanted to be cool, they should make anyone who wants to come here arrive wearing a blindfold. Then no one would know how to get here – not even the bar staff. Now that would be the kind of exclusive bar I'd like to go to on a regular basis.'

Alexa laughed lightly. On a scale of one to ten of sexiness she scored a perfect twelve.

'So?' I said, fearing another pause attack. 'What do you fancy doing?'

'What are the choices?'

'Cinema, drinking, eating, dancing . . . bowling.'

Alexa frowned wrinkling that nose again – it seemed to be getting cuter and cuter by the second. 'Bowling? Isn't that the kind of thing you do on dates when you're fourteen?'

'Probably,' I conceded. 'So this is a date, then?'

'Well, let's see,' she said coquettishly. 'Dating checkpoint number one: are both parties single?' She smiled. 'Well, we know about you.' I nodded coolly. 'And I'm not seeing anyone at the minute. So yes we're both single.' She sipped her Martini. 'Dating checkpoint number two: are both parties keen to get to know each other?' She looked at me and I nodded, cautiously. 'That's a yes from him and I can concur that it's a yes from me too.' She plucked the olive from her glass and dropped it into her mouth. Never before had I so wanted to be an olive. She continued: 'So I'd pretty much say that if we act like we're on a date and look like we're on a date then we probably are on a date.'

'Ah!' I said knowingly. 'But how do we know if we look like we're on a date? We've only got each other's opinions to verify that.'

'Let's find out.' Alexa turned to her left and tapped a stocky man in a long leather jacket on the shoulder. He was in the middle of a conversation with a young blonde dreadlocked woman in a trouser suit. 'Excuse me?' said Alexa. 'My friend and I were wondering if we looked like we were on a date. Do you think we are?'

Bloody TV presenters! While the rest of us were content to tell people what kind of a fun personality we have, people like Alexa always felt a need to prove it. I cringed with embarrassment. Fortunately, the man recognised her and couldn't wait to flatter her ego.

'You look like old college friends,' he said, humouring her. 'You look way too comfortable to be on a first date. What d'you reckon, Olivia?'

'I think you're wrong, Jez,' said his companion thoughtfully. 'They're definitely a couple. Look at the way they're sitting, look at the body language. This is more than companionship: this is about sexual chemistry.' She began laughing. 'I feel quite flushed just looking at the pair of them!'

'Thanks,' said Alexa. She turned to me in order to flash a wide, astonishingly suggestive grin in my direction. 'You don't know how useful your comments have been.'

I see a couple

We left the bar and Alexa put her arm through mine as we walked along leisurely in pursuit of food. She led me to a down-at-heel Indian restaurant off Charing Cross Road called Punjab Paradise, which according to her had become cool with TV and music-business types bored with posh expense-account restaurants and celebrity chefs. Over a distinctly ordinary chicken sagwalla and prawn bhuna we talked avidly about our lives, exchanging stories of our past that presented us in the best light possible. A few times I noticed she tried to steer the conversation on to past relationships, and when I could no longer avoid the issue without appearing rude, I told her simply that Mel and I had broken up because I couldn't marry her. She didn't react, and I think the serious tone of my voice revealed that I was far from over Mel, so she let me change topics.

At about nine thirty we left the restaurant and she suggested we go for a coffee somewhere nice. We reached a coffee bar in Soho, but it was packed full of the type of beautiful people that even she found tedious, so reaching for my hand she suggested that we go for a walk through Leicester Square instead. Convinced this was her being all TV presentery again, I tried to put her off the idea, reminding her that this late at night Leicester Square was turned over to an outlandish collection of tourists, bongo players and pickpockets, but she wouldn't listen. And anyway, a small shallow part of me was flushed with pride at the thought of being out and about in the centre of swinging London holding the hand of one of the most lusted-after women on television.

We walked around for a while, then Alexa said she wanted to sit down for a minute, so we bought two ice creams while we looked for a bench that didn't have someone sleeping on it. A few minutes later and we were sat down watching the crowds pass by. She turned to me fixing me with her deep brown eyes just a moment too long. 'You're quite a laugh really, aren't you?' she said.

'Really?'

'Not like you are on stage though.'

'What am I now?'

'The stand-up you is sharp, funny and slightly irreverent in a good natured kind of way. The real you is more serious, more awkward, like you're in a permanent state of embarrassment.'

'So, you're a TV presenter and an amateur psychologist. An interesting combination.' I smiled knowingly. 'You like to suss out people don't you? You've been doing it ever since I met you.'

'It's true,' she admitted. 'I like to know what makes people tick. It's the key to being a good interviewer.'

'So now that you've got me in a box, are you happy with what you've found?'

'I think so,' she said, and smiled sweetly. 'But I need to do some further investigations.'

Needing no further encouragement I weighed up the pros and cons of attempting to kiss her right there. (Pro: it was a warm night so she might think it was romantic; con: It was a street bench and she might think it was a bit juvenile.)

Before I could come to a conclusion she turned to me and with a mischievous glint in her eye said, 'Let's play Couple Analysis. Like those two people did with us in the bar. Let's make wild, completely unfounded assumptions about couples based on what they look like.' I have to admit I was a little disappointed that she was more excited at showing off her predisposition towards the wacky than having her wicked way with me, but I didn't let it show. In fact I found it amusing because it wasn't the sort of thing I'd ever have suggested doing with someone as gorgeous as her.

Alexa nudged me playfully and pointed to our first victims. They were both about eighteen, and wearing baggy T-shirts, jeans with large turn-ups and brightly coloured trainers. He had on a floppy hat that I suspected he thought made him look like a bit of a hardcase, and was carrying a rucksack that probably had his sandwiches in. She was dressed exactly the same, but had a skateboard tucked underneath her arm.

'They've been going out for six months,' said Alexa between licks of her ice cream. 'It's the longest relationship he's ever had. He thinks she's the best-looking girl in the world. They are in love without a doubt.'

I disagreed. 'Note the way that she's walking just that little bit faster than him. I think they've been going out about a year, but she's been seeing someone else called Darren for the last three weeks. She's just working up the strength to tell him.'

'That's a bit cynical, isn't it?' Alexa pulled a face. 'Give them a chance.'

I shrugged my shoulders. 'I'm just telling it the way I see it.'

She nudged me in the ribs again. 'Okay, your turn.'

I scanned the crowds for a suitable couple. 'Okay, how about those two over there?' I pointed to two Spanish kids who looked like they were fourteen, tops. 'They've been a couple for exactly four weeks. He's fancied her for the last two years. He'll be grateful for this moment for the next ten years. She's the one who's going to establish his pattern. Every girl he goes out with after this will in some way be compared to this one.'

Alexa laughed. 'You're serious, aren't you? Who am I going to be compared to?'

I smiled but didn't answer.

'I think you're wrong,' said Alexa. 'He's too pretty not to have queues of girls chasing him. I think she's been after him for ages, making subtle hints and suggestions, desperately hoping that he'll get the message. But he's too thick or self-absorbed to notice until now. So she makes her move because they're on holiday and he thinks that it's just a spur of the moment thing.'

'Okay,' I said. 'It's your turn. Only one more couple, though, and then we'll find somewhere to have another drink if you like.'

'Sounds good,' nodded Alexa in agreement. 'I see a couple.'

'Where?'

She ignored me. 'She's been very keen for a while. Dropping some serious hints, like that Spanish girl, but he doesn't seem to notice.' I couldn't see the couple anywhere. There was a shady-looking pair standing next to a nightclub entrance who looked like his 'n' hers drug dealers. 'He's not her usual type. He's a bit more down to earth, but she thinks that's good.' I watched a tall dark-haired woman in her late thirties walk past with her young lover. 'She likes him because he makes her laugh and because he's got a look in his eyes that's kind of keen, but then there's something about him that's not quite there.' A young couple with a terrier loitered in front of us as if waiting for friends. 'Like she's not got his full attention. She likes it though. Makes him more of a challenge.'

Well, of course by the time she'd stopped talking I'd stopped searching for this phantom couple and after a token deliberation I commenced what was to become my first public snog on a bench in well over fifteen years.

Like crazed adolescents we kissed in the taxi all the way back to Alexa's flat in Camden. All the time I was thinking, *This is fantastic – I'm snogging an intelligent beautiful woman who not only is not Mel, but has the added benefit of being TV's Hottest Totty.* I was okay with this thought for about ten seconds but then I let my imagination run away with me, wondering what would happen when we reached Alexa's flat. Inevitably, as happens in these situations, she'd invite me up for coffee. And though I hated coffee I'd agree to the idea, and as I sipped my Douwe Egbert's, she'd slip on Miles Davis's *Kind of Blue* and we'd take our clothes off and . . .

'What's up?' said Alexa. The taxi jolted as we pulled up sharply outside a large modern-looking apartment block. She was looking at me intently. I'd been so deep in contemplation that I'd failed to concentrate on the business at hand.

'Nothing,' I said quietly. 'I'll be all right.'

She stepped out of the taxi, paid the driver and held open the door for me to get out. 'Are you coming?'

'Where?'

'Up.' She pointed to her flat in case I didn't believe her. 'Fourth floor, on the right-hand corner, the one with the lights on.' I followed her finger with my eyes, and I couldn't have been more terrified if it had been a moonlit Transylvanian castle, surrounded by dark clouds, thunderbolts and lightning, with the screams of the undead rending the air.

'I don't drink coffee,' I confessed hesitantly. 'Hate the stuff.'

Alexa adopted a suggestive smirk, squinted her eyes and purred, 'Who said anything about coffee?' She lowered her voice to a stage whisper. 'I'm inviting you upstairs to my flat for . . .' she paused, briefly, barely able to control her laughter, and yelled, '. . . hot sex!'

I coughed nervously for the benefit of the cabbie. 'This is all a bit . . . what I mean to say is . . . listen, I've got to get up early in the morning . . . work and all that. I'll call you. Okay?'

'No way,' she said, grabbing my hand. 'You're coming with me.'

Alexa's bathroom was roughly the same size as my flat. It was huge. It had a large circular sunken bath with steps up to it in the middle, and mirrors and chrome just about everywhere. From my position by the wash-basin I could see at least fifteen different views of myself, which was disconcerting, but not as disconcerting as what would happen when I left this safe haven.

Alexa was busy in her kitchen actually making coffee, but I knew she was going to become suspicious if I didn't come out soon. The thing was, I didn't want to come out. I was prepared to stay in the bathroom until she fell asleep, got bored or retired from showbusiness at the age of sixty. I wasn't built to sleep with fabulously beautiful women. I was built to sleep with Mel. Not that Mel wasn't fabulously beautiful, especially when she wore my favourite dress. It's just this was definitely a case of more being less and Alexa was definitely too much.

Ridiculous things were going through my mind like, 'Could I survive the jump from a fourth-floor window?', 'I wonder if there's an air-conditioning tunnel I can escape along like Tom Cruise did in *Mission Impossible*?' and most absurdly, 'How many calories are in a bar of Ulay, because I'm bloody starving?'

Alexa knocked on the door sharply. 'Are you okay, Duffy?'

I scanned the room for something to help me make suitable busy-on-the-toilet noises. 'Yeah,' I shouted as I located a box of purple cubes by the bath, grabbed a handful and dropped them into the loo. 'I'll just be a minute,' I yelled and flushed the toilet. Big mistake. I watched in horror as wave after wave of dewberry-scented bubblebath foam erupted from the bowl like lava from a volcano. When the water finally stopped churning, Alexa's toilet and the surrounding area was covered in a mass of foam. *Surely*, I said to myself, scooping bubbles from the toilet into the bath and mopping the floor with a huge towel, *things can't get any worse*.

Alexa and I were sitting in the lounge. The lights were dimmed and we were gazing out through windows that spanned the room and looked down on to the calming moonlit waters of Camden Lock. She'd laughed until her stomach hurt when I finally confessed the bathroom saga to her, and told me I was the maddest person she'd ever met. She got up and put on some music by a band that I'd never heard of. 'They're playing a gig next week, we should go and see them,' she said as the mellow vibes of the tune washed over us. 'That is, if you fancy it.'

I nodded. 'Sounds great.'

She kicked off her shoes, curled her feet up on the sofa and cuddled up to my chest. 'This is nice, isn't it?' she said, sounding smaller, more vulnerable, more real than Alexa the TV presenter.

I had to agree that she had a point: this was nice. I could smell her hair, and feel the warmth of her body, and in this setting, with this music, things couldn't have been more ideal. We sat perfectly still for some moments, not speaking, barely breathing, just soaking up the atmosphere. And then she kissed me.

Then I kissed her back.

Then I kissed her front.

Then we fumbled about with each other's clothing.

Then we fumbled some more.

And then I noticed something I'd never noticed before.

As a semi-clad Alexa led a semi-clad me to her bedroom, I came to realise that 'something' was wrong, and that the 'something' resided in the department marked 'Boxer Shorts'.

There was nothing going on.

Nothing.

N.o.t.h.i.n.g.

N-o-t-h-i-n-g.

As barren and lifeless as the surface of Mars.

I wasn't just being pessimistic. I'd had this body twenty-eight years. No one knew it better than me. And I knew that no amount of coaxing, jostling or shouting was going to make a jot of difference to the situation.

'What's wrong?' said Alexa as we reached her bedroom door.

Everything, I wanted to say. *Everything*.

'Look,' I said, panic now having worked its way fully into my voice. 'I can't do this.'

'Yes, you can,' she said, smirking. 'It's really quite straight-forward.'

'No it isn't,' I remonstrated sadly.

She tugged my arm. 'Of course it is!'

I'm going to have to tell her.

'Alexa?'

'What's wrong?'

'It,' I said, looking down at my groin.

'What?'

I pointed silently.

'Oh!' she exclaimed, casting a pity-filled glance at my boxer shorts.

'Oh, indeed.'

'These things happen, don't they?'

'Not to me they don't,' I said despondently.

'I mean . . . I've read in magazines . . .' Lost for words, she tapped her finger on her lips as if thinking of a solution. She had none. 'Are you sure?'

'Of course I'm sure,' I snapped. I apologised immediately. 'Look, I'm sorry, this is just too embarrassing for words. Why don't I just go, eh? We'll put this down to experience.'

'Is it my fault?' asked Alexa. 'Have I done something wrong?'

I really did want to go home now. Go home, get into bed and never get up again. Ever. I did not want to stand here, in this flat, with very few clothes on, talking to a virtual stranger about something so intimate that the very thought of it had me reeling in anguish. 'Look, Alexa. In case you've forgotten, you're TV's Hottest Totty. It's not likely to be your fault, now, is it?'

She looked crestfallen. 'Well, I'm sorry anyway.'

'Not as sorry as me,' I replied, searching around for my trousers. 'Believe me, no one is as sorry as me.'

Not a sausage?

'Are you okay, Duffy? You seem a bit odd.'

It was the day after the sleepless night before and I was round at my sister's, lying across one of her armchairs pouting like a toddler who'd just broken his favourite toy. Charlie was in the garden mowing the lawn, while a now visibly pregnant Vernie was sitting with me, eating a bowl of ice cream and staring at me like I was slightly touched. Not many men would've gone to their sister's to talk over this sort of problem, but I had to talk to someone and there was no way on earth I was going to mention anything this sensitive to Charlie or Dan.

I needed a woman's perspective on this, because women, I reasoned, were more at ease with their bodies. Vernie certainly was. From the day she hit puberty she was forever discussing periods, swollen breasts and the benefits of evening primrose oil. I tried to tell her that as a young boy not even into his teens, I wasn't even vaguely interested. I used to cover my ears and sing loudly, but somehow the information seeped into my consciousness. Over the following years I eventually became so well informed about the technicalities of so-called 'women's problems' that girlfriends had in the past asked *me* for advice. It therefore required only a short leap in the imagination to conclude that although Vernie wasn't in possession of the same equipment as me, she might have a handy miracle cure or words of advice that would make everything all right.

'No, I am *not* okay,' I said, answering her question grouchily. 'I am *not* in the *least* bit okay. In fact right now I believe this is the *abso-bloody-lutely* least okay I've ever been.'

'What's wrong?' Vernie asked.

'Everything,' I said dejectedly, and proceeded to tell her about my evening with Alexa in all its gory detail.

Perched on the edge of the sofa my sister listened to my tale of woe carefully, and occasionally, in between huge spoonfuls of ice cream, let out gasps of 'Oh!', 'How awful!' and 'Poor you!' When I concluded my narrative she put down her empty bowl on the carpet and stared at my groin in disbelief. 'Are you sure?'

'You know in *Some Like it Hot* when Marilyn Monroe kisses Tony Curtis in that incredible dress and you think to yourself you'd have to be dead not to get excited about that? Well, this was a little bit like that, only about fifty billion times worse because it was happening in *my* pants.'

'Yeah, but are you sure? Maybe you're, you know, nervous because she's on telly.'

'Believe me,' I sighed, casting my mind back to the night before, 'I was totally relaxed.'

'Maybe you'd drunk too much?'

'I'd hardly touched a drop.'

Vernie got up, taking her bowl with her, and left the room. When she came back she was carrying an entire tub of Wall's Chocolate Swirl virtually fat free dessert with a spoon jutting out of it. She really was milking this pregnancy craving thing for all it was worth. She settled herself down and recommenced eating.

'Do you know what I think?' she said after two mouthfuls.

'What?' I said sulkily.

'You know how men always think with the contents of their boxer shorts?'

'Yeah?'

'Well, I think the contents of your boxer shorts are still in love with Mel.'

'You're joking, aren't you?'

'Think about it. It used to work, right?'

I opened my mouth as if to say something but Vernie put her hand up to silence me.

'Spare me the details, oh brother of mine. A simple yes or no will do.' I nodded. 'And it doesn't work now.' I nodded again. 'That's it, then. It's psychosomatic. Your . . . you know . . . is still in love with Mel!'

'That's absolute rubbish,' I said, quashing Vernie's eureka moment dismissively. 'And you know it.'

'Okay! Okay!' she said defensively. 'It was only a suggestion, Duff. There's no need to be so bloody touchy.'

'Well, if you've got any more suggestions like that, I suggest you keep them to yourself,' I said irritably and stood up to leave. 'I came round here for your advice, Vern, but if you think that I'm going to go and ask my GP for previous partner aversion therapy or pop down to Holland and Barrett's for some organic anti-Mel rescue remedy or ask at Boot's chemist counter for the ex-girlfriend equivalent of a nicotine patch, you've another think coming! This has got nothing whatsoever to do with Mel. Nothing.' I calmed down, having finally become aware how ridiculous my indignation sounded. 'I'm going to go now and do what I should've done in the beginning instead of coming round here. I'm going to sort out this whole sorry episode myself and when you see me next I will be a whole man once more. Goodbye.'

*　　　*　　　*

Over the following seven days, in an attempt to right the wrong that had happened to me, I saw Alexa twice. Both times we got on incredibly well. We'd laugh, flirt and have a great time, but the minute things started to get even vaguely heated, well . . . nothing. Bizarrely, she seemed keener on me than ever before. It was as if her reputation as TV's Hottest Totty was at stake and she was determined not to lose her crown. Time and time again she asked me up for 'coffee' and time and time again I said no, not wanting a repeat of that deflated Saturday night. The more I said no, the more she wanted me to say yes. This was a unique position for me to be in and one that would've been of great benefit in my youth. Had I managed to convince girls at sixth form that it was *me* refusing *them* sexual congress, rather than the other way round, my 'A' level life would've been considerably more bearable. None of this mattered, however: despite everything I'd done to try and alleviate the problem – purchasing baggier pants, eating Bran Flakes and browsing the female underwear sections of clothing catalogues – the problem remained.

'Are you okay, Duff?'

It was a week later and I was round at Dr Vernie's sexual ailment surgery once again. This time I was prepared to take her advice for a miracle cure, whether it involved leeches, losing a limb, or even my ex-girlfriend.

'No,' I said sulkily.

'Is it still . . . ? She pointed to my lap and raised her eyebrows questioningly.

'Yes.'

'Nothing at all?'

'Nothing.'

'Not a sausage?' Vernie doubled up with uncontrollable

laughter, barely stopping herself from falling off the sofa. She wiped the tears of mirth from her eyes and sniffed. 'I'm sorry, Duff, I couldn't help myself.'

'Yeah, I'm sure you couldn't.' I held my head in my hands in despair. This really was becoming a nightmare from which it was possible I would never wake up. 'Do you really think that it's got something to do with Mel?'

'Don't you?'

'I'm not sure. Your theory fits. It's just—'

The sound of the front door opening interrupted our conversation. It was Charlie coming in from work. He came into the lounge carrying two large plastic Threshers bags that were making excessive clinking noises. 'Bumped into Dan on the Tube,' he said to Vernie, explaining not only why he was an hour late but why he smelt of Guinness too. 'He's just nipped to the newsagent. He'll be up in a minute.'

'Is that right?' said Vernie, now unquestionably annoyed. 'Why didn't you phone to say you were going to be this late?'

A man after my own heart, Charlie pretended he hadn't heard her question and instead opted to create a diversion. 'What's so funny?'

'Nothing,' I said abruptly. There was no way I was going to let him use my current infirmity to get him out of trouble with Vernie.

Charlie refused to give up, though. His only hope was to harangue me into submission. 'I could hear you laughing from outside. Come on. What's going on?'

Vernie opened her mouth as if about to begin a sentence.

'No, Vernie!' I yelled and leaped over to cover her mouth.

Charlie looked at me and then at Vernie, clearly bewildered, but aware that with a little more pushing he'd be off the hook for good. 'I'll find out sooner or later, you know.'

'It's private,' I said with my hand still over Vernie's mouth as she giggled wildly.

She bit my hand forcing me to let her go. 'I can't keep secrets from Charlie, he's my husband,' she said, trying to suppress her laughter. 'We tell each other everything, don't we, Charlie?'

'Of course we do, darling,' said Charlie, adopting an angelic tone of voice in order to mock me. 'What is it that your dear, dear, brother doesn't want you to tell me about?'

'You are *not* telling him anything!' I barked at Vernie threateningly.

'Oh, Duffy,' pleaded Vernie. 'Charlie only wants to help. Anyway, I think it might help for you to talk it over with another man. He might have some advice on what to do in this type of situation.'

'What kind of example are you showing your unborn?' I pointed to her moderately pregnant stomach. 'He can hear you, you know. He's probably thinking to himself, 'Why's Mummy tormenting uncle Duffy like this? She can't be a very nice lady. I'm going to show my disapproval of her shocking behaviour by taking fifty-two hours to come out.'

'Any more than twelve hours and I'll drag you out myself!' yelled Vernie at her bump. 'Anyway, if the baby is a *he*,' she said patting the sides of her stomach fondly, 'he's learning a valuable lesson – not to be anything like his uncle Duffy. Baby Jacobs, when you grow up, don't keep things inside. Talk. You can talk to me. You can talk to your dad – though I wouldn't recommend it – and you can even talk to your uncle Duffy. One day the whole of the world's male population will spontaneously combust because they've kept too much stuff in for too long, and I don't want it happening to you.' She paused. 'If you're a girl, Baby Jacobs, let me tell you how very lucky you are. Life is so much easier being a woman. We're so much more . . . I don't know . . . unburdened.' Vernie then looked up at me smirking. 'Try it, Duff. Try a little unburdening. Share your problem with Charlie, he might actually be able to help you.'

Charlie looked at me eagerly while I grimaced at Vernie's attempt to be earnest. 'Has it happened to Charlie then?'

'Never,' said Vernie barely able to suppress a snigger. 'Not my stud muffin.'

A look of horror crept across Charlie's features as the unmentionable of all unmentionables reared its ugly head inside his consciousness. 'You mean your . . . y'know . . . oh mate, I'm so sorry. I had no idea.'

I bowed my head in shame.

'I've heard it's quite common,' said Charlie, clearly trying to bolster my spirits. 'I shouldn't worry about it, mate. Leave it alone for a while and it'll be all right.'

'Leave what alone?' said Dan, who had just entered the room carrying a family-sized packet of Quavers.

'Duffy's you-know-what,' said Vernie matter-of-factly. 'He thinks he's impotent.'

Dan shivered visibly. 'Oh, mate,' was all he initially managed to say by way of comfort, then he added shakily, 'I agree with Charlie. Leave it alone for a while. It's probably resting or hibernating or something.'

'You lot are hopeless!' chided Vernie. 'You and your "It's only a flesh wound" mentality. Go on, listen to Charlie and "leave it alone for a while" – just make sure when it drops off you bring it to him to fix for you, and not to me. Get yourself down to a doctor, Duffy. Doctors see people with things that are wrong with them all the time! That's what they're there for.'

'Nah,' said Dan warily. 'Bunch of quacks, mate. You do not

want to be lowering your trousers in a doctor's surgery. You don't know what might happen. One minute you're following orders, slipping on to the examining table with the paper towels on it and the next he's telling you all sorts of things have got to come off. Ignorance, my son, is bliss.'

'Oh, stop, it you two,' said Vernie finally taking pity on me. 'You can take a thing too far, you know. Duffy's worried enough as it is thinking that it's all got something to do with Mel.'

'What's it got to do with Mel?' asked Dan quizzically.

'Everything,' said Vernie.

'You know what you've got to do, don't you?' said Dan after Vernie had expounded her theory.

'What?' I said, expecting this to be yet another joke at my expense.

'Exorcise it.'

'Exorcise it?'

'Well not "it" exactly,' said Dan laughing. 'I don't think there's a priest in the world that would want that job. But I think you've got to confront your demons. Vernie reckons that you're like this because you still find Mel attractive, right? So if you stop finding her attractive you'll be okay, won't you?'

I nodded.

'You've been talking for ages about wanting the two of you to be friends, so all you've got to do is stop talking and start doing. Once you see Mel as a close friend rather than your ex-girlfriend your troubles will be over.'

'Makes sense,' said Charlie, his tone of voice revealing that he was somewhat shocked to discover Dan could make sense. 'It's the only thing you can do, mate.'

'He could have a point,' said Vernie, looking at Dan,

barely able to comprehend that she too was agreeing with him.

'Friends it is, then,' I said, looking at all three of them. 'I just hope it works.'

We should do this more often

'So how are you, Duffy?'

'Okay. And you?'

'Not bad. Not bad at all.'

It was mid-afternoon, that post-lunch pre-hometime period of the day when it's impossible to do anything at work but sleep, stare into space or phone your mates. I chose to phone Mel. During the call I updated her on Vernie's recent pregnancy scan ('It looks just like a wizened Winston Churchill only smaller and without the cigar'), and Charlie's continuing battle to get to grips with fatherhood ('He did the introductory quiz in *Pregnancy For Fathers* and scored three out of twenty') and Dan's latest attempt to reinvigorate his comedy act with a character called Trip Master Monkey ('He pretends he's a monkey that keeps falling over. You have to see it to believe it'.) Then for no reason at all Mel said, 'This is good. This being friends lark.'

'Yeah,' I replied. 'It shows that we're growing up. Maturing like cheese and fine wine.'

Mel laughed. 'I'm the fine wine. You're the cheese.' She paused. 'I'm glad we're talking like this, because I want to tell you something and you may not like it, but I think if we are friends I should tell you anyway.'

'Okay,' I said, my stomach muscles tightening, waiting for the blow. 'Go for it.'

205

'Rob and I . . . we're going to go on holiday to Tuscany next week with Mark and Julie.'

'Oh,' was all I managed as I imagined the two of them frolicking next to a sunkissed lake, laughing gaily, and later sitting down on their sunloungers to write a postcard that said, 'You wish you were here.' It was too much. 'I didn't realise you were at the holidaying abroad stage. We didn't reach that stage until year two.'

'That was only because up until then five days in the Lake District with me was about as much of a commitment as you'd make.'

'There's no need for that.'

'I'm sorry,' said Mel. 'You're right.'

'I've got some news of my own.' I'd been meaning to tell Mel about Alexa for a while and as we were being truthful, now seemed as good a time as any. 'Remember that woman who knew Mark who came to see my act . . . the one who's a presenter on *The Hot Pop Show* . . . well, we're kind of . . .'

'Oh,' said Mel and fell silent for a few moments. 'So how long have you and TV's Hottest Totty been . . . ?'

'A while,' I confessed. I didn't want to hurt her any more than she'd wanted to hurt me with her holidaying arrangements. We both knew life had to move on but that didn't make it any less painful.

'It had to happen some time,' she said impassively. 'I'm pleased for you. I really am. Does she make you happy?'

We were back to that old one. 'I wouldn't go that far,' I said reassuringly. 'We're getting on okay though.'

Silence.

'So now we've both moved on,' I said finally.

'Looks like it,' she replied.

'So this means we can be proper friends.'

'Yeah,' she said. 'I suppose it does.'

I paused. 'Will I get to see you before you go off on holiday?'

'I don't know,' she said. 'I've got loads on at work. I'll just check my diary.' Her voice disappeared for a while, leaving me alone with my thoughts. 'Thursday's the only night I can do.'

'Okay, Thursday.'

Mel tutted loudly. 'Oh, hang on, I've got a presentation Friday morning, so I'll have to work late.'

I really was disappointed. I hadn't seen her since the day I'd visited her at work, and I desperately wanted to see her. To see with my own eyes that we were friends. This wasn't about exorcising her memory from my pants, this was about consolidating what we had. I felt that unless we did, she'd return from her holiday closer to Rob1 and further away from me than ever.

'What about just a quick drink, then?' I suggested hopefully.

'I'll be too tired to be out in public,' she said dolefully. 'I'll tell you what, though, I can do better than just a drink. How about coming round to mine? You bring a bottle of wine and I'll bag something tasty from Marks & Spencer's chill cabinet.'

'Sounds great,' I said, brightening immediately. 'See you Thursday.'

It took me fifty minutes longer than my usual five to get ready to go to Mel's. My bed was covered in clothes that I'd been trying on and taking off for most of the evening. In the end I wore my jeans, trainers, a white T-shirt and my corduroy jacket. I looked a bit scruffy, but I didn't care because that was the point entirely. I had to make it known to Mel that I hadn't made an effort. She was an expert on the semiotics of my wardrobe. The slightest bit of an effort on my part would be immediately construed as a covert attempt to get into her pants.

I arrived ten minutes late (I was working my 'No Effort Theory' to the max), and rang the doorbell.

After some moments Mel opened the door. 'Hi,' she said and kissed me on the cheek. 'Come in.'

I followed her upstairs to her flat. She was wearing dark blue jeans, a shiny black top and a green cardigan. The look was understated, homely and comfortable. She obviously had a 'No Effort Theory' of her own. I handed her a bottle of wine, my contribution to the evening's meal. I'd bought it from Safeway. I didn't have the faintest clue whether it was any good or not. All I cared was that it had passed my three basic criteria of wine purchasing:

1) Does it have a nice label?
2) Do I know anyone who has holidayed in the country of origin?
3) Is it under a fiver?

The label on the bottle had a picture of a cedar tree on it, and it was made in Italy (a country Dan had visited on a school trip many years ago), but the thing that had really swung it for me was that it was £4.99 – not quite cheap and yet not exactly reassuringly expensive.

'I'll get the glasses.' Mel headed off into the kitchen, leaving me alone in the lounge. I looked around the room for any changes. There were some new curtains and she'd moved the large uplighter that used to stand next to the sofa over into a far corner. There were a couple of new videos in her collection – *The Big Blue* and *La Grande Illusion* (undoubtedly presents from Rob1) – but apart from that nothing had changed. This pleased me immensely and immediately set me at ease.

We sat down to eat at the kitchen table. There was a huge pile of bills, a Next catalogue and a copy of *Elle* at one end and us and a candlestick at the other. Mel really was a big fan of the 'No Effort Theory'.

I bet she's never this relaxed with Rob1.

I poured more wine into our now half drunk glasses and we began our meal which was undoubtedly the best thing I'd eaten since we'd split up. As I chewed a mouthful of fondant potatoes Mel apologised for not cooking something proper and I told her not to worry. Why? Because this was yet another thing she . . .

. . . would never do with Rob1!

The meal over, two empty wine bottles on the table and a third already open, we tucked into dessert, a summer fruits pudding for her and a cherry cheesecake (my favourite) for me. Everything felt relaxed. Everything felt . . . okay.

'This is nice,' said Mel, moving her chair next to mine so that she could sample my pudding as well as her own without stretching. 'We were always friends as well as boyfriend and girlfriend, don't you think?'

'Yeah,' I nudged her gently with my shoulder, 'buddy.'

She nudged me back, slightly harder. 'Yeah . . . mate.'

I nudged her in return harder still. 'Yeah . . . chum.'

She then proceeded to nudge me so hard that I fell off my chair. Laughing hysterically from my position on the floor I managed a 'Yeah . . . pal!' as Mel tried to help me up. Holding on to my hand, she lost her balance and ended up on top of me in a fit of giggles. Having determined that the wine was making it too difficult for either of us to stand up, I grabbed the remaining bottle from the table and on all fours we crawled our way to the living room to relax.

'So, you're okay?' I asked, slouching back on the sofa sipping another glass of wine. 'I mean, everything's good in your life?'

Mel didn't answer. I nudged her again. 'Yeah.' She shook her head as if waking herself up. 'Sorry, you must excuse me. I was just thinking . . . Sitting here, drinking too much wine, talking, laughing. This kind of comfortable doesn't happen overnight.'

'No.' I kicked off my trainers. 'You're right it doesn't.'

'People always go on about how fantastic relationships are in the beginning, and of course everyone hates relationships when they end, but what about the middles? The middles where you know everything there is to know. Where you can look at the person you love and know what they're thinking; see something on the telly and know how they'd react; when you know exactly what they'd wear to come round and see you.'

I smiled fondly. 'Did you know what I'd be wearing tonight?'

'Look under Fat Buddha's bum,' she said.

I slid off the sofa, crawled over to the mantelpiece and picked up the small ceramic Buddha Julie and Mark had brought back from a trip to Thailand several years ago. Fat Buddha used to be the butt of all our politically incorrect jokes about fat men when we were together. I picked him up by his neck and underneath was a torn out page from a pocket diary. It read, 'White T-shirt. Jeans. Trainers. Corduroy Jacket.'

'Are you trying to tell me that you knew exactly what I was going to wear?' I said, crawling back to the sofa.

'I'm not *trying* to tell you anything,' she laughed. 'I bet you've even got your marl grey underpants on.'

This was typical Mel. I remember her once telling me that as a teenager she'd been a massive fan of the pop band Wham! So much so that she knew every personal detail about George Michael and Andrew Ridgeley, right down to their shoe sizes. I'm sure back then she didn't question why she collected all this information – she did it simply because it made her happy, not realising that she was actually learning skills that she'd one day need in the future. Seventeen years or so down the line, she was still an avid collector of personal details, only this time round they were mine. In the four years we'd been together Mel had learned off by heart every detail about me – chest size, name of first girlfriend, favourite episode of *Dad's Army* – everything. I'd often wondered why she'd done this, but it was only now, as I sat on the sofa that I realised that there was indeed a method to her madness. To her, to know truly, was to be intimate. To be intimate was to know the person you love as well as you know your own self. She'd built up the information inside her head to the point where she had created a virtual me, a model which she could use to predict my behaviour down to the last detail – even to the choice of colour of underwear. I was impressed.

'Congratulations,' I mocked. 'When's your membership to the Magic Circle arriving?'

'Ahhhh,' she joked. 'Have I hurt your feelings?'

'No,' I said, faking a sulk.

Mel leaned towards me. 'Come here,' she said rubbing my cheeks. 'Let me make it all better.'

Then she kissed me.

Then I kissed her.

Then we fumbled about with each other's clothing.

Then we fumbled some more.

And life came back to where there had been none.

And so we did it.

Twice.

Okay, once and a half.

Rays of sunshine broke through the curtains, rousing me from my slumber. Consciousness came immediately, but I didn't move in case I woke Mel. Instead I slowly opened my eyes and carefully manoeuvred my body to face her. I quickly realised I needn't have bothered being so quiet. She was already up and making shower noises. I lay back on the pillow, arms behind my head, and savoured the sweet smell of victory.

I always knew we'd get back together. I knew it would just be a matter of time. We meant too much to each other to give up so easily. I think we'll take things slowly to begin with. See each other twice a week until we're safe. And then everything will carry on as it was before. Except this time I'll make sure that I never lose her again.

Mel entered the bedroom wearing her hooded white towelling dressing gown, brandishing her hairdrier sternly. Her hair was still wet. She didn't look happy.

'My hair drier's dead, Duffy,' she said. 'This is a sign.'

'Of what?'

'A sign to punish me for what we did . . . there . . .' she pointed to her bedroom rug . . . 'and there . . .' she pointed at a small peach armchair her gran had given her . . . and there,' she pointed to the bed. 'My hair, Duffy. What am I going to do? I can't go to an important meeting with wet hair.'

I sat up in bed and tried to do that sexy, ruffled look that characters in big Hollywood films always have the day after. I caught a glimpse of myself in the full-length mirror on the wall. I looked about as sexy as an alcoholic tramp. 'It's probably the fuse,' I said helpfully.

'You don't know that,' she snapped exasperatedly. 'You

know bugger all about DIY. Remember, you were the one who fitted a handle on my bathroom door upside down, and three years later it's still the same way.'

This was not the mood I'd expected. I was hoping for a little joy. Maybe even euphoria. Irritability at my presence expressed through a knackered electrical appliance wasn't really what I had in mind.

'I take it you regret last night.'

Mel flopped down heavily into her peach armchair. 'Regret? Duffy, this is beyond regret. I cheated on Rob! I can't believe I did that.'

I instantly felt relieved. She didn't regret last night at all, she was merely torturing herself because she felt bad that she was going to have to hurt Rob1 when she dumped him. She needed help. She needed Bloke Logic.

'There you are wrong, Mel,' I said pointedly. 'What you did . . . what we did, well, it's not cheating. Not really. It's just a question of timing. You were going to dump Rob1 anyway, so the fact that we did what we did before you'd told him, is at the very worst a grey area.'

Mel's face transformed from neutral to thunderous instantly. 'Point one!' she yelled. 'Will you stop referring to Rob as Rob1? It's really annoying! Point two: it's not a grey area, Duffy! It's very black and white. Point three: I'm not going to dump Rob. You and I should not have done what we did. It was very wrong.'

I felt my body deflate in humiliation. 'But I thought . . .'

'Well, you thought wrong. Has your position on together-ness changed?'

I didn't answer.

'Yes, well, mine hasn't either!' She stood up and came over to sit on the bed next to me with her head in her hands. Her anger disappeared as quickly as it had arrived. 'Now look what we've done,' she said. 'What about this friends thing we had going?'

'It's still there,' I said dejectedly. 'Just as long as we stay away from £4.99 bottles of red wine.' I searched around for my underwear. It felt ridiculous being the only one naked in the room. 'Can you pass my clothes, please?'

Mel picked up my jeans off the floor and threw them at me playfully. 'You did this on purpose, didn't you?'

'What?'

'You came around to seduce me. Looking all cute and worn out.'

'I did no such thing!' I protested.

She laughed. 'Why not? Aren't I good enough to seduce, eh?'

'What about you?' I said accusingly. 'You only invited me round here because you were jealous that I was together with Alexa. All this time I've had to listen to you go on about Rob1, but it was okay, because *you* had someone else. The minute I found someone else, though, you didn't like it, did you?'

I knew I shouldn't have said it. Yes, it was true. Yes, it scored a few points on the self-righteous scoreboard. But was it worth it? Not at all. Yet another 'LEAVE WELL ALONE' option that I'd failed to exercise. *Why do I always say the wrong thing at the wrong time?*

Mel didn't say another word to me. Instead she got dressed, put on her jacket and shoes, grabbed her briefcase and hermetically sealed the door with a slam so forceful something fell and crashed on the floor next door. I got up and looked into the living room. Fat Buddha was lying smashed on the floor with his head rolling towards the sofa. I picked up the pieces sadly and placed them on the coffee table.

I walked back to the bedroom and looked out of the

window. I watched as Mel got into her car, slamming the door shut behind her. It was a bizarre scene to watch, because all the time I kept thinking, *Her hair is still wet.*

. . . and your plan is?

'Duffy, it's Mel.'

'Hi,' I said cagily. It had been two weeks since I'd last heard from her. 'When did you get back from Tuscany?'

'Half an hour ago.'

'How was it . . . your holiday, I mean?'

'It was all right,' she said dismissively. 'I don't think the food agreed with me. I kept being sick all the time.'

Was it too much to ask for Rob1 to be ill too? A touch of gastroenteritis. A smidgen of dysentery. A tinge of beri-beri. 'Did Rob suffer too?'

'He couldn't go in the end. Something came up at work.'

Excellent! Better than disease – penalised by hard work.

'I'm sorry to hear that,' I said airily.

'I'm sure you are,' she said sardonically. 'But none of this has anything to do with why I've called. I've been thinking a lot about what you said last time we were together. You were right: I think I *was* jealous about you and Alexa. It was wrong of me to invite you round and to let what happened happen. I suppose I just wanted to see if you still wanted me, and if you're truthful you wanted to know exactly the same thing. You have to admit it, Duff.'

'No, I don't.'

'Of course you do,' she persisted, her voice revealing a complete lack of doubt. 'Don't forget how well I know you.'

217

'Okay, you're right,' I admitted finally. 'But where does that leave us? You still have feelings for me. I still have feelings for you. You want one thing, I want something else, and to top it all we're both seeing other people.'

'The way I see it,' said Mel authoritatively, making it clear that she'd given the matter a great deal of thought, 'we've got to face up to the fact that, irrational as it may seem, we still mean a lot to each other but want different things from life. We were together for a long time, and that kind of intense feeling isn't just going to disappear. We undoubtedly still feel the need to be part of each other's lives—'

I interrupted. I could feel that Mel was going into over-analysing mode – finding fifteen different ways of saying exactly the same thing. I'd had enough. I just wanted her to get to the point. '. . . and your plan is?'

'If only you knew how annoying that is, Duffy!' she snapped exasperatedly. 'My *plan* is that as we can't live with each other and we appear to be unable to live without each other, we have to do the mature thing. The adult thing.' She still wasn't getting to the point.

'And that is?'

'Well, the way I see it, one of us has a well-developed conscience while the other likes to pretend that he hasn't, even though I know he bloody well has. And so in the same manner that criminals are sometimes forced by courts to face up to their wrongdoings by meeting the victims of their crime, we should meet each other's new partners.'

I coughed nervously. 'You're joking, right?'

'It totally makes sense, Duff.'

'On Planet Psychotic perhaps, but here on earth I think you'll find that what you've suggested is deranged.'

Mel continued, unruffled. 'Once we meet each other's new partners they'll both become real. This way I can convert the image of Alexa as "that bitch off the TV who's sleeping with my ex-boyfriend" to "Alexa the human being who finds herself in the middle of this terribly entangled situation". She becomes real.'

'But aren't you forgetting one small thing?'

'What?'

'I've already met Rob1 "that tosspot who's going out with my ex-girlfriend", so I can be excused from this nightmare. He didn't become "Rob1 the unfortunate individual caught up between two people who . . ."' I chose my words carefully . . . '"have strong feelings for each other". I loathed him before I met him and totally despised him after the event. It's just the way it goes.'

'Let me explain this to you, Duffy,' said Mel, adopting a businesslike tone I suspected she used at work with difficult clients, 'in terms you can understand. We can't carry on being friends if we don't try to do something to rectify this situation. That's no phone calls. No meeting up together. No Letters. E-mails. No communication whatsoever. I know it'll be difficult but it's the only way if you won't do this.'

'You're serious, aren't you?'

'Yes, I am,' she said. 'Anyway,' her voice was much lighter in tone now she'd got my attention, 'you haven't met Rob properly at all. He's a really nice guy. He likes you. He told me so.'

It was all I could to do stop myself from tutting contemptuously. 'I bet he's told you he's not jealous that you phone me either; that he's happy we're still in each other's lives; that it doesn't bother him when you mention my name . . .'

'Yes,' snapped Mel.

'Mel, these are guy lies! Can't you see that? It's not in

our natures to like He-Who-Was-There-Before-Us. It's natural selection. The selfish gene.'

'Look, I'm serious. We have to do something. And we have to do it now.' She played her trump card. 'Have you got a better solution?'

'No,' I said.

'Then it looks like we're going with mine, then, doesn't it? Next Saturday night. You and Alexa come round to mine. I'll make something nice and we'll sort out this whole thing.'

'But won't they think it's suspicious that we're suddenly having this meeting? I mean, you're not going to tell Rob1 about what happened, are you?'

'You know what a terrible liar I am. I feel like I'm going to be struck down by a bolt of lightning every time I tell my mum that I didn't skip breakfast, but this would hurt Rob too much.' She paused. 'How would Alexa react?'

'She'd be really mad,' I lied. I hadn't the faintest clue what Alexa would think. 'Absolutely furious.'

It was the day of the dinner invitation and I'd just arrived at Alexa's. I was wearing a dark burgundy suit without a tie in a bid to look both smart and casual. Alexa, however, had insisted on dressing up. She was wearing a purple top that had all the seams on the outside by a Dutch designer whose name I couldn't pronounce, and black wide-legged trousers from Joseph. I knew all this information about the labels because she'd insisted that I accompany her on a shopping spree in New Bond Street for the whole afternoon. It was a truly frightening experience. Not only did she not bother looking at a single price tag the whole time we were out, but she deliberated over a pair of shoes for three hours and still didn't buy them. Shopping for soft furnishings with Mel was a doddle compared to this.

'Come in,' said Alexa, holding open her front door. I followed her into the lounge. 'Do you want a drink? I'm having a glass of wine.'

'Yeah, go on, then,' I said, sitting down on the sofa. I looked down at Alexa's feet as she handed me the glass of wine. 'Are those what I think they are?'

'Yes,' she laughed. 'The second I got home I knew I wanted them after all. I called a cab and went straight back to the shop and bought them. And even if I do say so myself, they look fantastic.'

'They do,' I said. I took a moment to take in her whole outfit. 'In fact all of you looks fantastic.'

'You don't look too bad yourself.'

She sat down next to me and took a sip of her wine. 'I've got to tell you something that I know you're not going to like,' she said.

'What is it?' I asked, hoping she was going to deliver the 'this isn't working out' speech. It had been obvious for quite a while that Alexa and I were never really meant to be. She was beautiful, fun to be with, and for all her pretensions actually quite down to earth, but she wasn't right for me. Though cured, I was still feigning impotence – a sign, if any were needed, that things weren't quite right – and when I'd explained Mel's suggestion to her earlier in the week she'd said yes without even blinking an eyelid. No one normal should want to meet their current partner's ex-partner that much. If it had been the other way round and Alexa had wanted me to meet any of her ex-boyfriends, there would've been no way I'd have done it. We just weren't suited. I didn't mind, though, because I really did think we could be friends – especially as, technically speaking, we hadn't seen each other totally naked.

'It's about the audition,' she said.

I stopped breathing.

'The executive producer called me about an hour ago to let me know she'd made her decision. I'm sorry, but you didn't get the job. I tried really hard to swing it for you. I really did, but they kept going on that you weren't what they were looking for, whatever that means. But they don't know anything. Don't worry about it, Duff. Something else will come up soon, I'm sure.'

I drained my glass of wine and didn't say anything. I purposely hadn't been thinking about the audition, because I knew that if I gave it any thought at all, by the time I'd finished churning out vast numbers of hope-filled 'what ifs', it would become the biggest thing in my life. Unfortunately, it was only now as I sat on this sofa, not saying anything and feeling like the whole world was collapsing around my ears, that I realised how misguided I'd been. Despite my efforts, the audition had been the biggest thing in my life this past few months. It had been the one thing keeping me afloat. It had been the best thing that had happened to me in the eight years of being heckled, ripped off and lied to. It hurt not to have it happen. It hurt more than I could bear. I looked at Alexa and then at the room that I was sitting in. None of this felt right. This was all wrong.

'You win some, you lose some,' I said eventually. 'Who got it in the end?'

She picked up a scrap of paper by the telephone. 'Some guy called Greg Bennet. I think I even met him at one of the auditions.'

'Grim-looking, balding man with a massive Napoleon complex, talks a lot about football?'

'Yeah,' she said, puzzled. 'Come to think of it, when I spoke to him he did say that he knew you too.'

I've had enough, I told myself. *This is the end.* 'I'm quitting comedy,' I said, letting my thoughts roam free. It felt odd saying those words at long last, and yet at the same time I was relieved.

'Not because of this stupid audition, surely?'

'Exactly because of this stupid audition. I've given this comedy lark my best shot for over eight years, and this audition was the biggest thing that's happened to me in all that time. Maybe it's a sign. I don't know, maybe it's time I realised I'm going to be one of the ones who doesn't make it. I'm not bitter.' I paused. I wasn't fooling anybody, least of all me. 'No, I *am* bitter. I'm as bitter as it's possible to be. I've given up everything chasing stupid dreams. Too much. Now it's time to bail out before it's too late.'

'This is a bad idea. You're really talented, Duffy. You've just had a knockback. We all get those once in a while. You wait. Take a few weeks off, forget all about the audition and then everything will look different.'

'Did you know,' I said, wondering how I was ever going to tell Alexa that I didn't want to see her any more, 'that Margaret Thatcher once said, "If a man finds himself a passenger on a bus, having attained the age of twenty-six, he can account himself a failure in life"?'

'No.'

'Yeah, she did. I read it in an article in the *Guardian* last year. I pinned it on the cork noticeboard in the kitchen'. I sighed heavily. 'Do you know how I get to work every day?'

'By bus?'

'For the last three years,' I said. 'I'm two years past Maggie's sell by-date and I'm still catching the bus. That's why I'm giving up comedy. I need to get real. I need to stop travelling on buses.'

'Come on, Duff. What would you do? Get a permanent office job? You'd be banging your head against the walls within a week.'

I shrugged. 'I could go back to college maybe. I don't know. Do something constructive.'

'You're just feeling depressed about not getting the job. Everyone knows what it feels like to be disappointed. There'll be other auditions, other opportunities.'

'Maybe.' I sighed again. 'And maybe not.'

'But that's not all, is it?' she said, her eyes searching my face.

'What do you mean?'

'Us.'

'Us?'

'Yes, us.'

Alexa had obviously developed the same mindreading technique that Mel possessed.

'Yeah, well, I was going to get round to "us". The thing is—'

'You're still in love with your ex.'

'That's not what I was going to say.'

'I know, but it's true. You were going to string me some old line about things not working out between us, because you're too scared to admit what's really going on. I'm no expert on love, but I am a woman. It's totally obvious you're still in love with Mel. There are only three reasons why any man would agree to go to dinner with his ex and her new boyfriend. One: he's mad. Two: he's stupid. Three: he's still in love with her. You're not mad or stupid, so what's left? You talk about commitment like it's an alien concept. This thing that you just can't do. But all this time hasn't it dawned on you that "commitment" is what you're doing right now? I read this brilliant thing once in a book: 'What's the difference between involvement and commitment? Think of eggs and bacon. The chicken was involved. The pig was committed." You, Mr Duffy, are, probably always were, and definitely always will be, a pig.'

Alexa's words slowly began to sink in. 'So what you're saying is I've been acting like a fool because I'm already committed to Mel . . .'

She nodded.

'So if I'm already committed to her, then it's ridiculous being afraid of commitment. So there's nothing stopping me from . . .' I stood up. 'I've got to go.'

'I know,' said Alexa.

'Aren't you mad at me or anything? I've led you a right dance: I've helped you spend hideous amounts of money on clothes you needn't have bought, and if that's not enough, I wouldn't sleep with you even though you practically begged me.'

'Well, now you put it like that . . .' Alexa started to laugh. She leaned forward and kissed me. 'Look, firstly I love buying clothes. Secondly, you're kidding yourself if you think me and my brand-new shoes are staying in tonight pining for you while you're proposing to your ex-girlfriend. And thirdly, rejection is good for the soul. Even if you are TV's Hottest Totty. Duffy, you're a nice guy, you really are, and I hope we can be friends, but the real reason I'm not bothered is because at the end of the day I'm just a sucker for a happy ending.'

In the back of a cab with a wet late-evening London whizzing past in a continuous blur I could hear nothing other than the sound of my heart beating. With the benefit of my new enlightenment, the key mistakes I'd made in all my time with Mel were suddenly clear to me in a way they'd never been.

For starters I'd entered our relationship determined to stay exactly the same – which I'll admit is pretty stupid, but at the beginning had made perfect sense to me. Changing meant that I wasn't the man I used to be, and I quite liked the man

I used to be. Mel, however, had taken me on a journey out of the wilderness I inhabited with Dan and led me part of the way to the land of the living, where there were three different types of shampoo in the bathroom, duvet covers that matched pillows and food that didn't come out of a tin or make its appearance accompanied by toast. Admittedly, sometimes I'd felt like I was slapbang in the middle of no-man's land – not quite my old self and not revised enough to be a new self – and yes, there were occasions when I found myself wanting to run back to what I knew. But I'd tried being a super stud of seduction and it hadn't worked, precisely because I was a changed man. In the past my deepest thoughts used to be about stand-up, music and women. Thanks to Mel's influence I'd expanded my repertoire of subjects to include life, the universe and everything.

Mel was the best girlfriend I could've asked for. She was funny, gentle and most of all, loyal. She was one of a kind and I'd nearly blown it for good because I had a problem with all the stuff that seemed to come with the relationship. Like IKEA. Like dinner parties. Like . . . marriage. The one thing she most wanted but the only thing I couldn't deliver.

Well, I could now.

Blue

The taxi pulled up outside Mel's and I sat motionless in my seat as my head occupied itself with the following problem: how on earth was I going to announce to her that I didn't just want to have dinner with her, I wanted to spend the rest of my life with her too? I looked out of the cab window for inspiration. Mel's 2CV was glistening brightly in the rain but I couldn't see Rob1's coolmobile anywhere. *He's probably got a taxi so he can have a drink*, I reasoned. A thought which led me to consider the bottle of wine in my hand. During my afternoon shopping trip with Alexa, in a bid to be wild and unpredictable like her, I'd abandoned my normal strategy for wine purchasing and picked a bottle at random in Selfridges and bought it. It had cost me £17.99, which to my mind meant that it had better be up there with the best the sensual world had to offer or I was asking for my money back.

Enough of the procrastinating, Mr Duffy, I reproached. *It's now or never*. I stood and watched the cab pull away. My legs felt incredibly unsteady, like I'd just run a marathon. It was amazing. They just wouldn't work properly. In addition to this, my saliva had turned tinny and watery. With each swallow the scales of digestion were tipping further and further towards projectile vomiting. I was comforted by this fact because it meant that both my conscious and unconscious selves were in agreement that this situation I was about to get myself into was a momentous one.

I rang the doorbell and waited, practising my proposal, so that when the moment came, at the very least I'd be word perfect.

Mel, I love you. Will you marry me?

Nice.

Mel, I've been a fool. Will you be my bride?

Okay, but a touch melodramatic.

Baby, I'm thinking me in a suit, you in a white dress and the vicar in whatever he wants.

Who am I, John Travolta?

I closed my eyes, breathing deeply, and tried to calm myself down. Eventually I heard the lock on the front door turning and I opened my eyes to see Mel standing there. She'd been crying.

'What's wrong?' I exclaimed, observing the traces of smudged mascara across her face. 'Are you all right?'

She wiped away a stray tear with the palm of her hand and said, 'You'd better come in.'

I followed her upstairs into the living room, wondering what could've happened. I thought that perhaps she'd had a row with Rob1, but it seemed to be more than that. Then it occurred to me that something might have happened to her parents. Mel's mum had suffered a slight stroke a couple of years ago and had been in and out of hospital ever since.

'Are you all right?' I asked when we reached the lounge. 'It's not your parents, is it?'

'No,' she said. 'They're fine.'

I put my bottle of wine on the table and scanned the room for evidence of Rob1's presence. 'Where's Rob?'

'He's been . . .' she said, sitting down on the sofa . . . 'and he's gone.'

228

I sat down next to her, and all I wanted to do was put my arms around her. 'Have you had some sort of row?'

'You could say that.'

'I'm sorry to hear it,' I said quietly. In a strange sort of way I actually meant it.

'There's no need to lie, Duff.' She smiled weakly. 'At least not for my sake. Me and Rob were never going to go anywhere. I've known that from the beginning. It's funny: I think I was only with him because he was so much the opposite of you.' She paused. 'Anyway, he's not the reason why I've been crying.'

'I don't understand,' I said, moving closer to her. 'What's upset you so much?'

'I'm pregnant,' she said, not looking at me.

I tried to grasp the meaning of what she'd said, but it just seemed to escape me. It was like my brain was stuck. I had no reactions at all. I was totally calm. I didn't say anything. I couldn't say anything. I couldn't feel anything and could barely hear anything apart from the sound of my own heart.

'Before you ask,' she said, 'it's not Rob's. Practical impossibility. Call me old fashioned, but I couldn't sleep with someone I didn't love, and I didn't love Rob.'

'When did you find out?'

She looked at her watch. 'Three hours and twenty-seven minutes ago. Not that I'm counting or anything. I was over a week late. I've been late before, but like they always say, this time I knew. I bought three tests, three different brands. Any less than three opinions isn't enough for a woman like me.' She laughed softly, stood up and walked over to the mantelpiece and picked something up. 'I thought I'd keep them as a memento.' She unwrapped a tissue and laid the three test sticks on the table one by one. 'Blue. Blue. And Blue. It's a baby all right.'

She looked at me expectantly. It was my turn to say something. The best I could muster was, 'I thought we . . .'

'That's life,' she said sharply. 'Accidents happen.' She began pacing the room nervously. 'If this is a shock for you, Duff, I'm sorry, but it's a whole lot bigger shock for me. It's turned my whole world upside down.'

'Listen, Mel,' I interrupted. I had to say something. I had to let her know that I loved her. That I wanted to be with her. That whatever happened *we* were going to be all right. 'I've got something I need to tell you.'

'Will you not do that!' she yelled, tears now streaming down her face. 'I'm speaking, Duffy! I'm fed up of you talking over me all the time. For once just shut up and listen!' She closed her eyes and breathed deeply. When she spoke again her voice was calmer and more controlled. 'I want you to know that I've made up my mind that I'm going to have this baby, Duffy. But I have to make it clear to you here and now that we won't be getting back together. That's what you were going to say, wasn't it? Let's get back together?'

'It's not like that, Mel. It's not like that at all. I want you back. That's what I came here to say. That's why Alexa's not here. Because I want to be with you.'

'Oh stop it, Duffy! Just stop it. Why won't you listen to me? I don't want you to do the right thing. I don't want us to be together because I'm pregnant. I wanted us to be together out of love, but it's too late. It's funny. In all the time we've been apart I've not once told you that I love you. We used to tell each other "I love you" every day. When we split up that stopped and I missed it more than anything. Instead we've been going on about how we "care" for each other and "need" each other, afraid to admit that we still love each other. Well, I love you, Duffy. I love you so much it scares me, but I can't do this any more. I just can't.'

'So what are you saying?'

'I'm saying that even though I love you it's over between us. I'm saying that right now I can't even handle having you near me. I'm saying that things have changed now beyond our control. I've always tried to do what's best for you but now I've got to think about me.'

I looked into her eyes, overflowing with tears, and could see that she meant every word, and as the tears filled my own eyes, I knew that she was right. If I'd thought that there was even the slightest chance I could change her mind I would've gladly spent every second from then on trying to convince her. But she was never going to believe me. It wasn't the situation that was impossible, it was her. I could see already from the way she spoke and looked at me that she'd created a barrier between us to protect herself, and she was never going to take it down.

Standing in front of her, my head swimming with thoughts and my heart overloaded with love, I pleaded with her. 'Please, Mel, I'm begging you. Is there anything I can do, anything at all that will change your mind?'

'No,' she said. 'Some things just aren't meant to be.'

Rituals are important. Nowadays it's hip not to be married. I'm not interested in being hip.

—John Lennon

The Italian Job

Friday. 11.30 p.m. The flight from Paris arrived three hours late into Heathrow's Terminal Four, which was just about typical of the entire torturous fourteen days I'd spent there. On my very first night in Paris I came up with the great idea of sleeping rough in the Gard du Nord, thus saving me the many francs I would've squandered on a room with such frivolities as a bed, toilet and running water. It was only when I saw the state of the premier Paris train station that I realised what a mistake I'd made. The air was thick with fumes from the trains, and even the pigeons cooing quietly in the rafters were a dirty, sootish grey. At three o'clock in the morning, which is when I arrived, the only place with a higher concentration of criminals would've been a prison. Within half an hour I'd been solicited by four prostitutes, offered hard drugs by a man wearing a dressing gown, and received threatening glances from a group of young men who had nothing better to do than hang around a train station at 3 a.m. After a sleepless night in which I did nothing but wish I was back in Muswell Hill, I booked into a hotel.

Over the next two weeks I saw all the sights that Paris had to offer: the Louvre, the Eiffel Tower, the flea market, the Left Bank, but without anyone to share them with, it all seemed kind of pointless. Everywhere I went there were couples smooching; gazing into each other's eyes; feeding each other food across restaurant tables. I knew Paris was supposed to be the city of love, but this was ridiculous – it was like going to IKEA on a bank holiday, only worse because there was no escaping it, and it all served to remind me just how alone I was.

Even checking in for the flight home was a nightmare. The woman on the desk had asked me if I wanted a window or an aisle seat and I told her that I wasn't bothered. The clerk tapped away at her computer keyboard and told me that all the window seats had gone for my type of ticket. Now that I couldn't have one, of course I wanted a window seat, I needed a window seat, I would've torn off my right arm for a window seat. Where did she put me? A middle-row seat right at the back of the plane. When she asked me if I'd packed my own bags I briefly contemplated telling her that my mum, the renowned diamond smuggler, terrorist and drug overlord, had done it for me, but I chickened out because I didn't know what other punishments she could inflict on me with her mighty seating computer.

All in all, I had a crap time from start to finish, but I suppose it didn't really matter where on earth I'd disappeared to, my mood would've been just the same.

Mel had absolutely refused to listen to reason. The night that she told me she was pregnant, I'd stayed round at her flat until four the next morning just holding her and crying. Nothing changed, though. She still believed that it would be best for both of us to go our separate ways. During my time away I'd tried really hard to put myself in her shoes. To understand what it was she was feeling. Here she was, twenty-nine, single and pregnant, with a ex-boyfriend whose track record for reliability wasn't exactly perfect. Of course she'd be scared to rely on me; to let me back into her life when she wasn't sure whether I had what it took to go the distance. Given my past performance, I'd failed her. Why would she believe in me?

That was only one side of the story though. My side was equally complicated. I hadn't set out to be unsure of my ability to love one person for the rest of my life – it had just happened. Unlike Mel, who seemed to have been handed a map and compass of her emotional landscape at birth, I didn't know what I was capable of, and it felt like I was being punished for my deficiency.

Mel and I were a badly dubbed, out of-sync kung fu movie, with Mel as the action and me lagging behind as the dialogue. I thought I'd never catch her up. But which was more important: us reaching the same conclusions, or us reaching the same conclusions at the same time? Mel had arrived at the idea of marriage before me, but now I'd reached the same point that she'd been at, she'd raced ahead again. Once again, it seemed, everything came down to timing.

Mel told me that she needed time alone, and I agreed that space was probably what I needed too. So I went home and told Dan everything that had happened – the splitting up with Alexa, abandoning comedy, my road to Damascus conversion to commitment, and of course my impending fatherhood. He asked me if there was anything he could do to help and I replied, rather melodramatically, 'I don't think there's anything anyone can do to help me now.' That's when I decided I needed to go away. Why Paris? Why not?

Initially I'd intended not to tell anyone when I was coming back home, but Charlie and Vernie wouldn't take no for an answer. They'd harangued me vigorously when they dropped me at the airport to catch my flight, so I gave in and promised to contact them from France. I wasn't trying to be enigmatic. I just didn't want to come back to England until I'd vaguely sorted my head out. This level of intense emotional trauma was all new to me and I hadn't the faintest idea how long a decent headsort would take, but given that I'd only packed twelve pairs of pants and loathed handwashing with a vengeance, my time away was always going to be limited.

In the end, the thing that made me come back (other than hating the food, boredom or running out of clean underwear) was Dan. Before I'd left he told me that he was thinking about going to Meena's wedding after all. He didn't ask me to go with him. He would never do that. But if at the age of twenty-eight I was allowed to have anything approximating the playground title 'best mate', then Dan was it, and I wasn't going to let him go through something like that alone.

As soon as I came into the arrivals lounge I found a phone booth and dialled Mel's number. I'd felt like calling her a million times a day when I was in Paris, but had always resisted for fear of making her feel like I was crowding her. The phone rang out and eventually her answerphone picked up. I put the receiver down without leaving a message and made my way to meet Charlie and Vernie outside the Sock Shop.

'How are you?' said Vernie. Her stomach was now so round with her pregnancy that I had to hug her from the side when she greeted me.

'I'm fine,' I replied unconvincingly. 'I'm still standing, as they say.'

'It's good to have you back,' she said, holding on to my arm. 'I wouldn't say this under normal circumstances, but because I'm about to pop a sprog any time in the next fortnight I think I can get away with it – blame it on hormone imbalances or something.' She paused and smiled. 'Baby brother Ben, I have missed you.'

'Me too,' said Charlie, giving me a blokey hug. 'It's been

weird coming home every day to find there's still food in the fridge, beers in the cupboard and no one hogging the remote control. It's unnatural, just didn't seem right.'

'Are you excited?' I said, looking at Vernie's stomach.

'Of course I am. I'm going to be a brilliant mother.' She paused. 'Talking of brilliant mothers, Mum's coming down to stay with us in a couple of weeks. Charlie can't get that much time off work, and when the baby arrives I'll be rushed off my feet, so she's volunteered her services for a while.'

'Great. With Mum only up the road there'll be no hiding how messy my flat is!' I protested jokingly. 'Mother's intuition doesn't stretch from Leeds to London, but Crouch End to Muswell Hill will be a doddle for her. She'll have psychic visions of the state of the kitchen and she won't be able to rest until she's nagged me to death to clean it up or done it herself. How much do you want to bet that when you pick her up from the train station she'll arrive with a mop, a duster and twenty quid's worth of cleaning products?'

Vernie laughed. 'Pregnancy might mean my brain is shrinking, but not even in this condition would I bet against a dead cert like that!'

Charlie wandered off, trying to remember which of the NCP car parks he'd left the car in. Vernie and I, meanwhile, sat down on a bench outside and waited. I could tell that she wanted to ask more about how I was feeling but was holding back for fear of her concern being interpreted as nagging.

'It's okay,' I told her. 'I can see that you've got something to say, so you might as well say it.'

'I just want to know that you're okay. You're the only baby brother I've got.'

'I'm fine,' I said. 'Admittedly I'm not brilliant but I am okay.'

'You don't look fine, Duffy. You look terrible.'

'Cheers,' I said sarcastically.

'I know you told me not to say anything to Mum, but with her coming to stay you know that you're going to have to tell her about Mel being pregnant, don't you?'

'Yeah.' Even the idea of telling my mum all about this made me feel ill. 'But not yet, eh?'

'If you don't tell her, she'll find out somehow. That what's mothers do best. If she does find about it by accident, it'll really hurt her that she didn't hear it from you.'

'I know,' I said. I glanced up at Vernie to see if she'd finished. 'I'll sort it out.'

'All right, mate!' yelled Dan triumphantly as I walked into the living room and dropped my rucksack on the floor.

'You look like a stick insect,' grinned Dan. 'I'll get you a lard drip feed to fatten you up while you're asleep. You look way too healthy.' He sat up and rubbed his head. 'How was it, then?'

'Not too bad,' I replied as he handed me a tin of Red Stripe. 'Six out of ten at a push.'

'I've got three pieces of news for you, all of which will make you believe that there is a force working for the greater good against all the evil in the world.'

'Give me the news that will make me most happy first.' I sloped into the armchair. It felt good to be back.

'Well, Alexa called while you were away. She said she had some news that she just couldn't wait to tell you. It turns out that the telly job Greg got wasn't as good as it sounded after all. Apparently the producers decided against using him to write gags and sketches, and instead preferred to utilise his skills as . . . wait for it . . . the voice of one of the programme's studio puppets! I taped it last week, and honestly, Duff, I nearly had a heart attack I was laughing so much. You can tell it's Greg from a mile off. Who says there's no justice?'

'What's the other news?' I said, laughing. 'It can't be anywhere near as good as that, surely?'

'Greg update number two. I bumped into The Lovely Anne last week in the Haversham, and guess what? She's dumped him!'

'Result! So she came to her senses after all?'

'Not exactly. It was more a case of her having no other choice. Get this.' Dan leaned towards me as if too shocked to impart the news in the normal way. 'Apparently Anne had thrown a party at their flat to celebrate Greg's new job and invited all their mates. Half cut on Jim Beam, who should try it on with Bethan Morgan – Anne's best mate – but Greg! Anne hit the roof and chucked him out!' Dan paused. 'I wish I'd been there.'

'So what's the third piece of good news?' I asked. 'Don't tell me you've got your own sitcom?'

'Better than that. Guess what's on in half an hour on BBC2?' he said, pointing at the TV with the remote.

'Dunno.'

'*The Italian Job.*'

'Nice one,' I said. It was mine and Dan's all-time favourite film. 'Any other phone messages?'

'Nah,' said Dan.

I was still hoping Mel would've called by now. I looked at my watch. *It's late – if she's gone out she'll be back by now. How many places can a pregnant woman be at this time of night?* Getting up off the floor I went to the phone and dialled her number. Her answerphone was still on. I left a message telling her I was back and that I'd try to call her again when I knew whether Dan and I were going to

Meena's wedding. Dan must have overheard the last bit of the message because when I turned round he was looking at me pensively.

'You don't have to come with me tomorrow, you know,' he said solemnly. 'I still haven't made up my mind about the wedding, but if I do go I'll be all right on my own.'

'I know you will,' I replied, 'so you won't mind if I tag along, will you?'

Realising that it was futile to argue, he laughed and said, 'Cheers. At least I'll have someone to talk to.' He sat up straight and turned off the TV. I looked at him questioningly, and he said, 'There's something else.'

'What is it?'

'We need to talk.'

'What about?'

'Us,' he said.

'Us?'

'Yeah, let's talk about us.'

'I don't know what conclusions you came to out in Paris about you and Mel or about what you're going to do with the rest of your life, but I've been thinking seriously about my own future while you've been away. I've also been thinking about you leaving comedy, and it's a really bad idea. The worst you've ever had. I know we've both got a lot of other stuff going on in our lives, but the comedy has always been a laugh. We're not too old to stop having a laugh, so what I'm trying to say is . . . I think we ought to try working together.'

'What do you mean?' I said. 'Be partners? Form a double act?'

'Like Abbott and Costello.'

'Morecambe and Wise.'

'Hope and Crosby.'

'George and Mildred.'

We ran out of double acts.

The only conclusion I'd come to in Paris was that Alexa was right. The minute I took any permanent job with no hope of escape I would be banging my head against the walls, constantly calling in sick or being escorted off the premises by security guards within a week. Some people can do the nine-to-five thing and not worry, but I knew I couldn't.

Dan took my hand and laughed. 'Do you, Benjamin Dominic Duffy, take Daniel Aaron Carter to be your lawful wedded partner in comedy?'

'I do,' I said, grinning like an idiot. 'Do you, Daniel Aaron Carter, take Benjamin Dominic Duffy to be your lawful wedded partner in comedy?'

'I do,' said Dan, adding, 'Then by the considerable power invested in me I now pronounce us officially a double act. Carter and Duffy. Has a nice ring about it, don't you think?'

'Not as nice as Duffy and Carter,' I replied, 'but it'll do for now.'

The groom's handsome too

I woke up with a start and studied the alarm clock carefully.
My stomach tightened and I put my hands behind my head
and stared at the ceiling, lost in thought. Today was the day.
Today was D-day for Dan. Before we had gone to bed (after
falling asleep halfway through *The Italian Job*) he had told
me that he'd definitely decided to go to the wedding. I knew
there was no point in trying to talk him round, so I reminded
him I was going with him no matter what, and went to bed
hoping that the intervening hours would bring him to his
senses.

Pulling on a T-shirt that had been lying on the floor, I
got out of bed, knocked on his door, yelled, 'Morning!'
and walked in. Though the curtains were closed, chinks of
light coming through the gap between them illuminated the
room enough for me to make out the shape of Dan sitting
up in bed. The sound of Marvin Gaye's album *What's Going
On* was coming from his CD player. He turned on his bedside light.

'Morning,' I said again.

'Yeah,' he replied unenthusiastically. He looked at his
watch but remained silent.

'I suggest that we stay in London, laugh at Greg on kids'
TV, meet up with Charlie for a drink and count our bless-
ings – and if you're really good we can go to that café on

Archway Road that does those fried breakfasts. I'll even pay.'

My transparent attempt to take Dan's mind off things failed abysmally. 'Not today,' he said, rubbing his eyes and stretching. 'I've a wedding to go to.'

'So you're still going?'

'What do you think?' he said.

I didn't reply.

'I didn't mean that sarcastically, Duff. I actually want to know what you think I should do. Do you reckon I should go to my ex-girlfriend's wedding?'

Even though I already knew what my answer was, I weighed up the situation as truthfully as I could and I still thought it was a bad idea. 'No,' I said finally. 'It's not going to do you any good whatsoever if you stay here and mope, and it's certainly not going to do you any good if you go there and watch someone you still . . .' I searched around for the right terminology . . . 'someone you still obviously have *strong feelings* for, marry someone else.'

'I knew you were going to say that, Duff,' said Dan, turning off Marvin Gaye. 'I knew it because that's exactly the kind of advice I'd give you. Thing is, we're both so crap at giving and receiving advice that I wonder why we bother. The easy thing would be not to go, which is exactly why I have to go. Sometimes it's not always about the easy life. I can see that now. All I've ever wanted was the easy life. Not too much stress, not too much boredom, a bit of a laugh here, some mucking about there. Nothing too strenuous. Now look where that's got me. It's got me losing Meena. It's got me living here with you for the last eighteen months and maybe for ever. It's got me living exactly the same life that I've always led. I've lost her, Duff. She's going to marry someone else and there's nothing I can do. So I'm going to act like I'm twenty-eight instead of eighteen. I'm going to go to the wedding and I'm going to wish her well, because it's the only way I'll ever learn.'

Dan put on a suit and tie, which made him look kind of odd. The last time I'd seen him in it was during a momentary lapse in his faith in comedy two years ago. He'd bought it from Burton's for a job interview with an IT company. Twenty minutes after he got the letter telling him he had a second interview, the suit was back in the wardrobe and he was back in the world of laughs, late nights and hecklers.

We caught the train to Nottingham and were silent for most of the journey. Dan was obviously wrapped up in thoughts of Meena. Meanwhile I was wondering how Mel was. I constantly worried about her and the baby, whether she was sleeping okay or how she was getting on at work. She was always on my mind, but it never felt like a burden.

At the station we caught a taxi to the registry office and twenty minutes later we were there. Large groups of people milled about with that wedding vibe about them: the smart clothes, the anxiety about what time it was, and the facial expressions that managed to combine 'This is so exciting' with 'These shoes are killing me'.

Dan and I sat on the wall of the registry office car park and loosened our ties. Although it was September and not exactly hot, I could feel the sweat running down my armpits, and I considered starting a discussion with Dan about the differences between antiperspirant and deodorant, but just at that moment Meena's brother, Chris, tapped us both on the shoulder. It was a matter of public record that Chris had wanted to give Dan 'the kicking of a lifetime' for the way Dan had treated Meena, and if there was anyone that you wouldn't want to receive the kicking of a lifetime from, it was Chris.

The only thing that had prevented him from killing Dan was Meena's protests that Dan wasn't worth it.

'Carter and Duffy,' he said flatly, making us sound like the veritable comedy double act we now were. 'There's a surprise.'

'All right?' said Dan. 'How's things?'

'I'm going to say this once and once only,' spat Chris. 'This is my sister's wedding day and you're not going to spoil it. If you do anything at all to screw this up I will spoil you beyond all recognition.' He jabbed a muscular finger into Dan's chest. 'Do you understand?'

'I'm not here to spoil anything!' protested Dan, consciously avoiding looking Chris in the eye, as you would any wild animal that was looking for an excuse to tear you limb from limb. 'I'm here to see a close friend get married. Okay?'

Chris glared at Dan and then glared at me and then combined his glares for the benefit of the both of us before walking off.

I turned to Dan, about to remark upon Chris's ability to walk upright without the aid of his knuckles, when we were interrupted again. Standing next to us was a balding man in his late fifties, with a full beard who was so large he reminded me of an off duty version of the wrestlers that my mum loved watching on a Saturday afternoon when I was a kid. The austere-looking woman next to him, in a matching cream suit and hat, I assumed was his wife. They just had to be Meena's parents.

'I would've thought you'd have had the decency not to turn up,' said Mr Amos to Dan. He raised his eyebrows when he said the word 'you' for emphasis.

'Your daughter invited me, Mr Amos,' said Dan. 'She's a friend. It would've been wrong not to have come. The coward's way out.'

'Well, you still shouldn't have come,' muttered Mr Amos, lost for words at his daughter's stupidity.

'Why?' asked Dan.

A look of confusion spread across Mr Amos's features. His huge eyebrows suddenly met in the middle, the furrows in his forehead deepened and his lips tightened.

Mrs Amos, obviously unfazed by the unexpected, stepped into the fray on behalf of her husband. 'Because you don't deserve to be here,' she said, and then added a loud, dismissive tut to back her husband's disapproval.

'Don't think you're going to mess things up for our daughter,' Mr Amos said threateningly. 'I promise you this: you will not spoil this day.' He looked at Dan with such scorn that I thought he was going to throw a punch.

'Look,' I said, and stood up, pushing him back gently, 'you've said what you wanted to say. Now leave it, eh?'

'You'd better take your hands off me, son, if you know what's good for you.'

The last thing on earth I needed was to get into a fight with anyone. Least of all a man with a son as preposterously homicidal as Chris was. However, he was threatening my friend, so I stood my ground regardless, despite possessing all the pugilistic presence of an eight-year-old girl.

'Just leave him alone, okay?' I said, trying my best to sound hard.

Throwing a look of disgust in my direction, he and his wife turned and walked away, leaving me to bask in the glow of winning such a potentially lethal face-off. I sat back down on the wall, my legs were shaking slightly.

'Maybe it wouldn't have been such a bad thing if he had hit me,' Dan said quietly.

'Nah,' I said. 'He would've knocked his wig off in the process.'

'You reckon he was wearing a wig?' Dan looked over his shoulder at the departing Mr Amos. 'Who'd have thought it, eh? I always knew there was something about the old git that didn't add up. Meena always told me he just didn't like having his hair cut.'

For a moment he almost seemed like his old self, but within a few minutes he slipped back into his New Dan depression.

I was just wondering what to do to cheer him up when a voice from behind us said, 'Feeling sorry for yourself?'

I looked round, semi-startled, at a tall dark-haired man whose distinctive attire singled him out as the groom. Next to him were two other men, who by their dress could only have been ushers. Without a doubt we were once again going to be threatened with violence. I handed Dan a cigarette, and took one out for myself.

'Don't,' said Dan, taking control of the situation by refusing to turn around. 'Just don't. There's no need to, Paul. You've won.' He inhaled deeply on his cigarette. 'You've got Meena, and watching the odd episode of *Casualty* and *The Bill* I can see that your acting career has indeed gone from strength to strength since we left college. Meanwhile, I've got no Meena, and as for my career . . . well, let's just say it's nowhere near as illustrious as yours. So, please, there's no need to prove your manliness with fisticuffs – I believe you. Let's just leave it at that, eh?'

One of Paul's ushers, eager to prove his solidarity with the groom, shoved Dan in the back, and would've followed it up with some other act of violence had I not stood up, dropped my cigarette and pushed him back forcefully. He lost his balance and fell into the other ushers. He was about to launch himself at me and tear me limb from limb when Paul held him back.

'Leave it, James,' he said. 'If we start anything here Meena will go mad.'

James calmed down, but not before spitting in my direction. 'You're a dead man,' he said, pointing at me threateningly. I nodded, smiled and gave him a silent but effective internationally renowned gesture of disdain. Where all this bravado was coming from I had no idea, but I was going to enjoy it while I had it.

'I'll leave you alone,' said Paul while Dan observed him coolly. 'I don't know what Meena ever saw in you. I really don't. You were a waster at college and you're a waster now.' He paused. 'It was Meena who invited you here and I've respected her wishes in having you here. But this I will say: do anything to spoil this day and you will regret it.'

'Why does everyone think I've come here to spoil Meena's day?' said Dan to me rather than the assembled besuited apes behind him. 'I loved Meena. Why would I want to spoil her day?'

'Paul, we'd better go, mate,' said the groom's only pacifist usher. And with that they walked off without saying another word.

The registry office was set on the edge of a park five minutes away, so for the remaining twenty minutes we wandered about looking at flowerbeds, sitting on benches and smoking too many cigarettes. By the time we made our way back to the registry office a large group of people from the last wedding party had just exited and were milling around with the guests for Meena's wedding. At five minutes past two everyone's attention turned towards the driveway as a white Rolls-Royce carrying Meena and her maid of honour came to a halt. Watching her get out of the car was a totally surreal experience. I was no expert on wedding dresses, but even I could appreciate that she looked absolutely stunning. Meena's father helped her out of the car and she held on to his arm proudly.

'I can't believe it,' said Dan, his voice faltering slightly. 'I'm jealous of Mr Amos. Meena's relying on his support to get through this. I want to be Mr Amos. I want Meena to rely on me, even if she is marrying someone whose finest hour was as bank robber number two on *The Bill*.'

The interior of the registry office was decorated in a soulless cream that made the room feel cold and impersonal. Dan and I thought it best to take seats at the back, well away from the groom, ushers and Meena's family. We sat down on cushioned plastic chairs that had seen better days, and smiled at an old lady dressed in orange taffeta who had moved along for us. The organist began playing Mendelssohn's Wedding March, and everyone stood up.

'She looks wonderful,' said the old orange lady to Dan as Meena and her father made their way up the aisle. 'The groom's handsome too.'

Dan nodded.

'I'm so happy for her,' said the old orange lady. 'Of course it nearly didn't happen. Her mother was saying that she had cold feet this morning. Wasn't going to go through with it.'

'Really?' said Dan. 'Why was that?'

'I haven't the faintest clue, but I'd love to know,' she said ominously. 'Apparently she's only been courting Paul for a year. Maybe that was the problem. Although, the way I hear it she's not had a very good track record with men altogether. According to her mother, Meena's previous young man was a bit of an undesirable.'

'I heard he was just a bit stupid,' said Dan. 'Didn't know a good thing when he had it.'

'He's meant to be here somewhere,' said Orange Lady

scanning the room, presumably in search of someone with hooves and a pointed tail. 'Apparently he had an invitation! Can you imagine the audacity of such a man? Turning up to Meena's wedding like this?'

Dan shook his head.

'Well, he doesn't matter any more,' said Orange Lady dismissively. 'The important thing is that she's here today. Whatever worries she had, she must have resolved them.'

I looked across at Dan, but his eyes were fixed to the front of the room.

Now, I'd seen *The Graduate* and countless Hollywood imitations. I knew that when the registrar got to the part where he says, 'If there's anybody here who knows of any reason why these two should not be married, let them speak now or forever hold their peace,' Dan was supposed to say something, anything that would mean that he wouldn't lose Meena, but he didn't. He just kept his mouth tightly closed and tried to hold back the tears.

Everyone clapped when Meena and Paul were pronounced husband and wife. I didn't at first, as a show of support for Dan, but then Dan started clapping and I felt a bit stupid being the odd one out.

Orange Lady looked at Dan sadly while the happy couple signed the register. 'It was quite emotional, wasn't it?' she said, handing him a tissue from her handbag. 'I hope you don't mind me saying, but it's very rare that men cry at weddings. You must have been very close to her.'

'Yes,' he said. 'I was.'

Like that bloke in *Groundhog Day*

Dan and I were offered a lift to the reception by two of Meena's old college friends, Jenny and Lisa. In the car they asked me how we knew her and I lied and told them we used to live in the flat above Meena when she lived in Muswell Hill. Dan wasn't really saying much about anything, and although I tried to make up for his reticence by talking all kinds of complete and utter rubbish, it quickly became obvious to them that he was acting a bit strange.

Eventually Lisa got annoyed enough to make a comment when an innocent question to Dan about what he did for a living was met with complete silence. 'I don't know what your problem is,' she said to Dan as the car pulled up at a set of traffic lights, 'but there's no need to be so obnoxious. Last time I looked, manners didn't cost anything.'

Without pausing for thought Dan opened the car door and got out, slamming it behind him.

'Er, d'you want me to pull over?' said Jenny, addressing me agitatedly, about to indicate. There was now a long queue of traffic either side of us.

'I didn't mean to upset him,' added Lisa apologetically. 'He was just being so strange. Don't you think you should go after him?'

'No,' I said quietly as I watched Dan dodging through the lines of cars to the other side of the road. 'No, I don't think

I should go after him, and no, I don't think you should pull over.'

They both looked at me as if they were witnessing the worst betrayal of friendship ever committed. Right now, however, Dan didn't need my opinion, sympathy or comfort, which is what these two strangers wanted me to offer him. What he needed was to be alone.

'He'll be all right,' I explained. 'He's just had a bit of a weird day, that's all.'

The white Rolls-Royce that had taken the bride and groom from the registry office to the reception at the Piermont Hotel, was surrounded by a gang of children. They were pointing and yelling, 'Chitty Chitty Bang Bang!' in unison at the car's chauffeur. They'd been at it for some five minutes now and I could tell from the look on the driver's face that he'd got to the stage where he was weighing up whether it was worth losing his job to enjoy the simple satisfaction of telling the lot of them to bugger off. The rest of the wedding guests milled around aimlessly on the hotel's front lawn sipping glasses of bucks fizz, chatting with friends and relatives they hadn't seen in years and generally wondering what would happen next. Meanwhile Meena and Paul and their immediate families were being herded around the hotel grounds by a team of wedding photographers keen to give the couple's day of happiness a varied selection of softly focused backdrops.

Jenny and Lisa had abandoned me in order to 'mingle' almost the very second we'd arrived, leaving me to loiter alone at the front of the hotel lobby examining the ornamental ivy growing up the windowframes like a dedicated amateur botanist. Quite obviously appearing bored out of my mind, I was approached by a number of people who all endeavoured to draw me into conversation. I chatted to Mrs

Kapur (Meena's great auntie) about the latest trends in men's ties, Samantha (the groom's second cousin's ex-girlfriend) about how much she hated the groom's second cousin, and Lucy (a six-year-old who hadn't the faintest clue what her connection to the bride and groom was) about what she was getting for her birthday in two weeks' time. Thankfully after half an hour of this an announcement was made for the guests to take their seats at the banqueting hall. There was no way I was going to sit down at a table of strangers, eating melon and swapping wedding anecdotes, and I had made my mind up to call a taxi and get the train back to London when I spotted Dan walking up the hotel drive, looking pensive.

'All right, mate?' I said as he reached me.

He nodded, hands dejectedly lodged in his trouser pockets. 'Yeah. I'm all right.'

'Let's sit down for a second.' I gestured to a wooden bench overlooking a large pond. 'These shoes are killing me.' Dan nodded and together we walked across the lawn, crunching sun-dried duck poo underfoot.

'Did you walk here?' I asked as we sat down.

'Got a taxi,' said Dan. He scratched the back of his neck animatedly. 'Sorry about . . . you know.'

'No, problem,' I replied, and there we sat, not moving or talking, just sharing a silence – a big, fat empty pause filled with nothingness. I'd forgotten how much of a strain it was constantly to have to translate the world and how I saw it into words for the benefit of those who didn't understand. It was nice to enjoy a moment when I could just sit back, relax and think about nothing.

'Duff?' said Dan, after having shared over half an hour's worth of noncommunication.

'Yeah?'

'Do you love Mel?'

I paused and lit a cigarette before answering. It was a big question to begin with, but the fact that it was Dan who had asked it, only seemed to make it even bigger. 'That's a bit deep, isn't it?' I stalled. 'Where did that come from?'

He shrugged indifferently, acknowledging both my attempt to sidestep the question and my right to do so. 'I was just wondering whether if I had the power to time-travel, I'd have done things differently . . .' His attention was distracted by the roar of an RAF jet passing overhead. He stopped and stared up at the sky momentarily. 'Do you know, I'm not sure I would. That's the thing about hindsight: over time you gradually forget how stupid you've acted in the past. Time and time again I've made the same mistakes. Like that bloke in *Groundhog Day*. Only I never learn. Knowing you've got to do the right thing doesn't amount to much if you never actually do it. I mean—'

'I thought I'd find you both out here,' interrupted a female voice from behind us. It seemed like everyone was coming up behind us these days.

Dan and I turned round simultaneously to see which new member of Meena's family and friends had come over to warn us off spoiling the wedding. My money had been on Meena's chief bridesmaid, because I'd noted somewhat warily that she was built like a professional arm wrestler, but it was the bride herself. She was standing there quite innocently, her wedding dress appearing much whiter than it had done before. Every now and again a shallow gust of wind caught the loose fabric of the skirt, giving it an almost liquid appearance.

'Hello, Dan, hello, Duffy. How are you both?'

'All right, Meena?' I said nervously. I stood up, preparing for evasive action. This was bound to turn into a Situation, and I really didn't want to be here when it did. 'I think I ought to leave you two alone. You've probably got stuff you want to talk about and you don't really need me hanging about, do you?'

'No,' said Dan firmly. 'I think you ought to stay, Duff. You need to hear this more than anyone else.' He stepped over to Meena and kissed her lightly. 'Congratulations,' he said warmly. 'It was a good wedding as weddings go.'

'Thanks,' said Meena. 'I'm . . . glad you could come.'

'Wouldn't have missed it for the world.'

'You two weren't at the lunch, were you?'

'No,' said Dan apologetically. 'It was all my fault. I had a bit of a wander around Nottingham and lost track of time.'

'There's more food if you want it,' she said, gesturing towards the hotel. 'There's loads of it knocking about. If you don't fancy it now you can always wait until the evening reception.'

'Are you having a disco later?' asked Dan, grinning.

'No,' laughed Meena. 'Paul's parents paid for the hire of a band. They're called the No Tops. They play all sorts, but they specialise in covers of cheesy Sixties Motown hits.'

'No disco,' said Dan with a hint of gentle sarcasm in his voice. 'No "Come on, Eileen"? No "Three Times a Lady"? Not even a "Birdie Song"?'

Meena laughed and held his gaze a few seconds longer than necessary or indeed appropriate for a recently married woman.

'So what's it like being married?' asked Dan. 'Do you feel any different?'

'I don't know,' she said thoughtfully. 'No, no different. At least not yet.'

'D'you remember that wedding we went to?' said Dan. 'It was one of your mates from the first theatre you worked at, what was her name . . . Lynne Hodges that was it . . . and there was that huge fight between the best man and her father-in-law.' He paused, slightly confused, as if he'd lost his train of thought. 'Do you think our wedding would've been like this? I can't help thinking it wouldn't have been. I think at least it might have been a bit smaller. My family's nowhere near as big as yours. My mum—'

'Don't, Dan,' interrupted Meena. 'Don't make out like we're old mates. Don't pretend that you're just another wellwisher. If there's one thing you can do for me, please just be honest.'

'I'm sorry, you know,' said Dan quietly.

'What for?'

'For everything. I know I've done everything wrong. I can't believe I let you go. I loved you when I lived with you, and I think I still love you now. I wish I'd had the guts to tell you all this yesterday. Or even this afternoon. When the registrar said, 'Does anyone know why these two people shouldn't be married?' I wanted to say what I felt.' Staring right into her eyes, he asked her a question that up until this point in my life I would never have imagined him saying. 'If I had spoken up,' he said, 'would you still have married him?'

She paused before answering. 'We'll never know, will we?' Then she looked away as tear after tear fell from her eyes and ran down her face. She wiped them away with her hand, smearing a dark line of mascara across the bridge of her nose in the process. 'After today I never want to see you again, Dan.'

'I know,' he said. 'That's why you invited me and that's why I'm here: to say goodbye.'

Meena looked at me for the first time since her hello. I felt embarrassed to still be here; I felt embarrassed to have witnessed this most private of moments; I felt embarrassed for being me.

'Have you got a spare cigarette?' she asked. I handed her the lit one that was in my hand. She puffed on it frantically for a few seconds as if she were more in need of nicotine than oxygen, threw it on the floor and walked away without saying another word.

Dan didn't move. He just stood and watched her walk off silently.

'C'mon, Dan, let's just call a cab and go home, mate,' I said, checking my pockets for change for the phone. 'You've done what you came here to do. I think it's best that we just go. Even you must have had enough by now.'

'We can't go yet,' said Dan, subdued.

'Why not?'

'Because Mel's here.' He pointed across to the hotel lobby where Mel was indeed getting out of a taxi with Julie.

'I can't believe this,' I sighed.

'What's she doing here?' asked Dan.

'Meena invited Mel and me ages ago – just when we'd split up. I told Mel that I wasn't going, so she obviously assumed that it was safe for her to come up here and wish Meena well.'

'Are you going to talk to her?'

That was a good question. After all that had happened today, I wasn't in the right mood to make small talk. Julie's presence was bound to wind me up, and the last thing on earth I needed was to start a row. Mel and I certainly needed to talk, but not here, not now, and certainly not in front of a million wedding guests. *No*, I decided, *this is going to be the one time that I actually choose the 'LEAVE WELL ALONE' option.*

'Let's just go,' I said quickly, 'before today gets any crappier. It will, you know, I can just feel it.'

'Earlier,' said Dan, staring at me with the same searching

look that he'd given to Meena, 'when I asked you if you still loved Mel, you didn't answer me.'

'I know,' I admitted reluctantly. 'What about it?'

'Well, do you?'

I nodded.

'So why don't you do anything about it?'

'Look, Dan, just let it go!' I said, losing my temper with him in a way I never had before. 'I've told you, Vernie and Charlie – all of you a million times – the reason why. Mel thinks I only want to be with her because she's pregnant. She doesn't want me.'

'Calm down!' said Dan. 'I'm not attacking you, Duff.'

'Look, I'm sorry, mate,' I apologised. 'I know you're only trying to help me out, but this isn't just about me any more. I've got to think about Mel and the baby too. I've messed her around too much in the past. There's no way I'm going to be able to convince her. It's just my tough luck.'

'No,' said Dan firmly. 'It isn't . . . well, at least it doesn't have to be. Look, you've seen what's happened to me today. I can't stand by and watch the same thing happen to you. She loves you, Duff. You know that as well as I do. You two, weird as it might seem, are made for each other. You've got to make her see that.'

'How? I've tried everything. I can't get through to her.'

'Look,' said Dan, 'there was no guarantee that if I'd spoken up in the church today that Meena would've changed her mind. In fact I'm pretty certain that she wouldn't have. But at least I'd have known that I tried. That's what really galls me, Duffy – that I didn't *try*. It's just like the day that she walked out. I knew I could've talked her round, I knew that I could have convinced her to stay, but it was easier to let it go. If you believe in something, Duff, you can't let it go without a fight. You just can't.'

* * *

'The Piermont Hotel welcomes you to the Halcyon Suite, for the wedding reception of Paul and Meena Amos-Midford,' read the sign outside the main banqueting hall. I opened the doors and scanned the room for Mel, but I couldn't see her anywhere at first. Eventually I spotted her sitting at a table in the far corner of the room. It was weird, but at that exact same moment she looked up, saw me and smiled.

I was halfway across the room, less than thirty feet away from her – less than thirty feet from asking her to marry me – when the best man began tapping his dessert spoon against a wine glass to get everyone's attention and announced that it was time for the speeches. I didn't want to stop, but I knew if I continued walking, the whole room would be watching me, so with my heart racing, barely able to concentrate at all, I sat down in an empty seat and waited.

'Hello again, young man,' said a voice next to me. It was Orange Lady from the registry office, holding a large glass of wine. 'Where's your friend?' she whispered loudly.

'Outside,' I explained. 'Doesn't like speeches.'

'Me neither,' said Orange Lady, then added, 'Do you know, this is my fourth glass of wine?' She leaned unsteadily towards me until we were almost touching noses, and whispered loud enough for everyone at the surrounding tables to hear, 'Very good stuff it is too. But I do believe it's gone straight to my head!'

The best man's speech was loaded with jokes about the groom's ex-girlfriends, acting skills and personal habits. Meena's dad thought this bloke was hilarious and kept patting Paul on the back heartily. The groom's speech was even worse: he just harped on about how wonderful his new family was. There was no love in evidence at all, only gratuitous backslapping. He finished by proposing a toast to the newest Mrs Amos-Midford in the world, and everyone in the room raised their glasses. There was a huge round of applause, and waiters appeared, filling everyone's glasses with champagne. The band started to play an uptempo version of 'I've Got You Under My Skin'. Paul and Meena made their way to the centre of the room for the first dance and began twirling around as if they'd been beamed straight from some 1930s cocktail party. During the whole time it took for all this to happen, Mel didn't take her eyes off me.

Edging around the wedding photographer and a man armed with a video camera, who were recording Meena and Paul's every move, I made my way to Mel's table.

'Hi,' I said, smiling. She looked beautiful. More beautiful than ever. Her hairstyle had changed yet again, and now it was short and messy in the kind of sexy way Meg Ryan could only dream of.

'Hi, Duff,' she said, standing up to hug me. 'How are you? How was Paris?'

'Fine,' I lied. 'And you? How's everything with you?' I'd wanted to ask about the baby too, but didn't want to bring it up in so public an arena.

'Okay,' she replied. She could obviously still read minds when she wanted to, because she then looked down at her stomach and added, 'Everything's fine there too. No need to worry.'

'Good.'

Silence.

'Didn't I see you here with Julie? Where is she?'

'She's just nipped to the toilet,' said Mel hurriedly. I could tell that she was lying, because she was fiddling nervously with her hair. She always did that when she lied. I took this as a good sign, however: Julie had obviously disappeared on purpose so that Mel and I could talk.

'Gone to look for more victims to turn into the undead, has she?'

'Don't start, Duffy,' reprimanded Mel sternly. 'Julie's having . . . well, she's having a tough time at the minute.'

What could possibly have fazed the mighty Julie? I wondered. Had they run out of polenta at her local Sainsbury? Had her Dyson vacuum cleaner spontaneously combusted? Or worse still, had she discovered that she and Mark would never be able to afford to live in their beloved Notting Hill Gate? I didn't ask any of these questions of course, because it didn't feel right baiting Julie without her being there.

'What's wrong with her?' I asked. 'Nothing too painful I hope.'

'I can't tell you, Duffy. At least not yet.' She paused. 'I've got some news of my own, but you might not like it. I was going to call, but since you're here I might as well tell you now. I told my bosses at work that I was pregnant and that I wanted to leave and they offered me a deal to make me stay.'

'That's good,' I said. 'If it's what you want.'

She smiled. 'It is . . . well, at least I think it is. The company has just taken over a group of radio stations in the North and I'll be overseeing the restructuring of their sales divisions. It's only a temporary project – around three months – but it's a step up into higher management and if I do well it could mean big things in the future.'

'Sounds like you've come up trumps. So what's the problem?'

'It's away from London. I'll have to spend Monday to Friday up there and then I'll fly back to London at the weekends.'

'Mel,' I said nervously, 'you're being vague on purpose. Whereabouts up North is it?'

'Glasgow.'

I didn't say anything. I couldn't say anything. I could feel a massive pause coming, until suddenly, from an unknown source, words came to rescue me. 'Don't go,' I said so quietly that I could barely hear myself.

'What?'

'I said, don't go. I don't want you to go, Mel. Stay here in London and marry me. I miss you. Whatever it is that makes you different from any woman I have ever met or could ever hope to meet – the very Melness of you – I miss that more than anything. It's just over four months since we first split up and since then a lot has happened that I need to explain to you . . .' I stumbled as I searched for the right words to express what I wanted to say.

'The reason why I didn't want to get married when you asked me was because I lacked faith in myself. I thought the minute we got married I'd feel trapped. I just couldn't get it into my head that marriage wasn't a conspiracy to hijack my independence. You knew that, and that's why you broke off the engagement, because you didn't want to make me do anything I'd regret. Well, I regret more than anything not marrying you. I regret that I'll never be able to have the time back that I've missed with you. I promise you it's not the baby that's changed my mind. I changed my own mind. I want to marry you because I can see now that the benefits outweigh the disadvantages. No, I don't mean that, what I mean is that . . . that . . .'

'I think what you're trying to say is that you're not scared any more,' said Mel softly.

'That's right, I'm not scared – okay, maybe I'm a little nervous, but I'll be all right. I'm not scared about sleeping with one person for the rest of my life, in fact I'm looking forward to it. I'll admit I still feel a bit shaky about going to IKEA, but that's something we can work out. The big thing is that I'm no longer scared I'll ever fall out of love with you . . .

or that you'll ever fall out of love with me. I have to commit to . . . I *am* committed to you because without you nothing makes sense. Without you I'm not even myself. Without you I'm nothing.'

That was it. That was my big speech. I'd given my all and now it really was up to her. I studied her face for clues to her state of mind, to see if I'd finally managed to convince her to believe. There was a look about her that I couldn't explain, but it made me feel that I'd managed to breach the barrier that had come between us. We were now standing barely inches apart.

Without speaking she reached for my hands, held them tightly and gazed deeply into my eyes, searching for the answers to everything she wanted to know. Then she started to cry.

'I want to believe you, Duffy,' she sobbed. 'I want to believe you more than anything in the world. I look at your face and I hear your beautiful words and I'm nearly there, Duff. But nearly just isn't good enough any more. How do I know that you really mean what you say? How can I be sure that those old feelings won't come back again?'

'I don't understand. You've always gone on about how well you know me. How you know me better than I know myself. And it's true. I've never met anyone who knows me like you do. So why can't you see that I'm telling you the truth when I say that I want to marry you? Why can't you read my mind?'

Her tears were in full flow and we had become the main attraction in this corner of the room. I didn't care. I couldn't see anyone but her.

'That's just it,' she sobbed. 'I don't trust myself any more. I don't trust myself to make a decision that will affect not just your life, or my life, but the life of our baby too. I can't tell what it is you're thinking because I don't know what I'm thinking and it scares me. I love you, Duffy, but I'm too scared to gamble everything when I can't be sure.'

I couldn't believe it. This was supposed to be our happy ending, the last reel of a romantic comedy, the point where the guy gets the girl, but somehow it had turned into *A Nightmare on Elm Street.*

'I know I have to make a decision one way or the other for both our sakes,' she continued. 'We just can't carry on like this any more. I know this is selfish of me, but I can't make this decision right now, so I'm asking you for more time – time to think things through and get my head round all of this.' She leaned forward and kissed me. 'My new job starts on Monday. I'll be up in Glasgow all week but I'll be back in London late Friday night and I promise you that by then I'll have an answer for you.'

Bet you're happy now

On the train back from Nottingham, frustrated at being unable to do any more than wait for Mel to make her decision, I formulated a plan. The perfect plan. A plan that would without a doubt convince her once and for all that she had nothing to be scared of, that I did love her and would always do so. The only drawback, however, was that it required the assistance of Julie. As in Mark and Julie. As in Nosferatu. As in the person who last time I checked ranked me lower on the evolutionary scale than pond scum. But that's great plans for you – they always carry with them an element of danger. By the time Dan and I got home from the wedding it was quite late so I decided to sleep on my plan in case I was being rash. When I woke up early on Sunday morning and still thought it was the best idea I'd ever had (totally eclipsing past highlights such as baked beans on cream cracker sandwiches and taping *EastEnders* while I watched it in case I thought of something clever to yell at the characters after it's over), I knew I had to do it.

Coming up the escalator at Shepherd's Bush Tube I worked out my strategy for dealing with what was bound to be an impossible situation:

1) Go round to Mark and Julie's.

2) Beg for her mercy.

3) If needs be, cry.

I didn't give myself the option of steps one to three not working. There was no plan B, and without Julie there'd be no plan A. Julie was essential. It was then, as I stood on her doorstep, my heart racing wildly and my index finger hovering over the doorbell, that it occurred to me that this was about karma. I was being punished for the sins of my previous life, the telling of ex-girlfriends that I was dead, the half-truths to Mel and the skeletons in my cupboards. It was as if life had decided that if I really wanted true happiness I was going to have to pay for my indiscretions.

I rang the doorbell and waited.

When Julie finally came to the front door she was wearing nothing but her dressing gown. 'What are *you* doing here?' she exclaimed.

I decided in the light of what Mel had said about Julie having some sort of crisis, that a delicate touch would be required. 'Hello, Julie,' I replied as chirpily as possible. 'I'm sorry I didn't get to talk to you yesterday at the wedding, but by the time you came back from the loo my taxi had arrived.'

Julie fixed me with a menacing stare as if I was some horrible practical joke writ large. 'Duffy,' she growled, 'it's eight o'clock on Sunday morning. It's freezing cold out here and I haven't got the patience or indeed the inclination to humour you. So I'll say this: I don't care that you didn't speak to me yesterday because I don't like you. I don't care if I never see you again because I don't like you. In fact I don't care about you full stop because I've never liked you. So now we've got that sorted, what do you want?'

'Is Mark about?' I asked innocently. I was hoping that his presence might soften Julie up a bit.

She bristled instantly. I knew that bristle. It was the bristle Mel used to use on me when I was in her bad books, just as, it would appear, Mark was in Julie's. 'He's in Los Angeles on a shoot,' she said sharply. *They've probably had a row about him going off around the world again,* I reasoned. *This is bound to be Julie's big 'crisis'. I'll give them two simpering twenty-minute transatlantic phone calls and they'll be back to their usual smug selves.*

'He won't be back in England for a few days,' she said and then added, 'Was it him you wanted to see?'

'No, Julie,' I said. 'It's you I came to see. I need your help.'

She was visibly shocked. All her facial expressions went into free fall. She looked very odd indeed. Then as quickly as the panic came it disappeared. 'You don't really expect me to persuade Mel to get back with you, do you?' she sighed dismissively. 'Not even you can be that stupid, surely?'

I coughed uncomfortably. 'I know we've not always seen eye to eye about everything, Julie, and I'm sorry about that. I'm also sorry about the time I was sick over your bathroom floor, I'm sorry that I've always been so rude about your dinner parties and I'm really sorry that I used to call you Nosferatu behind your back.'

'You called me Nosferatu?'

'Damn. I thought you knew. Well, now I'm really really sorry I called you Nosferatu. I'm sorry for just about everything, but please, I'm begging you for just ten minutes of your time while I explain what I need from you. Please.'

I studied Julie's face to see how many points I'd scored in my favour. Judging by her posture (defensive) and her facial expression (overflowing with disdain) I reasoned it was a figure somewhere near, as they say in Eurovision circles, to *nul points*.

'No way, Duffy,' said Julie firmly. 'Mel told me everything that you said to her at the wedding. And do you want to know what I advised her? I told her that she was mad to think that you were capable of growing up, let alone changing.'

I took a long deep breath and held it. I wasn't going to breathe again until the impulse to commit manslaughter had passed, which it did surprisingly quickly as it finally dawned on me what this was all about. Julie was protecting Mel in the same way that I would've tried to protect Dan had someone like Julie wormed their way into his affections. I had to convince her that I was good for Mel. That I'd do anything to make her happy. I took another long deep breath.

'Okay, Julie,' I said, pulling up my trousers at the thighs. There was only one person on earth for whom I'd normally do what I was about to do, and that was Mel. 'You want me to beg, well, I'll beg.' I got down on my knees, put my hands together as if in prayer and wailed at the top of my voice, 'Pleeeeaaase!'

Julie's first reaction was to check if the neighbours had started looking out yet (they hadn't), her second was to look at me as if I'd lost the plot (which to all intents and purposes I had), and her third was to take great pleasure in exclaiming loudly, 'No!'

'Please!

'No!'

'Please!'

By now the twitching-curtain brigade were out in full. Julie knew this. I knew this. It was just a matter of whose nerve would break first. She stepped back inside and slammed the door shut. Determined not to give up, I stood my ground and continued to yell at the top of my voice on Julie's front doorstep.

'Julie! I know you're still there and I'll stay right here on your doorstep keeping your neighbours awake for as long as it takes for you to let me in and listen to me. I don't care if you call the police. I really don't care. Not any more. So you see you've got two choices: let me in for five minutes and listen to what I've got to say, or have me carted away by the Old Bill and really give the neighbours something to talk about. Which is it to be?'

There followed a long silence in which I contemplated what a night in gaol would be like. It didn't seem that bad in theory. The main thing that bothered me was that they'd take the laces out of my trainers. It always took me ages to lace up my trainers. Julie opened the door just as I'd decided that if I did get arrested I'd give my trainers to the desk sergeant for safe keeping rather than unlace them.

'Okay, okay,' she said wearily. 'Come in. But you've got exactly five minutes and no more.'

She let me in and I followed her through to the lounge. The room seemed emptier somehow, less furniture. *Metropolitan minimalist chic agogo*, I commented to myself silently. Julie sat down on the sofa and rubbed her eyes. It was strange seeing her just-got-out-of-bed hair and and Clinique-free features, because although on the one hand she now really did remind me of one of the undead, on the other, for the first time ever she almost looked human. I decided to soften her up with flattery. 'You look fantastic, Julie.'

'No I don't,' she snapped. 'I look hideous. It's how people who have been woken up on a Sunday morning look. Don't flatter me. Don't make small talk. Tell me what it is you want and then disappear.'

'Okay, I'll be straight with you. I'm trying to butter you up because I've got a huge favour to ask. There's no reason in the world for you to do it other than that you're the only person who can help me. Please. I don't want to cry in your living room but I will if I have to.'

'What do you want?'

I outlined her role in the Plan, although not the plan in its entirety. She listened, didn't say anything one way or the other, and as soon as I'd finished looked just as unmoved as she had done before.

'Firstly,' said Julie, 'it's a ridiculous idea. Secondly, I don't think anything can convince Mel to spend the rest of her life with you, and thirdly . . . no. A plain and simple no. In fact, let me put it this way. Not now. Not ever. Let me tell you, Mr Duffy, you have put my best friend though hell. You weren't the one who had to console her when she was falling apart when you first split up. You weren't the one who had to watch your best friend get back together with the man you loathe most on earth. You weren't the one who had to mop up the tears when she found out she was pregnant. Why? Because you're never the one who has to clean up after the devastation you cause.'

'I know what you think of me,' I said, 'but there's another side of me, Julie. You've got to know that. I admit I've been selfish in the past, but I've changed.'

'You say that now,' said Julie passionately, 'but what about in six months' time? Men leave. That's what they do. They get tired of what they've got and they get up and go.'

I was confused. This was more than a general 'all men are crap, get a dog instead' speech. She sounded if she was talking about something specific.

'I don't get this, Julie. What are you trying to say?'

She shook her head. 'Nothing.'

'Mel told me that you're having a hard time at the minute.

She wouldn't tell me why. Is it something to do with Mark being in Los Angeles?'

'No.'

'Then what's wrong? I know it's not like me to show concern but if it's serious—'

'Mark and I have split up, okay?' she said without looking at me. 'He's gone.'

I was stunned. It was worse than when I discovered at the age of eight that Father Christmas didn't exist. At least then I still knew that I'd be getting presents from my mum, Father Christmas or no Father Christmas. But if the king and queen of togetherness couldn't make their love work, what hope was there for mere mortals? No wonder Mel was unsure about getting together with me: not only had I provided her with enough doubt, she was also having to deal with the fact that everything she'd idealised about Julie and Mark had been broken in two. 'I'm sorry, Julie. I really I am. I had no idea.'

'Well, now you know. He moved out about a month ago. I told Mel not to tell you because I knew what you'd say. I know you used to think that Mark and I were smug. What was the phrase you used? Oh, I remember now. "Keeping up with the Mark and Julies." Bet you're happy now.'

'No, I'm not, Julie. It's crap when things fall apart. I wouldn't wish it on anyone. I am sorry about you and Mark. Is there anything I can do?'

She shook her head.

I sat and watched her for a moment. A shadow of her usual venomous self, I found myself actually feeling sorry for her. As much as I'd derided Mark and Julie, I'd always thought that they were right for each other. I suddenly felt guilty sitting here asking her to help out my relationship when she was so obviously on the verge of falling apart.

'Listen,' I said, standing up, 'I'd better go.'

She pointed at the door. 'I think you'll find that's the way out.'

I wasn't going to say anything, I was just going to get up and leave, but then I thought about Mel and what was at stake and I suddenly got angry. 'There's nothing I can do to get you and Mark back together. If there was I'd do it. But can't you see that you've got the chance to help me and Mel? I know that I can't change her mind if she's doesn't want me, but I can show her that I meant every word I said when I told her that I loved her.'

'I don't believe in love.' Julie stood up in a bid to hasten my exit.

'Because Mark left you?'

'*Because* no one means anything they say any more. Because everything is temporary. Because nothing lasts. Because that's the way it is.' She looked over at me expectantly.

'It doesn't have to be,' I said, meeting her gaze.

'I think you've had your five minutes.'

'Yeah,' I said, wondering what I was going to do now. 'I suppose I have.'

This is little Elvis

'Are you cold?'

  'No, Mum.'

  'You must be cold.'

  'I'm not, Mum.'

  'These hospital waiting rooms are incredibly draughty and you're only wearing a shirt.'

  'But I'm not cold.'

  'You're bound to catch a cold. Why don't you go home and put on a cardigan?'

  'I'm fine, Mum,' I said, making contact with my inner Dalai Lama. 'Honestly I'm fine.'

  Three days had passed since Julie had ruined the Plan. Three event filled days that had begun on Tuesday with a telephone call and ended with me lodged on a hard plastic chair in a waiting-room in Whittington Hospital.

  It all began at the beginning of the week with a long and confusing answerphone message left by Pete Berry, a comedy promoter at the Chuckle Club in Hackney. In it he informed Dan and me that he wanted to book us for a gig in a fortnight because he'd been hearing good things about our new act. He then went on to reveal that if the gig went well he would consider us as a support slot for the previous year's Perrier Comedy Award Winner on a six date national tour he was organising. All of this was news to me because to the best of my knowledge Dan and I hadn't written a single joke together, and the only people who knew about Carter and Duffy the double act were Carter and Duffy the double act.

I had to wait two hours for Dan to get back from his weekly shopping trip to Muswell Hill Sainsbury's before I discovered that all this was his doing. 'If you're going to make a splash,' he said, 'you've got to make a few waves.' By 'waves', I think that he meant the following complete and utter fabrications:

a) that we'd been approached by Channel Four to develop a new sitcom called *Dexter's Plectrum* about a bunch of geeky no-hoper sixth-formers who turn out to be the next U2.
b) that we'd accepted a 'substantial five-figure sum' to do voiceovers for a series of adverts selling a well-known brand of cooking oil.
c) that a talent scout from a US talent agency had spotted our act and signed us up and we'd already been flown to Los Angeles for casting auditions in two Hollywood pictures as 'Limey bad guys'.

Dan had pitched his lies perfectly. In the world of comedy, where one day you could be bottom of the bill in the Dog and Duck and the next taking meetings in Hollywood, anything was possible, and our fictionalised success was just wild enough for anyone who heard it to believe every single word.

'Honestly,' said Dan, nearly doubled over in laughter, 'I told two of the regulars on last Sunday's bill at the Laughter Lounge in Hammersmith, and by Monday night the whole of the London comedy circuit knew about it. We are hot!'

The second event to occur was the arrival of my mum

at Euston station on Tuesday afternoon. One of the first things she'd said to me when Charlie and I picked her up from the station was that she was coming round to see where I lived first thing Wednesday morning. As the flat was in the worst state I'd ever seen it, I made Dan stay up with me until three o'clock in the morning so we could have it tidy for her inspection. In the process we discovered £7.86 in change down the back of the sofa, fungus the size of a small yukka plant at the side of the washing machine, and Dan's car-boot-sale copy of *ET* lodged behind the sideboard.

By the time we'd finished it looked like a completely different flat. My mum would've been well impressed by our efforts had she ever got to see them, which she never did because of the next big event: Vernie going into labour.

Mum called me from the hospital on Charlie's mobile to tell me. This was just about the funniest thing ever: my mum and 'newfangled technology' just did not go together, so for the first few minutes all she said was 'Can you hear me?', 'Am I speaking into the right end?' and 'Am I doing it right?' As it was 3.20 a.m. and I was on my way to bed after my cleaning fit, I told her that I'd be there before lunchtime on Wednesday. She promised to call me if there was any other news and I went to sleep.

As soon as I woke up I made my way to the hospital and I sat in the waiting room, listening to Mum's constant questions.

'Do you want a cup of tea or coffee from the machine?' she asked, her purse open to display a vast collection of coins of the realm. My mum liked to be ready for every sort of occasion and collected change like some people collect stamps.

'No thanks, Mum,' I said, refusing for my usual reasons.

'I was going to have a cup of tea,' she said, closing her purse, 'but I think I'll wait just a little bit longer as well.'

She dropped her purse into her handbag, rooted around a bit and pulled out a packet of sweets. 'Trebor Mint?'

'No thanks, Mum.' I smiled. 'You're nervous, aren't you?'

'Of course I am,' she said. 'Aren't you?'

That thought hadn't occurred to me. Was I nervous? I think I was. I was excited. I was going to be somebody's uncle. There was going to be a child who would have an uncle Duffy; someone to whom I'd be able to pass on the skills of making the perfect slice of toast, and read books Mum used to read to me as a kid. Someone to be around for when they wanted to talk about how much their parents drove them up the wall. This felt good.

It didn't require a huge leap in my thought processes to make the connection between what was happening here and what was happening in my own life. I was going to be somebody's dad too quite soon. I hadn't thought about it in France, or since I'd got back, or even when Mel had told me. It was easy not to think about it because it hadn't happened yet. But sitting here in this admittedly now chilly waiting room, it struck me: I'm going to be a dad.

Suddenly I felt sad. Sadder than I'd ever felt before. Not about the baby, but about Mel and me. Our having a baby was bound to be one of the best things that would ever happen in my life, and yet here I was not making the most of it. Whatever decision Mel made, nothing would change the fact that I was going to be responsible for a life other than my own. A greater privilege than that, I couldn't think of.

'Mum,' I said, 'I've got something to tell you.'

'I know,' said my mum.

'How do you know?'

'I don't know exactly what it is, but I can tell when you're troubled, Ben.' She handed me a mint, took another one from the packet and put it in her mouth. 'I've got something to tell you too. Two secrets, in fact. One big, one not so big. I'll tell you my secrets first – that way it'll make it easier to tell me yours.'

I was kind of perturbed by the whole situation. I couldn't imagine what kind of secrets my mum would have that she'd think I needed to know about.

She put her hand on mine and began. 'The small secret first: I may be moving down here to London permanently. Vernie's been asking me to come and live with her and Charlie since they knew about the baby. I told them I didn't want to, but she said that she didn't want the baby just to see her gran on special occasions. I told her I'd visit as often as I could, but then Charlie insisted too. I finally gave in, but I told them I'd give it a go for a few months first to see how it went. I'm keeping the house in Leeds until I'm sure.'

'That's great,' I said. 'Vernie will love having you around. Me too.' I couldn't think of anything more to say, so focused was my mind on secret number two. 'So what's the big thing you've got to tell me?'

'Confess rather than tell,' she said quietly. 'I don't know how to say this so I'll come straight out with it: when you broke up with Mel I was really worried about you. I know that you're a grown man and I should've kept my nose out, but I couldn't help thinking it was wrong: you loved each other – anyone could tell that. When you told me you'd split up because you weren't sure you could commit, I blamed myself. I hated the idea that you weren't getting married because of what happened with me and you dad. Which is why I wrote to him and asked him to get in touch with you.'

'*You* wrote to *him*?' I could hardly believe what I was hearing. 'You've been in contact with my dad?'

'I got his address from his sister in Tamworth and I told him that he had to get in contact with you and arrange a meeting to explain to you that you're nothing like him.'

It was odd being subjected to this much love. To think that my mum would open all sorts of painful memories just to try and make me happy. I gave her the biggest hug I could manage and she started crying.

'I was only trying to help, Ben,' she sobbed quietly. 'He wrote and told me that you never got back to him. I didn't want to upset you. I just wanted you to see that you were nothing like him. You're your own person. You always were and you always will be.'

When she'd finished crying I fetched a cup of tea for her from the machine and a coffee for myself so that she didn't feel like I was being left out. While it went cold I told her the story of Mel and me, right from the beginning, from when I first saw her four years ago through to the last time, less than a week ago at Meena's wedding.

Mum didn't say anything for a moment: I think the shock that in a few months she'd be a grandmother for a second time had left her speechless. She drank her tea silently. 'So Mel's going to make her decision in two days' time?'

'The arrangement is she comes back from Glasgow on Friday,' I explained. 'She'll call me as soon as she gets home. I'll go round to her flat and one way or the other we'll sort this whole thing out. We both want what's best for the baby, and for what it's worth, if she decides that she doesn't want to be with me, then at least I think we've learned enough from the past to make it work as friends.'

Mum looked at me and said in the manner that only mothers can use convincingly, 'Don't worry. Everything's going to be all right.'

'I know, Mum,' I said. 'I believe you.'

* * *

'Look,' said Charlie, holding up his daughter for mum and me to see as we walked into the delivery room. 'I'm a dad!'

It had taken ten and a half hours for Vernie to give birth, which according to the doctors was an 'easy labour'. Judging by the state of Vernie, who to be frank looked like she'd just ran a marathon, the phrase 'easy labour' was something of a misnomer.

Still holding the baby, Charlie pointed to me. 'This is your uncle Duffy! He's the one who'll be giving you your pocket money.' He pointed to my mum. 'This is your gran and anything you want she'll get it for you!' As he passed the wriggling bundle into Vernie's outstretched arms he introduced the baby. 'And finally everyone, the star of the show . . . this is little Elvis.'

'Don't start, Charlie,' sighed Vernie in a good humoured sort of way. 'No matter how much I love you, we're not calling our baby Little Elvis.'

'But she looks like Elvis,' said Charlie.

'She's bald, her head's a funny shape, and in case it has escaped your attention she is a little girl. Her name's Phoebe. You know her name's Phoebe because you helped choose it. If this child grows up thinking that her name is Little Elvis I promise you there will be trouble.'

Charlie smiled. 'Beautiful baby Phoebe.'

The next half hour was spent playing pass the baby. After Vernie it went to Mum, who then passed her back to Charlie, who then passed her back to Vernie when she started crying, who then quieted her down and then offered her to me.

'I think I'll pass this time,' I said, declining as politely as I possibly could. Babies always made me nervous – they were so fragile that I felt they'd fall apart in my hands if I so much as looked at them in the wrong way. Plus, I wasn't entirely convinced by the Theory of Universal Baby Cuteness that so many people subscribed to. I mean, she looked fairly okay, but not exactly what I'd call attractive. My main problem, however, with babies was that I couldn't reason with them. It was why I've never been all that keen on cats either. It's the ability to reason that separates us from the animals, and until Phoebe could talk, an animal she would remain. *She may well be my niece*, I thought, *but I'll wait until I can chat to her like a regular human being before I really bond with her.*

In the end Vernie passed Phoebe to Charlie who clearly couldn't get enough of her.

After five minutes she began crying again. 'She's crying again,' said Charlie needlessly to Vernie. 'What shall I do?'

Vernie smiled at him all sweetness and light and said, 'You're her dad. *You* do something.'

Ten minutes and two circuits of the ward corridor later and Charlie handed her back to Vernie in triumph. 'Somehow she's managed to scream herself into a sort of blissful state of peace,' explained Charlie.

As she lay in Vernie's arms, her eyes firmly shut and her tiny fingers flinching sporadically as she dreamed of whatever it is that babies dream of, I peered at her closely.

'She looks like you,' I said to Vernie.

'I think she looks like aunt Margaret sucking a sherbet lemon,' said Vernie. 'The likeness is uncanny.'

By the time I got home it was late afternoon. I felt totally drained and was just contemplating a long spell in bed when I heard the electronic beep of the answerphone. I listened to the messages: a sycophantic Greg congratulating me and Dan on our sitcom deal; Dan calling to see if the baby had been born yet; my old temping agency to see if

I was interested in a six-week block at an accountancy firm; and one other. I listened to the one other twice. Searched out my address book. Picked up the phone and dialled.

'Julie, it's Duffy here. I just got your message. You said you had something to tell me.'

I heard her taking a deep momentous breath. 'You know that thing that you asked me to do?'

'Yeah?'

'Well, I'll do it.'

I was stunned. Miracles could happen. The plan was back on. 'Excellent!' I cried a little too enthusiastically, and then added calmly but sheepishly, 'I couldn't ask you for another favour, could I?'

'What is it, Duffy?' sighed Julie impatiently.

'You couldn't meet me tomorrow after you've been to work, could you? I sort of need a lift.'

'Where to?'

'IKEA. A new addition to the plan.'

She paused. 'You want me to ask, don't you? Well, I'm not going to, because I don't want to know how that mind of yours works. Some things should remain a mystery.'

'So you'll do it?'

'I'll see you round at mine at six thirty sharp.' She paused again. 'Duffy?' she said, a hint of warmth entering into her voice. 'I really do hope that everything works out for you.'

'Thanks,' I said. 'I hope so too. Because to tell you the truth, I really don't know what else I can do.' It was my turn to feel uncomfortable. 'Julie?'

'What now?' she said with mock impatience. 'Do you want me to drive you to Marks and Spencer as well?'

'Not this week,' I returned quickly. 'I just wanted to ask: what made you change your mind?'

'I'm going to hate myself for saying this, but *you* did – *you* changed my mind. I thought about everything you've said and done recently, and I don't know why, but I really do believe that you love Mel and that you want to make her happy. All I've ever wanted is for her to be happy, and if that's what you do, then I'm all for it.'

'Cheers.' I sensed an awkward moment coming over the horizon. 'I'd better go, but I'll see you tomorrow at half six.'

'For what it's worth,' she said hesitantly, 'I just want you to know that what I said yesterday was wrong. Well, at least I've changed my mind. For better or worse I'm back believing in good old-fashioned love.'

Finally, everything was coming together. There was just one more thing that I had to do. I picked up the phone and made a call.

Monkeys

Here's how my first ever conversation with my dad went:

Me: Hello, is that George?

Him: Yes.

Me: It's Ben Duffy here.

Him: (Pause.) Hello. (Hideously long pause.) How are you?

Me: I got your letter a while ago. Do you still want to meet up?

Him: Yes, of course.

Me: How about tomorrow?

Him: Sounds good to me.

Me: Where shall we meet?

Him: Wherever you like.

Me: (Painfully long pause.) I dunno.

Him: (Excruciatingly long pause.) I don't know either.

Me: (Quite obviously siezing on the first thing that enters my head.) London Zoo!

Him: The zoo? Aren't you a bit old for that?

Me: (Brusquely.) Okay, you choose.

Him: No . . . London Zoo sounds fine. Eleven o'clock suit you?

Me: Fine. (Pause.) Okay, then, 'bye.

Him: 'Bye.

The zoo. The sodding zoo! I couldn't believe that I'd just arranged to meet the man who was half responsible for my conception, in a zoo. It had just flashed in my head like a beacon. Later I wondered if deep in my subconscious what I'd wanted more than anything while growing up was to be taken to the zoo by my dad. Well, here I was some two decades later and finally my dream was coming true.

I had made the decision to call him as I'd sat in the hospital waiting room with Mum and she'd told me how she'd contacted him for my sake. I didn't like the thought of her feeling responsible for something that had nothing to do with her. I already knew that I wasn't my dad. I already knew that unlike him I could do the commitment thing. But I felt that for Mum's sake, for my sake and for the sake of everyone whose dad just waltzed off and left them when they were kids, I had to do this one thing. And anyway, the parallels between my own life and that of Luke Skywalker in *Return of The Jedi* were so uncanny that I couldn't resist. Was I, like Luke, going to discover that my dad was someone powerful like Darth Vadar, or was he just going to be some old rent-a-dad, with regulation paunch, bald patch and extended nasal hair? When I was a kid I used to tell people that my dad was in the SAS and that was why he was never around. But then Mike Bailey got a book out from the local library on the SAS that said that they weren't even allowed to tell close family members they were in the crack army battalion, which pretty much blew my cover.

The next day I got up early and put on the suit that I'd worn to Meena's wedding. It was a bit crumpled but I wore it anyway. While I didn't really give a toss one way or another what my dad thought of me, I couldn't help but feel a little insecure. Something in me didn't want him to be disappointed when he saw me. I even put on a tie. The funny thing was, as I approached the entrance to the zoo dead on eleven o'clock I spotted him a mile off because he was wearing a suit and tie too. So there we were. Two grown men in suits and ties going to the zoo.

'Hello,' I said, giving him a short and very awkward wave. 'Are you George?'

'Ben,' he replied, offering me his hand. 'Good to meet you.'

I thought about correcting the 'Ben' thing but left it. He squeezed my hand very firmly in a handshake that seemed to last for ever. He was shorter than I expected. Both Vernie and I were quite tall, and as my mum wasn't, I'd always assumed that we'd got it from my dad. It felt odd discovering that we'd inherited our height from one of our less immediate ancestors. He had a full head of grey hair (so I couldn't blame my receding hairline on him either) and a kind of long, drawn-out face that along with his thick eyebrows and moustache gave him the appearance of an ageing TV private detective. The only thing we had in common was our eyes. Almond shaped, and dark brown. 'Shall we go in?'

'Yeah,' I said. 'Let's do that.'

He paid for the two of us at the kiosk near the entrance and we pushed through the turnstile into the zoo. As it was a damp Thursday in October and school half terms had not yet started, the zoo wasn't exactly crawling with activity. There were a few preschool kids with their mums dotted about the place, and that was it. Leading the way, George decided that we ought to go and visit the lions first. Which is exactly what we did.

It was the strangest thing, because we didn't talk about the missing years, his life or mine; instead animals dominated the conversation. Never have two people who so obviously know bugger all about the animal kingdom found so much to say about it. We read plaque after plaque, informed each other of nature documentaries we had seen in the past and dredged up all manner of ridiculous animal facts. ('No, I didn't know that whales give birth to live young. But did you know that the kangaroo has a forked penis?') After the lions, we visited the reptile house, the penguins in the pool, watched the llamas, the elephants, in fact everything there was to see.

We spent a particularly long time in the ape house, for my benefit. I was running out of stuff to say and the orangutans were so entertaining that we used them as a talking point for at least half an hour. The zookeepers had given the orangutans clothes to play with. One particular orangutan, who had to have the saddest, most mournful face in the primate world, was sitting on the ground next to a tree, with a lady's long raincoat over his head. His body was huddled up and his long hairy arms were wrapped around his back as if he were giving himself a hug. We watched him for ages as he began doing forward and backward rolls for no reason at all. If Mel had been here she would've wanted to cry.

After three hours of wandering around, we decided to take a break for lunch. Queuing up in the restaurant, George told me that he'd treat me to lunch, which struck me as very funny – I'd worked out on my way to the zoo that at the very least he probably owed me a few thousand pounds in backdated birthday presents alone. He chose a ham baguette wrapped in cellophane and I had a plate of French fries with three sachets of tomato sauce.

'Do you want a coffee?' he asked as we reached the drinks dispensers.

'I don't really do hot drinks,' I told him.

'Me neither,' he said, pulling a face. 'I hate things that are too hot to sip.'

As the sun had come out briefly, we sat at the tables outside the zoo's restaurant to eat, even though the plastic chairs were damp. As we chewed in silence, I could see how difficult this was for him, but it was hard for me too. There was this massive thing between us – a conversation that we both knew we had to have, but that neither of us particularly wanted to begin.

I was just about to offer up another animal fact ('Did you know that bulls see in black and white?') when George suddenly put down his half-eaten baguette. 'I was just wondering what made you change your mind?'

This is it. This is The Talk.

'About seeing you?' I asked, playing for time. He nodded. I thought deeply about his question and avoided eye contact while I spoke. 'I've just sorted out my life in a way I never thought possible. I've spent a long time avoiding stuff that I used to be scared of, and if there's one thing I've learned it's this: nothing is ever as scary as you think it will be.'

George laughed, a kind of big baritone laugh that made me envious, given that my voice was nowhere near as deep. 'I think it was Mark Twain who said, 'I am an old man and have known many fears. Most of which have never happened.''

'I think I prefer my version,' I said. 'It has a sort of awkward charm about it.'

'I prefer yours too,' he replied.

There was a big silence. 'I used to hate you. In fact I spent most of my life hating you. You made my life difficult for no good reason as far as I can see.'

'I deserve that,' he said. 'There's no good excuses for what I did. You're right I made your mother's life a mess and made things hard for you and your sister.' He paused. 'You said "used to hate". Does that mean that you don't hate me now?'

I swallowed hard. 'I think I've just come round to the idea that it's pointless hating you. When I was at school, most of my mates had absentee dads of some description. It was weird. Like a whole generation of men had held some sort of secret ballot and decided universally to bugger off pronto. They were all at it. Like the monkeys.'

'Monkeys?'

'Yeah,' I said and then proceeded to tell him Dan's dead monkey joke. 'You were just doing the dead monkey like everybody else, which is no surprise given that the difference between monkey DNA and human DNA is as little as one per cent.' This startling statistic forced me to take a moment of self reflection: *Where are all these animal facts coming from?* 'You weren't necessarily a bad person,' I continued. 'Just weak willed.' I looked up at George for the first time. He was watching me intently.

'You know I'm sorry, don't you?' he said. 'It's useless apologising – it's only words after all – but I mean it. I've missed your growing up and Vernie's growing up and it's stuff that I'll never get back. I tried not to think about you at all when I first left, which was difficult, but I knew your mum would give you everything you needed. Eventually it got easier and easier to forget that you existed. It was almost like you were a dream, or you were somebody else's life.'

Over the next half an hour we tried to cram in as much as we could about the last twenty-eight years. I told him about Vernie and the baby, my stand-up career so far, and even a bit about me and Mel and the baby (although I didn't go into too much detail).

In return George told me about his life. He'd remarried and divorced, never had any more kids and had spent his life in shoe sales. Now he was retired he spent most of his time in the garden of his house in Enfield. He seemed moderately happy with his lot, which annoyed me slightly, so I made up a stack of lies about my mum having won a modest sum on the National Lottery and her having a retired suitor who was forever taking her on exotic holidays to the Caribbean. Although I no longer hated George, there was no way that I didn't love my mum a billion times more than anything I'd ever feel for him.

'Well, I'm glad she's happy,' was all he managed to say.

'She is,' I replied. 'Very.'

We decided to call it a day when it started to rain. As we headed for the exit George talked about how this hadn't been as scary as he thought it would be and so we should do it again. However, I think he knew as well as I did that we were never really going to. We'd both done the thing that we'd been waiting a lifetime to do, and now we'd crossed it off our lists there wasn't a lot more to say other than goodbye.

'Goodbye, then.' I offered George my hand.

'It's been good to see you,' he said, shaking it firmly. 'For what it's worth, I think you're a fine young man.'

'Cheers,' I replied. I don't think he expected me to recipro-cate his compliment, but if he did he was sadly mistaken. His statement did, however, call for something more substantial than 'Cheers', so I found myself saying, 'I've got your eyes.'

'I know,' he said, taken aback.

'Mel thinks my eyes are the reason she fell in love with me,' I said quietly as it began to rain. 'I'll let her know that they're just like yours.'

He smiled gently. 'Meet up soon, then?'

'Yeah,' I said. 'I'll see you around.'

Every man has a poem in his heart

'Are you sure it goes in there?'

I looked at Julie exasperatedly.

'Maybe you've got it upside down or something? Have you tried wobbling that funny-looking thing?'

I gritted my teeth and wobbled irately.

'This isn't going to work, is it?'

Julie, I thought carefully, *may well have a point*.

Up until now everything in the Plan had gone like clockwork. As arranged I'd met up with Julie and we'd driven to IKEA. Half an hour and several hot and bothered assistants later and part one of the Plan was complete. In my pockets were parts two and three but on the way to Clapham I had a flash of inspiration and a potential fourth part of the Plan occurred to me. A quick detour via the freezer section of a nearby Safeway and my job was nearly complete. By eight o'clock we'd arrived at Mel's flat where Julie's role in the Plan came to the fore – she handed me the spare keys she kept to the flat. I'd told her I'd be in and out in under an hour. That was then.

'What time is it?' I asked, rubbing my temples gently whilst surveying the havoc I'd wreaked in Mel's living room. *It's going to take ages to tidy this lot away.* 'It feels like midnight.'

Julie looked at her watch and did the sort of comedy

double take that usually only ever happens in films. A look. Another look of disbelief and then another look just to check that the first two weren't part of some sort of hideous hallucination. 'It's one o'clock in the morning,' she said.

'You're joking?'

'I'm not. I'm deadly serious. Look, Duffy, we're going to have to go. I've got work in the morning. I can't stay up all night while you make a mess. I'm sorry, but I think we ought to tidy up and leave.'

'We can't go yet,' I protested. 'I haven't finished doing what I'm doing. Mel's going to be back tomorrow night. I wanted everything to be perfect . . .' I ran out of steam as the futility of my big plan finally hit me. 'This really isn't going to work, is it?'

'Look, it's just one part that's not going to work. The rest will be fine. Let's just tidy up and make the most of what you've done.'

'Will you put in a good word for me? Explain to her what I was trying to do?'

'Of course I will,' said Julie. 'The more I think about it, the better this idea of yours gets. It won't matter that you didn't get it all done. All that matters is you tried. Mel's not stupid, she'll know how hard you've worked. It's the trying that matters. She'll know how much you love her.'

Julie then did something she'd never done before. Something I never expected her to do in this lifetime or any other – she hugged me. At first, still somewhat shocked, my body went rigid with fear as if I'd come face to face with a black widow spider. Slowly, however, I overcame my initial reaction as I recalled the qualities of New Julie – the one who had gone out of her way to help me – and I found myself returning the hug. And there we stood, wrapped in each other's arms, sharing a moment that up until yesterday had been right at the top of the least-likely-event-to-occur-in-the-next-twenty-four-hours Top 40.

Just as I was wondering what the second least likely event might be, Julie whispered in my ear, 'I think someone's in the room.'

We immediately let go of each other as if we'd just been connected to the national grid, turned and stared wide eyed at the doorway to the living room. Standing there, holding a small suitcase and wearing a look of sheer bewilderment, was Mel.

'What are you doing here?' asked Julie, trying for all the world not to sound guilty. 'You're not meant to be back until tomorrow evening.'

'What am *I* doing here?' said Mel, switching on the main light. 'What are *you* doing here, more like? It's one o'clock in the morning, I'm knackered and I've just walked into my own flat to discover my best friend in an embrace with the father of my child. I don't think I'm the one who needs to be bloody explaining anything.'

'It's not how it looks,' I said sheepishly. 'Honest, Mel, this is all just a hugely hideous mistake.'

'Of course it's not how it looks,' Mel sniggered. 'Just look at the two of you! Terrified rigid that I'm going to accuse you of having an affair. Do you honestly imagine for one minute I'd think that?' She stepped into the room, and for the first time noticed the sheer havoc I'd wreaked in her living room. 'Okay,' she said, hand on hip. 'What's going on? And why have you decided to turn my flat into a bombsite?'

'Mel,' I began, 'It's not Julie's fault, it's all mine. I had a plan, something that was supposed to convince you how serious I was about you, but it's all gone horribly wrong . . .'

'It hasn't, Duffy,' prompted Julie sternly. 'Just do what you've got to do.' She walked over to Mel, gave her a hug and said warmly, 'Go easy on him. He's not half as bad as he seems.' Mel looked at Julie in silent amazement. 'My work here is done,' continued Julie, 'so I think I'm going to leave you two to sort this out by yourselves.' She went out, closing the door softly behind her. Now Mel and I were alone I knew this was it – my big moment.

'I've got some things to give you,' I began, as I felt my breathing quicken. My head started to feel slightly fuzzy as the blood rushed to my brain. 'The original plan was that you were supposed to come home tomorrow and just find them here in the flat. *I* wasn't supposed to be here at all. But since I am, I might as well give them to you myself. They're not gifts exactly – sort of non-gifts to be accurate – but they do all have something in common that I want you to think about.'

'This is all really weird Duffy, even for you,' said Mel. 'The fact that you've managed to rope Julie into your schemes worries me greatly.'

'Close your eyes,' I said, 'while I give you your first non-gift.' Mel closed her eyes. 'Put out your hands.' She did as I requested and I placed my first non-gift in her hand.

'Yeurgh!' exclaimed Mel. 'It's all soggy.'

'I know. I forgot to put it back in the freezer and put it in the fridge by accident. You can open your eyes now.'

'It's a bag of broccoli,' she said blankly, looking at me for explanation.

'I know, you left some in my freezer ages ago before we broke up. I threw it away but I've bought you some more.'

'Thanks. It's just what I wanted,' said Mel pulling a face. 'What's next?'

'You know the procedure.'

She closed her eyes and I handed her the second non-gift. 'It's the remote control for *my* television!' exclaimed Mel.

'Er . . . thanks very much! This is like some sort of twisted version of Christmas.'

'This bit's a little more complicated,' I said, ignoring her asides. 'You close your eyes again, but this time I'm going to have to guide you over to the other side of the room.' Holding on to her hand tightly, I navigated her carefully across the room. 'You can open your eyes now.'

'Great!' Mel looked around her. 'Bits of wood and metal. Now I know for a fact that unless you've been dismantling my furniture none of this is mine.'

'Ah you see bits of wood and metal,' I corrected. 'But I see *very* important bits of wood and metal. This mess here,' I pointed to a pile of short metal rods, two large door panels, a massive instruction sheet, and a pile of brackets and side panels, 'in my hands all amounts to a bunch of bits of wood and metal but in the hands of someone with more common sense than your average house brick they all fit together to make an IKEA wardrobe.'

Mel's faced changed as she began to get an inkling of what I was doing. She opened her mouth, about to speak, but I put my finger to her lips to silence her.

'Not now. You can speak when I've given the last of my non-gifts.' I searched around in my jacket pocket and knelt down in front of her. 'This is for you.' I handed her a small gift-wrapped package.

She tore open the wrapping paper revealing the box inside, and opened it hurriedly. She was quiet for some moments and then she looked at me with tears in her eyes and knelt down beside me. 'It's my engagement ring.'

'I know you're probably wondering what this is all about. You probably think this is just me having a laugh, and in a way it is. I love making you laugh, Mel, I want to be the one who makes you happy all the time, but there's a serious side to this too. You see, the broccoli *was* yours and I give it back to you. The remote control *is* yours but I used to use it most and so now I give it back to you. The wardrobe *should've been* yours on that day we argued in IKEA, so I give it to you now. And finally this ring, in your hand, which represents my heart, is, was, and will always be yours. Even if you turn me down, I can't ever take it back because it's yours for ever.'

I sat down on the hardwood floor, exhausted. 'Charlie once said to me that when it came to winning over the one you love, "every man has a poem in his heart". Well, this, Mel, was my sonnet. The only thing I regret about tonight,' I said, wiping a tear away from her cheek as she moved herself closer to me, 'is that I was defeated by that stupid wardrobe.' With that I closed my eyes like a blindfolded deserter about to be shot and waited for her answer.

There was a brief moment of silence, and then I felt Mel's arms around me, squeezing me tightly as she whispered the words, 'I love you,' into my ear.

'Will you marry me?' I asked tentatively.

'Of course,' said Mel as I opened my eyes. 'That's why I've told my bosses today that I couldn't carry on the job in Scotland and asked for my old job instead. That's why I came back a day early. I couldn't wait any longer. I didn't need frozen broccoli, a remote control, a ring or even a wardrobe to know that you love me. I just know.'

'You're sure?'

'Of course,' she said wiping her nose on the sleeve of her jacket. 'If it's really what you want.'

'Even though I can't build flat-pack wardrobes?'

'Especially because you can't build flatpack wardrobes.'

'Even though I still hate shopping in IKEA?'

'Especially because you hate shopping in IKEA.'

'Even though I don't always understand you, I wind you up with the stupid things I do and occasionally try to shush you when the TV's on?'

'Don't push it,' she said as she moved in closer to kiss me. 'Quit while you're ahead, Mr Duffy.' She kissed me again. 'All you need to know is that I love everything about you. I love you exactly the way you are. I don't want you to be like me and I certainly don't want to be like you. I want us to be the way we are.'

It'll reduce puffiness around the eyes

We set a wedding date for as soon as was possible, which turned out to be some four months away, and in the meantime I went back to temping, gigged like a demon with Dan up and down the country and fell more deeply in love with Mel than I thought possible.

Like these things do, the big day came up faster than either Mel or I had expected, but it was none the less welcome, and my last twenty-four hours as a single man went something a little like this:

12.30 p.m.
Took the afternoon off work and met up for a drink because Mel said I wasn't allowed to go out the night before the wedding, as the previous Thursday's stag do resulted in a ten-week ban from the Haversham. Dan, Charlie, myself and various other mates headed to the Haversham wearing joke-shop false moustaches.

3.10 p.m.
Landlord of Haversham saw through disguises instantly, and we were escorted off the premises. We headed for the Newton Arms, in Tufnell Park, the definitive old man's pub – Woodbines behind the bar, no carpet on the floor and grumpy-looking old men just about everywhere. We spent

the afternoon drinking bitter, laughing ourselves silly and smoking Woodbines with aforementioned grumpy old men.

6.00 p.m.
Mel's official cut-off point. As responsible best man, Dan let me know it was time to go. We all agreed that it was indeed time to go home.

6.10 p.m.
Okay, just the one.

7.10 p.m.
After this next one we're off. I mean it.

7.30 p.m.
No, really.

8.10 p.m.
Just as we were finishing what we promised ourselves would be our last drink, Charlie's mobile began an annoying electronic rendition of the 'William Tell Overture'. He answered it, expecting it to be work, but it was Vernie trying to find out where we were. Thinking on his feet, he told her that we were just on our way home, but his cover was blown by Dan and two of his new octogenarian best buddies, Albert and Reg, singing 'Can't Smile Without You' at the top of their hoary voices. Needless to say, Vernie pulled a strop, yelled loud enough for us all to hear and slammed the phone down. Now it really was time to go.

8.15 p.m.
Vernie called back and threatened Charlie with all manner of torture should anything untoward happen to me before my wedding.

8.32 p.m.
Dan, Charlie and I said our goodbyes to Albert and Reg and all our mates and and then grabbed a taxi home. Despite our protests, the driver insisted on keeping his car radio tuned to an easy-listening station which happened to be playing back-to-back Phil Collins. Though he clearly did not know the words, the driver insisted on singing along to 'Easy Lover', twice forcing me to correct his completely inaccurate rendition of the chorus.

8.51 p.m.
Thanked the very nice waiter at the Star of the Punjab in Kentish Town for taking our orders (onion bahjees, chicken vindaloo, prawn korma and chicken sagwalla). It was all Dan's idea. Honest.

9.01 p.m.
Vernie called Charlie on his mobile again and issued the severe reprimand: 'If anything happens to make Duffy late, ill or unpresentable tomorrow, you will never ever see me naked again in this or any other lifetime.' For the sake of Charlie's sub-duvet activities we asked the waiters to hurry up.

10.15 p.m.
Taxi arrived at the Star of Punjab and we bid fond farewells to Harpreet, Hassan and Steve, the Star of Punjab waiters. As they waved their goodbyes, they promised faithfully that they'd come to the wedding as I'd requested. We got the taxi to drop Charlie off in Crouch End first. Vernie came out the minute we pulled up, gave Charlie her best Death Ray look and peered into my eyes. 'I don't want my brother looking haggard on his wedding photos!' she berated loudly and then

handed me a Clarins bottle. 'It'll reduce puffiness around the eyes,' she added sagely.

10.25 p.m.

Dan and I arrived back at the flat. Our good moods in full swing, we decided to invite Will and Alice, the couple who lived in the flat beneath us, to the wedding in a gesture of niceness. At first they looked at us strangely, but when I eventually managed to persuade them that although I was drunk I was telling the truth, they said they'd love to come. We also considered inviting the couple who lived in the flat above us, Matt and Monica, but Dan still held a grudge against them because he was convinced it was they who had called the police round to pull the plug on our New Year's Eve party last year. I, however, was still overflowing with the milk of human kindness so I invited them anyway.

11.30 p.m.

Mammoth toast-making session. Dan and I toasted a whole loaf of Hovis just for the hell of it. Whilst opening a can of Red Stripe I had a brief tender moment with Dan. 'You know, you're all right for a Northern toast-muncher,' he said, buttering a slice of toast. 'And you're not too bad yourself for a soft southern git,' I replied. Touchy-feely moment over, we slipped into the living room to consume the fruits of our labours.

12.03 a.m.

Asked Dan who the mystery guest was he was bringing to the wedding, and he refused to tell me yet again. He'd asked me a month ago if he could bring someone. I'd said yes of course, but when I asked who it was he went all furtive, so I didn't bother asking again. Mel reckoned it was Fiona, the new girl who had just started working behind the bar in the Haversham. Charlie and Vernie were of the opinion he was bringing one of my ex-girlfriends as a surprise guest, but my money was on it being someone nobody knew – that was much more Dan's style.

1.12 a.m.

Tiredness came over me in a massive wave so I retired to bed. Before I did so, I wrote down on a notepad, 'Getting married tomorrow,' in case it escaped my memory, and then read and followed set of instructions pinned to my pillow by Vernie:

1) Set bedside alarm clock for 7.30 a.m.
2) Set Dan's radio alarm clock on the floor next to the bed for 7.30 a.m.
3) Set Mickey Mouse alarm clock at the bottom of the bed for 7.30 a.m.
4) Call BT and ask for 7.30 a.m. wake-up call.

1.22 a.m.

Attempted to sleep.

1.55 a.m.

Still not sleeping. Counted sheep.

2.28 a.m.

Ran out of sheep and began counting other farmyard animals.

3.30 a.m.

Called Mel and told her how much I love her. Her only reply was a very sleepy, 'That's nice.'

3.32 a.m.
I called Mel again in case she thought I was a crank caller. 'Of course I knew it was you,' she said patiently. 'Only you would do this to me!'

3.40 a.m.
Still unable to sleep, so I got up and flicked through Dan's videos in the front room. Selected Dan's car-boot-sale copy of *ET* to while away the early hours as I'd never seen it.

4.20 a.m.
Due to heightened emotional state caused by impending wedlock, *ET* had me in floods of tears. 'Why are people so horrible? He only wanted to go home.'

4.30 a.m.
Fast forwarded film to the end to make sure he wasn't really dead.

5.21 a.m.
Satisfied with happy ending, I suddenly felt tired and went to bed.

7.30 a.m.
Multiple alarms woke me and probably everyone in North London apart from Dan. I felt awful and wondered if I was in fact dead. Went back to sleep.

7.45 a.m.
Woken by doorbell. Eyes barely open I made my way downstairs to discover Mum, Charlie, Vernie and baby Phoebe on the doorstep dressed up in full wedding gear. They all came

upstairs and made themselves at home while I showered. When I emerged from the bathroom half an hour later, Mum was washing the dishes, Vernie was grilling sausages and Charlie had Phoebe on his lap and was watching *ET*. Dan, meanwhile, was still asleep.

9.00 a.m.

Cars arrived to take us to St Faith's in Barnet. Estimated Time of Arrival: 9.30 a.m.

9.30 a.m.

Stuck in traffic. ETA now 9.45 a.m.

9.45 a.m.

Still stuck in traffic jam. ETA now 9.55 a.m. I managed to convince myself that Mel wouldn't marry me if I was late, and that I'd be condemned to live with Dan until the day I died.

9.54 a.m.

Arrived at the church. Thankfully Mel hadn't arrived yet. Mum kept checking my suit for fluff and dusted me over every thirty seconds like one of her prized Capo Di Monte figurines. Remembered to ask Dan if he'd got the ring. Few panicky moments when after checking every conceivable pocket and orifice he still couldn't find it. Fortunately he discovered it on a piece of string around his neck just as I was about to kill him with my bare hands. Good man!

10.00 a.m.

Said hello to waiters from the Star of Punjab, Will and Alice and Alexa. No sign of the New Year's No Noise Neighbours, or for that matter my fiancée. Spotted Dan behind a Vauxhall Astra in mid-snog with his mystery guest . . . none other than The Lovely Anne, Crap Greg's ex-girlfriend. Hurrah for Dan indeed!

10.05 a.m.
Still no sign of Mel. Mum helpfully reminded me that it's a woman's prerogative to be late. Didn't reply for fear of being unable to locate my inner Dalai Lama. Julie came over and introduced me to her new man and former pottery teacher, Leon, who lives in Notting Hill Gate. Leon handed me a large gift-wrapped box on behalf of Julie. I tried and failed to resist taking a crafty peak. Typical! Dinner set from Habitat.

10.15 a.m.
Managed to convince myself that Mel had got cold feet and had done a runner. My mum just shook her head and told me me to 'stop being so ridiculous'.

10.21 a.m.
Mel's car is spotted by Dan coming up the road. She loves me!

10.25 a.m.
Following a brief moment for explanation from Mel's mum and dad (the car was stuck in the same traffic as us) we're nearly ready to begin.

10.45 a.m.
Standing at the front of the church, I turned to see Mel on her father's arm, striding up the aisle. It was like seeing her for the first time in my life all over again – that walk, that living

breathing version of Chrissie Hynde singing 'Brass In Pocket'
– even in a wedding dress and six months pregnant! When
she reached me I whispered in her ear, 'You look amazing,'
and she beamed and whispered back, 'Don't say things like
that, because I'll only cry and I'm desperate to look calm
and serene on the wedding video!'

10.55 a.m.
She said, 'I do.'

10.57 a.m.
I said, 'I do.'

10.59 a.m.
'I now pronounce you husband and wife,' said the man in
charge. 'You may now kiss the bride.'

11.00 a.m.
We kissed.

The Best Man

Ladies and gentlemen, on behalf of the bride and groom I'd like to welcome you to the wedding of Melanie Lara Benson, and of course, the one and only Benjamin Dominic Duffy! As best man it falls to me to come out with a lot of stuff about how wonderful the bride is and then crack a few jokes about the groom . . . and who am I to truck with tradition? No, seriously, although this is a happy day, in some way it's a sad day, too, because I'm going to miss Duff. Over the last couple of years he has been the best flatmate ever. He is easy going, reasonably house trained and never ceased to amaze me with his ability to make lost fridge food edible simply by scraping the fur off it and shoving it into the microwave. Someone said to me this afternoon that I shouldn't think of today as losing a flatmate, I should see it as gaining somewhere nice and clean to be invited for Sunday lunch – they may well have a point. Decent food apart, though, I hope I'll also be gaining another friend as good as Duffy. Mel really is the best thing that has ever happened to him and I couldn't think of a better person to hand over responsibility to for his supervision. And so, I ask you to join me in a toast to these two brave people – brave because no matter how much in love someone is, it is still a leap of faith to make the sort of promise they've made today and mean it. So I ask you to join me in raising a toast: to Duffy and Mel – Mr and Mrs Commitment.

The Bride

Hello, everyone. Due to thousands of years of patriarchal oppression women have been denied the right to make speeches at weddings and make jokes at the groom's expense. As a fully-fledged flexible feminist I'm not about to have my wedding day dictated to me by anyone – especially as I paid for half of it. Anyway, I've prepared a few words that I'd like to say. When Duffy and I first planned to get married, I'd had my heart set on a huge wedding. Now it's me who is huge and not the wedding. But to be serious for a second, I'm glad we've done it small – just the people we love and care for most. I couldn't have wished for a better day. Anyway, I'd like to thank everyone for coming: you really have made today a day to remember. I'd especially like to thank my mum and dad for all the hard work they've put in to making this day a success, and Julie for being there for me, and Charlie and Dan for making sure that Duffy didn't come to too much harm on his stag night; and to Duffy's mum for everything she's done, especially for sorting out the catering – you have her to thank for the wonderful Moroccan-style chicken starters. And finally, I've got a surprise for my husband. For the past few months he's been under the impression that we're having a band playing at this evening's reception, but we're not – we're having the Derek G Mobile Disco Experience instead. And yes, Duffy, I made sure before I hired him that he's got

'Come On Eileen', 'Three Times A Lady' and even 'The Birdie Song'. That's all I've got to say really, but before I sit down, I'd like to take this opportunity to thank my husband, who is the most special person in the world . . . he's kind, gentle and . . . and . . . a . . .

The Groom

That's exactly why women aren't supposed to give speeches at weddings – they just burst into tears. Mel, her mum, my mum, Vernie, have been shedding tears all morning. It's only because I shed all mine last night watching *ET* that I'm the only one in the house with dry eyes. There's nothing in the world that I want more than to be with Mel for the rest of my life. Now it's not my intention to shuffle off this mortal coil until I'm oh, what shall I say, eighty, ninety? I want to see for myself whether one day we will all be drinking blue drinks, wearing shiny silver spacesuits and taking winter breaks on Mars. I wouldn't mind living for ever, which of course will mean being married for ever. Which is as great as it sounds. This is what I've spent the whole of my life not searching for, mainly because I didn't know I needed it. A few hours ago Mel promised to love and cherish me for the rest of her life. She didn't say obey, which is okay, because I don't want to control her, I just want her to want to be with me and me with her. I know I sound like some sort of New Man, fully in touch with his emotions, able to cry at romantic comedies starring Meg Ryan and capable of having women as friends without harbouring secret desires to see them naked. It's not true – well, apart from the naked women friends thing – I'm still me. I still don't like it when she talks when the TV's on. I'll admit I don't understand her all of the time. But I know I wouldn't want it any other way, because I've seen the other ways. And so, I'd like for you to join me in a toast – to Mel, my wife, the best a man can get.

Three months later

She's gorgeous

'Isn't she beautiful?' said Mel holding her up for all to see.

'Gorgeous,' said Vernie, taking our baby in her arms. 'Absolutely gorgeous. Look at her eyes – the way they sparkle.'

'Duffy,' said Julie, 'don't you want to hold her?'

'Er,' I uttered noncommittally, 'I'm not sure about this. I've never held a . . . you know . . . anyway, she looks a bit fragile to me. What if I drop her? Maybe later, eh? When Mel's mum and dad arrive. Give them the chance to see their granddaughter in one piece before I start juggling with her.'

'No,' replied Mel firmly. 'You're going to hold her now. You've been making up excuses for the last two hours. It's time for the two of you to bond.'

'My hands are really sweaty. She needs to be held by someone with a better grip than mine.'

'Are you seriously intending not to hold her until she's more robust?' asked Mel. She turned to hand me my daughter. 'Here you go, Daddy.'

'It's not difficult,' reassured Julie as I took her from Mel's hands. 'Just be gentle with her.'

My baby was oblivious to the fact that someone new was holding her. Her eyes were firmly closed and her mouth was pouted just like her mum's when she's having a sulk.

'Have you thought of a name for her yet?' enquired Mum. 'I can't believe you've left it this long.'

'We wanted to wait until she was here before we named her. It didn't seem right calling her something without seeing her.' Mel looked up at me and smiled. 'We're open to suggestions. What does everyone think?'

'I don't know,' said Mum, 'I've never been all that good at thinking on my feet.'

'She looks like a Philippa,' said Julie. 'Or maybe a Jane. Or maybe even a Philippa-Jane.'

'Elvis!' said Dan and Charlie in unison.

'I reckon Jackie,' said Vernie, carefully balancing Phoebe in one arm in order to thump Charlie playfully with the other. 'There hasn't been a world famous Jackie since Jackie Onassis. The world needs another one as soon as possible.'

'What do you think?' said Mel, directing her question towards me. 'You're her dad, you should have a whole list of names by now.'

I looked fondly at the new addition to the Duffy family, who was still resting peacefully in my arms. *She's beautiful*, I thought. *No doubt about it. This has got to be the best-looking baby there has ever been. She needs a name that sums up her personality. Something that says, hello, I'm smart and funny and irresistible – just like my dad.*

'I know exactly what her name is,' I said, looking into her tiny face. 'Mel chose it a long time ago, and as ever, she was spot on. I think we should call her Ella.'

'I can't believe you remembered!' said Mel fondly. 'You're right, she does look like an Ella. So Ella Elvis Duffy it is.'

'Elvis?'

'Of course,' said Mel with a flourish. 'She's a Duffy, isn't she? So she's bound to be a star.'

My Legendary Girlfriend

and

Mr Commitment

Mike Gayle

HODDER

My Legendary Girlfriend first published in Great Britain in 1998 by
Hodder & Stoughton
A division of Hodder Headline
Mr Commitment first published in Great Britain in 1999 by
Hodder & Stoughton
A division of Hodder Headline
This Hodder paperbacks edition in 2006

A Hodder paperback

1

A CIP catalogue record for this title is available from the British Library

ISBN 0 340 82341 0

Printed and bound by
Clays Ltd, St Ives plc

Hodder Headline's policy is to use papers that are natural, renewable
and recyclable products and made from wood grown in sustainable forests.
The logging and manufacturing processes are expected to conform to the
environmental regulations of the country of origin.

Hodder & Stoughton Ltd
A division of Hodder Headline
338 Euston Road
London NW1 3BH

My Legendary Girlfriend

Mike Gayle

HODDER

For Claire

Acknowledgements

I would like to thank: for their help, Philippa Pride and all at Hodder, Jane Bradish Ellames and Emlyn Rees and all at Curtis Brown; for their encouragement, Joe and Evelyn Gayle, Andy Gayle, Phil Gayle, Jackie Behan, The Richards clan, Cath McDonnell, Charlotte and John, Liane Hentscher, Emma and Darren, Lisa Howe, John O'Reilly, Pip, Ben, Rodney Beckford, Nikki Bayley and the Four Winds regulars; and for their inspiration, Mr T, Dave Gedge, Kevin Smith, Mark Salzman, Xena, Richard Roundtree, Clive James, Oxfam and anyone who ever asked Mike.

FRIDAY

6.05 P.M.

'Mr Kelly, which football team do you support?'

As I strolled along the edge of the pitch clutching a football underneath each arm, I considered fourteen-year-old Martin Acker and his question carefully. He had been the last of my pupils to leave the pitch and I knew for a fact that he'd lingered with the specific intention of asking me his question, because amongst other things, not only was he genuinely inquisitive as to where my footballing allegiances lay, he also had no friends and had selected me as his companion on that long and lonely walk back to the changing rooms. He was quite literally covered head to foot in Wood Green Comprehensive School football pitch mud, which was a remarkable achievement for someone who hadn't touched the ball all evening. Of his footballing prowess, there was little doubt in my mind that he was the worst player I'd ever witnessed. He knew it, and he knew that I knew it, and yet I didn't have the heart to drop him from the team, because what he lacked in skill, he more than made up for in enthusiasm. This was of great encouragement to me, proving that for some, the futility of an occupation was not in itself a reason to give up.

While Martin was hopeless at playing soccer but excelled in its trivia, I, on the other hand, could neither play, teach nor fake an interest in this most tedious of distractions. Owing

3

to PE staff shortages and the need to impress my superiors, the mob of fourteen-year-olds that made up the year eight B-team was entirely my responsibility. The headmaster, Mr Tucker, had been much impressed when I volunteered for the task, but the truth was less than altruistic: it was either football or the school drama club. The thought of spending two dinner-times per week, aiding and abetting the kids to butcher *My Fair Lady*, this term's production, made football the less depressing option, but only marginally so. I was an English teacher – created to read books, drink cups of sugary tea and popularise sarcasm as a higher form of wit. I was not designed to run about in shorts on freezing cold autumnal evenings.

I peered down at Martin, just as he was looking up to see if I'd forgotten his question.

'Manchester United,' I lied.

'Oh, sir, everyone supports Man U.'

'They do?'

'Yes, sir.'

'Who do you support?'

'Wimbledon, sir.'

'Why?'

'I don't know, sir.'

And that was that. We continued our walk in silence, even failing to disturb the large number of urban seagulls gathered, wading and pecking in the mud, by the corner post. I had the feeling Martin wanted to engage me in more football talk but couldn't think of anything else to ask.

Martin's fellow team-mates were bellowing and screaming so loudly that I was alert to their mayhem before I even reached the changing room doors. Inside, chaos reigned – Kevin Rossiter was hanging upside down by his legs from a hot water pipe that spanned the room; Colin Christie was

4

snapping his towel on James Lee's bare buttocks; and Julie Whitcomb, oblivious to the events going on around her, was tucked in a corner of the changing room engrossed in *Wuthering Heights*, one of the set texts I was teaching my year-eight class this term.

'Are you planning to get changed?' I asked sardonically.

Julie withdrew her amply freckled nose from the novel, squinting as she raised her head to meet my gaze. The look of bewilderment on her face revealed that she had failed to understand the question.

'These are changing rooms, Julie,' I stated firmly, shaking my head in disbelief. '*Boys*' changing rooms, to be exact. As you are neither a boy nor getting changed may I suggest that you leave?'

'I would, Mr Kelly, but I can't,' she explained. 'You see, I'm waiting for my boyfriend.'

I was intrigued. 'Who's your boyfriend?'

'Clive O'Rourke, sir.'

I nodded my head. I hadn't the faintest clue who Clive O'Rourke was.

'Is he a year eight, Julie?'

'No, sir, he's in year eleven.'

'Julie,' I said, trying to break the bad news to her gently, 'year elevens don't have football practice today.'

'Don't they, sir? But Clive said to meet him here after football practice and not to move until he came to get me.'

She dropped her book into her rucksack and slowly picked up her jacket, as though her thought processes were draining her of power, like a computer trying to run too many programs at once.

'How long have you been going out with Clive?' I asked, casually.

She examined the worn soles of her scuffed Nike trainers

5

intently before answering. 'Since dinner-time, sir,' she confessed quietly. 'I asked him out while he was in the dinner queue buying pizza, beans and chips in the canteen.'

Hearing this tale of devotion which included remembering details of a beloved's lunch was genuinely moving. My eyes flitted down to my watch. It was quarter past six. School had finished nearly three hours ago.

'I'm afraid you've been the victim of a practical joke,' I said, spelling it out, in case the penny hadn't dropped. 'Somehow I don't think Clive's going to turn up.'

She turned her head towards me briefly before examining her trainers once again. It was clear she was more heartbroken than embarrassed, her eyes squinting, desperately trying to hold back the tears and her lips pressed tightly together, attempting to lock in the sobs trying to escape. Eventually, she allowed herself the luxury of a carefully controlled sigh, rose and picked up her bag.

'Are you going to be all right?' I asked, even though it was obvious that she wasn't.

With tears already forming in her eyes she said, 'Yes, sir, I'll be all right.'

I watched her all the way to the changing room doors by which time her grief was audible. Some teachers might have thought no more of her but not I. Her image remained in my head for some time because in the few brief moments we'd shared, I had realised that Julie Whitcomb was closer in kind to myself than anyone I'd ever met. She was one of us – one who interpreted every failure, whether small or large, as the out-working of Fate's personal vendetta. Clive O'Rourke's name would never be forgotten, it would be permanently etched on her brain just as my ex-girlfriend's was on mine. And at some point in her future, mostly likely after completing her journey through the education system right up to degree level, she'd realise that a life pining after the Clive O'Rourkes of this world had made her bitter and twisted enough to join the teaching profession.

The sound of a small boy emitting a noise roughly approximating, *Whhhhhhhooooooooorrrrrraaaaaaahhhh!!!* signalled that Kevin Rossiter had changed adrenaline sports and was now racing around the far changing room, naked but for his underpants on his head. I couldn't begin to fathom his motivation for such a stunt, let alone find the required energy to tell him off this close to the weekend and so, sighing heavily, I slipped unnoticed into the PE department's tiny office, closing the door behind me.

Rooting around in my bag I discovered my fags, slightly crushed under the weight of my year eights' exercise books – I had one left. I mentally totted up those that had fallen: five on the way to work, two in the staff room before registration, three during morning break, ten during lunch break. It was difficult to work out which was the more depressing thought: the fact that I – who had only in the last three years made the jump from social smoker to anti-social smoker – had managed to get through enough cigarettes to give an elephant lung cancer or that I hadn't noticed until now.

As the nicotine took effect, I relaxed and decided that I was going to stay in my small but perfectly formed refuge, until the last of the Little People had disappeared. After half an hour, the shouting and screaming died down to a gentle hubbub and then blissful silence. Pulling the door ajar, and using my body to block the smoke in, I peered through the crack to make sure the coast was clear. It wasn't. Martin Acker was still there. He was dressed from the top down but was having difficulty putting on his trousers, mainly because he already had his shoes on.

'Acker!'

Bewildered, Martin scanned the entire room nervously before locating the source of the bellow.

'Haven't you got a home to go to?' I asked.

'Yes, sir,' he said dejectedly.

'Then go home, boy!'

Within seconds he'd kicked off his footwear, pulled on his trousers, pushed his shoes back on, grabbed his things and shuffled out of the changing rooms, shouting, 'Have a good weekend, sir,' as he went through the doors.

The newsagent's *en route* to the tube was manned by a lone fat Asian woman who was busily attempting to serve three customers at once, while keeping an eye on two Wood Green Comprehensive boys, lingering with intent by a copy of *Razzle*, which someone far taller than them had thoughtfully left on the middle shelf. When my turn came to be served, without taking her eyes off the boys, she located my Marlboro Lights and placed them on the counter. It was at this point in the transaction that I got stuck; Twix wrappers, torn pieces of silver paper from a pack of Polos and fluff were the nearest items I had to coins of the realm. The shopkeeper, tutting loudly, put my fags back on the shelf and started serving the man behind me a quarter of bon-bons before I even had a chance to apologise. As I brushed past the boys, their faces gleefully absorbing the now open pages of *Razzle*, I berated myself for not having used my lunch hour more wisely with a visit to the cash machine on the High Street. Smoking myself senseless in the staff room had seemed so important then, but now, penniless and fagless, I wished with my whole heart that I believed in moderation more fervently.

Stepping out into the cold, damp, Wood Green evening, gloomily illuminated by a faulty lamppost flickering like a disco light, three women, approaching from my right, caught my attention, due to the dramatic way they froze – one of them even letting out a tiny yelp of surprise – when they saw me. It took a few seconds but I soon realised why these women were so taken aback: they weren't *women* – they were *girls*. Girls to whom I taught English Literature.

'Sonya Pritchard, Emma Anderson, Pulavi Khan: come here now!' I commanded.

In spite of everything their bodies were telling them, which was probably something along the lines of, 'Run for your lives!' or 'Ignore him, he's the teacher that always smells of Polos,' they did as they'd been told, although very much at their own pace. By the time they'd sulkily shuffled into my presence they'd prepared their most disconsolate faces as a sort of visual protest for the hard of hearing.

Pulavi opened the case for the defence. 'We weren't doing nothin', sir.'

'No, sir, we weren't doing nothin',' added Sonya, backing up her friend.

Emma remained silent, hoping that I wouldn't notice the furtive manner in which she held her hands behind her back.

'Turn around, please, Emma,' I asked sternly.

She refused.

'Sir, you can't do anything to us, sir,' moaned Sonya miserably. 'We're not under your jurisdiction outside of school.'

I noted Sonya's use of the word 'jurisdiction'. Normally I would've been impressed by any of my pupils using a word containing more than two syllables, but 'jurisdiction' was the type of word only ever employed by characters on shows like *Baywatch Nights* – which was more than likely where she'd got it from. 'Judicature', however, was the sort of word shunned by TV private eyes, tabloid newspapers and teenagers alike, and definitely would've earned her my deepest admiration.

'Okay,' I said, feigning acute boredom, 'if that's how you want it. But I wouldn't want to be you on Monday, though.'

It occurred to me that perhaps I was being a bit of a bastard, after all; they were right, this wasn't school time and this wasn't any of my business. The only answer I could think of to defend myself was that being fagless had turned me into a grumpy old sod who enjoyed annoying teenagers.

'That's not fair, sir,' moaned Pulavi rather aptly.

'Welcome to the real world,' I chided, rocking back on my heels smugly. 'Life isn't fair – never has been and never will be.' I turned my attention to Emma. 'Now, are you going to show me what you're hiding or not?'

Reluctantly she held out her hands in front of me, revealing three cigarettes sandwiched between her fingers, their amber tips glowing wantonly.

I tutted loudly, employing a carbon copy 'tut' of the kind my mother had used on me for some twenty-five years. All week I'd found myself doing impressions of people in authority: my mother, teachers from *Grange Hill*, Margaret Thatcher – in a vain attempt to stop them from running riot.

'You know that you shouldn't be smoking, don't you?' I scolded.

'Yes, Mr Kelly,' they replied in sullen unison.

'You know these things will kill you, don't you?'

'Yes, Mr Kelly.'

'Well, put them out right now, please.'

Emma dropped the cigarettes – Benson and Hedges, if I wasn't mistaken – on the pavement, and extinguished them with a twisting motion of her heel.

'I'm going to let you off this time,' I said, eyeing Emma's shoes sadly. 'Just don't let me see you at it again.'

'Yes, Mr Kelly,' they replied.

I picked up my bag and began to walk off, momentarily feeling like a Rooster-Cogburn-John Wayne single-handedly sorting out the baddest gang of desperadoes this side of Turnpike Lane, but after two steps I stopped, turned around and surrendered.

'Er, girls . . .' I called out. 'I don't suppose you've got a spare ciggy, have you?'

My good work went up in smoke. I'd balanced my job's requirement for discipline against that of my desire for a nicotine rush, and the Cigarette had won. As smokers, my pupils understood my dilemma; that is, once they stopped laughing. Pulavi delved into her moc-croc handbag and offered me one of her Benson and Hedges.

'You smoke Benson and Hedges?' I asked needlessly, taking one from her outstretched hand.

'Yeah, since I was twelve,' she replied, her face half hidden by her handbag, as she searched for a lighter. 'What do you smoke, sir?'

'Sir probably smokes Woodbines,' joked Sonya.

'Marlboro Lights, actually,' I replied tersely.

Pulavi discovered her lighter and lit my cigarette.

'I had a Marlboro Light once,' chipped in Emma. 'It was like sucking on air. You wanna smoke proper fags, sir. Only poofs smoke Marlboro Lights.'

Once again they all dissolved into fits of laughter. I thanked them and attempted to leave their company but they insisted they were going in my direction. Linking arms, they trailed by my side. I felt like a dog owner taking three poodles for a walk.

'We're going up the West End, sir,' said Emma bustling with energy.

'Yeah, we're off on the pull,' added Pulavi, smiling the kind of filthy grin that would have put Sid James to shame.

11

'Yeah, we're going to the Hippodrome, sir,' said Sonya. 'D'you fancy coming with us?'

Their question made me think about going out, not with them of course – that would've been unthinkable – but going out in general. I didn't know a single soul in London, and had nothing planned for the weekend, so it was still some wonder to me why, when a few of the younger teachers in the staff room had asked me if I was free for a drink after work, I'd told them I was busy.

'You've got no chance of getting in there,' I said, shaking my head knowingly, partly for their benefit but mostly because I was still reflecting on the sorry excuse of a weekend I had in store for myself.

'You're joking, aren't you?' squealed Sonya. 'We go there every week.'

'Don't you think we look eighteen, sir?' asked Emma.

For the first time during the conversation I recalled what had alarmed me so much in the first moments of our encounter. I knew them to be fourteen-year-olds, but the girls trailing after me were far more worldly than their biological years indicated. Emma had squeezed her frankly over-developed chest into a bra top, barely large enough to cover her modesty, matched with a short silver skirt. Sonya wore a lime green velvet cropped top, combined with an incredibly short blue satin skirt that, whenever she moved her upper body, raised itself an inch higher, instantly revealing more thigh than was strictly necessary. Pulavi had opted for a pair of leopard-print hot pants and a sheer orange blouse, through which her black Wonderbra was clearly visible to the world at large. I was truly mortified.

I thanked them again for the cigarette and rapidly conjured up a girlfriend I was in a rush to get home to. This was exactly the kind of moment which Fate liked to introduce into my life, to let me know there was still plenty of room for things to get worse before they got better. The girls began giggling and in a matter of seconds reduced my self-confidence to zero.

As I entered Wood Green tube station I checked my back pocket for my travel card. It wasn't there. Neither was it in any of my other pockets. Trying not to panic I rapidly developed Plan B:

1. *Try not to dwell on how much it will cost to replace travel card.*
2. *Buy one-way ticket to Archway.*
3. *Do not even consider worrying until 7.00 a.m. Monday morning.*

It was some moments before it occurred to me that Plan B was flawed by the fact that I had only sweet wrappers and pocket fluff to my name.

It began to rain as I put my card into the cash machine and punched in my Pin number: 1411 (the date and month of my ex-girlfriend's birthday). I checked my balance – £770 overdrawn. The machine asked me how much money I wanted. I requested five pounds and crossed my fingers. It made a number of rapid clicking noises and for a moment I was convinced it was going to call the police, make a citizens' arrest *and* eat my card. Instead it gave me the money and asked me in quite a friendly manner – as if I was a valued customer – whether I required any other services.

On the way back to the tube, I passed Burger King on Wood Green High Street. Emma, Sonya and Pulavi were inside, waving at me animatedly from their window seats. I put my head down and did my best to give the impression that I hadn't seen them.

At the station I bought a single to Archway and placed the ticket in the top pocket of my jacket for safe-keeping. As I did so, my fingers brushed against something: I'd found my travel card.

I reached the southbound platform of the Piccadilly Line just in time to see the back of a tube train flying out of the station. I looked up at the station clock to see how long it would be until the next one. *Ten more sodding minutes.* When it finally arrived, I sat down in the end carriage, put my travel card and ticket on the seat next to me where I could keep an eye on them and promptly fell asleep.

The train lurched into a station with a jolt, awakening me from an incredibly gymnastic dream about my ex-girlfriend. While mentally cursing the train driver for cutting short my reverie I looked up in time to realise I was at King's Cross – my stop. I grabbed my bag and managed to squeeze through the gap in the closing doors.

The second part of my journey on the Northern Line, as always, was uncomfortable. All the carriages were so littered with burger wrappers, newspapers and crisp packets that it was like riding home in a rubbish tip on wheels. The only pleasant event that occurred was the appearance of a group of exquisite looking Spanish girls getting on at Euston. They chattered intensely in their mother tongue – probably about why the Northern Line was so dirty – all the way to Camden, where they alighted. This seemed to be the law as far as the north branch of the Northern Line was concerned – beautiful people got off at Camden; interesting people got off at Kentish Town; students and musicians got off at Tufnell Park; leaving only the dull, ugly or desperate to get off at Archway or thank their lucky stars they could afford to live in High Barnet.

Halfway up the escalators at Archway, I searched around

in my top pocket for my ticket and travel card. They weren't there. My hugely expensive one-year travel card was now stopping at all stations to Uxbridge on the Piccadilly Line. I shut my eyes in defeat. When I opened them seconds later, I was at the top and thankfully no one was checking tickets at the barrier. I let out a sigh of relief and thought to myself: *Sometimes, life can be unusually kind.*

Opening the front door to the house, a depressing atmosphere of familiarity overwhelmed me. For five days this had been home. Five days, but it felt like a decade. I pressed the timer switch for the hallway light and checked the mail on top of the pay-phone. As I put the key in the door to my flat the lights went out.

7.20 P.M.

'Ahhh! You've been burgled!'

These were the words my ex-girlfriend, Aggi, used to turn and say to me every time she saw the state of my bedroom. It was our favourite running gag which, in spite of its asthmatic tendencies, used to have us in stitches every time.

Aggi and I split up exactly three years ago, not that I'd been counting the days or anything. I was aware of precisely how long it had been because she dumped me on my twenty-third birthday. And despite everything I'd done to forget the day I was born and the occasion of her dumping me, the date remained locked in a brain cell that refused to die.

I was woken that fateful day by the sound of silence; Simon and Garfunkel got that spot on: silence had a sound. Back then at my parents' house, if anyone was in and not comatose, silence never got a look in. Every action of the occupants was pursued without regard for the sleeping: washing machines at six in the morning, clinking cutlery, breakfast television, 'Have you seen my shoes, Mum?', shouting, and occasionally laughter. Living in the aural equivalent of Angola, I quickly learned to filter out the white noise of lower-middle-class family life.

Later, when my parents had gone to their respective places of work (he: Nottingham City Council; she: Meadow Hall

17

Retirement Lodge) and my kid brother, Tom, to school, the house was allowed to drift back into a restful peace. My brain, no longer filtering out anything more threatening than the occasional starling chirping in the garden, woke me up – silence was my alarm clock.

On top of my duvet lay a solitary brown manila envelope. Whenever post arrived addressed to me my dad would leave it there before going to work. I think he hoped the excitement of seeing it there would somehow galvanise me into action. It never did. Nothing could. At the time, I didn't receive many letters because I was a hopeless correspondent. It wasn't so much that I never wrote letters, I did frequently, I just never posted them. At any one time there were dozens of sheets of notepaper littered around my room with barely legible 'Dear so and so' scrawled across them. With nothing happening in my life I had very little to say beyond 'How are you?' and to have documented even the smallest slice of my mundane lifestyle ('Today I got up, and had Frosties for breakfast . . .') would have left me too depressed for words.

I was well aware of the contents of the envelope on my bed before I even opened it, as the day in question was Significant Wednesday, the bi-weekly religious festival that heralded my salvation – my Giro. My parents were, to say the least, not the happiest of bunnies when I, their first born, returned to the family nest to languish on the dole. Four years earlier they'd driven me – along with a suitcase, hi-fi, box of tapes and a *Betty Blue* poster – off to Manchester University, expecting me to gain a first-rate education, an ounce or two of common sense and a direction in life. 'We don't mind what you do, son, as long as you do it to the best of your ability,' they'd said, not bothering to hide the extreme disappointment in their collective voices when I announced that I intended to study English and Film Studies. 'Whatever for?' asked the two-bodied, one-headed guardians of my soul. Neither were they impressed with my explanation which basically boiled down to the fact that I liked reading books and I liked watching films.

Three years later, I concluded my journey on the educational conveyor belt and quickly gained a realistic perspective of my position in the world at large: I was over-educated in two subjects that were of little use outside of university without further training. Having only just scraped a 2:2, and bored with the education process as a whole, I bundled 'further training' into the box marked 'out of the question'. Instead, I applied myself to reading a few more books, watching a lot more films and signing on. I maintained this pattern for a year or so, until the bank got tough with me during a short-tenancy in a shared house in Hulme. In a two-pronged attack worthy of Rommel, my bank manager withdrew my overdraft facility and made me sign an agreement to pay £20 a week into my account to bring the overdraft down to 'something a little more reasonable'. And so, like a homing pigeon, I returned to the parental home in Nottingham and holed up in my bedroom, contemplating the Future. Both parents pulled any number of favours to help me get on the career trail, while my Gran telephoned with regular monotony informing me of jobs she'd seen in the local paper. Needless to say all their hard work was wasted on me. I wasn't interested in a career, I had a roof over my head and, I reasoned, as long as I had the love of a good woman being poor didn't much bother me.

I say 'much', because occasionally my impoverished state did in fact work me up into a frenzy of bitterness. Fortunately, I learned to express my powerlessness by scoring as many points against Them – as in 'Us and . . .' – as I could. These minor acts of guerrilla warfare included the following:

19

- Obtaining a NUS card under false pretences.

- Using the aforesaid card to gain cheap admission to the cinema.

- Altering out-of-date bus passes.

- Damaging fruit in Tesco's.

- Driving a car without road tax or insurance.

- Drinking complete strangers' pints in night-clubs.

I did anything which, generally speaking, kept my mind alive and made me feel like I was chalking up another point on my side of the great scoreboard of life. But it was Aggi who kept me sane. Without her I would have dropped off The Edge.

Aggi really was quite brilliant, the most wonderful person I'd ever had the pleasure of meeting in my life. When we first started going out together I used to walk her home and while we were kissing and hugging good-bye on her door step, my favourite thing to do was to concentrate my whole mind on capturing the Moment – her smell, the taste of her mouth, the sensation of her body pressed against mine – I wanted to photograph it and keep it forever. But it never worked. Within minutes of walking through the damp streets of West Bridgford, with drizzle in my hair and an ache in my loins, she was gone. I could never recreate the Experience.

We met in a charity shop during the summer break. Aggi was eighteen then and had just finished her A levels, while I'd just completed the first year of my degree. She worked at an Oxfam shop in West Bridgford which I'd been frequenting on a twice weekly basis, because of its high turnover of quality junk. I'd been waiting patiently for the doors to open since

9.25 a.m., but as the shop didn't officially open for another five minutes, I'd whiled away the time pressing my nose against the glass door pulling faces purely for my own amusement. Aggi had noticed one in particular – my impression of a gargoyle in mental distress – and had opened the doors two minutes early, laughing as she did so. We were alone apart from an old lady at the back of the shop listening to *Desert Island Discs* as she sorted clothes. That day Aggi wore a short-sleeved green dress with small yellow flowers on it and a pair of sky blue canvas baseball boots. The overall effect was, to be truthful, a little twee but somehow she made it look marvellous. I positioned myself in front of a few old Barry Manilow albums and pretended to look through them, because the rack that housed them was the ideal location for me to steal as many glances at this incredibly beautiful girl as I liked.

I was sure that she would feel my eyes watching her every move, because after a while I gave up all pretence of being interested in any of Barry's greatest hits and just gazed at her longingly instead. I smiled as I approached the till with my sole purchase, an Elvis mirror, the type found only at fun fairs, where something skilful with an air gun, dart or hoop has to be done to win one. Thanks to Aggi, I'd cut out the middle man. Elvis was mine.

'The King of Rock 'n' Roll.'

Those were the first words she ever said to me. I went back every day that week and over the following months and subsequent conversations we got to know each other well.

Me: Hi, what's your name?

Her: Agnes Elizabeth Peters. But it's Aggi to you.

Me: Why do you work here?
Her: My mum works here sometimes. I'm bored of staying at home so I help out sometimes, it's my contribution to helping humanity evolve. (Laughs) Plus it looks good on CVs.

Me: What do you do?
Her: I'm about to go to the Salford University to do Social Science.

Me: Why?
Her: (Looks slightly embarrassed) Because I care about people rather than money. I think it's wrong that people in this day and age should be homeless. Call me old-fashioned but I'm a socialist.

Me: Do you believe in platonic friendship?
Her: No. 'Platonic friendship is the moment between when you meet and your first kiss'. Don't applaud, I didn't say it first.

Me: Do you think Elvis really is dead?
Her: (Laughs) Yes. But his memory lives on in the hearts of the young, the brave and the free.

Me: What's your favourite film?
Her: This might sound a bit pretentious but I think film as a medium is nowhere near as expressive

as the novel. Having said that I must admit a distinct liking for Audrey Hepburn in *Breakfast at Tiffany's*.

Me: What's the weirdest thing you've ever thought?
Her: If there are an infinite number of parallel universes, containing all the alternate decisions I could've made, how would my life have turned out if I'd accepted Asim Ali's proposal of marriage when we were six?

Me: When was the last time you cried?
Her: Probably when I was six, after turning down Asim Ali. I don't know – I don't really do emotional histrionics that often.

Me: Do you love me?
Her: I love you so much that when I think about how I feel about you my brain can't begin to comprehend it. It's exactly like infinity. I don't understand it, but those are the limitations of my love.

Between the first question and the last was a period of about five months. We got together between 'Do you believe in platonic friendship?' and 'Is Elvis really dead?' which was the opening topic of conversation on our first proper date, in the brightly lit, overcrowded, not-in-the-least-bit-romantic lounge of the Royal Oak. Deep down, I always liked to believe that I knew things wouldn't work out between us. Nothing could have been that perfect unless it had its première on terrestrial television. The thing that swung it for me, the one thing that made me so sure, was our first kiss. It wiped away my fears and insecurities in an instant.

At the end of our first date I'd been unsure about where we stood with the boy-girl relationship thing. Yes, we'd held hands occasionally and flirted a great deal, but we hadn't kissed, at least not properly. At the end of the night I'd kissed her lightly on her left cheek, as I would my Gran, and made my way home after I'd made her promise to see me again. I'd spent the entire week prior to our next date in a tortured state of limbo. What had happened, exactly? We'd gone out together, yes, but had it only been a date for me? Perhaps for her it had been nothing more than a night out with a nice guy? Had I spent the last seven days dreaming of her unceasingly, while she could barely remember my name? I wanted an answer. I needed an answer. I even called her once to ask her, but my courage had faded and I'd put the phone down. I couldn't think of how to say what I wanted to know, which was basically: Am I your boyfriend?

'Am I your boyfriend?' is the kind of question a nine-year-old asks another nine-year-old. It had no place in a sophisticated relationship. I knew the rules – I was meant to be cool and relaxed, laid back and casual. At first maybe we'd 'see' each other (which meant that she'd still 'see' other people), then maybe we'd date (which would mean that she wouldn't see other people even though she might want to) and then finally we'd be boyfriend and girlfriend (by which time she wouldn't want to see other people because she'd be happy with me).

When the day of our second date finally arrived, we met outside a record shop, Selectadisc, as arranged. The plan, such as it was, revolved around spending the afternoon in the square outside the town hall feeding the pigeons (her idea). Only it didn't happen like that. The first thing she did on seeing me was to wrap her arms around me tightly and kiss me so fervently that I literally went weak at the knees. I'd never felt passion like it before. And this was the best bit: *she* looked straight into my eyes and asked *me* if she was my girlfriend. I said, 'Yes, you are my Legendary Girlfriend.'

The end of everything we had, everything we were and everything I'd hoped we'd be, also arrived with a kiss, one which I found myself reliving two or three times a day years later. It was my birthday and I'd only been back in Nottingham for a couple of weeks, while Aggi had been there all summer since graduating and was waitressing in a restaurant in town. We'd arranged to meet outside Shoe Express in Broad Marsh Shopping Centre. Aggi had got there before me, which should've set alarm bells ringing as she was frequently punctual but never early. She was empty-handed but the significance of this didn't occur to me until much later.

We had a glorious afternoon celebrating my twenty-third – maybe a little too glorious – wandering in and out of stores pretending to be a recently married couple furnishing our love nest. The conversation and humour made me feel alive, really alive. It didn't matter that I didn't have a job, future or money – I felt at peace with the world. I was happy.

Driving home I sat next to Aggi in her mum's Fiat Uno as we made our way through the city centre. Ten minutes before we should've been at her mum's house she pulled into Rilstone Road, a cul-de-sac near Crestfield Park, and stopped the car. Undoing her seat-belt, she turned her body towards mine and kissed me. There was no mistaking it – it was a 'good-bye' kiss.

It was a 'this isn't working' kiss.

It was a 'this is hurting me more than it's hurting you' kiss.

All I could think was: 'This is The Last Kiss.'

She said that for a long time she'd felt that I wanted more from her than she had to give.

She said I needed someone who could guarantee to be around forever.

She said that, while she did love me, she didn't think that was enough any more.

She said that she was twenty-one and I was twenty-three and that we should both be living our lives to the full but instead we'd got stuck in a rut.

She said that for a long time she'd had the feeling that we weren't going anywhere.

I said nothing.

At 5.15 p.m. I'd been a perfectly happy young man with everything to look forward to. By 5.27 p.m. my life was over. It took twelve minutes to dismantle three years of love.

I got out of the car, slamming the door behind me, walked to the nearest cashpoint, took out £50 and headed for the Royal Oak. There, despite my embarrassingly low threshold for alcohol, I drank three double Jack Daniels, a Malibu and Coke (out of curiosity) and a double gin and tonic (because it was the first drink I had ever bought Aggi).

On a whim, I got a taxi back into town and continued drinking, despite throwing up twice. Around midnight I ended up in a club called Toots, with a group of people whom I vaguely knew. Much of what then happened is hazy, although I do recall stealing at least three strangers' pints. Some weeks later, while bruising peaches in Tesco's, I was pounced upon by a fat, angry Irish girl who filled in the rest of the details. She claimed to have been at the club that night and said that I'd danced with her, shirt unbuttoned to the waist, to Abba's 'Dancing Queen'. According to her version of events, half an hour later she discovered me in a stall in the Ladies', lying curled at the side of a toilet bowl, crying desperately. My good Samaritan, worried that an earlier refusal to kiss me had had this effect, put me in the back of a taxi, but not before I'd thrown up over her shirt and told her that I loved her.

7.45 P.M.

It's a soul-destroyingly depressing fact that when you live in a place on your own, nothing moves. When I'd left the flat on Friday morning it had resembled Dresden after a flying visit from the RAF. Suitcases lay open, their contents spilled out across the floor. Cardboard boxes full of junk occupied valuable floor space. Soiled underwear lay abandoned in the oddest of places – the window sill, on top of the wardrobe, underneath the phone – while dirty crockery bred rapidly all around. And now, some twelve hours later, things were still pretty much the same. Maybe the air was a little staler or the dust on the TV a bit deeper, but on the whole nothing had changed. Back home in Nottingham, however, if I left my room – sometimes for as little as an hour – something always changed. Usually it was because my mother had kidnapped the dirty clothes off the floor, or sometimes because of my kid brother's general snooping; once, even my Gran got in on the act – playing detective. Inspired by a report on Young People and Drugs on *This Morning with Richard and Judy*, Gran had decided my sleeping in late and general lack of motivation was a result of drug abuse. In search of hard evidence she set about my room, but the nearest she got to crack was a yellow and blue tin that said Myoxil, and even then she still insisted on taking it to Boots to check it really *was* athlete's foot powder.

Dumping my bag on the sofa, I contemplated cleaning the flat. It was the sort of idea – along with ironing, visits to the launderette and letters to friends whom I hadn't seen since university – which I was inclined to conjure up when I had nothing better to do. The idea, however, was taken no further because I spotted a novel in one of the boxes which I'd given up on months ago, and decided that now was as good a time as any to finish what I'd started. I was about to pull out the sofa-bed – in order to delude myself that I was going to recline and read, rather than recline and sleep – when I decided that I might be hungry. There was nothing that my mother, or for that matter a dietician, would've construed as 'proper food' in the kitchen, but I lit up a cigarette from the emergency pack stashed in my suitcase to stave off immediate hunger pangs, and checked out the fridge for the sheer hell of it.

The yellowing refrigerator in the corner of the kitchen gurgling vociferously, as if suffering from a heavy bout of indigestion was, at a guess, probably a decade older than myself, as was virtually everything in the flat. The cooker, wardrobes, sofa-bed, carpet – the rigours of age had consumed them all to such an extent that it had rendered them useless unless you had the know-how. For instance, to get a ring on the cooker to work, the control knob had to be turned on and off twice; to open the wardrobe door, pressure had to be applied to the top right-hand corner. Had I noticed all that was wrong when I first saw the flat, I wouldn't have taken it, but at the time getting a roof over my head had seemed more important than checking wardrobe doors, and my landlord, Mr F. Jamal (at least that was the name I wrote on the rent cheques) had known this. His skills in interior design were so shoddy that he must have graduated with honours from the Rachman school of landlords. Every surface in the flat had been painted in cheap cheerless white emulsion some time in the last fifty years, which the passing of time and countless smokers had managed to downgrade to a pale orangey-brown. The only furniture in the room was a sofa-bed in fawn velvety material pitted haphazardly with cigarette burns; a tile-surfaced coffee table against the far wall which had the TV perched on it; and two small white Formica wardrobes along the wall opposite the window. To try and cheer the place up – an impossibly futile task – I had stuck my favourite photo of Aggi on the wall near the sofa-bed and an Audrey Hepburn poster on the wall in the bathroom.

I'd spent two solid weeks searching for accommodation. They were the second most depressing weeks of my life, requiring me to get the 07.15 National Express coach from Nottingham to London four times, in order to traipse around the slum districts of the capital. In this time I learned the two laws of looking for accommodation in London:

1. **Never trust a landlord while he's still breathing.**
2. **The only good landlords are four dead landlords.**

The only place I saw, could afford and which didn't have drug dealers in the vicinity was Flat 3, 64 Cumbria Avenue

– aka – N6. A luxurious self-contained studio flat with own kitchenette, bathroom/shower

– aka – a glorified studio flat, minus the glory, on the second floor of a decrepit Edwardian house in crappy Archway.

To be truthful, Mr F. Jamal hadn't advertised my abode in *Loot* or any other free ad newspaper. He hadn't needed to. He had a kind of word of mouth thing going amongst people in the know in the lower end of the accommodation food chain, so much so that his many properties were consistently snapped up within seconds of becoming available. I, however, became aware of his legendary status not by being in the know – but through Tammy, my friend Simon's girlfriend. She'd told him about Mr F. Jamal after I'd been moaning to Simon about the difficulty I was having. I'd looked at nine places, all complete and utter toilets 'five minutes' from the tube, the worst of which was a place in Kentish Town. The landlord arrived half an hour late for our appointment, by which time five other people had turned up to view the place he'd promised me first refusal on. It wasn't anything to shout about, just a double room with a shared toilet and kitchen. He told the assembled crowd that the man living there had changed his mind and wanted to stay, but he was going to put an extra bed in the room and did anyone want it. At this point I'd walked off in disgust but three of my fellow house-hunters were desperate enough to stay behind. Tammy gave Simon Mr F. Jamal's phone number. One call later and I was signing the lease. I had thought about thanking her for her effort, but as Tammy and I couldn't stand each other I hadn't bothered. I'd assumed her assistance was some kind of perverse tactic to get one over on me.

I opened the fridge door and peered in. The light didn't come on. I suspected it probably hadn't done so since the Apollo Moon landings. Peering amongst the abandoned items within: marmalade, margarine, tomato ketchup, a five-day-old can of beans and an onion – I spied a jar of olives and smiled heartily to myself.

Lying on the sofa in the main room, I lanced an olive while attempting to write my name on the cushion with my index finger – all the down strokes followed the flow of the material so half of it was missing. Time flowed by. I ate another olive and stared at the ceiling. More time flowed by. I ate another olive and tried to read my book. Yet more time flowed by. I ate another olive and let the brine drip off the end of the fork onto my chin and dribble down to my neck. At this point I decided it was time for action. I considered all the things that needed doing and chose the least painful: a begging letter to the bank. On a page of notepaper using a green Berol marker pen I'd stolen from school, I wrote:

Dear student banking advisor,

Having recently qualified from a teacher training course I'm now ready, at the age of twenty-five (nearly twenty-six) to take my place as a fully functioning member of society. I have a job but am living in London, and it is so ridiculously expensive to live here that I'm not sure why I bother. To this end please would you extend my already extended overdraft a bit more, because otherwise I may faint from starvation in front of a class of fourteen-year-olds.

Yours forever,

William Kelly

I chuckled aloud. I was just about to add 'PS and don't think that I've forgotten that you stitched me up when I needed you most', when I noticed the red light of the answering machine blinking away.

Next to the Walkman, I considered the answering machine to be one of man's truly great achievements. It allowed you to keep abreast of the latest developments in your social life *and* screen calls. Brilliant. My love for this particular piece of technology was inspired by a message Aggi left on my Aunt Susan's when I was house-sitting for her in Primrose Hill during the summer vacation of my second year. At the time, Aunt Susan lived in London, where she was beauty editor on *Woman's Realm* or some other similar magazine that had knitting patterns.

Aunt Susan, it must be said, was more unlike my mother than I thought possible for people who had shared the same womb. Twelve years younger than my mother – almost a generation apart – she had more in common with me. She hated work, was one of the first in her road to have cable television, and adored the third series of *Blackadder*. She used to tell me that she'd never get married because then she'd have to grow up. The summer after I came to house-sit, however, she got hitched, had my cousin Georgia, gave up journalism and moved back to Nottingham. On the occasion in question, she'd gone on holiday with Uncle-Bill-to-be, and said I could do whatever I wanted with the house as long as the police weren't involved. Fortunately for her all I did was watch videos, eat crisp sandwiches and walk her dog, Seabohm – hardly activities worthy of the scrutiny of the local constabulary. I'd been out walking the dog on this particular day, when I returned to the house to discover there was a message for me from Aggi:

You're not in! This is not how it was supposed to be. All I wanted to say was that I dreamt about you last night. We were in a field and the soundtrack to 'Singin' in The Rain' was playing in the background. We lay on our backs just staring at the moon. I want you to know I won't stop loving you. I promise you, I won't.

I listened to it over and over again. I wanted to keep it forever but it was sandwiched between a call from a PR called Madeline inviting Aunt Susan to the launch of a new range of Boots nail varnishes, and one from my mother checking to see if I was eating properly. When my aunt heard Aggi's message she said, and I remember this quite clearly: 'That sounds like Ms Right to me.' When I got back to Nottingham, I asked Aggi about the message but she refused to discuss it. That was just her way.

I played the messages back:

Venus calling Mars. Come in, Mars! Why are men so bloody competitive? Discuss. Hi, Will, Alice here. If you have an answer to this eternal conundrum, or indeed just fancy a chat with your best friend in the whole wide world – call me now!

Er, hi. This is Kate Freemans here. (Voice falters) I used to live in your flat. (Starts crying) I was just wondering if there was any mail for me. (Attempts to stop crying, instead snuffles loudly) The temp agency I was working for posted my cheque to the wrong address. I'll try and ring later. (Begins crying again) Thanks.

Listen, I've got something really important to tell you. Call me as soon as you can. It's urgent. Really urgent . . . oh, it's Simon by the way.

Will, it's Martina. I don't know why I'm leaving this message, I think your machine is broken, this is the third one I've left this week. Assuming that you've got it fixed, hello for the first time since Saturday night! Er, ring me, please. We need to talk. Bye.

Hello. This is Kate Freemans again. I'm just ringing to say sorry about my message. Just ignore it, okay? I'm really sorry.

My first thoughts were about the girl who used to live in my flat. It felt weird hearing a stranger's message on *my* answering machine, let alone one in which she was crying. As she hadn't left a number there was little I could do bar sit and wonder why my answering machine had reduced her to tears. Next up, I thought about Martina, even though I didn't want to. There was no way on earth I was going to return her call because she, as far as I was concerned, was a first rate nutter of the *Fatal Attraction* variety and I had no intention of playing Michael Douglas to her Glenn Close in her sordid little fantasy. I checked my watch. It was too late to catch Simon now, as I knew for a fact that his band would be on stage at the Royal Oak. Anyway, the message was so typically Simon — overblown and melodramatic — that it completely failed to pique even an iota of interest. And so by process of elimination, Alice's was the only message left worth returning, qualifying on the grounds that it was the only one that made me feel better.

I'd first met Alice on my sixteenth birthday. I'd been standing in the Royal Oak, discussing the finer points of the British soap opera compared to its weaker, less attractive Australian cousin, with two attractive fourteen-year-old girls who had taken it upon themselves to follow Simon's first band, Reverb. The girls had got it into their heads that Simon was good-looking and interesting, and I was busily trying to persuade them that I was a far better option, when I felt myself slipping away from the conversation. While my body gibbered away on terra firma, the important bit that made all the decisions focused its attention on a girl who looked like the French foreign exchange student of my dreams – dark-red hennaed hair, a beguiling smile and beautifully tanned skin – standing alone at the end of the bar observing Reverb's exceptionally abysmal cover of The Buzzcocks' Ever Fallen In Love. My brain alerted my body to its new discovery and both made their excuses to their captive teenage audience.

Chatting up girls had never been one of my strong points. Some people had that certain something needed not to look like a pillock while doing it. Simon, for instance, had it in abundance. I, however, didn't. On most occasions I would've resigned myself to this fact, content to gaze longingly at her rather than take up my desires and run, but this time was different. In a matter of half an hour I was convinced that this girl was the person I'd been looking for all my life – there was no way I was going to give up without trying.

At the end of the gig I approached her, using Reverb's performance to open up the conversation. She told me she thought they were terrible but the singer was quite cute – I was devastated. Right on cue, Simon, guitar in hand, strode across the room and introduced himself. 'Who's your friend?' he asked me 'casually'. I told him I didn't know and she smiled, offered her hand to him and introduced herself: 'My name's Alice. Alice Chabrol.' And that was that. I wasn't so much edged out as completely ignored. Admittedly I did receive compensation by way of a birthday kiss, 2.2 seconds of red-lipped perfection pressed against my cheek with the delicate touch of an angel's wing.

Simon and Alice went out for a total of two weeks before she came to her senses and realised that he could never be as interested in anyone as he was in himself. 'I hadn't thought it was possible,' she'd told me over coffee the day after she'd dumped him. 'Everything he says is *me me me*.' Alice and I, however, became best friends. Over the following years I fell in love with her several times but never felt compelled to tell her, there was no reason to – she never seemed the slightest bit interested in being anything more than friends. If I'd seen the faintest glimmer of hope I would've gone for it, but faced with Alice's lack of interest and the memory of her choosing Simon over me I gave up, thus cultivating the following theory:

Kelly's First Law of Relationships:

No woman who finds Simon attractive will ever be interested in me.

As if to prove this as fact, when Alice went to university at Oxford she fell for Bruce (a surrogate Simon if ever I saw one), a Maths postgraduate who bore more than a passing resemblance to Steve McQueen in *The Great Escape*. With the exception of his total expertise in every field known to impress man, his most annoying trait was his ability to make me feel like a eunuch without even trying. He wasn't so much a man as a hyper-man, masculinity dripping from his every pore. He worked out three times a week. He knew what an exhaust manifold was. He owned an autographed photograph of Bruce Lee. Honestly, even Sean Connery would've felt like a bit of a girl around Bruce.

Fortunately my blossoming inferiority complex began to fade once I came to see Bruce as my best friend's boyfriend instead of six feet four inches of tosspot, and Alice as my best friend rather than the woman I most wanted to see naked. I adapted so well to my new role that my earlier mini-infatuations – which at the time had seemed more important than life itself – now felt like boyish crushes from a bygone age. I still didn't like Bruce, but it was no longer personal. When you have a friend of Alice's calibre, you come to realise there's no way anyone in ownership of a penis will ever be worthy of her.

After Alice got a job as marketing manager for British Telecom, she and Bruce moved to Bristol and led the kind of life that involved expensive restaurants, shopping trips to Bond Street and weekend breaks in Prague. I considered being jealous of her quite a few times but I couldn't. Though she earned more in an hour than I used to get in my entire fortnight's Giro, she was still the same person inside: kind, patient and understanding. As a rule, I disapproved of successful people, especially those of my generation, but I couldn't resent her. Success not only suited her, it appeared to be made for her.

* * *

'Hello?' said Alice.

'It's me,' I replied.

'Will! How are you?' she said, genuinely excited. 'How's the job?'

'Oh it's crap. Kind of just what I expected only worse.' I felt a yawn rise up from deep inside me. I attempted to stifle it by gritting my teeth. 'Much worse.'

'Is that possible? I thought your motto was "Think of the worst thing possible and multiply it by ten".'

'Obviously I didn't think things could be worse than even *I* could possibly imagine them,' I replied, reflecting on how, since Aggi, it had become my personal philosophy to look on the dark, half-empty, who's-nicked-my-silver-lining side of Life.

'It's horrible,' I said, noticing that the photo of Aggi had fallen down. 'A total nightmare. I can't coast or take it easy for a second, otherwise they'll skin me alive. I can't show any weakness. The kids, they can smell weakness from a mile off. Once they catch a whiff it sends them wild. They're like a pack of hyenas pouncing on a wounded antelope. Sarah, another newly-qualified teacher, broke down in tears in front of a class on Thursday.' I fiddled with the Blu-tac on Aggi's photo and put it back up. 'I give her another week before she's looking at other career options.'

Alice laughed.

'It's not funny, you know.'

'No, of course it's not funny.'

It wasn't the least bit amusing because I'd had some bitter experiences of my own during the past week. On Monday three year-eleven boys had walked out of my class; Wednesday I'd returned to the staff room to discover that one of the little gits had spat a huge 'greenie' on the back of my jacket;

and Thursday I'd left my bottom year-eleven set's English books back at the flat.

'It can be like that,' said Alice adopting a tone of voice reminiscent of a reassuring rub on the small of the back.

I wasn't comforted. I wasn't happy. I was fed up. And Alice would never understand this. She had a 'career', whereas I had a 'job' and that was the difference between us. 'Careers' are about personal challenges, whereas 'jobs' are about survival. Granted, Alice's chosen occupation might have been stressful at times, but her targets were realistic and she had the grand resources of a multi-national at her disposal. As a teacher, I had to deal with ludicrously ambitious targets, zero resources, school inspections and sociopaths who thought spitting on a teacher's back was right up there with Monty Python's parrot sketch.

'How do you do it?' I wondered aloud.

'How do I do what?'

'You know,' I said, searching for the right word. 'That . . . work stuff. How do you cope with it all?'

'Experience, Will, experience,' said Alice warmly. 'I don't want to seem patronising but come on, Will, you put a lot of this pressure on yourself by expecting results too fast. I've been working four years now, but this is the first job you've ever had.'

Alice, to be frank, was being more than a bit of a cheeky cow, as she was well aware that I'd spent an entire summer working in the Royal Oak. I knew what hard work was: I'd shifted barrels of beer, brought up huge crates of mixers from the cellar and worked twelve-hour shifts, all of which I reminded her.

'It wasn't the whole summer,' said Alice, sniggering. 'It was four weeks, and you got sacked for continually being late, if I remember correctly.'

41

She was right, not just about my employment history but about my attitude to work. I wanted everything to be perfect straight away, because the thought of it taking time and patience to learn how to control these animals made me feel sick.

During the course of this part of the conversation I'd become aware that something about Aggi's picture didn't look right. It was only as Alice told me some gossip about a mutual acquaintance who had been caught shoplifting, that I realised the photo was sloping a little to the right. I took it down to readjust it but creased it in the process. This was my favourite picture of her – taken before she'd had her bob; her long ringlets of auburn hair, which at times overwhelmed the delicate features of her face, were tied back leaving her beautiful green eyes, kissable lips and delicate nose on full display. She was leaning against a wall outside the university library, reading *The Beauty Myth*. She looked perfect.

My feet began to itch. I took off my sock and gave my toes a rub.

'Do you think you'll stick it out?' asked Alice. 'I mean, you sound pretty stressed out.'

I told her I didn't know and explained the crux of my problem – teaching in the training year was nothing like teaching was now. This was For Real. The kids were depending on me to help them pass their exams. The ramifications of my being a crap teacher were terrifyingly immense.

'Imagine thirty kids fail their English GCSE because of me – thirty kids who will get a rubbish job or no job at all sucked into the poverty trap. Five years later, half of them will have kids and be living off social security. Multiply that by a couple more years of me teaching, and before you know it I'll be responsible for increasing unemployment in the UK more than any government, Conservative or Labour, since the war.'

'You're overreacting,' said Alice. 'You've got to face facts, Will. You're a grown-up. Grown-ups have responsibilities.'

'You know what I mean,' I said, while pulling off my other sock and rubbing between the toes on my now naked foot. 'These kids won't know anything unless I teach it to them. What if I'm a crap teacher?'

I sensed Alice was having problems seeing my perspective. Too tired to continue making my point, I changed discussion topics. Over the next half hour – in which time I'd put my socks back on but taken my trousers off and draped the duvet around me – Alice told me how she was working out of the Peterborough office for a month and living in a Novotel in the city centre because of a project she was overseeing. The only time I'd ever been to a hotel was when Aggi and I had saved fourteen coupons from the *Daily Telegraph*, which had got us a half price night at the Nottingham Holiday Inn. We stole the shampoos, shower caps and even the miniature kettle before vacating the room the next day. It had been brilliant. I was about to remark how cool it must be to live in a hotel at someone else's expense when it occurred to me that Alice probably saw things a bit differently.

'What about Bruce?' I asked, remembering the times I'd really missed Aggi, like when she went on holiday to Austria for two weeks with her mum, or when she had her wisdom teeth out and had to stay in hospital on my twenty-first birthday. Both times I'd missed her so much I literally thought I'd die. 'Isn't he missing you?'

'Yes, he is,' she said sadly. 'At least I think he is. That's what my message on your machine was about. I think he feels threatened by the fact that things are going so well at work for me at the moment. He's been throwing himself into his work as if he's got something to prove to me – I don't know – that he's the main bread winner. As if I cared! He's been working late most nights, even some weekends. Once this project is over I'm going to ask for a transfer to a less frantic department. Maybe then he won't feel the need to compete and we can just be happy.'

I got the impression that Alice was unsettled for the rest of our conversation – I wished I hadn't reminded her of Bruce's absence. Hiding her sadness under the guise of a merry gossip she told me about the gym she'd joined and how her friend at work, Tina, was having an affair with her supervisor, and how she and Bruce were planning to go to New York over Christmas.

Before she finished the call she brought up the subject of my birthday.

'I know you hate birthdays, Will.'

'And Walkers prawn cocktail crisps . . .'

'But I . . .'

'And totalitarian governments . . .'

'. . . really wanted to . . .'

'And sticky-outty belly buttons . . .'

'. . . do something . . .'

'And Alfred Hitchcock films.'

'. . . special . . .'

I ran out of things to hate.

'I hope you don't mind,' said Alice.

I tutted softly and told her I didn't. She refused to elaborate on what 'something special' would entail, said good-bye, and promised to call me on my birthday. As I replaced the phone I whispered a small prayer of thanks to whoever was responsible for introducing this angel into my life.

10.01 P.M.

Peak time Friday night. Office workers, labourers, cleaners, architects and all, wash themselves free of the fetid stench of Work. This was the moment they were finally allowed to forget they were office workers, labourers, cleaners, architects or whatever, and remember, perhaps for the first time in five days, that first and foremost, they were people.

All week I'd been a Teacher. But what I wanted now was to be a Human Being.

I should've been out there with the office workers, labourers, cleaners and architects.

> I should've been getting my round in.
> I should've been making jokes about my boss.
> I should've been onto my sixth bottle of Molson Dry.
> I should've been dancing somewhere.
> I should've been out on the pull.

But I wasn't . . .

While everyone in the Western hemisphere was *out* having a great time, I was *in* having a crap time. This of course explained why none of the second-division friends in my sodding address book – people whom I only ever contacted

45

when really, really desperate – were in. Of the six calls made I got one no answer, two requests to enter into dialogue with answering machines and for the rest, I got the unobtainable tone. I refused to leave any messages on the grounds that there was no way I was letting anyone – least of all friends I rarely spoke to – know I was in on a Friday night and desperate for their company, while they were out starting their weekends with a bang.

I looked at my watch and wondered optimistically if it was telling the wrong time. I called the speaking clock:

At the third stroke it will be Ten-o-six-and-fifty-seconds.

Not altogether dissimilar to the time on my watch.

At moments like this, when loneliness seemed like my only friend, the only place safe to hide from the world at large was under the sheets. It was time to get out the sofa-bed.

The sofa-bed was pretty diabolical as a sofa and not that much better as a bed; the fact that these two nouns were joined together by a single hyphen failed to make the object they described any more comfortable than Dralon-covered paving stones. I threw its two cushions to the floor to reveal the depressing sight of the bed's underside. It always required more strength than I thought I had to pull the bed frame out. I took a deep breath and pulled. It slowly creaked into action, unfolding stubbornly.

Leaving my socks and shirt on, and pulling the duvet off the floor, I lay on the bed and tried desperately to forget the cold and the reason I'd retired there in the first place. The need to hear another human voice became paramount in my mind.

I turned on the radio on my hi-fi, hoping that *The Barbara White Show* would be on. I'd been listening to her show on Central FM all week. Barbara White was the 'larger-than-life' host of a phone-in show where assorted nutters, losers, weirdos and plain helpless cases called in with their problems. Barbara – a woman about as qualified to advise as I was to teach – listened, made the appropriate sympathetic noises and then came up with answers so facile she honestly had to be heard to be believed. The fact that she was American was probably the only reason she got away with giving such screamingly obvious advice.

Barbara was talking to Peter, a student from Newcastle-under-Lyme, who had just finished his A levels and had got into his local university to study Engineering. He wasn't happy, though. His girlfriend of seven months was going to university in Aberdeen and he was worried that the huge distance would drive a wedge between them.

It occurred to me as I listened to his pitiful story that Peter was being naive in the extreme. He'd been in a relationship for less time than it takes to make a baby and here he was wanting to make commitments. If I'd been his age I would have been over the moon at the prospect of hitting university as a single man – able to do what I want, when I want, with thousands of like-minded individuals who also think they've just invented sex, alcohol and staying up past 2.00 a.m.; people who'd want to party, party, party 'til they were sick and then party some more. Peter was guaranteed to have three years more exciting than my next ten.

I was so entrenched in my bitter attack against Barbara's caller I managed to miss most of her solution. All I heard her ask was, 'Do you love this girl?' and he replied he didn't know – he thought he did but probably wouldn't be sure until it was too late. As Barbara announced she was going to a commercial break, the phone rang.

I knew it wouldn't be Simon – his gig didn't finish until eleven; it was too late for either of my parents; I'd just spoken

47

to Alice and as far as I knew no one else had my number. The odds were, of course, that it was Martina, because my life was like that: too much of what I didn't want and a permanent drought of the things my heart desired most. I hoped with all my strength that it wasn't Martina, because as well as not feeling up to listening to her complain about how terrible her life was, I especially didn't want to dump her, at least not right now.

Ring!

Please don't let it be Martina.

Ring!

Please don't let it be Martina.

Ring!

Please.

Ring!

Please.

Ring!

Please. Please. Please.

Ring!

Please. Please. Please. Please!

I answered the phone.

'Hello?' I held my breath and waited for the first sounds of Martina's placid yet disturbing voice.

'Hello,' said the female voice on the other end of the phone, which clearly wasn't Martina's. There was a school-girlish enthusiasm about it that would've been refreshing had it not been me she was talking to. *Whoever this person is*, I thought, *this call is going to disappoint her*.

'Can I help you?' I asked politely.

'You can indeed,' she replied. 'I'm sorry to call so late but I thought if you're anything like me it's better to have a call late at night rather than early in the morning. My mum tries to ring me at seven in the morning sometimes just to tell me I've got a letter from the bank. Mind you, I'm never in at that time these days because I'm on my way to work, but if someone rang me on say, my day off, then boy, would they be in big trouble.'

She was rambling. The more she rambled the more adorable she sounded.

'I was wondering,' she continued, 'whether you could help me. I used to live in your flat up until a week ago . . .' She paused as if reaching the punch-line. I suddenly recognised her voice. She was Crying Girl from my answering machine. 'I was wondering . . . has there been any post for me? I'm expecting a cheque to arrive. I was doing a bit of casual office work for a temp agency and they've sent my cheque to my old address, even though I'd told them a million times that I was moving to Brighton.'

'Mmmm,' I said, thinking it sounded sympathetic.

There was a long pause.

I was about to offer another 'Mmmm' to fill the gap in the conversation when she spoke again. 'Well . . . is there any post?'

Instead of answering her question I deconstructed her voice. It was quite pleasant, really. The sort of voice that made me feel at ease; it was a bit well spoken at the edges but far from aloof. No, this girl sounded like she was definitely worth investigating, especially as there was the small point of her tearful message. I wanted to ask about it but couldn't quite work out how to do it.

'Sorry?' I said.

'Is there any post?' she repeated. 'I'm sorry for phoning so late but the cheque's quite important. I need it to pay this month's rent.'

I finally woke up. 'Oh, sorry. No, there's no mail for you. There's a big pile of stuff downstairs that no one's touched all week. People who used to live here ages ago, I think. But I've been through it and I didn't see any addressed to this flat.'

'Really?' she said disappointedly.

'Really. Tell me, what's your name?' I asked, quickly adding: 'So I can check again, if you like,' so that it didn't sound like a chat-up line.

'Katie,' she said. 'Or Kate rather.' She laughed. 'No, that's Kate Freemans, not Kate Rather!'

'As in the catalogue,' I quipped and then desperately wished I hadn't.

She laughed.

'Right,' I said. 'I'll just be a second while I nip downstairs and check them again.'

'Oh, thanks,' she said gratefully. 'It's nice of you to go to all this trouble.'

I put the phone on the bed and raced down the stairs in my boxer shorts, socks and shirt ensemble. Picking up the discarded post, I shot back upstairs, slamming the door behind me.

'There's loads for Mr G. Peckham,' I said, breathlessly shuffling through the letters. 'He's got a lot of stuff from the AA.' This was small talk of the tiniest variety, but I didn't have any other choice if I wanted to keep talking to her. 'There are two letters for a K. D. Sharpe, all with New Zealand stamps, and the rest is boring junk mail stuff. Sorry, nothing for a Kate Freemans.'

'Well, thanks for looking,' she said stoically.

'Maybe it'll turn up tomorrow,' I replied in a cheery tone which was very un-me. 'The post's pretty crap around here. It's my birthday on Sunday and I haven't received a single card yet. If they don't arrive tomorrow I won't have any on the day.'

'I'm sure you will,' she said, her disappointment at being cashless seemingly evaporated. 'How old will you be?'

'Do you really want to know?' I knew it was a stupid question the moment it slipped off my tongue and into the conversation. She wasn't going to say no, but it wouldn't be a truthful yes, either. She wasn't honestly going to give a toss about how old I was.

'Yes,' she said, so clearly, so confidently, so joyfully, that I was totally convinced she'd told the truth. 'But don't tell me. I'll guess. Are you thirty-one?'

'No.'

'Older or younger?'

'Younger.'

'Twenty-nine?'

'Lower.'

'Twenty-six?'

'Got it in one! Well, three actually. But well done anyhow. How did you guess? Do I sound twenty-six?'

This, of course, was stupid question number two. Where all this inanity was coming from I couldn't begin to guess, perhaps, I mused, I'd become a portal between Earth and Planet Stupid.

'I don't know,' she said. 'How does a twenty-six-year-old sound?'

'Although technically speaking,' I explained, 'I'm not actually twenty-six until Sunday, they do happen to sound a lot like me. The male variety, of which I consider myself to be a prime specimen, tend to whinge a lot about receding hair lines, loss of physique, life, work, love-life (or lack of love in their life) while constantly harking back to some golden age, usually their university days. It's quite a monotonous sound but comforting all the same.'

Kate laughed. With my hand on my heart, and a finger hovering over the self-destruct button marked, 'Cheesy Similes', I swear that her laughter perfectly captured summertime – the sun on my neck, birds singing in trees and cloudless skies – all at once.

'And what about you?' I asked. 'How old are you?'

She didn't speak.

'Okay,' I said. 'You're twenty-one or twenty-two?'

'Nope.'

'Higher or lower?'

'What do you think?'

'Lower.'

'You're right.'

'Twenty?'

'Er, nope.'

'Nineteen?'

'Yup,' she said. 'But I'll be twenty in November.'

There was a long pause.

The long pause grew longer.

The long pause grew so long that unless one of us said something soon, the only thing left to say would be good-bye. I panicked and said the first thing that came into my head.

'Ahhhhh.'

There was another long pause.

'What does "Ahhhhh" mean?' enquired Kate, mimicking my 'Ahhhhh' note perfectly.

I hadn't a clue what to say next and was running out of plausible ideas at an alarming rate. 'Nothing really. Well not much anyhow. It's just that . . . I used to know a Katie at junior school. She was the fastest runner in the whole of our year until she was ten. It was amazing. I've never seen a girl go so fast. I've often wondered whether she ever made it to the Olympics or anything like that. You're not that Kate, are you?'

''Fraid not, Mr Spaceman,' said Kate.

'Spaceman?' I repeated.

'I don't know your name.'

'No, you don't, do you?' I thought of making one up purely for my own amusement, but somehow the honesty and the purity of her voice shamed me into not being so pathetic. 'Names are irrelevant. They're just labels. I mean, how can you tell what a child should be called before they've even had a chance to do anything?'

I was well aware of how pompous it sounded, because I'd thought exactly the same thing when I heard Simon say it to a girl at a party. The reason I was employing its use now was that I desperately wanted to ape the fantastic results he'd got using it.

'Don't you like your name?' asked Kate.

'It's all right,' I said nonchalantly. 'But it's not the name I would have chosen.'

She laughed, which wasn't exactly the reaction I'd been looking for. I asked her what she found amusing and she said something about boys being all the same and then asked me what name I would've chosen, which proved unfortunate as I couldn't remember which name Simon had used.

'I . . . I don't know,' I said nervously. I jammed the phone up against my ear with my shoulder, leaving my hands free to frantically tear the letter I'd written to the bank into little pieces.

'I think I'd call you James,' she said playfully.

I was intrigued. James? I listed all of the cool Jameses I

could think of: James Bond (shaken but not stirred cool), James Brown ('soul power' cool) and James Hunt (daredevil motor racing cool) – in spite of my list and the fact that the odds were a million to one against, I couldn't help feeling she had a different James in mind. James Baker, to be exact, a small lad in the year below me in junior school who perpetually had scabs around the edge of his lips.

'Why James?' I asked defensively.

'I don't know,' she said whimsically. 'You just sound like a James. But if names are irrelevant why did you ask me what mine was?'

'Because I wanted to know how wrong your parents were.'

'And how wrong were they?' asked Kate guardedly.

'Only quite wrong,' I answered. 'Not far off the mark, I suppose. Three out of ten for effort.'

The rude streak that dwelled within me had risen to the surface. I'd like to pretend that my obnoxiousness was part of my seduction technique but it wasn't. It was sheer blatant crapness. My mouth always ran away with itself, intoxicated by the power it wielded. It happened any time I came face to face with genuine niceness, as if scientifically testing the limitations of my chosen subject's pleasant nature – to see how far was too far.

'Are you trying to be offensive?' she asked, more stunned than hurt.

'No, I'm sorry,' I said, apologising profusely. 'Forgive me, I'm stupid. It's just . . . it's just that I'm just having a bit of a rough time at the moment.'

'What's the matter?' asked Kate, genuinely concerned.

I tried to stop myself but couldn't.

'It's my girlfriend,' I said. 'She dumped me.'

'Oh, I'm sorry to hear that. I know how you feel. It's terrible when things like that happen. I feel terrible. Your girlfriend's just dumped you and here I am wittering on about cheques.'

'Oh, don't worry,' I said cheerfully, momentarily forgetting my grief. 'It's not like she's just done it.'

'So when did it happen?'

'Three years ago.'

The whole story came out. During the appropriate breaks in my narrative, Kate made supportive 'uh-huh' noises which made me feel even worse. Here I was wasting the time of an interesting, velvet-voiced and quite possibly good-looking girl, telling her about my ex, when any man with any sense would've been trying their best to chat her up.

When I'd finished my story, roughly an hour later, without pausing she told me that I ought to be strong. She herself was recovering from a recent break-up of a relationship.

'That's why I was crying on your answering machine – thank you for not mentioning it, by the way – phoning the flat reminded me of living there, which reminded me of being there with my boyfriend, which reminded me of the fact that he had dumped me.'

I thought she was going to start crying, but she didn't. Instead she took her turn in what was quickly becoming a miniature self-help group for that small but vocal strata of society known as The Dumped. Her boyfriend – whom she refused to refer to as anything but 'my ex' or occasionally 'that heartless bastard' – had dumped her three weeks earlier, totally out of the blue. They'd been together for six perfect months.

'I lost the plot for a while,' said Kate, 'I really did. I used to lie in bed just staring at the ceiling. I even unplugged the phone just in case he ever tried to call me again. I didn't eat because I knew that I'd throw up. I didn't see anyone – not even friends – for nearly two weeks. I just stayed in watching telly and eating Hobnobs.' She laughed. 'Talking of which . . .' I listened to a packet rustle and the sound of an oat-based biscuit being delicately masticated. She made a satisfied kind of cat noise and continued: 'That's better. And then one day I just woke up. I said to myself, I can spend the rest of my life mourning his loss or I can get on with my life. Which is what I did.'

I marvelled at her confidence. She'd managed to do the one thing I could never do – she'd moved on. But the more I thought about it the less impressed I was. There was no way she could have loved her ex the way I loved Aggi, otherwise she'd be as crippled by misery as I was. The two cases weren't comparable.

Kate continued: 'I've never understood why people insist on saying things like, "There's plenty of other fish in the sea." My mum actually said that to me, you know, after I was dumped by the person formerly known as 'my boyfriend'. There's me crying my heart out and all she was offering me by way of consolation was a fish metaphor! She wouldn't have said that if that heartless bastard had died horribly in a car crash. She wouldn't have said, never mind Kate, there are plenty of other boyfriends out there who have the advantage over your ex of not being dead.'

She had a good point.

Just as I was wondering what to say next, out of the blue she said, 'Between grief and nothing, which would you choose?'

I recognised the quotation straight away. I knew it because me, Aggi, Simon and his then girlfriend, Gemma Walker (shelf-life three weeks, two days) had spent one Saturday afternoon, four years ago, watching *Breathless*, the Richard Gere version of Godard's *A Bout de Souffle* as research for an essay I was writing on Hollywood adaptations of non-English speaking films. I'd chosen the title because it meant I got to watch *The Magnificent Seven*, too, although the downside of that was having to endure *The Seven Samurai*, as well, which, to put not too fine a point on it, was about as meaningful as my moderately flabby arse. In one scene, Gere's girlfriend – played magnificently by Valerie Kaprisky – reads aloud a passage from a book and then drops it as she kisses him. Simon and I spent five minutes advancing that scene frame by frame to find out what the book was, because the passage made such a lasting impression on the both of us.

'That's from *The Wild Palms*,' I said excitedly, as if Kate was in a position to award ten house points *and* a gold star. 'William Faulkner.'

'Is it?' said Kate. 'I didn't know. That heartless bastard wrote it in a letter he sent after he finished with me.'

'Oh,' I said awkwardly.

'Well, what's your answer?' she asked.

I told her my answer would be nothing. She didn't believe me. But it was true. If I had to do it all again I wouldn't have gone out with Aggi. I would have walked straight out of Oxfam that day, albeit without my Elvis mirror, but thankful in the knowledge that at least my sanity and self-respect would be intact in years to come.

'But what about the good times?' probed Kate. 'You must've had some good times, surely?'

'Yeah, we had some good times,' I said, quickly flicking through some of them in my head. 'But at the end of the day what have I got? Nothing but memories. I'm twenty-six and I constantly live in the past. I've been without Aggi longer than I was with her and I still can't get over her. Ignorance, compared to this, would be bliss.'

Kate was beginning to tire of me. I could feel it. I wanted to tell her my whole life story. I wanted to tell her everything that was inside me. But I was convinced I was boring her.

'Am I boring you?' I asked, trying to make the question sound casual.

'No, why should I be bored?' Kate asked.

'No, well, maybe just a little bit,' I confessed. 'It's appalling that you have to listen to me droning on like this. Sometimes I'm so boring even I stop listening.'

She laughed. It still sounded like summertime.

'Kate, tell me about you,' I said, lighting up a cigarette. 'Tell me something I don't know about you.'

'Like what?'

'I don't know, anything you want.'

'I can't think what to tell you,' said Kate. She paused. I took a deep drag on my cigarette. 'Okay, I've got it. Ask me three questions that you want answers to and I'll ask you three.'

I agreed. My mind was racing, trying to think of questions that would be intriguing, sexy and yet devastatingly witty.

'Where do you live?'

'Good question,' said Kate. I tried to detect the irony in her voice. There was none. 'Let's sort the geography out.'

Kate lived in a flat in Brighton with her best friend Paula. Paula was out with her mates from work, which pleased me immensely because I liked the idea of the two of us being alone, talking conspiratorially late at night. Kate had stayed in because she had no money. She'd dropped out of her first year at the University of North London, where she'd been reading East European Studies ('We were known as the "Euro Studs"').

'So why did you leave?'

'Because I was going to get kicked out anyway,' said Kate, sighing. 'I hardly went to any lectures. I was in love. It seemed more important to be with my ex than learn about the history of the European trade agreements or have a social life. He was always having to go away and then I'd miss him so much that . . .' Her voice began to falter. She took a deep breath and the tone of her voice changed, as if she'd made a conscious decision to try and never think about him again. 'He's history.'

'Do you miss London?' I asked, adding: 'This is my second "official" question, by the way.'

She laughed and said: 'I don't miss London at all. It's too expensive, it's grimy, it's dirty and it's unfriendly. It reminds me of him. I like Brighton. My flat's only five minutes from the sea. And I love the sea.'

I thought long and hard about my third question. I thought of funny things to ask, I thought of poignant things too, but there was only one thing that I wanted, almost needed, to know. It was about her boyfriend. A subject that was now clearly off limits. As usual I succumbed to my compulsion.

'What was your ex like?'

'He was just a guy,' replied Kate without hesitation. 'Just a guy who thought he meant the world to me and was right. But between grief and nothing, I'd take grief.'

She refused to say anything more.

'I know you only said three,' I said, almost, but not quite, shyly, 'but I've got another question.'

'Ask away,' said Kate.

'Will you phone me again soon?'

'I don't know,' she replied. 'We'll have to see.'

11.45 P.M.

When she'd put the phone down I tried to dismiss her from my mind but I couldn't – she wouldn't go. Instead I went over the answers I'd given to her three questions.

Her: Who was the first girl you ever fancied?

Me: Vicki Hollingsworth. I was in my early teens. It didn't work out. Too many complications.

Her: What's your worst habit?

Me: Making pot noodle sandwiches. (Pause) Smoking. (Pause) Lying. (Pause) Thinking about my ex-girlfriend.

Her: Why do you want me to call again?

Me: Because.

Her: Because what?

Me: Because.

I considered returning to the entertainment of *The Barbara*

White Show, but the early morning rise to work – still something of a shock to a body that preferred to run on dole time – was beginning to take its toll. It took roughly an hour, door-to-door, to get to school in the mornings. It wouldn't have been so bad if I could have strolled in at the same time as the kids, but it was frowned upon by Mr Tucker if members of staff weren't on site by 8.15. So unless I wanted his miserable, wart-ridden, beardy face chastising me on a daily basis, I had to leave the flat at 7.15 – requiring me to get up at 6.45! It was a killer. I tried a variety of methods to cut my getting-ready-to-go-to-work time down and thus lengthen the time spent in bed. I stopped brushing my teeth and instead squirted the toothpaste directly into my mouth; I showered in the evening instead of morning; and wore my trainers on the journey to work in case I had to sprint at any point. Somehow, no matter what I did, I always ended up leaving a half-eaten bowl of Honey Nut Loops in the kitchen sink and chewing a piece of toast while jogging up Holloway Road.

Off went my shirt and socks as I got back into bed. They landed in a crumpled pile next to my trousers. These clothes, my School Clothes, were completely alien to the real me. Until I started on my teacher training course, I'd managed to avoid going into branches of Burton's, Next or Top Man for over a decade. There was something about High Street men's shops that I despised more than fascism, landlords and neighbours who parked their cars outside my house. The combination of half-wit YTS trainees, terrible decor and the clientele – adolescent boys with clothing allowances, engineering students, and girlfriends with Zero Taste looking for a 'nice' jumper for their boyfriends – was all too much for me. All my clothes were second-hand, purchased from Imperial Cancer Research shops and the like. I had two wardrobes full of what Simon and I referred to as 'Dead Men's Clothes' – the sort of items only widows and bitter divorcees throw away. My whole wardrobe – consisting of literally dozens of items – had cost less than fifty quid in total, but it wasn't the money that mattered, what really counted was that it added to my sense of individuality. The look I was working towards was a cross between Clint Eastwood in *Magnum Force* and Richard Rowntree in *Shaft*. While I freely admit I wasn't exactly there, I was close enough to feel different from the rest of the crowd. Teaching, unfortunately, was about conformity, and even I could see that a complete fashion rethink was in order if I was ever going to get a job.

The trousers were from Burton's. They were black and had turn-ups. Looking down at them from the bed, I noticed that the seat was going shiny. The shirt was from Top Man (urrgh!) and was one of five purchased one size too small. As I handed over my money, the youth at the till had asked me if I was sure they were the right size. I said yes, because he was a seventeen-year-old with acne and I was a graduate in English Literature and Film Studies which, I considered, made me infinitely more qualified in the intricacies of shirt sizes than he was.

I got out of bed and turned off the light. Light from the street lamps in Friar Avenue, which ran along the end of the garden, made the curtains glow spookily, casting shadows around the room. As I put my head down I lifted it back up immediately and picked up the clothes off the floor to put underneath my head. One of the items I'd forgotten to pack was a pillow, and as I wasn't entirely sure which sort of shops sold pillows I'd managed without. I made a mental note to ask Kate about it if she ever phoned again.

Kate is definitely an interesting girl, I thought, hoping I might dream about her. *She sounds like she'd be fun to be with. She seems different from other girls. Not like . . .*

The phone rang.

'Hi, Will, it's me,' said a voice I knew only too well belonged to Martina. All things considered she sounded reasonably chirpy.

'I hope you don't mind me phoning so late,' she said meekly. 'It's just that . . . well . . . you haven't returned any of my calls this week. I thought perhaps it might be your phone playing up but I got the operator to check that the line was working properly.'

It was time for some quick thinking:

a) Amnesia?
b) Too busy?
c) Answering machine not working?
d) The truth?
e) All of the above?

'I didn't know you'd phoned earlier,' I lied, trying with all my strength to sound surprised. 'I don't think the answering machine is working. I'm really sorry.'

'It's okay,' she said hushing my apologies, 'it's not your fault, I'm sure you'll have been too busy making new friends to call me back until the weekend. It must be so exciting, Will. More exciting than anything I could offer you.'

Martina had got into the habit of speaking to me like that – putting herself down in order, I think, to elevate me even higher in her esteem – from the moment I'd kissed her. It was a manipulative trick which pathetic people, myself included, used to make the object of their affections say something nice about them. Martina wasn't fishing for compliments – her earnestness was such that I just knew she was one of those people who meant every word they said and never said anything they didn't mean.

I ignored her bowing and scraping. 'So, how have you been doing?'

'Not too bad,' she sighed, making the 'oooo' in 'too' sound like an asthmatic owl. 'I still haven't found any work yet. I've signed on with some teaching agencies though – they think I might be able to get something quite soon. But as for a staff job, I don't think there'll be any of those going until after Christmas.'

I hated to admit it, but she did sound genuinely sad, lost and very lonely.

'How's it going at your parents' house?' I asked.

'I hate it, Will,' she said bitterly. 'I really hate it. I wish I was in London with you. Wouldn't that be brilliant? I could get a flat downstairs from you and I could make you dinner and we could watch that TV series you're always telling me about.'

'*Blackadder*,' I prompted.

'Yes, *Blackadder*,' she said wistfully. 'That would be my dream come true, Will. It really would.'

This wasn't some off-the-cuff remark, like 'Oh, wouldn't it be nice if . . .' She was serious. She'd probably transported herself to this scene in her head thousands of times as she sat in her bedroom filling out application forms. I knew this, of course, because I'd spent a lot of my own spare time imagining similar scenarios with Aggi.

'It won't be forever,' I reassured her. From my position on the bed, I craned my head trying to see the night sky through the bits of window that were visible because the curtains didn't meet in the middle. 'You'll get a job. You've got very good references. You'll . . .'

'I miss you, Will,' interrupted Martina.

There was no time for thought. The tone of her voice demanded an immediate reaction. Here was my chance. I could break her heart without saying a single word or I could make her day. I had this power – this all-consuming power – and I didn't want it. I didn't want it more than I'd ever not wanted anything because, metaphorically speaking, I was going to have to look down at this human manifestation of a seal pup, all big eyes and cuteness, and bludgeon its brains out.

'I miss you too, Martina,' I whispered quietly, hoping that neither her nor my conscience would hear me.

She sighed heavily with relief.

This couldn't carry on; I knew this of course. I'd made another huge mistake. She didn't want my pity – she wanted my affections. And I had none to give. I had to tell her the Truth.

'Martina?' This time the tone of *my* voice must have given the game away because she didn't reply. I could feel her tensing down the phone line, bracing herself for the blow, waiting for her world to end. I'd seen the family dog, Beveridge, do a similar thing when he thought I was going to tell him off. He refused to come when I called him, but waited, savouring the last few moments of Life as it Was before it turned into Life as it Is.

What was I going to say?

Martina, I'm sorry, but this just isn't working out.

Too harsh.

Martina, it's not you, it's me. It's all my fault.

Too soft. She'd just think I was having a bad day.

Martina, I don't know how to say this so I'll come straight out with it, this isn't working out.

Straight to the point. Firm but fair. Nice one.

'Martina,' I began, 'I don't know how to say this . . .'

'Don't say it, Will,' said Martina. 'I know exactly what you're going to say and I feel the same way too.'

'What?' I exclaimed.

'I feel the same way, Will,' she continued, spilling her confusion down the line. 'I know we've only been together since last weekend but what does time matter? Will, I love you too.'

I was well aware how large my active vocabulary was, and yet not a single word or phrase sprang to my lips in my own defence. I was speechless, although I'm sure she took the length of time I took to respond as a sign that I was inwardly returning the sentiment, too overcome with emotion to vocalise my affection. I just couldn't work out why she was telling me she loved me when all that we'd shared was the briefest of brief encounters over a week ago.

'Look, Martina . . .' I began, but stopped mid-sentence. Even fired by anger I couldn't allow myself to get straight to the point. 'Martina, it's late. I'm tired. It's been a really long week. I'd like to go to sleep now. I'll talk to you tomorrow, okay?'

'Dream of me,' she whispered sweetly.

'Yeah, all right. Whatever,' I said, shaking my head as I put the phone down.

Martina was bad news of the worst variety. She was a terrible idea that was even worse now it was running loose in reality. She was Satan in Gossard underwear. How had I ended up like this?

Nikki and Cathy, two girls from my teacher training course, were good friends with Martina. On a night out during the second week of our year-long course they'd told me about a number of complimentary comments Martina had made about me during lectures, which all added up to the fact

67

that she fancied me rotten. At first I was flattered because Martina was far from ugly; she was tall, naturally blonde and had a manner about her so elegant that she almost seemed to float. That evening I'd tried talking to her a few times but it was obvious, even then, that though she was keen we had nothing in common.

I didn't say another word to her until the weekend before I came to London. I'd been discussing with Alice how soul-destroying it was looking for LOVE in the Nineties, when she suggested that the reason I hadn't found it had nothing to do with demographics, and everything to do with the fact that I was TOO UPTIGHT FOR MY OWN GOOD. I had to admit, she had a point. While, all around, my peers indulged in one-night stands, two-timing antics and three-in-a-bed-scandals, I was too busy to join in because I was searching for the Other One, to take the place of Aggi (the One). It was easy to see what Alice was getting at. I was practically walking around with a sign around my neck saying: 'Wife wanted.' I was looking for a replacement Aggi with a lifetime guarantee and nothing else would do.

So Martina was it. She was my experiment. The Franken-stein monster of my own creation. My one attempt at a casual relationship, and now I was paying for it dearly. One phone call was all it took. In the back of the taxi after an evening dining at Los Locos, she'd made it clear to me as I frantically stuffed my hand up her top and ran my fingertips along the edges of her bra, that *she* wanted a relationship. I'd mumbled something along the lines of, 'Yeah, me too,' before she swamped me in deep, passionate kisses. Now, because of that, my regret threatened to overwhelm me – which wasn't all that hard to do. On a good day, I felt guilty for things that most people didn't give a second thought – not giving to the homeless, not buying a Lifeboat sticker, killing moths trapped in net curtains: guilt had always been a key feature of my life. And now, thanks to Martina, I felt completely and utterly guilty for things I knew for a fact had nothing to do with me. Hiroshima. That was my fault. The sinking of the *Titanic*. That was me too. Han Solo getting stuck in carbonite in *The Empire Strikes Back*. Blame me for that one, Princess Leia.

Already my conscience was suggesting that I should go out with Martina as an act of penance. After all, Catholics had it sussed – erase all guilt by turning the pain of the guilt in on yourself, because at the end of the day, dealing with your own anguish is easy enough when compared to dealing with the pain you've caused. It was a nice theory, but it wasn't the answer. The situation would only get worse. This was my problem: I had to get rid of her, but I didn't have it in me to dump her. I'd never dumped a girl in my life. Yes, I'd behaved so badly that they'd had no option but to get rid of me, but I'd never done the deed myself. I just couldn't tell another human being that I didn't like them the way they liked me. Thanks to Aggi, sometimes I felt like I was the only person in the world who could say, 'This is going to hurt me more than it's going to hurt you,' and really mean it.

12.50 A.M.

Martina, or more accurately, thoughts of Martina were denying me the right to sleep, as they raced around my head as if the inside of my skull were a miniature Silverstone. Inevitably, they slowed down, converging at one point – Aggi. How long had she wondered – just as I was doing with Martina – how to break it to *me* gently? She must have known that whatever she said, and however she said it, I'd be totally torn apart.

Weeks afterwards, when I could actually get my head around the concept of her not being there any more – about as easy as coming to terms with waking up a paraplegic – it occurred to me that she might have been trying to tell me how she felt for weeks, maybe even months, and I'd been too stupid to notice. It hurt to think that all that time I'd been under the illusion, thinking she felt the same about me as I did about her – and now I didn't know what to believe in. The questions I should have asked at the time never got asked, and by the time I'd got around to feeling I could ask them without falling to pieces, she'd cut off all contact.

Maybe she'd decided that very morning, or when I met her outside Shoe Express, or as the milk in our coffee began to separate in the café, or as she drove through the barriers of the car park, or as she pulled into Rilstone Road, or as she leaned over and kissed me to say . . .

71

That's enough. I closed my eyes tightly, hoping that sleep would come soon. *That's enough thinking for now*. I was never going to get to sleep at this rate. I looked through the gaps in the curtain, the night sky appeared to be fading into morning – I wondered if I'd fallen asleep without knowing it, and checked my watch. Night-time was still a very long way from being over. I lay back on the bed and stared at the Artexed ceiling, hoping to drop off out of boredom. I could barely see the ceiling without my glasses, the world was a blur and for this I would always be grateful.

I was twelve years old before I realised people were supposed to see the world clearly. My vision had been in a state of deterioration for at least two years. As a twelve-year-old that was a sixth of my life, or if I only counted the important bits when I could talk and at least do a portion of thinking for myself – at least a fifth. It wasn't like I was on the road to Damascus or anything, it just sort of sneaked up on me. I thought it was the way things were.

My first pair of glasses were a hideous affair that I bucked, railed and tantrumed against when informed of their impending entry into my life. I took one look in the mirror at the optician's and burst out crying. There were only two good role models for four-eyed youngsters back then: Brains from *Thunderbirds* or Joe 90, and even then, everyone assumed you were clever.

My peers, without any need for provocation, took it upon themselves to abuse both me and my spectacles at every opportunity. Even Sandra Law, who had a pink plastic pair, felt able to join in. I had to take the 'brassings', as we used to call it, for over a week until, thankfully, they found another child to torture. Craig Harrison's younger brother had shown his tackle to a group of girls in the gully that ran along the back of the school. Admittedly, they had goaded him into it, but that was no excuse. That boy had no shame.

During that dreadful week Simon had stood by me. This didn't exactly mean that he defended my honour – that would've only attracted abuse in his direction – but I always had someone to play with and knew that there was at least one person in the world who would never call me 'speccy-four-eyes'. It was during a lunch-time break, while playing Galactic Head with Simon, our personal vision of future space travel, that it dawned on me to incorporate my spectacles into the game.

I Sellotaped a Bic biro to the right arm of my specs and thus my glasses became an intergalactic communicator. It was an immediate success. I started off the biggest playground craze seen in years – bigger than the Slinky Spring, *Return of the Jedi* trading cards and fastening the top toggle of a duffel coat around your neck to make it look like Batman's cape. That afternoon my glasses were practically passed around the whole of the school. By the end of the following week people were bringing sunglasses into school for me to customise. The craze, and my popularity as a whole, took a nose-dive when Gareth 'Stiggy' Evans, brought in his dad's bifocals for me to transform. His dad later told the headmaster that Gareth had 20/20 vision, so it was 'no bloody wonder' he tripped over and smashed them while playing keep-it-ups with Arthur Tapp.

Four years after that my own glasses shared a similar fate during a Scout camping weekend in the Derbyshire hills. There were five of us to a tent and before we'd gone to sleep Craig Butler – who was sleeping in the middle – had convinced us that a man would try and sneak in during the night, and steal our body parts using a sharpened butter knife. By the time he'd finished winding us up only the unceasing clenching of buttock muscle kept the contents of my bowels from exploding. I was at the zip end of the tent, so there was no way I was going to take off my specs. When I woke up in the morning my glasses had disappeared but I didn't have to look far to find them. They were lying on the floor, crushed under the quivering buttocks of Fat Nigel.

The lead Scoutmaster, a man called Mr George, suggested Sellotaping the arm back on. Mr George had obviously never been a teenager because otherwise he would have realised how stupid his suggestion was. Sellotape may have been all right for Galactic Head, but I was only a kid back then. Now that I was thirteen, there was nothing on earth that could make Sellotaped spectacles cool. Thus, I decided, it would be far easier on my ego not to see anything at all, so I spent the rest of the weekend – that's all of Saturday *and* most of Sunday – being pointed in the right direction. When I got home, my mum made me go straight to the optician's to choose another pair of glasses. But how could I? It was like being asked to choose another nose. After three hours in the shop, trying on the whole range of children's spectacles, I settled on a black pair. I took them home and showed them to all my friends but I couldn't shake the feeling that they'd always be a second best to the pair I'd broken.

The thing about that weekend without glasses was that what I could see looked really nice. Nothing had any definition about it. Colours merged. It was like constantly being caught in the sort of cheesy soft-focus normally reserved for swooning heroines, all the rough edges smoothed away, all the blemishes blurred out of existence. Real Life seemed far away.

In my retrospective mood, lying in bed staring at the ceiling, I was reminded of the first time that Real Life and My Life collided in my head. I'd just completed a rather excellent picture of my mother. I'd painted her with a red smiling face and blue hair – most importantly of all I'd given her a neck. I'd noticed that those of my peers whose talents lay in the world of art rather than the sand pit, had drawn portraits of their mothers – specifically commissioned for Mother's Day – without necks. Some had big round heads, others even had hair, but not a single mother had a neck. I knew my mother had a neck, so I gave her a neck. It was a long slender green one. It made me very proud.

After painting time, we were forced into our afternoon nap. The beds were set out in rows across the far end of the classroom. I usually ran to the one by the door so I could feel the draught come in and pretend that I was on a boat at sea. This particular day, I ran to a bed that faced the large window which spanned the side of the room. It looked out onto the trees in the yard near the playground. I wasn't sleepy but I liked lying down. I could've run and jumped and played twenty-four hours a day, but I conceded this battle every time because the afternoon nap gave me a chance to think. Back then I rarely thought proper thoughts because I was too busy playing. Time was always NOW, in big, bold, upper-case letters. The future just wasn't my concern.

I closed my eyes tightly and waited until I saw the red and orange floaty things that always appeared before my eyes when I did this. They were beautiful, but I could never look at them directly otherwise they disappeared and would only reappear once I'd stopped looking for them. After five minutes or so, I began to think about my mum. She had dropped me off at the nursery, as she had done every day since September. I was completely happy with this arrangement. I had no problem with being left alone with strange adults and a bunch of children I didn't know. If my parents were trying to give me a head start on the advancement of my social skills then they should have asked me and I could have told them that I got along with everyone.

That morning I'd kissed mum good-bye but as I lay there that wintry afternoon, I began to think about where she was. I couldn't explain it, but I suddenly wondered if she was real. I'd sometimes dreamt things that felt so real that they couldn't possibly have been dreams. I once dreamt I could fly and, even now, can still remember what the city looked like from up in the sky and how the wind felt in my hair and against my skin. But when I woke up I couldn't fly.

Lying on the bed thinking these thoughts, I concluded that my mother was just a really nice dream. I could remember the softness of her cheek that I'd kissed that morning and how smooth the tissue that wiped away her lipstick felt. I could remember her smell, which was warm and summery in contrast to the bleak day it really was. I remembered it all, just like I remembered that I could fly. Right there and then, I convinced myself that my mum didn't exist, that both she and my dad, my bedroom and toys – all that I loved didn't exist. Nothing existed except me and what I could see.

I opened my eyes, looked out of the window, saw the branches of the trees blowing in the wind and started to cry. Not loudly for attention, but softly, very softly. My eyes filled up and warm tears ran across my cheek onto the hand resting beneath my head. Within minutes I was in full flow. I felt sad and empty. I was an orphan. The teacher, Mrs Greene, a lovely lady who smelt of Pears soap, gave me a hug and stroked my hair, but I was inconsolable. 'My mum's not there! My mum's not there!' I shouted through my tears, but it wasn't actually what I meant. What I wanted to say was, 'My mum's not real!' In the end I cried so much that she had to call my mum at work from the telephone in the school office. When she explained to my mum what the problem was, she passed the telephone down to my outstretched hands to let me speak to her. As soon as I heard her voice, the tears stopped. My mum was real. It wasn't a dream. Everything was all right.

I'm in my flat, only it's not my flat. It's a better one but not too flash – let's keep it within the realms of reality. And for argument's sake let's say that I'm still in London and I'm still teaching – although why I don't know. The flat's tidy and the cold water tap on the kitchen sink works. My records and CDs are in alphabetical order and I've got a state-of-the-art flat screen digital TV with cable.

Right. I'm busy in the kitchen. I'm chopping parsley and sprinkling it over a dish which I return to the oven for twenty minutes to crispen – well that's what it says in my Delia Smith cookbook, anyway. Playing in the background is Elvis – Live From Madison Square Garden – it just fits the mood I'm in tonight – triumphant, jubilant, ready to please the faithful. There's a knock at the door. I brush parsley from my hands and slip on my jacket which has been sitting on the back of a kitchen chair. As I enter the hallway I catch a glimpse of myself in the mirror. Looking good. I'm wearing a dark blue suit from Paul Smith. It looks expensive but not obscene, chic and 'with it'. No, scrub that. The suit's too formal – where am I going? A funeral? No. I'm in something casual that could only have been bought on a shopping trip to New York. Let's see. A checked Calvin Klein shirt and a pair of Chinos from

79

Bloomingdales. No, no, no, no, no. It's just not me – only models in GQ wear that sort of stuff. Okay, I've got it. I'm in a plain white T-shirt and a pair of old Levis and – here's the best bit – I'm not wearing any socks! Nice touch, she used to like my feet.

I open the door and there is Aggi.

For a millionth of a second neither of us moves, frozen in time and space, our eyes saying more than words can communicate. I'm overcome by a sick and dizzy sensation that doesn't last very long as it is soon overwhelmed by euphoria. I wrap her in my arms and squeeze. Her warm tears trickle down the back of my neck. I pull my head back, still pressing her close to me, and look deeply into those big, bad, beautiful, deep-green eyes I've missed so much.

'William . . . William!' she sobs. 'I'm sorry. I'm so sorry.'

Saying nothing, I increase the pressure of my grip so tightly that she almost feels faint, but she doesn't resist, in fact she wants me to hold her tighter, because my embrace is declaring aloud the one thing she most wants to hear – 'I forgive you.'

I relax my grip around her slender waist as she takes my hand and looks down, ever deeper, into my soul.

'I thought I could live my life without you,' she says, trying desperately to hold back her tears. 'I can't. I've tried and I can't do it, Will. I've been so unhappy for so long. I thought you'd never forgive me. These last three years without you have been awful. I've been to hell and back.'

No. Definitely too melodramatic. More Barbara Cartland than Brontë. Okay, take it from, 'these last three years without you have been awful . . .'

'As soon as I'd ended our relationship I knew that I'd made the biggest mistake of my life.' She stops, her eyes

well up with tears and her bottom lip trembles. The pause is not for dramatic effect – it's for mercy. 'I wouldn't blame you if you hated me right now. Really, I have no right to be here. I gave up that right the moment I extinguished our love. But do you think that we could . . .? Do you think that we'll ever . . .?'

She notices how little I've said. The tears flow rapidly. 'Aren't you going to say anything?' she screams. 'You hate me, don't you? Don't you?'

I throw her a look I'd seen Nicolas Cage use on Laura Dern in Wild At Heart: *intense, deep and unambiguous as if to say, 'Baby, you're mine – I'm yours – forever!'*

She tells me she's grateful I've invited her around for dinner. She says that she didn't think I'd agree to see her. And I say something like, 'Why ever not?' And she looks down at her lap and then at her skirt, as if realising for the first time just how much she's let herself go. Though I hate to agree, she doesn't look like her old self. She knows it. I know it. And she knows I know it. It's almost as if she'd gone to her wardrobe and plucked out her best glad rags to realise that she was only half right. While reassuring her that she looks wonderful, I pull out a tissue from a box of Kleenex man-sized on the coffee table and gently dab the tears away. At one point, she smiles at me gently as my hand accidentally brushes against her cheek.

We move into the lounge. I offer her a seat on the sofa next to me. I get the feeling that she wants to move closer and very slowly she edges her body nearer to mine. Just at the moment she's close enough for me to feel the warmth of her breath against my skin, the radiation from her body and the smell of her perfume – Chanel No 5 – I evade her intimacy, announcing that I've got to look after the food.

Right, let's skip the boring bits and get to the point

where we're just about to eat. On the plates (from Habitat) are a wild mushroom and yellow pepper lasagne, and a selection of vegetables. Not your plain and simple peas and carrots affair, no, these are the kind of exotic veggies Sainsbury's have in little white containers covered with cling film. She tells me that I shouldn't have gone to all this effort because she's not a vegetarian any more, and I tell her that the effort was all for me, as I've not eaten meat in roughly three years.

I pour her a glass of red wine and tell her how this particular blend of grapes will complement the food wonderfully. I'm tempted to let her cup overflow symbolically but I don't. She says 'When' absent-mindedly, just as the wine reaches the edge of the glass. I pour myself one, our eyes meet, she raises her glass to her lips and is just about to sip when she says, 'What am I doing?' Her glass in the air, she says triumphantly: 'Here's to us! Here's to love conquering all!'

We clink glasses.

We're in the lounge again, back on the sofa. Two table lamps illuminate the room, creating a 'relaxed' atmosphere. There's no music in the background, although it does cross my mind to put on something laid-back like Tori Amos or Kate Bush. We sit down and I light a cigarette, not because I want one, but because I want her to know that I now smoke. Things have changed. Things have moved on. I'm the same man she fell in love with and yet different.

She tells me how dismal her life has been without me. How she gave up on her aspiration to be a social worker to work as an office junior in a firm of accountants. Recalling how her life lost direction after she dumped me, she sobs that she has felt adrift ever since. She even confides that despite her best efforts she has been unable to form a relationship with anyone new – ANYONE AT ALL . . . okay, one bloke, but she didn't sleep with him . . . okay . . . there have been a few: Paul, Graham and Gordon but none of them understood her like I did, especially Gordon who had ginger hair and Paul who had taken her to see Chris Rea twice against her will. I hold back the information that I've been dallying with a few girls' hearts, but she can see – Aggi can see them dancing in my eyes. And what she can also see is that I was over her the minute she told me it was over. Maybe even earlier.

The phone rings. I ignore it. Aggi moves to answer it and I hold my hand up, signalling that whoever is calling is nowhere near as important as she is. The answering machine clicks on and a refined voice – not altogether dissimilar to that of Audrey Hepburn – says, 'Hi, Will! It's Abi here. I just wanted to have one of our late-night chats but you're not in! What's a gal to do? Oh well. What are you doing next Thursday? I've got tickets for the theatre. It's Love's Labour's Lost. *It'll be wonderful. Do say you'll come. We can have dinner at my place again afterwards. Ring me soon. Please! Bye!'*

Aggi and I sit in silence. She takes my hand and places it between her two. They look small and artistic, just the right length for piano playing and stroking my hair. Thankfully she has stopped biting her nails. The wine flows freely and we chat and laugh and flirt with each other avidly until the Moment arrives. I know it's coming, I can see it a mile off. Once again, she slides herself closer to me, I feel the warmth of her chest pressing against mine, her eyes are closed, her faced turned towards me, her pale sensitive lips pursed to perfection and I prepare myself to relive all our kisses and . . . nothing. Nothing happens.

1.17 A.M.

The phone rang, denying me the opportunity to wallow in the depressing inadequacy of my imagination. I wondered who it could possibly be, but after a few seconds I made the decision to stop wondering, on the grounds that it was both pointless and stupid. I tried to argue back that neither of those reasons had ever stopped me before but I ignored myself and answered the phone.

'Hello?'

'It's only me.'

It was Martina.

I checked my watch, trying to gauge how outraged I should be. This late at night most normal people would either be a) not in b) fast asleep or c) having sex. As I wasn't normal I wasn't doing any of them – but I wasn't going to miss out on a sterling opportunity to lose my rag, dump Martina *and* fill the yawning chasm of boredom stretching out in front of me. This was obviously some sort of gift from above – maybe I'd done something right today.

'Martina,' I began. 'It's nearly three in the morning. Why are you telephoning me at three in the morning? Are you insane? I thought it was my mother ringing to say that my Gran was dead. How can you be so cruel?'

I don't know how I managed to say all that without laughing.

I especially liked the bit about it being 'three in the morning' – exaggeration always was my favoured weapon in wars of words.

Martina was so stunned that she literally didn't know what I was talking about.

'I . . . I . . .' was all she managed in her defence.

'You what, Martina?' I looked around for my conscience. It was nowhere to be seen. 'It's three a.m. Martina. You can't go phoning people at three a.m. Look, this has got to stop. Yes, I know we had a wonderful time last Saturday. And I'll always remember it.' I wondered where my conscience had got to and decided it must have had an accident and drowned in one of the many pools of self-pity dotted around my internal landscape. This was the kind of mean-spirited, hard-hearted, totally selfish, self-centred thing that Simon would do. Finally, after all this time I was totally and utterly devoid of guilt – I was Sean Connery as James Bond. I could love them and leave them and not care because, at last, I didn't give a toss about anyone but me. Shaken and not stirred! 'Martina,' I continued, limbering up for the kill, 'I've got to tell you something. Look it's not you it's . . .'

'I'm late,' said Martina abruptly.

'It's nearly four in the morning,' I replied, 'of course you're late. London's not in a different time zone, Martina, half four in the morning in Nottingham is half four in the morning here too. This isn't Australia, you know.'

She made small confused noises to herself. My efforts at biting sarcasm were obviously falling upon deaf ears.

Martina sighed heavily. 'I'm late, Will. As in, you know, *late.*'

I hadn't the faintest idea what she was on about. After some moments of confused silence I concluded she'd either finally parted company with the last of her depleted stock of marbles, or she'd been helping herself to her mum's Harvey's Bristol Cream.

'Martina,' I continued, 'I know you're late. I've got a watch. The big hand's on twelve and the small hand's pointing at the five. You don't need to tell me you're late.'

'Will, I'm . . .'

'If you tell me one more *bloody* time that you're . . .'

'Pregnant.'

I nearly coughed up my lungs in shock. This was quite literally the last thing I'd expected. The events of last weekend had been consigned to the annals of ancient history as soon as they'd occurred. And now I was being called back to take responsibility for something that, mentally speaking, happened decades ago. The entire point of one-night stands was supposed to be that they lasted *one* night. They were not allowed to come back seven days after the event and tell you they were . . .

'Pregnant?'

'Yes,' she whispered.

'But how?' I cried sulkily.

She started a sentence which I believe, had I let her finish, would've given me the text book explanation similar to the one I'd received thirteen years ago from Mr Marshall, my school biology teacher.

'Don't, Martina,' I said firmly. 'Just don't.' Huge droplets of sweat jettisoned from my every skin pore, so much so that my hands, wet with perspiration, lost all grip. The phone slipped from my grasp, smacking against the edge of the bed on its way to the floor. I sat and stared at it, carefully listening to the sound but not comprehending the meaning of the miniature Martina coming from the earpiece.

I picked the phone up. 'You're *late*?'

She didn't know what to say after the way we'd been

going round in circles. 'Er . . .' she began tentatively, 'yes, I'm late.'

'How late is late?' I barked. 'Later than I was to pick you up on Saturday? Later than the average British Rail train?' I started getting hysterical. 'I mean, should I start looking for a good secondary school for our child?'

'My period . . .' she began. I shuddered – an involuntary reaction cultivated in my youth intrinsically linked to the mere utterance of *that* word '. . . was due on Monday. I've never been more than a day late in my life.'

I crossed my fingers and hoped that this was the kind of biological freak of nature that would've gained her an entry in the *Guinness Book of Records* rather than the mundane result of a fertilised ovum.

'It's not fair. It's not fair. It's not fair. It's not fair. It's not fair. It's not fair. It's not fair. It's not fair. It's not fair . . .' I repeated, beginning what would've become a five minute mantra had Martina not intervened.

'Are you okay, Will?' she said kindly. 'Look, I don't want you to worry. Everything's going to be okay. I just don't want you to worry.'

I tried to think of something sensible to say, but, inside, my brain had turned to pure wibble. For all her faults Martina was being spectacularly calm, dignified, almost regal about the whole thing. I was entering my second childhood just as she was turning into the Queen Mother. She was unshakeable. This, I decided, was one of those moments that separated men from boys. And without a doubt I was standing on the prepubescent side.

'Don't worry,' she said again. 'Will, don't worry.'

I cast my mind back to The Event, but this time not through the eyes of the greatest fan of the most spectacular sexual athlete the world has ever seen. No, this time I went back as one of those disaster experts who sift through plane wreckage trying to piece together evidence of what went wrong.

While we had used a condom, I had to admit that I may have been just a teensy weensy bit careless. I kind of got carried away with the excitement of it all – after all, the one-night stand was uncharted territory for me. And for some reason the thought of doing it on her sofa while her parents slept in the room above us turned me on so much that I thought I'd pass out with the excitement. So, there *might* have been the slightest possibility that I *might* have torn the foil packet rather carelessly, but it had seemed okay to me when I'd wrapped it in its Kleenex coffin and flushed it away after The Event. I mean, I didn't put it through the sort of rigorous testing that had got it its kite-mark but it hadn't leaked. At least I hadn't thought so . . .

Part of me (that which would sooner hack off its own head than take responsibility for the fact that it may have screwed up) wondered if she was lying. After all Martina's favourite book was Hardy's *Jude The Obscure*. And while she probably fancied herself as the ethereal Sue Brideshead, she could well have been Arabella Donn trapping the unsuspecting hero with a false pregnancy. It was a nice theory but for the huge gaping holes in it. It just wasn't Martina's style to lie. She wasn't the kind to make waves even when trying to save herself from drowning. This was real. She was with child. I was the father. And it was highly likely that it was all my fault.

'Are you sure?' I said. 'I mean, do you know for sure?'

'No,' she whispered. 'I don't know for sure.'

'Then there's still hope.'

'Maybe.'

'So you haven't had a pregnancy test yet?'

'No.'

I couldn't believe what I was hearing. 'Why not? What's

wrong with you, Martina? Are you insane, woman? You are, aren't you?'

She fought back her tears but I could hear them in her voice. 'I . . . I don't know, Will. I'm scared. I'm scared what the test will say. I'll never get a job if I'm pregnant. I'll be stuck here with Mum and Dad, surrounded by nappies, watching gardening programmes for the rest of my life. I've been trying to phone you all week to tell you,' her voice faltered. 'I can't go through this on my own.'

I lay down on the bed, phone in hand, and stared at the ceiling. My earlier reincarnation as James Bond had all but disappeared by now. I'd had my licence to kill revoked. It felt good to be back in the familiar territory of the Realm of Regret, positioned on top of my favourite pile of ashes and sporting the latest designs in sackcloth. Martina had been worrying about this all week and I'd been too wrapped up in my own worries to notice. Lower than a snake's arse? Really, it just wasn't possible to feel more despicable.

I tried my best to comfort her, but at the back of my mind I knew something was up. I was carefully choosing every word I said, refusing to admit liability, in case one day soon it would be thrown back in my face. So I didn't say anything rash like 'I'll be there for you' or 'Let's see how our relationship goes' or 'I'll support you in whatever decision you make'. I made no mention of the future and instead opened my bumper book of meaningless platitudes and showered her with them from a great height. She seemed comforted. This, after all, was the nicest I'd been to her since promising to call as I'd warmly kissed her good-bye on her doorstep late on that fateful Saturday night.

We talked some more about things totally unrelated to the situation at hand: what was on telly right now; what she was doing in the morning; why teaching attracts such manic personalities; and then made ready to say our good-byes. She said that she was going to buy a test kit first thing in the morning and I told her to phone me as soon as she knew more. Before the call ended, reverting to her old self she said: 'Whatever happens, this doesn't change the way I feel about you.' And I said, 'Yeah, me too,' and put the phone down.

In a way I was both disappointed and elated at my sperm's performance. While in denial (which I surely was), it was quite possible to enjoy that exhilarating flush of pride in knowing that one of the little fellas had fulfilled its destiny. I'd kind of imagined them to be miniature versions of myself – slightly overweight, lazy, dysfunctional. It was hard not to laugh out loud at the mental picture I had: a group of them entering into a discussion halfway up Martina's cervix about whether it was time for a fag break. All, bar one diligent little fella, vote yes. 'I gave 'em up last week,' he says. 'No fags. No booze. I'm feeling so healthy that I think I'll carry on.'

It was funny. But not that funny. That one conscientious tadpole of love, so eager to live out its potential, was about to cause my downfall and there was nothing I could do about it. It was one of those classic moments when you wish that you really could turn back the clock. Even so, had I managed to go back in time, to that moment just as I was unzipping Martina's dress, not even the Ghosts of Christmas Past, Present and Future could've stopped me. Passion is depressing. A man in a French film once said, 'I resist my temptations in order to feel that I am free.' Though it was said by a character in a French film – which by definition means you can't take it entirely seriously – the truth of the words resonated clearly.

Sometimes the effort to resist can be as passionate as the compulsion to succumb.

The opening and closing of one of my close neighbour's front doors broke my concentration. I stood up and looked out of the window. Next door's dog – a black Labrador – barked at my window. Turning back into the room I scratched my stomach and tried to work out how I felt. I wasn't entirely sure. I looked at the alarm clock. It was late. Rather than being exhausted I had the munchies in a big way. Though not hungry enough to eat the proverbial horse, given two slices of bread, a bottle of ketchup and an hour or two longer without sustenance, even Champion The Wonder Horse would have looked snackworthy. My stomach specifically desired ice-cream. Then it occurred to me that perhaps I was having sympathetic cravings, just as some men have sympathetic pregnancy pains. Whatever the reason, I wanted ice-cream and I wanted it now.

This was one of the few instances I found living in the capital to have its advantages. Nottingham had nothing at all resembling the all night shop, which was a shame, because the 7-Eleven (so called because it's open 24-hours a day, seven days a week. Well done, Misnomer Man!) was a pretty good idea, probably in the top ten most brilliant ideas humanity has ever had – not as good as the Walkman or the answering machine, mind – but for that matter not that far behind either.

Fumbling through the clothes that constituted my pillow I located my trousers and proceeded to look for a jumper. The only one I found that would protect me from a bout of hypothermia was a cable-knit sweater Gran had made me a long time ago. It was during her frantic phase of making things out of wool: dolls for her next-door neighbour's kids, a bobble hat for my dad and a pair of trousers for Tom who, even at the age of ten, had the good sense to realise that woollen trousers were the kind of fashion mistake that followed you about for the rest of your life. Despite the cold I didn't bother with socks as I couldn't find any of the little sods. Instead, I pushed my bare feet into my laced-up burgundy brogues, ignored the sound of my mother tutting as she said, 'No wonder all your shoes fall apart if that's how you treat them,' and went out of the door.

The silence of early hours Archway was beguiling. Take away the sound of far-off traffic and the odd taxi or bus and this was the quietest North London ever got. The coldness of the night air heightened my sense of isolation – no one would be out in weather like this unless they were mad or in search of ice-cream. My ankles were so cold that they felt like they had ice cubes rubbing against them. Standing on the door-step, I watched the vapour from my first outside breath disappear heavenwards before launching myself into the night.

The streets were empty. Most of the revellers from the Irish club up the road would have been asleep for at least an hour or two. The chip shop on my side of Holloway Road was closed but the one farther down, past the dry cleaners, was still open, although technically speaking, it wasn't a chip shop – the name on the front of the shop being Mr Bill's Fast Food. The nearest they had to chips were French fries which, five minutes prior to ordering, lay in a bag with thousands of other grim-looking bits of frozen potato.

Walking briskly I reached the top of the road in a new personal best of eight minutes and thirteen seconds! A couple were huddled together in the doorway of the snooker hall near the intersection of Holloway Road and Junction Road. The man was in his mid-thirties, but it has to be said that I'm notorious for not being able to tell the age of most people over the age of eight. I once thought one of Simon's ex-girlfriends was fifteen, when she was actually twenty-five. I spent weeks congratulating myself on how liberal I was being, not asking her how she was getting on with her GCSEs or being less subtle and referring to her as jail-bait.

It began to rain as I walked along Junction Road and passed the Athena Kebab and chip shop opposite the tube station. There were no customers inside, but one of the men behind the counter stared at me menacingly as he diced cabbage. For some reason this scene seemed so ridiculous that I burst out laughing like some care-in-the-community patient.

Mr 7-Eleven didn't look up from his magazine as I entered, but I got the feeling that he saw me anyway. Simon once had a job working behind the till of an all-night garage off Jarvis Road. He insisted that while working night-shifts he discovered an uncanny ability to predict the make and colour of the next car to pull onto the petrol station forecourt. It was pure rubbish, of course – the sort of thing he'd write a song about one day – but, I supposed, it was possible to find out all manner of strange things about yourself if you spent all that time on your own while the rest of the world was sleeping.

Walking past the magazine rack and the early Saturday editions of the *Sun* and the *Mirror*, I made my way straight to the freezer chest, opened it up and sucked in the pseudo-Arctic air. The smells and tastes of all the produce that had ever been there lingered like spectres: I could taste the ghosts of frozen peas; I could smell the ectoplasm of spilt Alabama Fudge cake. It was spooky.

The choice was limited: Raspberry Ripple, Chocolate, Vanilla or Tutti Frutti. Tutti Frutti caught my eye but I suspected – correctly as it happened – that it contained melon. I felt the same way about melons as I did about girls who said they'd love me forever and then dumped me. A box of no-name choc ices in the corner of the freezer cried out for attention but try as I might, they failed to seduce me, forcing me to opt for a tub of Wall's Soft Scoop vanilla. You know where you are with vanilla. Its reputation, like that of Mother Teresa and Alan Titchmarsh, was spot free, which was highly useful, because at this particular moment, this close to the Edge, more than anything in the world, I couldn't afford to be disappointed.

The man in the kebab shop – keeping his steely glares to himself this time – had ceased cabbage shredding and was locked in conversation with his kebab-slicing comrade. The kissing couple had gone only to be replaced by an old man with matted – possibly brown – hair protruding from underneath a lime-green woollen hat. His overcoat pocket was ripped and, even in this light, I could see it was heavily stained. The closer I came to walking past him, the more I began to think I could smell him.

He's going to ask me for money.

At the height of my political awareness – five minutes into my first week at university – I'd made a pledge always to give to the homeless, even if it was only a penny. These days – since Aggi had left me, to be precise – in spite of my promise and acute sense of guilt, I no longer felt obliged to be nice to the needy. This wasn't so much a change in my personal politics as a sudden realisation that I didn't give a cack.

I set my eyes to a steely glare similar to that of the kebab chap, but the old man didn't say a word to me. I spent the rest of the journey wondering why he hadn't asked me for any money when he was so obviously in need of it. That thought carried me through the front door, into my flat and right into bed – leaving the object of my quest untouched and slowly melting on top of the TV.

SATURDAY

I woke up with a start. I deliberately didn't move for what felt like a long time, trying to fake that just-woken-up feeling. I closed my eyes tightly, then relaxed them, repeating the action, squeezing out all traces of daylight from my irises, but there was no getting back to sleep. Instead, I pretended to be unable to move my limbs, and, after some moments of great concentration, even the slightest movement became an act of considerable determination.

Freshly squeezed thoughts dripped down from my brain, pleading for an audience. I put any questions re impending fatherhood to the very back of my mind. *Maybe I'll wrap them up*, I thought, while slowing down my breathing. *Wrap them up and put a note on them saying, do not open – ever. Some things are, after all, better left unthought.* None of the topics for debate that remained – familiar faces all – stood out from the crowd, which was pleasing because mornings, especially Saturday mornings, shouldn't be over-whelmed with stuff to think about.

Waking up the morning after the day Aggi dumped me – a Saturday morning no less – had been a terrible ordeal, not least due to the horrible taste in my mouth and the smell of sick on my pillow. I'd dreamt that Aggi and I had swum across a tropical ocean to lie on a Bounty chocolate bar type island.

I clearly remembered feeling the sun on my back and neck, the sand clinging to my feet and the cooling sensation of the wind against the droplets of water on my skin. It seemed so real. Then suddenly I was awake. The essence of the dream only lingered for the duration of the journey from deep sleep to total consciousness, but for that short time I experienced the sensation I imagined others felt when they said they were on top of the world. Then WHAM! The nail-bomb exploded. Aggi was gone. She didn't want me. It was finished. Over the following weeks, my first waking moments followed the same pattern – an overwhelming feeling of ecstasy followed closely by the distressing hollowness of reality. Gradually, the length of time it took for me to realise Aggi was gone grew shorter and shorter, until one day I woke up crying. By then, I think, the Message had finally made its way through to my heart.

I turned over, squashing my face into my makeshift pillow. It was too late. My brain was in gear. Saturday had begun.

I'll have to tidy the flat.
I'll have to phone people.
I'll have to mark 8B's books.
I'll have to sort out my life.

I rolled over onto my back. Staring out of my left eye I checked the time on the alarm clock. I'd set it for 1.00 p.m. hoping to sleep most of the weekend away. The digital display, however, confirmed with its authoritative blinking eye that I'd been way too optimistic.

A huge, unnatural, pulsating pain throbbed its way across the front of my skull as if the rear wheels of a Shogun were running backwards and forwards over it. The severity and suddenness of this migraine attack had me worried. As I rarely got so much as a headache, within half an hour I'd selected a brain tumour from a list of maladies that included: beriberi, encephalitis and Lhasa fever, as the chosen explanation for my throbbing temples. Death by brain tumour was, after all, an unfulfilling way to die. While the most popular characters in soap operas got to die in car crashes or at the hands of mad gunmen, those at the other end of the scale were always written out after coming down with a mystery illness that, surprise, surprise, turned out to be a brain tumour. One bald haircut and a chemotherapy storyline later, and they were gone forever. This was exactly why I was going to die this terrible death. I was being written out of existence by a medical condition that was the disease equivalent of a pair of flares.

Attempting to endure the pain by diverting my attention to the state of the room, the thought entered my head that, possibly, a little bit of suffering would make me a better person. This wouldn't have been particularly hard as, thanks to Martina, I was more overloaded with self-loathing than usual. Sometimes, I thought, *I'm born to suffer.* This, I noted, was the second time I'd contemplated Catholicism in the last twenty-four hours. I'd always thought I'd make a great Catholic. I quite liked Italy *and* found the smell of incense reasonably relaxing. If I had converted – from what I didn't know – I could've been up there with the greats: Joan of Arc, St Francis of Assisi, William of Archway – patron saint of crap housing.

Fortunately for me, my aching head and the Pope, my mother had packed a bottle of paracetamol in one of the boxes scattered around the room. Lacking the motivation to phone Nottingham to see if she could remember exactly where she'd put them, I found what I was looking for, but not before I'd emptied the contents of all four boxes on to the floor. My hand was forced. Now I really would have to tidy the flat.

I gazed longingly at the translucent brown bottle in my hand. The name on the front, Anthony H. Kelly, was my dad's. He'd had them prescribed for him when he'd had flu two years ago, which was precisely the last time he'd been ill and the first time in twenty-five years, so he told me, that he'd had a day off work through illness. The bottle was virtually full. That was typical of Dad, he loved to suffer more than I did.

I popped two paracetamols on my tongue and raced to the kitchen sink. The water which came out of it was brown and had been all week. I let it run – the two tablets now clung to my tongue like magnets – but there was no change. Cursing Mr F. Jamal for all I was worth, and myself for not reporting it to him the day I'd moved in, I managed to convince myself that brown water wasn't poisonous, but in the end I lacked the courage of my convictions. I was nearly sick as I struggled to swallow the tablets aided only by chalky saliva and a stomach of iron. I could taste their powdery slug-like trail along my oesophagus and into my stomach long after they'd gone to work alleviating my aching head.

Now that I was in the kitchen it seemed natural to start breakfast. Today, I decided, was not a Honey Nut Loop day. Instead, I opted to create a minor Sugar Puffs mountain in the only clean bowl left in the cupboard. Sat on the bed with my back propped against the back of the sofa, I pulled the duvet over my legs and turned my attention to breakfasting. I'd forgotten the milk *and* the spoon. Too hungry to wait any longer, I grabbed a handful of Sugar Puffs to satisfy my immediate craving and shoved them in my mouth; they too clung to my tongue like magnets, but *they* were sugary, satisfying and instantly cheering.

There were no clean spoons in the cutlery drawer, so the only option was to wash one using the brown tap water. Though, technically speaking, washing in the water was not the same as drinking it, my qualms about its safety remained, so I over-compensated in the cleaning process by using three extra squirts of Fairy Liquid as if it were some kind of germ napalm.

Opening the fridge door, I searched high and low for the milk. There wasn't any. It all came back to me. I'd thrown the last of it away yesterday, after pouring at least a quarter of its rancid contents over my Honey Nut Loops. There was no salvage operation. I had been so dispirited that I'd put the whole thing (bowl included) in the bin and had breakfast from the Italian newsagent's up the road – approximate waiting time for a Mars Bar and a packet of Skips: four minutes. Now I was going to be disappointed again.

Fully aware that this day was doing its very best to torture me with the constant dripping of small, but perfectly formed disasters, I placed two slices of frozen bread in the toaster. I hovered above the slot until the heating elements glowed orange, as this week's other little trick had been to pop in a couple of slices of frozen bread, go away for two minutes only to be greeted by – cue fanfare – frozen bread, because I'd forgotten to plug in the toaster.

Returning to the problem at hand, I tried to work out my next move. I couldn't possibly eat a whole bowl of cereal without milk – I just didn't have that kind of high-level saliva production in me. The other option was to dash to the shops to get some but, I suspected, if I was in possession of enough energy to 'dash' – which I strongly doubted – I'd probably have the wherewithal to have something more exotic than Sugar Puffs for breakfast. Out of the corner of my eye I spotted the answer to my problem. I opened the tub of ice-cream I'd been so desperate for the previous night – now a rich pale yellow froth – and poured the contents of my cereal bowl in.

Thoroughly pleased with my own ingenuity, I patted myself on the back and got stuck in.

Twenty minutes later, I finished about a third of my concoction and started to feel sick. As I lay back on my bed, letting the contents of my stomach settle, I listened to the postman struggling with the letter box downstairs. I got excited. As far as Birthday Cards that weren't going to be Late Birthday Cards were concerned, today was D-Day.

Reasoning that it was too early for the rest of the residents in the house to be up, I nipped out of the door and downstairs in a T-shirt and boxer shorts, only stopping to put my shoes on as I didn't like the look of the hallway carpet. There was a small hillock of letters on the Welcome doormat, most of which had been crushed mercilessly. There were yet more letters for Mr G. Peckham from the AA, a bundle of 50p off Pizzaman Pizza deliveries coupons, a postcard for the bloke in flat number four – Emma and Darren were having a wonderful time in Gambia – and a lot of other stuff I couldn't be bothered to look at properly. After flicking through the pile twice I found four envelopes addressed to me and one for Ms K. Freemans. Too lazy to put the discarded mail on top of the telephone where it normally congregated, I created a very poor artificial post hillock underneath the letter box, sat on the stairs and opened the cards:

Card 1
Description: Painting of a bunch of flowers.
Message: *'Have a wonderful day, son. All my love, Mum.'*

Card 2
Description: Gary Larson cartoon of cow leaning on a fence as car whizzes past.

Message: *'Have a wonderful day, Grandson,*
                  love, Gran.'

Card 3

Description: Photo of Kevin Keegan circa 1977
                  with a full shaggy perm wearing a
                  No 7 Liverpool shirt.

Message: *'Have a great birthday! Love and*
                  kisses, A.'

Card 4

Description: Gustav Klimt's 'The Kiss'.

Message: *'Have a simply wonderful birthday.*
                  Thinking of you every second of
                  every hour, ever yours, Martina.'

I arranged the cards on the carpet in front of me, stood back
and took stock of the situation.

*Tomorrow I'll be twenty-six years old. For the first time
in my life I'll be closer to thirty than twenty; I'll be officially
in my late-twenties, and quite possibly a father to be. By no
stretch of the imagination will I be young and if that's not
enough this is what I'm reduced to: four cards. Two from
relatives. One from a woman I'm trying to dump. And a
crap 70s footballer from Alice!*

I looked down at Alice's card again, an intense sense
of disappointment slowly spreading throughout my entire
body. This couldn't possibly have been what she meant by
'something special'. I could trust Alice. She'd never let me
down. There had to be something wrong.

The postman.

I'd always had a deep mistrust of the British postal service ever since they'd returned a letter I'd written to Noel Edmonds when I was eight just because I hadn't put a stamp on it. Putting two and two together I decided that my postman had either lost, stolen or forgotten Alice's present. Whatever the reason, I was going to get it back.

A tall, wiry man in his mid-thirties was standing five doors away, shovelling mail through a letter box. The very sight of him sent me into a frenzy of anger, transporting me to a world where the only colour was red and there was no such thing as 'keeping things in proportion'. A yobbish 'Oi!' was all I needed to grab his attention as I ran towards him.

'Come on, where is it?' I asked, adopting the no-nonsense manner of the TV 'tec who uses unorthodox methods but always gets results.

The postman studied me nervously. 'Where's what?'

'My sodding present.'

I got the feeling that he wanted to run but terror rooted him to the spot. 'Your what?'

'It's my birthday tomorrow. Where's my present?'

He looked bewildered. A look of relief drifted across his face and his eyes darted about feverishly, presumably looking for the *Beadle's About* spy cameras. When he didn't find any his look of terror returned. 'Er . . . Happy birthday.'

'I don't want your congratulations. I want my birthday present.'

My eyes dropped down to his postbag. He followed my line of vision and draped his arm over it protectively.

'It's illegal, you know – tampering with the post. I'll call the police.'

'Not if I call them first.'

I was about to make a lunge for the bag when a red, white and blue Pizzaman Pizza moped pulled up next to us. Its engine purred with all the raw power of a Braun hairdryer.

'Nice day for it,' said the white jump-suited pizza delivery man, nodding in the direction of my boxer shorts.

I joined his gaze and then looked up at the postman sheepishly. As if awakening from a sleepwalk, the ridiculous nature of my temporary insanity became instantly apparent. 'Look, I'm sorry,' I said to the postman. 'It's just that a friend of mine was supposed to be sending something in the post. I jumped to the wrong conclusion when you didn't bring it. Sorry.'

The postman's whole body shook in a paroxysm of laughter. 'What do you look like!' he said, shaking his head. 'You need to work out, son. A couple of sessions down the gym will get rid of that.'

'Ah yes,' I said humouring him, 'very funny.'

He wiped a mirthful tear from the corner of his right eye. 'Tell us your name and I'll check my bag if you like.'

'William Kelly . . .'

'Flat 3, 64 Cumbria Avenue?' asked the pizza delivery man.

The postman and I both turned and looked at him.

He explained all: 'I only stopped to ask directions. House numbers around here are difficult to follow.' He got off his moped and handed me his clipboard. 'Just sign this for me, please.'

I signed.

He reached into the pizza carrier on the back of his moped and gave me a large cardboard pizza box.

'Cheers, mate,' he said mounting his moped, laughing. 'You've really made my day.'

The postman and I looked at each other in amazement.

'Go on then,' he said, pointing at the box.

I was about to open the pizza box when a Parcel Force van pulled up next to us.

'Everything all right, Tone?' asked the driver suspiciously.

'It's just that it's not every day I see you talking to a bloke in boxer shorts holding a pizza at . . .' he looked at his watch pointedly, '11.55 a.m.'

'Everything's fine,' said the postman. 'I'll tell you all about it when I get back to the depo. The lad's just having a bad day. We've all had those.'

Hoping to diffuse the situation I walked across to the van.

'Will Kelly,' I said offering my hand. 'Sorry about all this.'

'Will Kelly, Flat 3, 64 Cumbria Avenue?'

Despite the fact that this sort of occurrence was fast becoming commonplace the postman and I looked at each other in amazement for old times' sake.

'Parcel for you,' said the man in the van.

He handed me a small shoe box sealed with brown tape, waved to his colleague and drove off.

In the middle of our momentary not-quite-sure-what-to-do-next silence an Interflora van pulled up. The man in the van didn't bother getting out.

'Will Kelly, Flat 3, 64 Cumbria Avenue?'

'Yes,' I said warily.

'Thought so.' He handed me his clipboard to sign. 'I've got these for you.' I exchanged the clipboard for a large bouquet of lilies and he drove off.

'Looks like I can go now,' said the postman.

I offered him my hand. 'What can I say?'

'No problem,' he said, shaking my hand. 'This'll make a great story for the lads down the pub tonight.' He turned and began trudging back up the road. 'Many happy returns of the day!'

Alice had excelled herself.

She'd completely transformed the formerly tedious birthday experience into a festival of happiness; a carnival of joy; a moment to remember for the rest of my life.

The Pizza

Extra cheese, pineapple, mushrooms, peppers, fish fingers and peas. The recipe of our Pizza – Pizza for the Dumped. Alice and I first created it when I visited her in Bristol a fortnight after Aggi and I had split up. I hadn't wanted to go, citing my newfound determination to grow a beard and forgo all human contact for the foreseeable future, as the reason. However, she had insisted to the point where she said that if I didn't arrive on her doorstep she'd drive up to Nottingham and take me back with her forcibly. (My hesitancy was odd, especially in the light of the fact that I ended up sleeping on her and Bruce's sitting room Futon for two whole weeks before reluctantly returning home.) On my first night at Alice's she'd asked me what I wanted to eat and I told her I didn't want to eat because I was too sad (Bruce, as luck would have it, had gone out so I could be as pathetic as I wanted). After much bullying on her part I relented and requested pizza. She flicked through *Yellow Pages* until she found a listing for a pizzeria that delivered. The entry read:

> **Luigi's – home of the pizza**. Luigi's Pizza
> Special: Two 7" pizzas and a selection of any
> six toppings, garlic bread and two soft drinks
> £7.99. Any delivery over thirty minutes late
> – FREE!

We called on Alice's speaker phone.

'A Luigi Pizza Special, please,' asked Alice.

'What toppings do you want?' enquired a distinctly un-Italian but disturbingly pubescent voice.

Alice turned to face me, her furrowed brow a visual question mark.

We took it in turns to make suggestions. As I was the guest I set the ball rolling.

'Extra cheese.'

'Pineapple.'

'Peppers. Only no green ones.'

'Mushrooms.'

'Fish fingers.'

'And peas,' said Alice with a flourish.

I laughed for the first time in what seemed like years (which was in fact only two weeks). For that brief moment Aggi didn't exist.

Baby Luigi tried to tell us that we could only order from selected toppings. Alice informed him that it didn't say that in their advert and if they refused to make our pizza she would be prepared to sue them for misrepresentation because not only was she a solicitor, she was also a solicitor who'd had a very bad day.

Forty-one minutes later (we'd set Alice's jogging stop watch the second we put down the phone) our free pizza arrived.

Reclining on the sofa, a slice and a Coke in our hands, we turned to face each other as though the situation required something momentous to be said.

Alice raised her Coke cup. 'May the mozzarella of our respective pizzas remain forever entwined.'

I took a sip from my cup before raising mine because I'd suddenly become incredibly thirsty. A mouthful of Coke and I was ready to speak.

'Ditto.'

When all that was left of my pizza were several crusts, fish finger crumbs and a number of peas that had managed to escape the glutinous grasp of the extra cheese I opened the shoe box.

The Shoe Box Parcel

Inside was a thick padded envelope and twenty packs of duty free Marlboro Lights. My entire stock of blood made a mad dash to my skull at the thought of being in such proximity to so many cigarettes. Alice was the world's healthiest person. She jogged, hadn't eaten meat since she was seventeen and even knew what her cholesterol count was. (It was low. Very low.) Not only did she not smoke, she was the most vehement anti-smoker I'd ever met, and yet her love for me was such that she was prepared to indulge me in my so-called filthy habit to the tune of 400 cigarettes! This act of charity propelled

Alice way beyond the parameter of best mate. She had excelled all definitions of cool. She was out there and unapproachable.

Propping my cigarettes on the window sill, so I could look and marvel at them wherever I was in the room, I tore open the padded envelope. By now Alice had whipped me up into such a flurry of excitement that I was half expecting to find it stuffed full of fivers with a note attached saying: 'Bruce and I had a collection for the poor. We don't know any poor, so we're giving it to you!' Sadly there were no bank notes only a colour photograph of a donkey, some stapled sheets of paper and a letter which read:

Dear William Kelly,

You are now the proud sponsor of Sandy the donkey.

Sandy, a twelve-year-old donkey, was discovered in a barn in South Wales by the RSPCA in July suffering from severe neglect, malnutrition and blindness in one eye. Following the rescue he was brought to The South Devon Donkey Sanctuary where he was looked after and nourished back to health.

Sandy is now a lot better and will be able to live out his days in the open fields of the Sanctuary grounds.

Thanks to your sponsorship we will be able to continue looking after the food and shelter needs of Sandy for a full 12 months.

Please find enclosed your sponsorship papers and
special certificate. As a valued sponsor, your name
will be placed on a plaque outside Sandy's stable for
12 months.

Thanks for your support,

Carol A. Flint
Director South Devon Donkey Sanctuary

I couldn't believe that somewhere in Devon there was a
donkey with my name on it. I fixed Sandy's picture to the
wardrobe door with Blu-tac and examined him in detail.
Though donkeys are supposedly the most miserable of
animals, Alice had somehow managed to find me a happy
one. His good eye almost sparkled, although that might
just have been the reflection of the camera flash going
off, and his mouth was fixed in an expression much like
a wry grin. His light brown coat looked healthy and sleek
and from what I could see in the picture, he appeared
to have more than enough field to roam around. Sandy
was fantastic. He was better than fags. He might be a
one-eyed donkey, but he was *my* one-eyed donkey and
that was all that counted. I examined his papers and
noticed that he was particularly fond of carrots. As I was
now responsible for Sandy's welfare I decided that from
now on his birthday would be the same day as my own. I
made a mental note to send him a fiver's worth of carrots
as a belated birthday present – a thought which resulted
in the following miniature day dream:

*I'm visiting Sandy for the first time. He's in a small
paddock with some of his donkey friends. On seeing*

me he trots towards the fence. I reach down to get his birthday carrots out of a carrier bag and realise that there's a small child standing next to me. I offer her a carrot, pick her up and let her feed Sandy. I look down at her smiling face and she says, 'Thanks, Daddy.'

I shook my head violently hoping that the image would somehow fall out of my ear and disappear into the farthest, darkest reaches of the underneath of the sofa-bed. Once the coast was clear I took a deep breath and examined the flowers.

Ten White Lilies

The lilies were perfect. But not as perfect as the message written on the card which had accompanied them:

Dear Will,

Ten years of whingeing, sarcasm, toilet humour, cynicism and misanthropy. Here's to ten more!

All My Love

Alice

Simon had been in my life longer than any of my friends and yet he still wasn't even sure when my birthday was. Only Alice would have done something like this; the flowers, donkey, fags and pizza – things she knew would please me immensely – delivered to my door within minutes of each other. I wondered what I'd done to deserve her and after a number of minutes concluded that I'd done nothing whatsoever. She was in my life without reason. She was there in spite of myself. Good things could happen to not so bad people.

I put the flowers in the only receptacle in the flat that looked anything remotely like a vase – the electric kettle – and climbed into bed with the telephone so that I'd be comfortable while I thanked Alice for her presents. I dialled her number but her answering machine was on, so I left her a message telling her to ring me asap because she was wonderful.

I looked around the room again at the fags, flowers and donkey and tried to imagine my life without Alice. Without her I'd be a rambling bearded tramp yelling expletives at young women and children while trying to beg enough money for my next can of Special Brew. The fact that she was always there to listen to me made a real difference to my life, especially at times of crisis – when Aggi dumped me my self-confidence completely imploded. It was Alice who had rebuilt it brick by brick, until I was back to my miserable and bitterly sarcastic old self. Of all the damage repair work she had undertaken on my bruised, battered and bloodied psyche one thing in particular had helped me more than anyone or anything to realise there was life after Aggi.

She had sent me a letter.

It arrived the day after I told her that Aggi had dumped me. It came in a sky blue envelope which my dad had put on the bottom of my bed as I lay there, pretending to be asleep so that he wouldn't ask how I was, because I didn't want him to see his twenty-three-year-old son crying like a baby and telling him that he felt like dying.

I took the letter out of a folder in my suitcase. It was one of my most prized possessions. I read it whenever I woke up feeling crap and wondered what the point was.

The paper was wearing thin along the edges where it had been folded. I flattened it out carefully and re-read it even though I was as familiar with every word as I was with Alice herself. The letter captured perfectly the rhythm and pattern of her speech. It was almost like having her here with me.

Will,

There's a part in Frank Capra's It's a Wonderful Life®, *right at the end when all of the families are bringing in money to save the Bailey Building and Loan company which gets me every time I watch it. I think it's his brother that says it: 'Here's to George Bailey – the richest man in town.' I hear that one line and I'm in tears. I tell you this because I suppose in a way that's how I feel about you. I think you're the richest man in town. There's a lot more I could say but I won't because I don't want your head to swell.*

Alice

PS
I've always thought that Aggi was a silly bitch with an over-inflated sense of importance who didn't appreciate how lucky she was and now she's proved it!

That last bit in Alice's letter always amused me. Up until then Alice had put on such a convincing show of civility in Aggi's presence I'd been convinced they were on the verge of becoming best friends. Strangely I'd never really got to find out what Aggi truly thought of Alice, as she'd always changed the topic of conversation whenever her name came up. I'd pretended to get the message and left her to it, reasoning it was some sort of 'women's thing'.

My thoughts were full of Alice, Alice and more Alice when it suddenly dawned upon me that I was probably experiencing one of the best birthdays witnessed since records began.

And then the phone rang.

Simon and I were mates from way, way back, even further than primary school. On our first day at nursery school he had tried to steal a packet of tomato-flavoured Snaps from my lunch-box while I was completely engrossed in a game of *Stingray* in the water bowl with Stephen Fowler. Something, possibly a sixth sense, made me look over at my satchel at the very moment Simon's thieving digits were delving into it. With the spirit of Troy Tempest within me, I ran across the room, snatched back my snack and punched him in the mouth. Mrs Greene didn't take kindly to me taking the law into my own hands but there was no further trouble. Because from that day forward Simon and I were best mates.

Twenty-odd years later, Simon was more interested in singing and playing guitar in his band, Left Bank, than women, life or tomato-flavoured potato snacks. Music was his life. He once told me that if forced to choose between music or women he'd sooner Bobbitt himself with a Bic disposable than give up his guitar. According to him it was only a matter of time before they, as he said in his own words, 'made it big'. I was both amazed and ashamed on his behalf when he'd said this, because not only was he deadly serious, he'd also managed to say 'make it big' without even the faintest nod in irony's direction.

While I spent my youth watching TV, reading books and going to the cinema, Simon had spent his – at least from the day he saw Duran Duran on *Top Of The Pops* sporting more make-up than Max Factor – studying and emulating the eccentric and obsessive personalities of rock 'n' roll folklore. In his final year at Beechwood Boys' Comprehensive, he took to wearing an earphone – not even attached to the pocket transistor radio it had come with – because it was the nearest thing he could find to the hearing aid his beloved Morrissey was sporting at the time. In the sixth form he discovered reggae and literally overnight every sentence he spoke started with the words 'I and I'. Within a week he was referring to anyone in authority – the head of sixth form especially – as 'Babylon'. He knew people thought he was weird, but he was also well aware that these same people, especially girls, thought he was cool in a sort of 'out there in deepest space' kind of way. It was all part of his master plan. One day a music magazine would ask him about his school days, and he'd pause, take a deep drag on his Silk Cut and say, 'I always felt like an outsider.'

He knew everything there was to know about music, and yet, it was this fact that was his band's downfall. Left Bank were dull, plodding and overly worthy because Simon was so steeped in rock 'n' roll history that he found it impossible to distance himself from it. It wasn't enough for him to write a good song, he wanted, in fact he needed, to write a 'classic' to impress all the musical heroes that lived in his head; lyrics that would make a pre-electric Dylan raise an eyebrow, tunes that would make John Lennon tap his toes seven-feet under, and a stage presence that would blow away Hendrix at his playing-guitar-with-his-teeth best. Nothing short of Beatlemania would do. I was firmly of the opinion that Left Bank mania would never become a word the music purchasing general public, let alone the *Oxford English Dictionary*, would ever become aware of. It was an awful name, conjuring up images of berets, fifties jazz, filterless cigarettes, beatnik poetry and tosspots who discuss Sartre without having read him (which Simon hadn't but I had – and was none the wiser for having done so). They were lumbered with this ludicrous moniker by Tammy, Simon's girlfriend and Yoko Ono in-waiting. She was three years younger than him and not his usual type at all. He always claimed to be 'a bit of an arse man' but she was a beanpole, with about as much arse as a stick insect.

Mine and Tammy's hatred of each other was pretty much instantaneous, but we were civil to each other because we had Simon in common. While he and I were pretty open with both our conversation and criticisms of each other, there was an unwritten rule never to make comments about each other's girlfriends. Even after I'd split up with Aggi he understood that only I could slag her off; if he'd joined in I would have felt obliged to beat him to a pulp or die trying.

When Simon called around to my house the day after Aggi had finished with me, he was completely unaware of all that had occurred. There wasn't a lot he could've done if he'd known anyway, apart from giving me 'space' and lending me his favourite Leonard Cohen album. To console, he needed to be a good listener and Simon didn't like to listen as much as he liked to talk; the ability to cook wouldn't have gone amiss either, although the key feature he lacked was a pair of attention-diverting breasts – to rest on, hug against and admire from a distance. I wanted Alice but she was in Bristol. When Simon asked where Aggi was I lied and said that she'd gone to see her cousin in Wolverhampton. The truth would come out sooner or later. It had to. I just didn't want to be there when it happened.

On his way out, having borrowed my brand new CD (*Elvis*

– *That's The Way It Is*) which I'd purchased with the sole aim of cheering myself up, he'd asked me what Aggi had got me for my birthday. It was then I remembered what had unsettled me so much when I'd met her outside Shoe Express – she hadn't brought a birthday present with her. Like the Dutch boy with his finger in the dam I tried my hardest to keep my tears at bay but the pressure behind my eyes rose steadily. Finally, when I could take no more, the most painful, animalistic, high-pitched squeals and groans released themselves, and before I had time to even think about being self-conscious I was crying like a baby. Snot gurgled loudly at the back of my nose as I opened and closed my mouth, attempting to form a sentence: '*Snort-gurgle-snort*-she's-*snort*-*snort*-*gurgle*-*gurgle*-duuuuuu-mmmped-*gurgle-gurgle*-meeeee!' Simon had looked around the room for something, anything, that might help me get through this anguish. Drawing a blank, he'd taken a deep breath, put his hand firmly on my shoulder and said: 'It'll be all right, mate.' With snot running down my chin and bent double in convulsion, I'd nodded in agreement, and told him I'd be all right and that we ought to go for a drink at the weekend. It never happened, a band practice came up at short notice. When I finally saw him weeks later, part of me wanted to thank him for being there, but the majority of me wanted just to forget it.

'You definitely missed a blinder,' Simon boomed down the phone, referring to the previous night's gig. 'Things are looking up for us.'

And they were too. Earlier in the week, Left Bank had received an excellent review of their last London gig in *Melody Maker*. Simon had blown it up on his dad's photocopier on to an A3 sized sheet of paper and sent me a copy, underlining in blue felt-tip pen phrases like; 'Kerosene fuelled attitude', 'the perfect antidote to the post-modern condition', and, my favourite, a sentence describing Left Bank's songs as, 'ergonomically crafted for those who like their music to fit the late twentieth century snugly'. Worse still, was the fact that Left Bank actually had a record deal. Last year they'd signed to Ikon, an off-shoot of EMI. Their first advance brought in enough money for Simon to buy a new guitar and sign off. The dole office almost threw a party when he told them the good news.

'That can't be your earth shattering news, surely?' I said incredulously. 'Come on, what's so important?'

Simon coughed shiftily. 'Listen, forget it. Temporary madness – that's all. It's no biggy. Forget it.'

And so I did because that was exactly what Simon didn't want me to do. If he felt the need to play games, the least I could do was annoy him with fake apathy.

'So how's it going?' I asked, not really wanting to hear the answer. I wasn't in the right frame of mind for Simon, or to be more accurate, I wasn't in the right frame of mind to hear he'd had an excellent week.

'Great. Really cool,' enthused Simon. 'You know we'd been demoing new material in London for the last couple of months? Well, it's all finished. A little bit of polish and our first single will be ready to be unleashed. I was talking to our press officer last week and she reckons we're creating a real buzz in the industry. Some woman at the *Guardian* might even do a feature on us. Wicked.'

'Yeah,' I said, trying to imitate sincerity but falling far short of the mark. Until the record deal, Simon's life had been my sole source of comfort when feeling guilty about Not Getting A Life. While languishing on the dole in Manchester I was constantly cheered by the thought that though I wasn't doing anything constructive, at least I wasn't him, at least I wasn't killing myself, putting all this energy into something so hopelessly futile as a band. *We hate it when our friends become successful.* Indeed. It was frustrating. I had more talent than Simon could ever dream of. I just didn't know where my genius lay, and in my latest incarnation as a secondary school English teacher it wasn't likely I'd find out either.

'How are things between you and Tammy?' I asked.

'Couldn't be better, my son.'

He was lying. Tony, Left Bank's drummer and West Bridgford's most notorious alcoholic, had told me over a double whisky chaser in the Royal Oak, that Tammy and Simon had been fighting with alarming regularity for the last couple of weeks.

'Oh,' I said casually, but not all that casually.

'Oh what?' said Simon coolly – his interest piqued.

'Fifteenth letter of the alphabet. At least I think so.'

I didn't need to say any more. My job was done. Happier, now that he wasn't quite so smug any more, I allowed him to change the topic of conversation.

'How's school?' Simon enquired. 'It sounds weird saying it like that. Like you're back at Beechwood Comp.'

'Fine,' I lied. I wanted to give him a run for his money in the fantastic-week-stakes. 'School's good. The kids think I'm cool because I've got a pair of Nike trainers. London's not as bad as everyone makes out y'know, there's a lot going on. I've been so busy I haven't been in a single night all week.'

'Sounds good,' said Simon. 'If things work out then the band might move down your way soon. I've been down there so long in the last six months, what with gigs and recordings, that it almost seems like home.' He hesitated as if weighing up something in his mind. 'How's the flat?'

'All right,' I said, wondering where his question was leading.

He was strangely silent. I wondered if he wanted me to thank him again for helping me get a roof over my head.

'Oh, don't forget to thank Tammy for finding the flat for me,' I said. 'It was uncommonly kind of her.'

'Yeah it was,' replied Simon absent-mindedly. He paused. 'George Michael signed his first record contract with Innervision at a café on Holloway Road just down the road from you. I always fancied going down there to see if there are any early eighties Wham vibes floating about, but I never got round to it.' He paused again, more than a little embarrassed, and fired off a diversionary question intended to win back the point lost by my earlier volley. 'So, anyone new in your life?'

Whether I'd had someone new in my life or not, I would've conjured up the perfect woman instantly, just to deny him his moment of self-satisfaction. However, as fate would have it, there was no need to break the truth when bending was all that was required. 'I've been seeing a girl called Martina. Stunning. An absolute babe. We met in Bar Rumba, in the West End. She's one of the reasons I'm so knackered. I've seen her every night this week, in fact she'll be coming round here soon.'

The only reason I even knew there was a club called Bar Rumba was because Aggi had once talked about driving to London just to go there and I'd said that I didn't fancy it, and she said she was going to go on her own, and I said fine, and she said fine, but she ended up not going anyway.

'That's good news,' said Simon. 'It's good to see you happy again.'

'Why?'

'Well, because it is.'

He meant Aggi.

'Oh, you mean Aggi?' I said.

'Yeah, well I didn't want to mention her,' he said, fumbling over his words. 'I know how sensitive you still are about her.'

'I'm not sensitive,' I said. 'Aggi? Lucky escape, if you ask me.'

'Come on, Will,' sighed Simon impatiently, 'you can't mean that?'

'Oh, yes I do,' I replied. 'She was a total control freak. No, this was definitely a lucky escape, mate. Martina's definitely the girl for me. Nice, down to earth and very beautiful.'

I carried on like this, rubbishing Aggi and extolling the virtues of Martina, so that soon it began to sound like a truth, if not quite up to the same standards as the Truth. It had been *three years* since Aggi and I had been together – a lifetime ago to any normal twenty-six-year-old. She was nothing but memories to me, and for what it was worth *she* might as well have been a figment of my imagination. Martina, on the other hand, was real. She was real, quite stunning and most of all I didn't have to do anything to please her because she liked me the way I was.

The more I spoke, the more I realised that if I could get Simon – who had heard me moan about missing Aggi all this time – to believe I had never loved her, then maybe I could pull the wool over my own eyes too. And then I'd finally defeat Aggi and drive her from my head and my heart for good.

'I never loved Aggi.'

The words cut dead the thread of our conversation. It sounded so unreal that I said them again.

'I never loved Aggi. I just thought that I did. I think that at the end of the day I'd just grown used to her. It was nice having her around, and yeah, losing her and leaving university did kind of turn my world upside down for a while, but I'm over it. Those three years we had together meant nothing to me. Nothing at all.'

'Nothing?' asked Simon. The tone of his voice indicated that he didn't believe me for a second.

'Not a thing, mate.'

It felt good to lie.

Simon put on his agony uncle head and I wondered whether he'd been listening to *The Barbara White Show* too. 'Are you sure that you're not just saying that because you think that you've finally got to get over her?'

I hated the way he thought he could suss out a situation in seconds. He was the only person in the world allowed to be unfathomable. The thing was, everything he'd learnt about life had been culled from music. That was his biggest failing. He hadn't realised that life couldn't always be reduced to a three and a half minute pop song.

'No,' I lied again. 'Not at all. Look, she was all right, I'll give you that, and we did have some fun times.' I looked at her photograph on the wall and considered tearing it up as a show of strength. 'And, yes, I was distraught when we split up, but you've got to remember that I'm the man who went into mourning when I heard there wasn't going to be another series of *Blackadder*.' I chickened out of tearing up the photo and instead grabbed a marker pen, blacked out a tooth and drew a beard, a pair of glasses and bushy eyebrows on her face. 'Me and Aggi, well, we had different agendas right from the start. She wanted to be ethereal and I wanted to be down to earth. She wanted to go out and experience life and I wanted to stay in and watch it happen on TV. We were doomed from the start. We had nothing in common.'

I gave myself a standing ovation.

Simon's only response was, 'Well I'm glad you're over her.'

'Over who?' I joked.

We both laughed but Simon's sounded forced, as if trying to bolster my spirits.

'Listen,' he said. 'I'm glad you've told me all this.'

'Yeah,' I said, mellowing not only to Simon, but to the thought of being without Aggi. 'It's been good to get all this off my chest. You know how it is when you keep things bottled inside. It's not good for you.'

'No, you're right, it isn't,' he admitted.

Simon paused theatrically. More theatrically in fact than the entire cast of a Harold Pinter play. His sense of drama was another extension of his rock 'n' roll persona. Life to him was something that happened so that he'd have something to write songs about. He was always in search of an Experience he could dilute into a verse-chorus-verse structure. I was sure that was why he'd had so many different girlfriends and behaved like a git to all of them. There wasn't a lot of song mileage to be had from successful relationships and a nice personality.

'I've got to tell you something,' he said. 'It's the reason I called last night.'

I wondered whether he was cheating on Tammy again; it wouldn't have surprised me as he'd done it before. As far as I knew, he hadn't been seeing anyone on the side, he'd been too busy working on his masterpiece in London to bother with women.

'I'm sorry, mate,' he continued, playing the scene for all he was worth. 'I don't know how to say this, so I'll just come out with it. I had a bit of a "thing" with Aggi.'

'You did what?'

I'd heard exactly what he'd said and understood it all too clearly, but I needed to hear it again if only to torture myself more than was strictly necessary.

'I had a bit of a "*thing*" with Aggi.'

His voice was throaty, like he needed a glass of water and a good cough to clear his air-passages.

130

I asked him, 'What kind of a *"thing"* did you have with Aggi?' My voice was emotionless, at least, that's the way I remember it.

'The kind of *"thing"* that you wouldn't have been very happy about at one time,' he replied.

Strangely, my emotions appeared to have gone AWOL. My brain was getting ready for a bit of a scene but there was nothing happening on an adrenal level. Maybe I'd got my wish. Maybe I *was* finally over her. I stared across at her graffitied photo and smiled weakly.

'It's no skin off my nose,' I said. 'What Aggi does with whomever is her business. I just thought . . .' This time it was my turn for a dramatic pause, because I hadn't got a clue what I thought. 'I just thought that perhaps you could've been a bit more sensitive about it. I know it's been three years since she and I split up but even so, it's a bit much. You're meant to be my mate. What are you going to do next? Jump in my grave before I get there? And what will you say, "Oh, sorry, Will, didn't know you were going to use it"?'

'It's been and gone,' he said, refusing to react to my sarcasm. 'It's all over. It happened a long time ago. I just wanted to tell you because it's been weighing on my mind recently. I only wanted to be fair. We've been mates for too long to let a girl come between us.'

'You should've thought about that before you started . . .' I couldn't bring myself to say it. Giving it a name would only have made it more real than I could handle.

'I'm sorry,' said Simon quietly. 'Will, I really am sorry.'

'Forget the apologies,' I said, ejecting one of Left Bank's early demos from my cassette deck and throwing it to the floor. 'I told you, I'm over her. All I want to know is exactly how long ago was it?'

'A while ago,' he said, barely audibly.

My brain was in overdrive but my emotions were still nowhere to be seen.

'Exactly how long ago is "a while ago"?' I asked.

'It was . . .' He was loving every second of this. 'It was while you were still going out with her.'

Suddenly, my emotions returned home from their package holiday. The pain was physical and emotional all at once, as if a huge invisible fist had sent me across the room like in the 1982 Spielberg-produced horror film, *Poltergeist*. I felt sick, I felt faint, my knees went weak. I couldn't understand why he was telling me now after all this time. Ignorance wasn't just bliss, it was the pillars that kept the roof of my sanity from crashing down.

Simon, meanwhile, was waiting for a response. I didn't know what to say. He was right, a response *was* called for, something brutal that would cut him down to size, something that would make him feel as low as I felt, a guilt trip so far off the map he'd never find his way back. I drew a deep breath and put the phone down.

2.38 P.M.

When Simon had given me the copy of Left Bank's demo tape which I now held in my hands, he'd described it as 'a piece of rock 'n' roll history' that would one day be priceless. Clearing a space amongst the clothes, dirty crockery and exercise books, I placed the tape on the floor and looked feverishly around the flat for an instrument to aid me in my actions. In the kitchen I discovered a bread knife and a saucepan which had the remains of Thursday's spaghetti hoop dinner encrusted to its non-stick surface. I smiled at them both maniacally like Jack Nicholson in full 'Here's Johnny' mode.

Standing with Simon's 'priceless' work of art positioned at the foot of the bed, I raised the saucepan over my head and brought it crashing down against the tape, repeating the blows until it shattered into a million pieces. On roughly the twentieth blow the saucepan and its handle parted company, at which point I fell to my knees panting heavily. Someone, presumably the bloke from downstairs, whose roof was my floor, knocked on my door loudly. Ignoring him I began bundling together what was left of the magnetic tape before attacking it with the bread knife – shredding it into three weddings-worth of confetti. This complicated procedure took ten minutes to complete because halfway through, my temporary dementia still raging, I had decided that no piece of magnetic tape should be longer than half an inch and forced myself to begin again. Once I'd finished, I gathered the bits into a pile and scooped them into an envelope – the one I'd stolen from the school stationery cupboard specifically to send to the bank with my begging letter – and, using the same marker pen I'd used to graffiti Aggi, I scrawled Simon's address on it, sealed it with Sellotape, and added a first class stamp.

I got dressed and pulled on my heavy grey cashmere over-coat (bought from a jumble sale at Beeston Methodist church hall for £2.20, knocked down from £5.00) though I hadn't a clue what the weather was like. In my head it was the harshest Siberian winter on record, and in my heart it was a rainy night in Georgia – it had to be heavy grey overcoat weather. I picked up the envelope from the floor, slipped my *A–Z of London* into my coat pocket and walked out of the flat.

I needed to walk. I had too much anger in me to sit and watch TV, which was the only other thing I could think of doing bar getting the train to Nottingham, borrowing my dad's car and leaving tyre marks across Simon's chest. As a rule I wasn't a violent person, but I amazed even myself by the murderous thoughts rocketing around my head. Smashing the tape had helped to a degree, but I wanted something more, something that would bruise, bleed and make him beg for mercy. Simon was considerably bigger than me, but I felt invincible, like I was in full Jackie Chan *Drunken Master II* kick ass mode. I would've smashed his face in.

I wanted to know when it had happened.
I wanted to know how it had happened.
I wanted to know why it had happened.
I wanted to know everything.
But most of all I wanted Aggi back.

Simon's news at least had an upside: I now knew how point-less it was trying to pretend that I didn't still feel something for her. It didn't make sense to love her. I'd weighed up the pros and cons a million times, and the results were always the same: I needed her. She was no good for me, she didn't want me to be part of her life, but there was nothing I could do about how I felt. I loved her. I couldn't lie to myself, though it was the one thing I wished I had the strength to do. I couldn't forget about her. The passage of time had, if anything, made her more important to me now than ever. I couldn't replace her with another girl without constantly comparing them to her and finding them lacking. I couldn't move forward and I couldn't reclaim the past. I was stuck in an ex-lover's limbo with nothing but happy memories to keep me company.

Looking around me for the first time I realised my feet had taken me to the Italian newsagent's near the top of Holloway Road. I put the envelope in the post box outside, decided against going into the shop to buy chocolate and continued up the road. My mission, petty as it was, had been accomplished, but I didn't want to go home. That was why I'd brought the *A–Z* with me.

Simon thinks that all Archway's got to offer is some café where George-bloody-Michael signed a record contract, I'd thought, while getting my coat on, ready to leave the flat. *Well, Marx's grave is near here somewhere. Now's as good a time as any to find it.*

With my *A–Z* open and my finger on Archway Road, I crossed the traffic lights at the tube station and navigated my way to Highgate Road. As I came to Whittington Hospital, an ambulance pulled out in front of me which led me into a long and protracted daydream:

Simon has contracted a rare blood disease. I'm the only

person on earth that has the right blood type to save him. 'Will, you're the only one who can save me,' he whispers weakly, clutching at my hand.

'Should have thought of that before you started poking my girlfriend,' I reply.

Five minutes and a fag-break later, I checked the *A–Z* again. It didn't look too far now. Across the road I could see an old church marked on the map which had been converted into a set of yuppie apartments and a bit farther up was the entrance to Highgate Park. The park was empty apart from a middle-aged woman in green Wellingtons walking a Yorkshire Terrier. As I passed the pond in the middle of the rolling landscape, I walked into a swarm of midges, inhaling quite a few of their number. Normally this would've set me off on a tirade of abuse against the animal kingdom but even this didn't phase me. I was a man with a mission and Marx's grave was my holy grail. There everything would become crystal clear.

I came to the gates on the far side of the park and turned left. There it was – Highgate Cemetery. There was a small white hut positioned two yards past the gates, on which was pinned a small hand-written sign revealing that tickets were 50p per person.

What has the world come to when you can't even visit deceased left-wing thinkers without having to pay for the privilege?

Disgruntled, I paid the far too chirpy elderly woman residing within her blood money. She asked me if I needed directions, I said no, in case she wanted to try and sell me a map.

The cemetery was peaceful and almost as silent as Archway had been the previous night except, if I strained really hard, I could hear the occasional lorry, so it kind of made sense to stop straining. Ridiculous as this might seem, it occurred to me that this was definitely a cemetery. All around me were graves. Marx was in the company of a lot of people whose deaths spanned over two hundred years. Time had caused the older gravestones to blend in with nature; ivy and erosion now made them seem at home. The newer headstones, though, looked depressingly incongruous, like shiny marble bookmarks stuck into the ground. I made a mental note to remind my mother that I wanted to be cremated. If I left my funeral arrangements up to her she'd get me the shiniest marble headstone money could buy, with the specific intention of embarrassing me for eternity.

Wandering aimlessly around the cemetery, occasionally stopping to read the odd inscription, I stumbled across the grave, or rather tomb, I was looking for. There was no mistaking it, a huge metal cast of a balding, bearded man's head rested on top of the pale stone tomb. Even if I'd never seen a picture of Marx I would have known who it was; he looked exactly how I expected the father of modern Socialism to look: a little sad, a little world weary; sort of a cross between Father Christmas and Charlton Heston, but with a twinkle in his eye, as if he was constantly on the verge of working out the meaning of life. The inscription on the tomb in gold lettering read:

> *'The philosophers have merely interpreted the world. The point is to change it.'*

As expected, his tomb had become a Mecca for Marxists worldwide, just as Jim Morrison's grave in Paris had become a home from home for half-arsed Euro-poets. Scattered around the edge of the marble base were a number of artificial roses and scraps of paper containing messages. I stood over one and read it:

'Thank you, from those of us still fighting for freedom all around the world.'

It wasn't signed.

I studied the inscription on the tomb again and felt ashamed. Marx had tried to change the world and make it a better place. He wanted workers to be able to study philosophy in the morning and go fishing in the afternoon. He wanted an end to tyranny, based on the belief that all men were equal. All I wanted was to get my ex-girlfriend back. It was a selfish pursuit benefiting no one but myself. Even as these self-chastising thoughts entered my head, I felt my shoulders automatically hunching up into a 'so what' shrug. I wondered if every man was like me. Give a man a noble cause and he would fight to the death for what he believed in, but get the woman he loves to leave him and his once honourable principles would cease to be quite so important.

I was standing so quietly, wrapped up tightly in my thoughts, that a robin flew down from the branches of the oak above Karl's head and landed on the ground right beside my feet. Straight away it began tugging at a twig over twice its own body length. For over five minutes it struggled, lines of determination etched onto its beaky little face, before it gave up and flew off to a silver birch branch four trees to the left to recuperate. That robin was me. I was that robin. And Aggi was that twig. Those five minutes the robin had spent tugging at that twig, well, those were the three years I'd spent trying to get her back. Like God and McDonalds, Aggi was everywhere.

I decided it was time to go when huge raindrops fell from the sky in their thousands, drenching me in seconds. My hair was soaked through and small rivulets of water ran down the back of my head, along my neck and into my shirt. I turned the collar on my overcoat up and pulled my head into its protection as far as I could, which didn't really help because now I couldn't see anything as my glasses had completely steamed up. To make matters worse, for the last few minutes I'd been monitoring a distinct rise in the smell of old men coming from my coat. Too cheap to bother getting it dry-cleaned when I'd bought it, I was now paying for the tightness of my wallet as the essence of the coat's previous owner came back to haunt me; it was sweet and musty, like stale urine mixed with the contents of a cat's litter tray.

I was wet, cold and smelling like the tramp from my late-night 7-Eleven trip. It was the rain that depressed me most of all. A walk in the rain might possibly have been fun if I'd had somebody to get wet with. I could've splashed gaily in puddles, swung on lamp-posts and sung a song or two, but I was alone. Drowning in torrential downpours on my own had no romance about it whatsoever. Gene Kelly wouldn't have been quite so annoyingly smug if he'd just found out his best mate had been sleeping with *his* girlfriend.

By the time I reached the house I felt lower than I'd done all week. Oblivious to the elements, I waited shivering by the garden gate, unsure about what to do next. It was still only Saturday afternoon, roughly speaking there were another thirty-six hours to fill until Monday. Even if I slept for as much of it as possible, there was still too much time, time I would spend imagining Aggi and Simon together: having sex; exchanging secret glances; laughing conspiratorially. Once I opened the front door the outside world would be locked out, leaving just me and my thoughts.

The hallway was depressingly dusty. Mr F. Jamal had promised me all communal spaces would be cleaned every Friday. I eyed a scrap of silver paper from a pack of Polos that had fallen out of my pocket onto the carpet yesterday morning, and shook my head sadly. Walking up the stairs I strained my ears, listening out for evidence of life in the other flats – people alone like me – people who might like to talk. The house was silent. Dead. When eventually I reached my door I fished around in my soggy overcoat pockets for my keys and also discovered the following:

> Three squashed Rolos (still in wrapper).
> Two bus tickets.
> Bakewell tart crumbs.

I scattered the crumbs on the threadbare carpet outside my door. A year ago I'd carried a solitary Bakewell tart in my coat pocket for less than a minute and since then I'd been removing crumbs by the thousand like modern day loaves and fishes.

I looked around the flat. Nothing had changed. N-O-T-H-I-N-G. I wasn't sure what I had expected to happen (someone to have fixed the kitchen tap? A miracle? A message from

Aggi?) but I'd desperately wanted something, anything to have changed. Instead, time had stood still and waited for my return.

To keep my brain ticking over I tried to work out who the last human being I'd spoken to in person was. There was one proviso, I could only count people whom I'd choose to go for a drink with. I'd left Nottingham the previous Sunday from my mum's house. Technically speaking, my mum and my brother had been the last human beings I'd spoken to. But while I liked them both, I didn't know whether I'd go as far as to say that I'd go for a drink with either of them. Next in line was Martina on Saturday night, but as I was trying to erase that encounter from my memory, she didn't meet the requirements. Casting my mind back further I recalled that on Friday I'd gone for a quick one in the Royal Oak with Simon, but as he officially no longer existed as far as I was concerned he didn't count either.

I pulled the emergency cord on this particular depressing train of thought and turned my attention to the phone. There were no messages on the answering machine. It wasn't even on, I'd forgotten to set it. After dialling 1471 – the number that tells you the last person that called – I wished I hadn't. At 2.42 p.m. precisely, Martina had phoned. She had to be pregnant. I called her parents' house but she wasn't in. They asked me if I wanted to leave a message and I said no. Shifting a pile of clothes and books aside, I made myself comfortable on the carpet, lying stomach downwards, and concentrated on the phone, willing it to ring.

For a while Aggi and I had lived under the delusion that we were psychic, after one occasion when we tried to phone each other at exactly the same time. The thought of our separate electrical impulses simultaneously hurtling down a fibre optic cable towards each other had meant so much that we spent a whole afternoon trying, quite seriously, to project images into each other's minds. It never worked.

I emptied the pockets of my jeans onto the floor because my keys were jabbing into my groin. After two minutes of intense concentration the phone still hadn't rung. I thought perhaps it was because I was being too general, trying to get anyone (bar Simon) to call.

Minutes passed and nothing really happened. Next door's dog, for some unknown reason, began howling like a wolf, but with the exception of that minor interruption life continued to pass me by. More minutes passed uneventfully. I considered calling Martina again and maybe leaving a message like 'Tell her everything's going to be okay' – something that would bolster her spirits if she was feeling scared or lonely, something that would imply that I cared without going overboard. It was wrong of course. I couldn't give her hope where there was none. If she thought she'd found true love after a drunken sexual encounter seven days ago, her warped mind would turn a message of solidarity into a proposal of marriage.

The telephone that I had in my hand was one I'd bought in Argos during my final year at university. It had come in three colours: grey, cream and white and I'd chosen grey because I thought it wouldn't show up the dirt as much as the others (although the grubby mouthpiece caked in minuscule deposits of dried saliva was testament to the fact that most things show up dirt if you don't clean them). Everyone in the house I shared had chipped in to buy it, but I'd got to take it home when we graduated because I won it in the house lottery. Tony (whom I hadn't seen or heard from since we all moved out) won the toaster, Sharon (whom I hadn't seen or heard from since graduation) won the plug-in TV aerial, and Harpreet (whom I hadn't seen or heard from since I left Manchester) won the electric kettle. I was really chuffed to win that phone; the hours I'd clocked up on it talking to Aggi probably ran into months. Some of our best conversations had been on that phone, like the one when she'd told me I was the kind of man that she wanted to marry one day. That phone had made me very happy.

It rang.

'Hello?'

'Hello.'

It was Kate.

'Hi, Kate. How are you?'

'I'm fine. I hope you don't mind me calling.'

'No, not at all,' I replied, happy that it was Kate and not Simon seeking forgiveness.

'Are you sure I'm not disturbing you?' she asked. 'You answered the phone very quickly. You must've been sitting on it. Were you expecting a call from someone else?'

'No, I was just passing,' I lied. 'I've only just got in. I went to Highgate Cemetery with some friends to see Marx's grave. Very cool. Definitely worth seeing.'

I wished I hadn't described Marx's grave as 'cool'. I was sounding too nerd-like for words.

'Do you know I lived in that flat for over a year and never got around to going there? It's a shame, I'll probably never get to see it now.'

'Maybe I'll let you visit me some day,' I replied, only half joking.

She laughed.

I laughed too, but only because I was wondering whether I was stretching the point to describe her laugh as 'flirtatious'.

'You'd better be careful what you say,' she said wistfully. 'I might take you up on that.'

Simultaneously I ran out of saliva and witty come-backs. I changed the subject. 'So, what've you been up to today?'

'Nothing much,' she said. 'I watched kids' TV this morning and then went into town. I managed to get an extension on my overdraft, so I spent most of it on a pair of trainers and a skirt. I shouldn't be spending money like I do but it cheered me up.'

'I think your cheque came today,' I told her, spying her letter on top of the TV. 'Well, there's a letter for you anyway.'

'Brilliant. That's fantastic news. Oh, what time is it? Quarter past three? I've missed last post then. Oh well, at least it'll get here on Tuesday. Better than it not coming at all, I suppose.'

She sounded happy.

'So would you like to talk some more?' she asked.

'Of course,' I said. 'How many times did I beg you to call back yesterday?'

'What do you want to talk about?'

'Anything,' I said happily. 'Anything at all.'

I actually had a topic that I wanted to discuss if she couldn't come up with one. It was a question I'd been mulling over on the journey from the cemetery. I wanted to know whether she thought the most beautiful people in the world (Cindy Crawford, Mel Gibson *et al*) ever got dumped. And if so, did this mean that no one, no matter who they were, was safe from getting dumped? I was thankful when she said she'd got a question, because I was sure mine would've eventually ended up about Aggi.

'This is kind of related to what you did this afternoon,' said Kate, revealing her question. 'Where do you stand on death?'

'I'm against it,' I joked.

We both laughed.

'You know what I mean,' she said. 'What do you think about death?'

'I think that when you're dead you're dead,' I said matter-of-factly. 'This is it as far as life goes, so we'd better make the most of it while we've got it. Although having said that, I think I'd be kind of disappointed if what I've spent the last twenty-six years experiencing was really all there was to life.'

'Okay, well my question for you is this: how would you like to die?' said Kate, as if she was a waitress asking a diner how they liked their eggs done.

'This is all getting a bit strange, isn't it?' I said.

'Strange? You should hear the things that me and Paula talk about at five in the morning after our eighth triple vodka! Question is, are you man enough?'

'I'm more of a man than you,' I protested mockingly.

'I should hope so!' said Kate.

'You'll never find out,' I retorted, wondering if this banter we were engaging in constituted flirting or simply joking around.

'Seriously, how would you like to pop off?' she asked.

'I don't know,' I said, gratefully returning to the subject of death. 'I'll need some time to think about this one. In the meantime, what about you? How would you like to die?'

'I thought you'd never ask!' she said laughing. 'Me and Paula have discussed this many times during our late night chats. My answer is all ready. Are you?'

'As I'll ever be.'

PART ONE OF A TWO PART CONVERSATION ON DEATH: HER WAY OF THINKING

Now this is going to sound morbid, in fact it's going to sound very morbid. I suppose it is morbid, really. What must you think of me? You don't know me that well, so I suppose you're probably not thinking all that much. Well, here goes. Every now and again I like to think about my own funeral. I know it sounds weird but it's true. People don't think about death very much these days, do they? They seem to spend their whole lives avoiding it. Pensioners on the other hand think about it constantly. They've definitely got the right idea. I suppose it's because they're so much nearer to the End than the rest of us. They keep a little bit of money in a post-office account to make sure there's enough cash around to pay for a decent funeral, coffin and finger-food for afterwards. That's how it should be. Then of course you've got the ancient Egyptians. They spent their entire lives thinking about death and when they went it was like the biggest party ever: good clothes, possessions and even slaves buried in the roomiest coffins in the world. Egyptians, old people and me – we've all got our priorities right.

The first thing to work out is exactly how I'm going to die.

147

Sometimes it's drowning, other times it's an aeroplane crash, but at the moment it's dying in any manner at all as long as it's for someone I love.

Okay, so you want me to explain? It's really simple. I'm desperate to die for someone I love. That's all there is to it. I don't know what the situation is. The important thing is that when I die the person I save lives on because of me. That's all that matters. I know it won't surprise you to know that I've already constructed a purpose-built scenario for this!

I'm nearly twenty. I've not done an awful lot with my life so far. I've been to school, gained a couple of A levels, gone to university and dropped out, and, um, that's about it. Pretty self-centred, wouldn't you say?

I got the idea from a black and white film I saw one Saturday afternoon the week before I moved out of the flat.

Here's the sitch: there's a cad, a French aristocrat, and a beautiful girl who's madly in love with the aristo. Anyway, the Cad falls in love with Beautiful Girl. On a trip to France the Aristocrat gets caught by the children of the revolution, who put him in the Bastille. The Cad goes to France and visits the Aristocrat in the Bastille. Now here's the good bit: the Cad knocks out Aristocrat, swaps places with him and goes to the guillotine in his place! D'you see? Cad loves Beautiful Girl so much that he's prepared to sacrifice his own life so that she can be happy with Another!

That film left me in shock. I've only seen it once. I don't even know what it's called – I mean . . . well . . . I did know, but now I don't. Being dumped does that to your long-term memory, doesn't it? Oh, it doesn't matter what it was called, it moved me. It really moved me. I mean, what does it mean? Is that love or is it obsession? Will any man want to do that for me? I'm asking a lot of questions. I apologise. I think Dirk Bogarde was in it.

Where did we begin all this? Oh yeah! My funeral.

It's been a great worry of mine that all of the people that I want to invite to my funeral won't be invited due to my own lack of foresight. There's no one person amongst my friends that knows all of my other friends. My friend Lizzie knows most of the people who went to our school who were friends with me, but she wouldn't know people like Pete or Jimmy or Karen or any of the small number of friends I made at university, and she wouldn't know any of the people from when I lived in Cardiff last summer like Mrs Grosset, or the lads who used to come into the Lion on a Tuesday night. A couple of times I've made a definitive list and posted it to Lizzie with strict instructions for it to remain sealed until my death. Lizzie is a mate, but I just know that she's opened it. Well, you would, wouldn't you? But it doesn't matter because I revise the list every now and again when certain people get too much for me. I'll add you to it if you want me to.

I suppose with all this talk about funerals you'll think I'm being really vain but it's something we're all guilty of. I just want to know that my passing will be mourned big time. I don't want people to be philosophical about my death. I want them to grieve for a decent period. It's good for the soul, you know?

PART TWO OF A TWO PART CONVERSATION ON DEATH: MY WAY OF THINKING

It'll be of little comfort to you but you're no weirder than me. I know what you mean when you say you want to die for someone else. When you look back at your life you want to have meant something. I've got a friend, or rather had a friend, and it's just possible that through some quirk of fate he might become famous. And I bet he thinks that if he gets this goal, i.e. fame and fortune, his life will have meaning. But it won't. The only way life can really mean something is if you give it away. It's a shame though because if you do give it away, you don't get the chance to fully appreciate the splendour of it. That's the main flaw of the ultimate selfless act – you never get the chance to be around to take your bow.

I had my first encounter with death at the age of five. I'd been given a junior gardening kit by my parents which consisted of a small shovel, rake and watering can. My mum had bought me some red Wellington boots to go with it and my dad had let me choose a packet of carrot seeds from a huge row of seed packets at the local gardening centre. At the time I had a big thing about carrots. I thought that if I grew some they'd lure Bugs Bunny to my garden. I lived in

151

hope that one day I'd see my carrots disappearing under the ground and then I'd know that Bugs was real. Then I'd peer down the hole where my carrots had been and he'd look up at me, twitch his whiskers and say, 'What's up, Doc?'

It was an incredibly hot summer's day when I decided to do my planting – my dad completely ignored the advice on the packet, which said to sow from March to late May – just to make me happy. Within half an hour of starting work I'd dug the soil, planted my seeds and watered them. My job was done, but I carried on digging for the sake of it in a patch of ground away from the carrots. Once in a while I'd find a worm. The first one startled me a little – I think it was because they didn't have eyes – but after that, every time I came across one, I picked it up on the edge of my spade and popped it in my little yellow bucket. I decided to have a competition to see how many worms I could collect in an afternoon. I promised myself that if I'd collected enough by the end of the day I'd try and make my own wormery like the one I'd seen in the solitary copy of *The Encyclopaedia Britannica* (Washington – Yam) we'd received free for joining a book club.

At about one o'clock my mum called me in for lunch. I was quite relieved to finally take a rest because I was beginning to feel a bit dizzy from the heat. Inside, the house was cool. On the table was a ham, lettuce and tomato sandwich and a glass of Ribena. I drank and ate and felt content. In fact I felt so content that I fell asleep on the living room sofa. Two hours later I woke up. By now it was time for the kids' programmes on telly. I watched my favourite cartoons until my mum ordered me to sort out the mess in the garden. It was then that I remembered the worms. I examined the bucket expecting to see a writhing mass of slimy worms bent on revenge. Instead all I saw were very grey, very stiff, very dry, dead worms. Why weren't they moving? I wondered. Why had they stopped being worms? Eventually I worked out that their few hours in the sun might not have been particularly beneficial to their welfare, so I rushed to the kitchen and filled a Tupperware beaker with water from the hot tap, poured it into the bucket and waited. I expected the worms to be instantly re-animated, but they weren't. Instead they floated on the surface of the water, rocking gently to and fro as steam rose up against my face.

I asked my mum why the worms had died and she gave me the technical answer about them losing moisture and dehydrating. But that didn't really answer my question. Why were they dead? The real answer, and the answer that I kind of worked out there and then, was this: the worms died because everything dies eventually. That's what life is all about.

The only attractive prospect about dying is that if I do it soon enough there's the possibility that Aggi might finally see that she and I were meant for each other. Of course, her realising this once I've popped my clogs makes the whole thing kind of pointless, but at least this great wrong would at last have been righted.

And now to funerals: I've done more than plan the guest list. First off there'll be twenty-two wailing women, dressed in black, standing at my graveside; girls whom I've fancied at various points in my sad life but who had ignored my advances, only to realise, now that I was dead, that I had been their perfect man all along.

My mum would be weeping like mad; I can't imagine that she'd be in any state other than suicidal. I think she's desperate to die before either my brother Tom or me, and I'm inclined to agree that it might be for the best. My mother takes great comfort in the status quo, as does my dad; they like things to be just the way they found them, though that didn't stop them getting divorced last year.

I find it hard enough to deal with twenty-six years of life, so the thought of dealing with an eternity of death fills me with dread. I can barely motivate myself to get out of bed these days. I wasn't always like this. I wasn't like this at all.

Look, I'm feeling a bit tired now. Thanks for calling. You're certainly an interesting person to talk to, but right now I've got to go. And no, it's not because I want to be a moody boy loner, although any mystique, even hackneyed moody boy loner mystique, would be useful. It's just that I'm talking all manner of weirdness to you straight off the cuff. I need to sit down and work everything out a bit. I found out today that the only girl I had ever loved cheated on me with my best friend and it kind of shook me up. Look, I promise I'll phone you back soon.

My neck was killing me.

During the course of the conversation I'd changed position several times and, by the time I'd put the phone down, I was lying half on the bed and half on the floor with my neck supporting more weight than it was designed to. It was a little unsettling to be suddenly thrust back into The Real World. A gust of wind sent a sheet of rain crashing against my window, as if I needed reminding that I wasn't meant to be happy. I picked up the phone again to see if Kate was still there. Sometimes, if the other person hasn't put their phone down, they can still be connected. When I discovered this, I used to do it to Aggi all the time. She'd always be the first to put the phone down and then she'd pick it up seconds later to call someone else and I'd still be there. When she cottoned on to what I was doing, she made me put the phone down first whenever we spoke. With hindsight, of course, she probably did it so she could phone Simon.

I reflected on the conversation I'd had with Kate. I hadn't told her the whole truth – I hadn't told her about my fantasies about Aggi's untimely passing. For ages the only way I could cope with Aggi's absence from my life was by pretending she was dead. I scattered her ashes by our oak tree in Crestfield Park, and when I occasionally visited her, I'd lay a few daisies at the base of the tree and tell her how life was. It was great when she was dead because at last I was free from worry. I always knew where she was and what she was doing; she always listened attentively and never argued.

Her funeral was wonderful. Lying in the coffin at the crematorium, her face was pale and fragile, her body stiff and wax-like – the complete opposite to how she'd been alive. Many of her previous boyfriends were present at the service but while they were all grim-faced and stiff-upper-lipped, I was the only one who openly shed tears because she would've liked that. Like Kate said, the last thing you want at your own funeral is people being reserved – the more wailing and gnashing of teeth the better.

Mrs Peters had cried too. She was one of the few people who could understand the pain I was going through. Although we hadn't spoken at the crematorium, when she'd bumped into me in town weeks later, she revealed how she'd always had a soft spot for me and said things like Aggi must've taken leave of her senses to dump me. She promised to put in a good word for me with Aggi when she got back home, unable to grasp the concept that her only daughter was dead.

Aggi had died from natural causes. I admit I'd considered murder, but it wasn't very me, although for a while it was. 'If I can't have you then nobody else can either!' It would've been amusing to have seen the look of horror on her face as I uttered those terrible words while haphazardly shoving cartridges into a shotgun. I'd have seen the terror in her beautiful green eyes as she realised that finally, after all these years, I did have a backbone and, unfortunately for her, my new Arnold Schwarzenegger-like persona would be the last thing she'd ever see. I couldn't shoot her though – too messy – and I couldn't stab her – which is what a crime of passion really called for, because that was messy too, and if I'd used a blunt instrument, I would've ruined that face that I loved so much. No, Aggi had died naturally from something the doctors didn't have a name for. Of course there was no antidote or cure but I didn't let her suffer. I offered her the choice of any of my organs if they could help matters, but alas they couldn't. After a week of suffering I kissed her good-bye and she fell into a coma. A month later Mrs Peters and I turned off her life-support machine to give another human being the chance of life.

I was devastated – the love of my life, felled in her prime by a mysterious disease! I spent morning, noon and night crying and shaking uncontrollably. My dad had said things like, 'It'll be all right in the end, son,' and told me to keep my strength up. Tom hadn't known what to say, but had given me a small smile of solidarity whenever our eyes met. Mum was the best of the bunch. She'd been very understanding, saying that whenever I was ready to talk, she'd be there to listen. Alice had phoned and told me that although she hadn't liked Aggi she was sad she was dead, and I had said it was okay and that it was good just to hear her voice. I'd telephoned the dole office and told them I wouldn't be in to sign on for the next couple of weeks, and even they, Nazis that they are, were extraordinarily nice, saying it was okay, rather than asking me to bring her body in as evidence, as I thought they might.

I rubbed my neck. It still felt sore. As I raised my arms to rub further I caught a whiff of my armpits that made my nasal hairs recoil. School sweat smells like nothing else on earth, the nearest thing I can compare it to is the smell of rancid milk and grass cuttings. I hadn't showered since Thursday evening – I had over thirty hours' worth of school sweat plus three hours' worth of its fouler smelling cousin, gym sweat, clinging to my skin. Fortunately, the shower was the one thing in the flat that had been modified since 1970. The water blasted out of the nozzle of my Gainsborough 1500 series like a mini police water cannon. I stayed there, enclosed by the shiny plastic shower curtain, for half an hour, lost in a world of steamy waterfalls, cleanliness and soap with labels that remained stuck on until the very end.

Standing on the cold lino post-shower, I rubbed myself down with a green hand towel – the only towel in the flat, because I'd forgotten to pack any others. Every time I showered I'd leave it hanging on the wardrobe door, praying that it would dry in time for use next day. By Wednesday morning it couldn't have been any wetter if it had been in the shower with me.

Dressing leisurely, I pulled my jeans back on and slipped on a clean, dark blue shirt. As I did the top buttons up, my hand brushed against what felt like the beginnings of a spot on my chin. I wanted to give up. I was undecided as to which was the more depressing thought: the fact that at twenty-six I still got spots, or that I was wishing I was at home so I could borrow my mum's foundation to cover it. It was impossible to tell exactly what stage it was at – minor blemish/hurts like buggery/custard pustular/bleeding scab – because I'd broken my Elvis mirror on Monday, the only mirror in the flat, having trodden on it as it lay hidden underneath a pile of clothes. *Seven years' bad luck*, I'd thought to myself. I added them to my last three years of misery, to make a nice round number.

The phone rang.

I gazed at it emptily, still wrapped up in thoughts about spots and my Elvis mirror, as if unsure where the sound was coming from. Once my brain got into gear, I whispered a silent prayer. I don't know why I hoped it was Kate. After all I had been the one who'd finished our last conversation prematurely and, as well as that, she'd given me her number so I could call her any time. No matter, I still hoped it might be Kate.

'Hi, Will, it's me.'

Like a spoilt child in need of – as my dad would put it – 'a good slapping', I was unreasonably annoyed that Martina had been out when I'd called. So out of sheer spite I pretended not to be sure who it was.

'Who?'

'Will, don't you recognise me? It's me, Martina.'

'Oh, sorry. I didn't recognise you for a second. You sound different on the phone.'

'Oh, do I?' she said, genuinely surprised. 'I just wanted to find out if you received my card.'

I tried to work out whether she sounded pregnant or not. There were no signs of stress in her voice but neither were there signs of relief. What's more she was asking me pointless questions about birthday cards when she knew full well that I was waiting to find out whether I'd fertilised one of her eggs and was going to spend the next thirty years in mourning. There was no way, of course, that I was intending to ask her. That was out of the question. She was playing games but I didn't care. If she'd ever seen the ruthless way I played Monopoly she'd know it wasn't worth her trying.

I cast my mind back to the birthday card and briefly contemplated denying its existence, because what Martina was really asking me was had I read and fully comprehended the ramifications of the message she'd written in it? She was making sure that the escape route marked 'Ambiguity' was blocked off for good.

'Yes, I got it,' I said.

'I've always wanted to send that Klimt card to a special person,' she said. I pictured her in my head, long blonde hair falling over her face. I'd watched her in lectures almost hiding behind that hair, as if it made her invisible. It was one of the few endearing things I'd noticed about her. 'Someone like you, Will. I think it's a really beautiful picture, don't you? It's got so much passion in it. I've got a poster of it in a clip frame. I spend hours looking at it.'

As she continued to sing the praises of Klimt and several other classical painters, I wondered whether I'd been too harsh with her. After all, she was kind and meant well. It wasn't her fault alone that she might be pregnant. She was certainly attractive and most of all she thought incredibly highly of me, in spite of everything I'd done to persuade her otherwise.

'Martina . . .'

I'd never used her name like that, not with any sort of softness or tenderness behind it that wasn't driven by lust. To her, my saying her name like that was a prelude to heaven. Wielding this sort of power was unsettling – I felt like a god, albeit a minor deity – all I had to do was utter a few small words and I could make Martina's wildest dreams come true.

'Martina, how would you like to die?' I asked, eventually.

'What do you mean?' she said, obviously confused. This wasn't what she had been expecting at all.

'I mean exactly what I said,' I replied gently. 'Taking aboard the fact that one day we're all going to die, when the big event comes – how would you like it to arrive?'

'I don't know the answer to that sort of question,' she said uncomfortably. 'I don't like thinking about, you know . . . passing away.'

'Yeah, well think about it now,' I said. My gentleness and sympathy evaporated. I was annoyed but only momentarily, because a second later I was overcome with guilt.

'I'm sorry,' I apologised. 'I didn't mean it.'

'No, *I'm* sorry,' she said bitterly. 'I'm obviously annoying you. I'll have a think right now. Let's see . . .' She paused, and made audible thinking noises. 'I'd like to go in my sleep,' she said, once she'd regained her composure. 'I don't want to know about it when it happens. I had a great aunt who died in her sleep and she looked very peaceful, like she was enjoying a good nap.'

I didn't know what to say next. I'm sorry to say that I didn't care about her answer. Martina wasn't Kate and she wasn't Aggi. We were never going to work out. It just wasn't meant to be.

'The test,' I said firmly.

'Negative,' she whispered. 'I'm not pregnant. I wanted to tell you. I just didn't know how. I'm sorry I dragged it out. I know you're angry. Please don't hate me, Will. I wasn't trying to upset you. I just didn't know . . .' She started to cry. 'Will, I was so scared. I really was. I was terrified. I wish you were here.'

I stood up and looked out of the window. It was raining. Next door's dog was sheltering underneath the silver birch at the bottom of the garden.

I was disappointed. Yes, I was disappointed. I wasn't going to be a father. I wasn't going to have to think up exotic middle class names for our child. There'd be no trips to Mothercare. My parents wouldn't be Gran and Granddad, nor for that matter would Gran gain her stately 'Great' prefix; Alice wouldn't become a godmother. After all that mental speculation everything would remain the same. I thought I'd have had a little girl. If Martina had voiced no objections we would've called her Lucy. When she'd reached five she would've gone to my junior school – hopefully Mrs Greene or someone equally nice would have been her teacher.

This is so hopeless.

'Will, I've got something to ask you,' whispered Martina,

ignoring my silence. 'I know you've probably been really busy this week, going out with your new London friends and all that, but I wonder . . .' Her voice grew quiet. An endearing blend of shyness and humility. 'I wonder if I could come and see you next weekend? I really miss you. I haven't been out all week because I've had no one to go out with. Nearly all of the friends that I managed to keep in contact with have moved away, and I swear if I have to spend another Friday night watching gardening programmes with my parents I'll go mad. I won't come if you don't want me to. I know that it's quite early on in our relationship and, well, with this scare things haven't been easy but . . .'

That 'but' hovered in the air for an unreasonably long time. I couldn't work out if she'd actually intended to finish her sentence or whether she'd left her 'but' lingering with intent. I decided she wasn't cynical enough to be that manipulative. I was genuinely moved. This girl was displaying a distressing lack of self-respect that only a master of these kind of indulgences such as I could truly appreciate.

I told her that I didn't really know what I was doing next weekend and that I had a lot of school work on. It was only after I'd said this that it occurred to me I might sound a little insensitive, what with her being an unemployed newly-qualified teacher. I told her that the best thing would be for me to ring her during the week and see how things were looking then.

She seemed to believe me and didn't say anything more about it. Before I said I had to go I promised her again that I'd call during the week. She sighed quietly, more to herself than anything, but clearly enough to let me know that she was disappointed I hadn't just said yes. Seizing the opportunity to start an argument in which I could end it all, I asked her if there was anything wrong. She hesitated before carefully answering 'No' in the chirpiest voice she could muster – which was in fact exceptionally chirpy. I said good-bye and put the phone down.

Martina had depressed me.

I really did want to make her happy. I did. But if her happiness involved my being with her until death did us part, there was nothing I could do for her. Pointless as it was, I bitterly wished I hadn't got off with her. I wished it hadn't happened at all. At least then, maybe I could have been her friend and helped her out; spoken to her on the phone for hours at a time; said yes immediately to her coming to stay; drunk too many bottles of wine and showed her my very poor impression of Sean Connery. But now none of this could ever happen. She'd never be satisfied with a demotion to being 'just good friends'.

Hunger drove me to the kitchen in search of sustenance. The best I could muster from a frantic search through the cupboards was an unopened bag of Tilda brown rice. In the end I opted for a cigarette and two slices of bread which I slipped into the toaster while I went to the toilet.

With my trousers around my ankles and the initial push of the first defecation of the day almost upon me, Martina's tearful face flashed inside my head with the persistency of a Belisha beacon. *That's how she'll look when I give her the push. Tearful. Like I've killed her Mum's Yorkshire Terrier with my bare hands and she's next on the list. Why can't she just get the message? Why is she making me do this? Why hasn't she got any self-respect?*

Get some, Martina. Get some self-respect before you end up like me.

Two days after Aggi had kicked me out of her life I was still very much in denial. The afternoon of the day in question, I found myself wandering along the booze aisle in Safeway, working out the most economical way to numb the pain with over a week left until my next Giro. Traditionally speaking, the situation – spurned lover seeking brief alcoholiday – cried out for vodka or whisky, but getting intentionally drunk on spirits, early in the morning, lacked the romance of, say, cheap wine, as it smacked too much of the real desperation of tramps and alcoholic wife-beaters. Plonk could always be explained away to my conscience as nothing more sinister than over-indulgence and so wine it was, two bottles of Safeway's own brand of Lambrusco. I barely got through the automatic doors at the exit before I'd unscrewed the cap off the first bottle and taken a deep swig. By the time I'd reached home on the bus over half the bottle had disappeared.

Wobbling up to my bedroom, I had dumped Aggi's letters out of the Nike trainer box where they lived and spread them over the floor. In between sips, I pored over each one, ninety-seven in total. This was the first time I'd ever read them collectively. Beginning with her first (twelve pages of feint-lined hole-punched A4) and ending with the last (a single sheet of green writing paper sent to me three weeks earlier), I built up a picture of our relationship different to the one in my head. The letters reminded me of how our relationship had really been, untainted by the events of the past few days. While the themes varied, after a year, they were pretty much all about the same thing: how much she loved me. I remember thinking to myself that the girl in these letters adored me and it was that girl, and not the girl who had dumped me, whom I loved so deeply. The other girl was just an impostor.

Hours went by as I filed them all in chronological order, even though some of them weren't dated. I amazed myself by working out when she'd written them by the kinds of things they mentioned. For example two letters were signed, 'Love, Mary Jane'. At the time that she'd sent them to me (March, roughly two-and-a-half years ago) I'd had a real thing for *Spiderman* comics and Mary Jane was the web-slinger's girlfriend. This and thousands of other tiny details sparked off so many wide-screen Technicolor memories that I felt like they'd only been written yesterday. By the time I'd re-read them all, I'd finished both bottles of wine and floods of tears were silently streaming down my face. I went for a walk to get some fresh air and ended up on Aggi's front door-step.

Mrs Peters opened the door, ushered me into the front room she kept for best and offered me a cup of tea. She told me that Aggi wasn't in but that she'd be back in half an hour as she'd only nipped out to the library down the road. She chatted at me (rather than to me) for every minute of that excruciatingly long half-hour, while I barely spoke a word in return, the Lambrusco having wreaked havoc with my ability to form simple sentences. She asked if Aggi had invited me over for Christmas dinner, which told me at least that Aggi had been too scared to tell her mum she'd dumped me. Her mum thought the world of me, and I of her. It took all the strength I had to stop myself accepting the invitation on the spot.

The scratch of key finding keyhole signalled Aggi's return, and in what felt like an instant we were standing in front of each other. She looked as beautiful as ever. She was wearing jeans, a checked shirt and a wine-coloured corduroy jacket that used to be mine. She was so shocked when she saw me that she almost dropped the books she was carrying. Mrs Peters slipped out of the room, sensing that we'd had some sort of tiff and were in the process of making up. Before leaving the room she said, 'Do you want another cup of tea, love?' I told her I didn't.

'You're drunk,' said Aggi aggressively. 'I can smell it all over you. How dare you come to my house in this state.'

I motioned drunkenly to her to sit down, which only served to infuriate her even more. I didn't say anything for a few seconds. The floor was spinning so wildly that I was desperately searching with my eyes for something solid to hang on to.

'You're beautiful,' I slurred eventually, gripping onto the arm of the sofa, 'but at least I'll be sober in the morning.' I thought I was so funny that the resultant fit of hysterics caused me to fall back into the sofa.

She moved towards the sofa until she was standing over me. I looked down into my lap to avoid her gaze, ashamed that we'd come to this. She told me I'd got to go and tried to pull me up by my arm. The sulky five-year-old that dwells within every melancholy drunkard freaked out and told her that she wasn't allowed to touch me any more. I think that scared her, she sat down in the armchair opposite me and did her best to hold back her tears.

'What do you want from me, Will?' she asked, taking her turn to avoid making eye contact. I searched her face for signs that she recognised me – the man she used to love – and found none. 'What can you possibly want to say to me? It's over and there's nothing that you can say to change my mind.'

'Nothing at all?' I asked, still trying to catch her gaze.

I told her that I wanted answers, I needed to know what I'd done to make her stop loving me.

These were her exact words:

'It's not you, it's me. I've changed. I thought I could be the person that you wanted me to be. For a while it was what I wanted too. I wanted to feel love like it is in the movies and you gave that to me and for that I'll be grateful forever.'

It didn't make sense. She was saying all these wonderful things about me but the message she was sending added up to little more than, 'Cheers, I had a really nice time.'

'But what did I do wrong?'

'You didn't let me grow, Will. I've been going out with you since I was nineteen. I'm not the same girl! You've stayed the same though, you haven't changed at all – you didn't grow with me – that's why we're different people. And now I can't breathe. I feel stifled. I feel like you're trying to trap me.'

I tried to explain to her that I wasn't trying to trap her. I told her that whatever freedom she wanted she could have. But she told me it was too late. She wanted a new beginning.

One thing she said really cracked me up though. 'It's like that song,' she said, completely straight-faced, '"If You Love Someone, Set Them Free."' I couldn't believe it. It wasn't enough that she was wrecking my whole life. She was quoting Sting to me too.

To be crueller than was strictly necessary I began singing in what I thought was a close approximation to the former Police star's vocal style. She wasn't amused. I knew our conversation would draw to a permanent close unless I could do something, anything, to make her see what a huge mistake she was making. As hard as I tried, I couldn't think of anything. Worst of all, I was beginning to sober up when all I wanted was to be drunk again, if only to give me an excuse for crying in her sitting room.

She stood up as if to say that she'd had enough. I stood up too and walked to the front door and opened it. She followed me into the hallway. Standing outside on the door-step, with eyes full of tears I said to her, 'Aggi, what do you want? And why aren't I it?'

She looked at me blankly and closed the door.

I flushed the toilet and pulled my trousers back up. Back in the kitchen, the toast had long since popped up and gone cold. I hate cold toast.

In my reckoning if Aggi and I hadn't split up when we did, we probably would've remained together. At least I hoped so. With the combined income from two professional jobs maybe we'd even have had the London equivalent of Alice and Bruce's place, a smart flat in nearby Highgate, instead of a poorly decorated shoe box in Archway. Of course, I didn't know this for a fact, but I often liked to imagine that somewhere out there existed a parallel universe where things had turned out okay.

I'd always longed to take my turn at playing house. At the age of thirteen (although, looking back, I could well have been fourteen) I was deeply besotted by Vicki Hollingsworth, to such an extent that I felt ready to make a huge commitment to her and I told her as much. It was a Tuesday dinner-time, I was in the canteen watching, mesmerised, as one by one, she consumed the jam sandwiches that constituted her lunch. A smear of strawberry preserve adorned her top lip and I remember feeling an overwhelming urge to lick it off. Instead, keeping my adolescent awakening in check, I got up from my table and strode across the room until I was standing in front of her. Emma Golden, Vicki's best friend, had just got up to scrape the remains of her dinner into the huge bin by the main door, leaving the two of us alone. With my eyes to the

171

ground, I spoke to her. 'Vicki,' said the teenage me, 'I don't know if you realise this but we were made for each other.'

I'd heard those very words spoken, less than twenty-four hours earlier, on the Monday evening episode of *Crossroads*. The second they'd come out of our Pye television set and into my world, they seemed to me the most magical, beautiful words ever spoken. Momentarily looking up from my shoes, I studied her face as she mulled over my proposition. I could almost see my words tumbling from one ear, past the back of her hazel eyes, to the other ear and back again, as she vacantly tipped her head from side to side. After a minute of this she met my gaze briefly, before running off in the direction of the main exit. My eyes remained fixed on the chair where the buttocks of this vision of loveliness had once been. I sat down in Emma Golden's chair and surreptitiously placed my hand on the seat Vicki had vacated. It was still warm.

In any one of the thousand times I'd played this scene over in my head, Vicki had been so overcome with emotion at my line that she'd clutched me to that region of her chest that would one day become her bosom and whispered, 'I love you.' I'd imagined happy teenage years, safe and secure in the knowledge that I had someone to love who loved me in return.

When, minutes later, I saw Vicki walking back across the canteen I snatched my hand away from her seat guiltily and stood up. Gary Thompson, a confirmed head-case from the year above, and unfortunately the nearest thing Vicki had to a boyfriend, was by her side. He was a whole twelve inches taller than me, never smiled and had small marks on the back of his hands where, rumour had it, he'd stabbed himself with an HB pencil trying to give himself lead poisoning. As Gary took a step towards me, I shuffled backwards to accommodate him.

'I'll count to ten,' said Thompson menacingly.

'Okay,' said the teenage me, resisting the urge to tell him it was lucky he wasn't wearing mittens.

'And if you're still here, you're a dead man.'

I didn't need to be told twice.

I didn't say another word to Vicki for the rest of my school career. When I saw her in the Royal Oak, two years ago, I still half expected Gary Thompson to pop up from nowhere and give me a Chinese burn for being in the same pub as she was. After a protracted period of exchanged glances she came over and spoke to me. She asked me what I was doing with my life. At the time I was very much on the dole, so I told her that I was a surgeon at a teaching hospital in Edinburgh. She was impressed. When I asked her how she was doing, she told me she was married to a forty-six-year-old lorry driver called Clive and had three kids, one of whom wasn't Clive's but he didn't know that. I asked her if she'd got what she wanted from life. She looked at the gin and tonic in her hand, raised her glass and said, 'Yes.'

Gary Thompson, I thank you.

The thing is, I never learned my lesson. Even after Vicki, all I ever wanted from a girl was stability. My sole aim in life was to find a girlfriend who would make me feel so secure that I'd never have to worry about relationships again. But it was always my fault that it never worked out with the girls I dated. I always underestimated the depths of my insecurity. It had nothing to do with poor self-image – I actually considered myself quite a catch – the problem was, I never trusted the women I was involved with to tell the Truth, because the Truth never changes, but as I knew so well, people did. I knew it wasn't everyone, some women did have Staying Power, but it was impossible to tell which ones they were.

Women should come labelled – it would make life so much simpler.

If Aggi and I had still been together, I would've asked her to marry me. She would've turned me down, of course, because in our final year together she'd told me that she didn't believe in marriage any more. I was informed of her decision while sitting in the middle row of screen two at the Cornerhouse cinema, right in the middle of a screening of a new print of *The Seven Year Itch*.

'Will,' she whispered into my ear, 'marriage is a stupid idea. It'll never catch on.'

'It already has,' I told her.

'Not with me, it hasn't.'

And that was that. I like to think she said it to stop us from drifting into matrimony by accident, as so many couples do after university, but it was probably more of a built-in escape clause, a bar-code on our relationship which, while giving me the impression that our love was open-ended to eternity, was in fact doing the opposite, stamping a coded sell-by date on our love that only she could read.

After I graduated, I actually did ask her to marry me anyway. The conversation went a little like this:

Me: Aggi, let's get married. I mean, will you marry me?

Aggi: (Firmly) No.

Me: Why not?

Aggi: I wouldn't like it. It'd be too constraining.

Me: How do you know? You've never been married.

Aggi: No, but I did live with a lover for a while.

Me: You did what? You had a . . . you lived with a . . .

Aggi: I shouldn't have told you. I knew you'd be uptight about this.

Me: (Angrily) Uptight? Uptight? I think I've every right to be 'uptight' since discovering that my girlfriend has in fact been 'shacked up' with some bloke. Who was it? Have I met him?

Aggi: No . . . well, yes.

Me: Who? Come on. Which one of them was it?

Aggi: Martin.

Me: (Ranting) Martin? Martin! But his eyes are too close together. You can't have lived with a man whose eyes are too close together! You've obviously made some mistake.

Aggi: Will, you're being hysterical.

Me: I'm not being hysterical. I'm being me. You ought to try it some time.

I knew about all her ex-boyfriends because I'd made her tell me about them after our fourth date. Out of all seven of them, Martin was the one I liked least. Aggi was only seventeen when she met him at a night-club in Nottingham. Three weeks later she moved into a room in his student house, and eventually into his bedroom. He was twenty and was studying Politics at the poly. He was a walking tragedy, the best reason to Eat The Rich I'd ever seen. He'd spent the ages between zero and eighteen at boarding school where he collected stamps, rowed and played Dungeons and Dragons. Rejected by Oxford after dismal A-level results, he ended up at what was then the Polytechnic. Realising that he was liable to be beaten to death by the mob of Socialist Workers who stood guard outside the student union selling *Militant* every day, Martin – posh, useless, waste of space Martin – decided to reinvent himself as the Ultimate Smiths Fan. Out went his chinos, V-necked jumpers, button-down shirts and nondescript haircut, and in came all things Mozzer-like. He had the stupid Morrissey quiff, the stupid Morrissey overcoat, the stupid Morrissey shoes but how he ever found a pair of stupid Morrissey glasses to fit his beady, too-close-together eyes I'll never know.

The reason I knew so much about Martin was that on my third coach trip to London in search of accommodation, the gods of misfortune allocated me a seat next to the git. We'd met once before, about four years earlier in the Royal Oak, when Aggi had been forced to introduce us because, unbeknown to Aggi and me, his Smiths' tribute band, The Charming Men, were playing a gig there. For the entire journey to London (five sodding hours!), all he talked about was Aggi and how much she'd changed his life.

What really offended me about Aggi's 'shacking up' experience was the fact that she didn't think it was a big deal. She'd lived with him for three months before she dumped him for another student, at a different night-club, and moved back to her mum's. I saw the whole episode as a threat to everything we had. When all you have is 'you', to give 'you', seven days a week, twenty-four hours a day, so casually, *is* a big deal. She'd been prepared to do that for three months with beady Martin, so why wasn't she prepared to have a go at spending the rest of her life with me?

If I had known that one day I'd be in a flat with Aggi for the rest of my life I could have relaxed – I'd have been happy. I'd have taken up a hobby. Maybe even tried and liked football. I'd have been NORMAL. But Aggi wasn't here and chances were she never would be. She was the one I wanted. The only one. She was made for me. I was made for her. She was my Legendary Girlfriend and I'd miss her for as long as I lived.

I got up from the bed, opened the window and sat on the ledge with my legs hanging outside. Lighting a cigarette I gently let out a silent fart. Chuckling heartily I sucked in some of the cold, damp air with my nicotine, causing me to cough and gurgle phlegm. It felt good to open up the window. I hadn't realised it, but the air in the flat had grown so stale I could almost see it trying to escape. The glowing end of my ciggy looked warm and inviting. A long column of ash fell onto my jeans. I brushed it away and after a while I thought about food again. Stubbing out my cigarette, I left my perch and went into the kitchen. Opening a can of spaghetti hoops and dropping them into a pan I turned the heat on the cooker up to maximum. I was just about to light another fag when the phone rang.

```
6.08 P.M.
```

'Are you all right, dear?' said Gran.

'Not too bad,' I replied. 'Can't complain. Are you all right, Gran?'

'Yes, thank you, dear. And you?'

'Not too bad. And you?'

'Fine. And you?'

'Dandy. And you?'

'Lovely!'

My Gran wasn't senile, and neither was I. This was just our little joke, although I wasn't all that sure whether Gran was quite up on the concept of irony. As far as I was concerned, this was our way of defusing tension caused by the fact that we had nothing in common, other than Francesca Kelly (my mother). We could talk to each other perfectly well face-to-face for hours on end, but on the phone, the importance of words always got blown out of proportion. I like to believe we spoke in clichés because it was much safer that way, but if my Gran wasn't entirely in on the joke, all it probably meant was that I was an evil grandson with a crap sense of humour.

'Your mother's not in,' said Gran.

'Isn't she?'

'So where is she then?'

'I don't know, Gran. She's probably out or something.'

179

'Oh.'

'Oh.'

'Oh.'

I introduced a new topic. 'Nice weather we're having, aren't we?'

'Not particularly,' said Gran. 'It's raining cats and dogs here. Mrs Staff across the road says it's the coldest September on record.'

'Is it really?'

'Coldest on record.'

'Well I never.'

'Happy Birthday for tomorrow,' said Gran. 'I would've phoned you tomorrow dear, but Mrs Baxter has managed to persuade her husband to take a couple of us up to the Lake District. I hope you're not offended, my love.'

'Of course not, Gran, don't you worry. Have a great time. Bring me back some Kendal Mint Cake, eh?'

Gran got excited. 'Oooh, you like Kendal Mint Cake? I shall have to get you a job lot!'

'Yeah. That'd be nice.'

'Well, I'd better be going, son. Take care and have a lovely birthday.'

'Yes, Gran, I will.'

'Oooh, before I forget I must tell you that your card will be late. I was trying to phone your mother all day yesterday to get your address. I've missed last post now anyway. It'll get there by Tuesday. Never mind, eh? Better late than never.'

'Yes, Gran. Better late than never.' I glanced across the room at the card she had sent which was perched on top of my hi-fi. Perhaps she was going senile after all.

As I put the phone down wondering what exactly to do with the lifetime's supply of Kendal Mint Cake she was sure to purchase, I realised that my spaghetti hoops were burning. The reason why

I'd suddenly recalled my dinner was that the smoke currently working its way under the kitchen door had already
reached the smoke alarm, which was now belting out the
mother of all high-pitched screams. I'd been in the flat
five days and already heard it six times. It was far too
sensitive; let toast crispen a little too much and on came
the siren. Once this happened, the whole household played
the I'd-rather-burn-to-death-than-leave-my-poxy-studio-flat-
and-turn-off-the-alarm game of endurance. The rules were
simple, if a little cavalier: see how long you can stand the
alarm before you're compelled to get out of bed and turn
it off at the control box on the ground floor. There were six
residents in the house – I'd done it once, the residents of
the two ground floor flats had done it twice each and the old
man on the top floor had done it once. The man at number
four on my landing, and the woman at number six on the top
floor, hadn't done it at all, which to my mind either meant
that they were deaf or took the playing of bloody-minded
Russian Roulette-style games very seriously.

In spite of the noise, the problem at hand still had to be dealt
with – the burning spaghetti hoops. Opening the door to the
kitchen fully, I half expected to be faced by a scene from *The
Towering Inferno* and was pleasantly surprised merely to choke
violently on thick black smoke. My eyes began to water almost
immediately; I shut them tightly, reached out to the cooker
controls and turned off the ring. Using a souvenir Bournemouth
tea towel of my mother's, I carefully manoeuvred the saucepan
out of the kitchen, opened the window in the main room and laid
it to rest on the sill outside, closing the window behind it. There
was nowhere for the smoke to escape to now, it lingered in the
flat like one of those ridiculously foggy evenings in the Basil
Rathbone Sherlock Holmes films. It was time for another walk.

As I reached the front door, the woman from downstairs

came out of her flat, dressed in a white towelling dressing gown and huge Garfield slippers, a black cloud of pure annoyance hanging over her head like a garland of hateful intent. Standing on the tips of her toes – poor Garfield's head squished unhappily against the grime-laden carpet – she attempted to press the reset button on the control box. I smiled at her in a neighbourly fashion. She scowled back. Within seconds of reaching the garden gate, the alarm stopped.

It was raining again. Archway looked more miserable than usual, all its colour had drained away, leaving only shades of grey and dog poo brown. I pulled my neck as far as I could into the collar of my coat (which still smelt) and headed in the direction of the newsagent's up the road.

The newsagent's on Holloway Road was owned by an old Italian woman with white hair and skin like a barbecued chicken. According to the sign on the door her sons were also involved in the operation, but as I'd never seen them, I couldn't exactly confirm this. My problem with her, and the reason she was on my mental hit-list (sandwiched in the lower ranks between my bank manager and Foster menswear) was that she had the kind of attitude problem Mussolini would've been proud of. Every morning that I'd gone into her shop she'd been umbilically attached to a pay-phone on the counter, wilfully ignoring customers until an appropriate pause in her conversation, which as I'd found on Tuesday could be anything up to six minutes. I hated that woman, and still fuelled with Simon-inspired bitterness, reasoned that now was a particularly good time to exact revenge.

As usual, she was behind the counter, and as usual she was talking very loudly into the pay-phone, every now and again repeating the same word in Italian, while shaking her head emphatically. No one else was in the shop. It was just the two of us. *Italian Granny Vs William The English Teacher. Ding! Ding! Round one.* I don't know what came over me but I secreted two Yorkie bars, a pack of Rolos and a copy of *Cosmopolitan* into my overcoat pocket and walked out without paying, not even bothering to pretend that I couldn't see the item I'd wanted to purchase. Though she didn't look up from her perch as I made my way to the door, this didn't stop me, once outside, from running like the proverbial clappers all the way to the flat, imagining that she'd suddenly realised my crime and stopped her conversation mid-sentence, in order to summon her sons to stab me to death because the honour of their family name was at stake.

I hadn't shop-lifted sweets in over sixteen years. Not since Simon and I had grabbed a handful of fizz bombs each from the newsagent's around the corner from our junior school, and stuffed them down the front of our trousers, reasoning that should we ever get caught, the police would never think of looking there. It felt good to have a bit of raw excitement in my life again, a bit of cut and thrust, a bit of living life by the seat of my pants. Stealing a pack of Rolos wasn't quite Raffles' standard, but I was happy nonetheless. The important thing was that I'd got one up on Crusty Old Italian Woman. 1–0 to me.

Back at the flat most of the smoke had managed to escape to the place where smoke goes to die. I checked the answering machine (no messages), and took a look at the spaghetti hoops on the window ledge. The saucepan had stopped smoking now. Not all the spaghetti hoops had died in the fire, there were a number of survivors floating on a sea of ruby sludge. I dipped my fingers in to taste a mouthful. They were cold and wet with rain rather than tomato sauce, but as long as the carbonised seam of hoops underneath remained undisturbed, they didn't taste too horrific. The saucepan on the other hand was knackered, which was unfortunate, as I'd 'borrowed' it from a set of three, against my mother's express wishes. I ate the Rolos and Yorkie too and then felt sick and sorry for myself.

I searched for the phone, called Alice's number again and left another message telling her to call me as soon as she got back in even if it was 3.00 a.m. because it was an emergency.

I turned on the TV, an action which I'd been trying my very best to avoid all week. As much as I loved to watch TV, the very thought of wasting hours doing it made me feel sadder and even more desperate, as if I were giving in to becoming a total loser without a fight. My mum had bought the portable TV for me as an early birthday present before I went to university. She'd said, and I quote: 'It'll be like a friend. Something on in the background in case things seem a bit empty.' It was a nice thing for her to say but ever since I'd been terrified that, if I wasn't careful, the day would come when I really would consider the TV to be my friend.

There was nothing on anyway. I flicked across the channels waiting for something good to happen. Sport, something about art history, news, horse racing and a nappy ad. Desperate, I decided to look for amusement elsewhere, but left it on in the background while I composed another letter to the bank:

Dear Sir,

I am writing to you to explain my current financial position. I have just started a job teaching in London. Due to the expense of moving to the capital and the fact that I will not be paid until the end of September, I would be very grateful if you would

184

further extend my overdraft by £500 until the end of November.

Sincerely

William Kelly.

As I put the full stop after the 'y' in Kelly, and wondered if it actually warranted a full stop, I glanced up at the TV and then scanned the room searching for confirmation of what I was feeling. I returned my eyes to the page, having found my answer. I was bored. When I was small and I used to tell my dad I was bored, he'd tell me that one day I'd find out what boredom was really about and then I'd be sorry. At that moment, sitting there in the flat, with the will to do anything at all almost crushed out of my body, I realised that I'd finally found out what it was like to be bored and I *was* really sorry. When I was bored as a kid, I had a whole lifetime ahead of me. I could easily afford to spend a few years here or there doing Nothing. But now, with a twenty-sixth birthday looming in the background, I no longer had time to waste that wouldn't come back to haunt me, as those two years on the dole did every time I heard about someone from my degree course getting a job writing on *Empire*, earning over £30,000 pa, or simply getting a life.

I changed channels. The walls of the flat were far more interesting than what was happening on screen, so it was there my eyes lingered, soaking up the years of desperation caked on to the wallpaper, before finally coming to rest on Aggi's defaced photograph. Crawling underneath the duvet, shedding trousers and socks on my journey to the pillow, I settled in bed. And there I lay, not thinking about anything at all, for quite a long time.

6.34 P.M.

In the right-hand corner of the room, just above the curtains,
a cobweb caught my attention as a steady draught whistling
its way through the poorly-constructed window frame tried
its best to dislodge it from the wall. It looked a bit flimsy,
as though it existed for decorative rather than practical purposes. Whichever spider had created this silken trap I decided
was going to go hungry because no self-respecting house fly
was going to be caught in a web as crap as this one. Even
Mother Nature it seemed was capable of creating creatures
as lazy, apathetic and half-hearted as me.

The telephone rang, preventing me from taking thoughts of
spiders, flies and cobwebs any further. It rang three or four
times before I climbed out of bed to answer it, as I was busy
working out the odds of who it might be:

Aggi (1000–1)
Alice (5–1)
Kate (3–1)
Martina (2–1, odds on favourite)

'Hi, it's me.'
'Hi,' I replied, ashamed that in spite of myself I'd still backed
the rank outsider. 'What've you been up to?'

187

'Nothing,' replied Kate. 'How about you?'

I recalled my promise to phone her back and considered feeling guilty, but then it occurred to me that she had phoned me in spite of my non-action. Kate actually *wanted* to talk to me. I instantly felt more relaxed. In the distance I could hear the siren of a police car.

'I'm sorry I didn't call back when I said I would. I fell asleep.'

'I love sleeping,' said Kate. 'It's kind of a hobby of mine.'

She gave a little laugh and I joined her, but whereas hers was joyous and summery, mine was nervous and shifty because I'd been busy wondering whether she slept naked or not.

'What are you doing tonight?'

'Nothing,' replied Kate. 'I've got no money. Anyway I don't fancy going out. I thought I might stay in and watch TV.'

'Good idea,' I said, nodding needlessly.

'What's on?'

I located the remote control hiding under a pair of grey M&S pants. The red light on the front of the TV flickered momentarily, and there before me was an episode of *Dad's Army*. I relayed this information to Kate and together we watched in silence; she in Brighton, I in London, unified by the wonder of television. Private Pike was on top of a huge pile of furniture on the back of a lorry next to a telegraph pole. As far as I could work out there was a bomb lodged up there and it was his job to get it down.

'I love *Dad's Army*,' I said quietly, half hoping that she wouldn't hear me.

'Yeah,' said Kate. 'It really makes me laugh.'

We sat in silence (apart from occasional laughter) watching Private Pike get stuck up the telegraph pole, and Captain Mainwaring's attempts to extricate him from this situation. It wasn't an uncomfortable silence at all. I felt as close to her as if she had been sitting on the bed next to me, absent-mindedly offering me crisps from a packet of cheese and onion, with her head resting on my shoulder, happy to be doing something as mundane as watching TV.

'What else is on?' asked Kate after a while.

Switching channels, I discovered a documentary on BBC2, about hi-tec thieves stealing computer chips from companies in Silicone Valley and was instantly drawn in. Excitedly I told Kate to turn over and join me and in the following quarter of an hour we learned about the Mafia's involvement in the multi-billion dollar black market in stolen chips. Kate wasn't half as interested in the programme as I was, and despite wanting to return to *Dad's Army* almost immediately, she continued watching BBC2 for my sake. I was touched. Eventually (once the micro-chip programme had finished), we switched over to Channel Four because the news was on ITV and neither of us considered news entertainment, which was all we were looking for. While a car advert played, Kate and I tried to think of as many ridiculous names for cars as we could in a minute. Our top three were:

1. The Nissan Nipple.
2. The Vauxhall Prostate.
3. The Ford Oooh!.

The ad break finished and the voice-over woman said something like, 'And now for something completely different,' in a soft Southern Counties accent she probably considered amusing. The credits for a TV show I'd never seen before came on. It was obviously some kind of fashion/music/style/youth-oriented programme because brightly coloured graphics were flashing up on the screen, battering my irises into submission in time to the thumping bass line of the theme tune. What it was called I never found out, because just as I was about to switch over to *Noel's House Party*, I caught a glimpse of something on the screen that instantly crash-landed all feelings of contentment.

'Dave Bloomfield!' I screamed at the TV.

'Who?' said Kate.

'The biggest tosser in the universe.'

Dave Bloomfield, aka 'the biggest tosser in the universe', I explained, was on my course at university. He was tall, half Spanish and a quarter Iroquois (so rumour had it), with hazel eyes and floppy, jet-black hair that made him look like some kind of Edwardian fop. He used to sit in the canteen on the top floor in the English Department reading the *Guardian* from cover to cover – always a sign of a tosser in the making – sipping black coffee and smoking filterless Camels. The female population of the department (lecturers included) doted on his every word, so much so that he even pulled *and* dumped Annette Francis, the most gorgeous creature on our course, a woman so aloof that the one occasion I plucked up the courage to talk to her by asking her the time, she point blank refused to tell me. Oh, and to make matters worse he got a first. Kate couldn't quite understand why seeing an over-achieving former university colleague presenting his own TV show was winding me up so much and so I tried to explain.

'Some things just come too easily for some people,' I raged. 'While the rest of us mere mortals have to make do, *they* get it all on a plate.'

I was surprised at my bitterness, particularly as I'd never harboured any urges to be a TV presenter. My problem with Dave Bloomfield was that he represented everything I hated about the successful: he was good-looking, clever, witty and, worst of all, motivated. Dave Bloomfield was everything I wasn't. Dave Bloomfield was the anti-me.

I explained this to Kate. 'It's just like anti-matter and matter, if Dave and I ever meet again we'll explode, killing thousands.'

Kate laughed. 'You put yourself down too much. You know you can do whatever you want if you put your mind to it.' She paused, as if thinking. 'What do you want, Will? What do you really want to do with your life?'

I lay down on the bed and pulled the duvet over my legs. I hadn't thought about what I wanted to do, in any serious manner, for such a long time that the answer didn't come quite as speedily as I felt it should have.

'I'd like to make films,' I said with a lack of conviction. I was ashamed that I'd done so little to push myself in that direction. I once filled out, but never posted, an application to Sheffield University for an MA in Film Production. It was still in the drawer of my desk at home.

'Really?' said Kate. 'That's brilliant. Why don't you do it?'

'Well, it's not that easy, you see,' I began. 'You need money and you need to be in with the right people. It's full of nepotism, the film business, and with my mum working at the retirement lodge and my dad doing whatever it is he does all day for the council, I can't imagine that either of them can open the doors of Paramount for me.'

'What about writing scripts?' offered Kate. 'Those don't cost a thing and you could do them in your spare time. A mate of mine's brother works on *Coronation Street* and his dad runs a chippy.'

I wasn't encouraged. 'I've enough problems teaching without trying to do anything in my spare time other than complain,' I said, getting out of bed and finding a comfortable space to lie on the carpet. 'Have you ever tried marking thirty poems on snowflakes? Believe me, if you had you'd be praying, just like I am, that global warming's going to get a lot worse.'

I wondered whether my excuse sounded like an excuse.

'That sounds like an excuse to me.'

I ignored her comment. 'So what about you? What do you want to do?'

Taking a deep breath she told me how she had always wanted to be a nurse. That was one of the reasons (apart from her ex) she'd dropped out of university. She'd realised that her course was pointless and wanted to do something that would help people. In five months she'd be starting nursing college at a hospital in Brighton which was why she was currently languishing on Boots' perfume counter. The more she spoke, the more I found myself admiring her spirited determination to lead a fruitful life and I even told her so. I think she might have blushed but I couldn't be sure over the phone.

'Do you mind if I ask you a question?' said Kate eventually.

'No. Not at all.'

'Are you sure you won't be offended?'

I wondered if it was going to be an embarrassing question along the lines of 'When was the last time you saw a man naked?'

'Look,' I said, 'at the rate of excitement I've been indulging in this weekend, being offended would be positively welcome.'

'What are you scared of?'

I paused, relieved that I no longer had to tell her about the occasion when I'd disturbed Simon and Tammy on their kitchen table, naked but for the melting contents of a tub of Cookie Dough Dynamo Häagen-Dazs.

'You think I'm scared of life, don't you? Well, I'm not. I'm not scared of failure either. After all I'm a failed teacher and I haven't killed myself yet. What I'm scared of is this: that at twenty-six, I'm too old to make my dreams come true. It's so hard not to feel envious of you. I know I'm going to sound like an OAP, but at least you've got the potential to do what you want to do.'

'Whereas you . . .'

'Whereas I haven't. My course is set. Unless something drastic happens this is it for the rest of my life.'

'What about becoming the next Scorcese?'

She wasn't getting the message. 'Orson Welles had written, produced and directed *Citizen Kane*, one of the world's greatest films, by the time he was twenty-six.'

'Forget Orson Welles,' exclaimed Kate. 'The TV genius that is Tony Warren was only twenty-three when he came up with the idea for *Coronation Street!*' Kate stopped herself, immediately realising she wasn't helping matters. 'I'm sorry. I'm not being very helpful, am I? My mate's brother who works on *Coronation Street*, he told me that amazing fact. It's been waiting there for the chance to escape ever since.'

'I'm not getting into a debate about whether *Coronation Street* is better than *Citizen Kane!* That's not the point. The point is, I'm twenty-six! All I've done is smoke cigarettes, watch TV and moan about my ex-girlfriend. Even if I started now, I'd be lucky to direct a school production of *Joseph and his Technicolor Dream Coat* before I'm thirty. Sometimes you've got to face facts.'

Kate wasn't convinced. 'You can do anything you want. If you've got talent it'll shine through in the end. You've got to believe in yourself.'

Her positivity was depressing. The similarity of her words to those I might have uttered at her age was surprisingly accurate. Little did she know that I was she, six years down the line.

'Look, Kate,' I said in my best let-me-give-you-a-few-words-of-advice voice. 'It's taken me this long to just get here. How long is it going to take to get anywhere else? Three years ago, maybe I had a chance. Maybe I could've done all the things I wanted.' My voice became higher, louder, more aggressive. 'It's too late. Sometimes you've got to know when enough is enough!' Out of frustration I kicked the ice-cream tub containing my Sugar Puffs breakfast and immediately regretted it. Creamy yellow froth and puffed wheat seeped onto my overcoat, which had been lying on the floor next to it. Now I really would have to get it dry-cleaned.

'It's never too late,' said Kate quietly. 'Not while you still believe.'

I was moved by the kindness of her words and for a few ecstatic seconds, deep in my heart I was convinced she was right. Then my brain kicked in. She was wrong. In spite of everything I'd done to prevent it, my course *was* set and there was nothing I could do about it. I'd spent the whole of my life wondering what I was going to 'be': at the age of five I'd wanted to be a lorry driver; at eight I'd desperately wanted to be Noel Edmonds; in my teens I'd flirted with every profession from a psychic to a chef, before deciding in my twenties that I sort of, possibly, wouldn't mind making films. So what had I done to set myself on the right path? I'd sat on the dole and then done a teacher training course. And because of that one mistake I was going to 'be' a teacher even if it killed me.

'Thanks, it was nice of you to say that,' I said kindly. I wanted to apologise for getting so wound up but I couldn't find a way to say it comfortably, so I changed the subject. 'What's your favourite film?'

This was a naff question, only surpassed in naffness by, 'So, what music are you into?' but I was desperate to know. Kate and I were sharing so many things that I felt were binding us together. It was hard to believe that as someone who adored films I hadn't asked her already.

'It's *Gregory's Girl*,' she said despondently. 'I know it's not as cool as some of the films that are bound to be your favourites. It's not *Taxi Driver*, *Reservoir Dogs* or *Apocalypse Now*, but I like it all the same. It's sweet, it's . . .'

I tried to contain my excitement. 'You're wrong, Kate. So wrong. *Gregory's Girl* is my favourite film. It's fantastic. Better than *Taxi Driver*, *Apocalypse Now* or even sodding *Citizen Kane!*'

Time ceased to have any meaning as we tried to recall the best bits of a film full of best bits. Her favourite parts were when Dorothy, the object of Gregory's desire, was being interviewed for the school paper in the dressing rooms, followed by the bit where the lost penguins keep getting redirected around the school.

'Let's dance,' I said.

She knew what I meant immediately.

Lying on my back, elbows resting on the carpet and wrists in the air, I began to move as if dancing as Gregory and Susan had done in the park scene near the end of the film. My ear kept moving away from the phone, but there was no mistaking the fact that Kate was participating because she was laughing so loudly that I could still hear her.

'What if Paula comes back? She'll think I've completely lost it!'

'Don't worry!' I yelled at the receiver, still dancing and feeling the happiest I had in a long time. 'Just go with the flow.'

I was on a roll. My words couldn't trip out fast enough. Kate made me feel like jabbering away until Monday morning. What was most impressive was the fact that she wasn't bored, sitting there in her Brighton flat, listening to a complete stranger talk about his life. I wanted to confess everything: how I couldn't swim but could bend my thumb back until it touched my wrist; and how, until my first day at Wood Green Comprehensive, I'd never bought a pre-packaged sandwich (I don't know why, I just hadn't). I wanted her to know everything.

'Tell me some more,' said Kate.

'What?'

'Tell me more about you.'

'Er, well. No,' I said uneasily. It was hard saying no to a girl who made me want to say yes to anything she suggested, but one of the cover lines on my 'donated' copy of *Cosmopolitan* kept flashing up in my head: 'Why men love talking about themselves.' Now, I decided, was my turn to listen.

'Tell me about *you*,' I said, smiling needlessly. 'You've heard enough of me surely? Anyway, my mother always told me never to talk to strangers and until I know more about you, a stranger you will remain.'

'It's quite nice being a stranger,' said Kate. 'I could be

anyone I want to be. Unfortunately I'm me. I work at Boots. I have to get there at 8.00 a.m. and I leave at 6.00 p.m. I work every other Saturday and get one day off during the week if I've worked a Saturday. That's it really.'

'I worked in a pub for a couple of months shifting crates of beer from the cellar. I hated every second of it. If it's anything like that, I bet it's soul-destroying.'

'Not really,' she said chirpily. 'A mate of mine, Daniel, he works for a firm of accountants in Oxford, and his job is what I'd call soul-destroying. He's constantly under pressure to produce results. Last week his doctor told him he's got a stress-related ulcer. He's only twenty-four. He earns quite a bit, mind. But no amount of money is worth all the rubbish he has to put up with. I'd never want a job like that. Boots wouldn't be so bad if I didn't have to get up so early. Anyway, I told Daniel this and I'll say it to you. There's no point in getting stressed about work. If a job gets on your nerves then leave it. No one's got a gun to your head.' There was a knocking noise down the phone line followed by a loud click. Kate's voice disappeared. I panicked. I thought she'd gone forever. 'Sorry about that, Paula's just come in. She took me by surprise. I dropped the phone! Where was I? Ah, yes. I used to want to have a high-powered job. I can't remember what kind exactly; I mean, I had phases where I've wanted to be everything from a news reader to a Crown Court judge, but I came to the conclusion that I couldn't really see the point. Do you know that I once got it into my head that I wanted to be a professional tennis player?'

'Were you really good at tennis?'

'No, I hated it,' said Kate dolefully. 'I just liked the skirts.'

We both laughed. I wondered what she looked like in a tennis skirt.

Kate continued. 'My driving ambition now is to fall in love, be a nurse, and have babies. That's all I want my life to be about now. Once I've got those three things in that order I'll have everything I want. It's true.'

I wasn't convinced. 'How are love and babies going to make everything all right? Aren't you forgetting some key points here, like babies costing money, love being hard to find, people falling out of love as easily as they fall in?'

'I know all these things,' she said, testily. 'But that's my ambition. I didn't say it was practical or even possible. We've all got our dreams.'

'Yeah, you're right,' I said, by way of apology.

'Do you think I'll get what I want?' asked Kate.

I couldn't help looking at the photograph of Aggi's bearded, bespectacled, scarred, toothless face on the wall. Even a defaced Aggi was better than no Aggi at all.

'Yeah,' I said. 'The babies part is easy enough. The world's crawling with sperm donors, as long as you're not too choosy. And the job seems to be sorted. It's the love part that I think might be problematic. In my opinion, you can only say that love truly is love once you're both dead, because it's only then, once you've managed to go your entire lives with each other and there's nowhere for you to go off to or anyone to go off with, that it finally becomes real. Anything else is more or less just infatuation. I'm serious.' The door to one of the neighbouring flats slammed shut, shaking my windows. I crawled into bed. 'Everybody loves a lover but too many people lack Staying Power. Love should be fatal. You should never recover from it. If you can, then it wasn't love.'

'Really?' said Kate, as though she had another question lined up. 'So what about you and Aggi? Was what you had love?'

'It was love. I loved her and I continue to love her, despite everything I do to make myself stop.'

'*You* might love *her*, but what about the fact that *she* doesn't love *you*? Is love really love if only one person stays true to the cause? That sounds more like infatuation to me. No offence intended.'

Kate was showing a side of her that I hadn't noticed before. She was capable of seeing straight through my sweeping statements and had by now probably realised that my authoritative manner was as fake as everything else about me.

'I don't know,' I said, lost for words. 'I think you've actually made quite a good point there. This must mean that I'm as sad as every other loser out there.'

'You made up the rules,' she joked.

'Yeah, I did.' I was getting tired of this now. 'He who lives by the sword dies by the sword. What goes around comes around. I've made my bed so I'd better lie in.'

'It?' prompted Kate.

'No, just in.'

We both laughed.

'I tell you what though,' I said. 'Aggi did love me.'

'How do you know? Did she tell you?'

'Yeah, she told me a million times but . . .'

I was going to tell Kate about something Aggi had done which proved beyond any reasonable doubt how much she felt about me, but I couldn't get the words out. This was a private memory and neither time nor space had made it mean any less to me. What Aggi and I had done was ridiculous in a silly sort of way, but I had forgiven myself long ago on the grounds that we're all allowed to be 'silly' once in a while, especially when in love. And I suppose it's true that even the most ridiculous things can carry more poignancy than all of Shakespeare's sonnets rolled together.

At the time of the event I was thinking of, I was twenty-one and Aggi was twenty, ideal ages to be hopelessly romantic. It was a Tuesday afternoon during the summer holidays, a year after we'd first met. Aggi had called around at my house. I was still in bed even though it was two in the afternoon. The sun was shining brightly through the chocolate fabric of my bedroom curtains, turning everything inside golden brown and warming up the air until it felt like a greenhouse. All the sounds coming in through my open bedroom window – birds chirping, next door neighbour's kids playing Swingball; the far-off jingle of an ice-cream van – were surprisingly life-affirming. And yet, there I lay, sweating under the duvet flicking through a number of books looking for ideas for my dissertation.

Tom must have let Aggi in because I only realised she was there when she knocked on my door from inside the room. She must have been standing there for ages because she didn't say anything for a minute or two and seemed a little embarrassed when I looked up from my book, completely avoiding all eye contact. She'd said, 'Let's go to the park.' And after I'd put on some clothes and had a brief wash, that's exactly what we did. On the way there she didn't say much, as if going over something in her mind that she was trying not to forget. When we got to Crestfield Park by the large oak tree – the very same oak tree where I'd later scatter her imaginary ashes – she sat down on the freshly mown grass and tugged at my sleeve, signalling me to take a seat. And this is what she said:

'I woke up this morning and knew that I loved you more than ever. Sometimes I get scared that this feeling will slip away into something less than the wonderfulness it is now. So I've got a plan. Let's capture how we feel right now and keep it forever. I've got some scissors in my bag and I'm going to cut off a lock of my hair and then you'll cut off a lock of your hair and we'll twist them together. Then on a scrap of paper I'll write down everything I feel about you and then you'll do the same. Then we'll put the lot in one of those plastic containers you put film in and we'll bury it right here. What do you say?'

What could I say? It didn't seem a 'silly' thing to do at all. It seemed like the only thing that made sense. It's easy to feel that everyday love isn't like love in the movies because successions of mind-numbingly dismal, modern romantic comedies – stand up *French Kiss, Sleepless in Seattle* and *While You Were Sleeping* – have succeeded in turning everything that's wonderful about love into cheese. People are too literal about love now and it's all because, thanks to these films, there's little space left for symbolism in real life. What Aggi and I did was slightly strange and the kind of thing that only lead characters in a Shakespearean tragedy could pull off convincingly, but I loved every second of it.

Aggi took her mum's orange-handled scissors from her bag and chopped off a lock of hair, scribbled on a piece of paper and put it in the container. I cut off some of my hair from the back, wrote on my piece of paper and then twisted our hair together and dug into the dirt with my hands. The hole, as deep as my hand, was more than big enough for the container. Together we packed the leftover soil on top of it, then stood up and stared at the mound, not speaking. We kissed right there and then went back to Aggi's.

I didn't know what Aggi had written and she didn't know what I had written, and that was what made the whole thing so mystical. Looking back, sometimes I like to joke with myself that the whole thing was some kind of voodoo trick, and that our messages and twisted hair were what was keeping me bound to Aggi all this time, but even I couldn't take it that seriously.

Over the next few days I couldn't get what we'd done off my mind. I had to know what Aggi had written about me. Nearly a week after we'd gone to the park, I returned, determined to dig up the container. I felt awful. I was betraying her trust. But I needed to do it. Because I needed to know.

When I reached the spot I immediately knew something was wrong because the mound had been disturbed. I clawed at the soil, but the container wasn't there. Had Aggi dug it up because she'd changed her mind? Had she been afraid that I might do what she'd actually done herself? Had someone else dug it up? I didn't know and I never found out. It was another of those questions that I never got to ask Aggi. Something inside me makes me think that she had second thoughts and just didn't like the idea of our declaration being out there – because then I would've had evidence that I was as important to her as she was to me.

seated in, kept all the muscles in my legs rigid so I looked like
one too.

Over time she began to get used to me and after we'd done all the
mini exercises where we'd just sit and wait without much else being
gained, she'd move to the bath. I thought, reassured,
to enjoy the reunion. Then I'd travel further, reunion would
not come to start but for both of us and then to relax.

Slowly I watched my speed up gradually until I am trying
this, working the muscles that in turn had been help, then I couldn't
accept that the impossible was going to be too easy, then it up
because once I started learning that she was more confident,
more work that she relaxed more, I had to learn to release
the grip upon which I relied and now I said too it was and out
of there she said that I have got to do what. Something
finishing, makes me aware that she, in a second thought
and still enjoyed the idea but only the result a being not
know — because that I would be released more than I was
unconfident, her grasp was tight.

9.47 P.M.

We'd been talking for a long time. My lips were as close to the phone as humanly possible. A small but not insignificant pool of moisture had formed in the mouthpiece. I swear if I could've slipped into that pool and slid down the telephone line right into Kate's flat I would've done. Gladly. To be with her, to be touched by her presence would've made my day. It would've made my decade. A huge wave of loneliness sprang up from nowhere, threatening to overwhelm me. *I think it's time to go.*

'I think it's time to go,' I said.

Kate was hurt. 'Oh, I'm sorry.'

'No, it's not you,' I said, desperately wanting her to believe me. 'It's not you at all. It's me. I've enjoyed every second talking to you. You're really . . .' I couldn't finish the sentence without saying something totally clichéd. 'You're really . . .'

'I'm really . . .'

'You're really . . .' I flicked through my lexicon of top quality compliments. Thanks to a world brimming over with cheesy films, cheesy books, cheesy music and cheesy TV – reducing the greatest human emotion to the lowest common denominator – they all sounded too jaded, too un-Kate, too, well, cheesy.

'You're special,' I told her. 'I think you're special.'

205

She laughed.

'And you're wonderful. I think you're wonderful, Will.'

'Goodnight.'

'Sleep tight.'

Back to reality.

The phone had never looked as lonely as it did when I ended that call. Lying there stiffly in its cradle, after it had had so much life flowing through it, it looked like it was dead rather than dormant. I picked it up and dialled Kate's number to make sure it was still working but put it down before it had a chance to ring. I felt bleak and empty, as if it wasn't quite worth the effort to take another breath. In these kinds of situations, I'm embarrassed to say, I often indulged myself in a little fantasy, believing myself to be a tortured poet rather than just a sad git with too much time on his hands. I once wrote fourteen volumes (i.e. fourteen W H Smith exercise books) of oh so very terrible poetry, entitled *To Aggi with Love*. I put them out for the bin men the week before I came to London as part of the first stage of my New Start policy, which I later abandoned when I realised it meant getting rid of my photo of Aggi too. Fortunately, the urge to conjure up a bit of blank verse for Vol. 15, was beaten to the finish line by the impulse to take a slash.

Before the house was turned into flats, my room had obviously been a large bedroom, part of which Mr Jamal had sectioned off to construct a plasterboard prison otherwise known as my bathroom, which was the reason it didn't have any windows. So, in order to see what I was doing in the bathroom, I had to switch on a light, which automatically started an extractor fan. I wasn't dead keen on stinky smells as such, but the extractor fan was the main cause of my flat-inspired frustration; it drove me up the wall. Every time it came on my heart sank. Something inside it was broken, so instead of a gentle hum like a far-off mosquito, I had to endure a sound similar to a tabby in a Moulinex liquidiser, and worse still, the fan continued to extract air – and my patience for that matter – for the next twenty minutes, even after I'd switched the light off. By Wednesday, I was so obsessed with never hearing it again that I attempted crapping in the dark. While it was nice to enjoy the silence, there was something disconcerting about sitting on the toilet, trousers and boxer shorts around ankles, in a darkened room. I once read a newspaper article that said the average rat was quite capable of swimming up a toilet U-bend from the sewer. The thought of coming cheek to cheek with a rodent depressed me so much that, in the end, I saved all bowel movements for the privacy and comfort of the school staff toilets which, I hasten to add, were virtually the same standard as the kids', but with marginally better quality toilet paper.

While washing my hands in the kitchen sink using a bar of soap I'd found under it, I was suddenly struck by the significance of my actions. The bar of Imperial Leather that I was fondling, caressing and generally playing about with had probably been left here by Kate. Looking at that gorgeous rectangle of glycerine resting in the palm of my hand, I smiled warmly and consciously indulged myself in thoughts of Kate. Five minutes I took over washing my hands – five of the best minutes I'd had all day. When I finally came to my senses (the warm brown water in the tap having reached coffee-making temperature), I began to feel claustrophobic. The walls of the flat weren't exactly closing in on me, but I did feel incredibly constrained by them. I was in a prison where I had the key, but no reason to use my freedom. *I need to go out*, I thought. *I need to go out to the pub where I can mix with real people instead of the ex-girlfriends who haunt me and strange women at the end of the telephone.* Before I could change my mind I was out of the front door.

The public house I had in mind was only ten minutes away from the flat but far enough from Holloway Road not to attract tramps, drunks, nutters or any permutation of all three, which that dreadful stretch of road regurgitated late at night. I'd discovered it earlier on in the week while trying to find out how many off-licences in the area sold Marlboro Lights (answer: none).

It was so cold outside that I was able to watch my breath rise gently in the dark blue sky, so I whiled away the majority of the short journey attempting to defy the laws of nature by blowing smoke rings without smoke. When I reached my destination, the Angel, I stood outside and peered into the huge windows that spanned the side of the building. From what I could see it looked reasonably friendly, by which I mean it wasn't so empty that I'd feel any more conspicuous than I was already feeling, but not so full that I'd feel like a loser even before I walked in the door.

I'd never felt the need to go to a pub on my own before. There had always been someone to go for a drink with, even if it was only Simon or friends from my teaching course. My experience of what I was about to do was strictly second-hand, and yet I felt quite confident, having watched one too many American movies where sad (in both senses of the word) men in trilbys drown their private sorrows in public bars, talk drunkenly to bar-tenders, and offer to buy wanton women (they were always wanton) drinks because it's their birthday even though it isn't. Well it was as good as my birthday, and as I pushed my way through the swing doors into the lounge area, I hoped the next hour would offer me an interesting chat with a barmaid or two, a couple of pints to take the Edge off life and, of course, my allotted quota of wanton women.

I tried not to meet anyone's eyes as I made my way to the bar, but I couldn't help looking at a couple of denim-clad Heavy Metal-type blokes playing pool noisily in the corner of the room. Their significant others were sitting at a table behind them, casting the odd glance at the table but essentially more interested in their nails than in who was winning. I felt sorry for these women, not because they'd made such poor choices in their love-life, but because they were both probably really happy. Vicki Hollingsworth Syndrome was everywhere. Sometimes I got the feeling I was the only person in the world wondering if there was a meaning to life, and people like these girls were undermining my faith that it was a question worth finding an answer to. *Maybe I should ask them if they're happy*, I thought.

Or maybe I should just shut my mouth and get a drink.

Two men were being served at the bar as I got there. Bald Bloke on my left was being served by Weasel Man (features too small, beard too thick) while Bomber Jacket Boy on my right was being served by a woman whom I was instantly attracted to. She wasn't my usual type – by this I suppose I mean that she didn't look like Aggi – she was some considerable years my senior and far more womanly than any female I had ever known. She looked a lot like Kim Wilde in her *Kids in America* phase – all blonde highlights and heavy make-up, yet strangely lithe and earnest but, of course, a lot older. *I want to be served by her*, I decided. *I need to be served by her*.

Weasel Man was pulling two pints of bitter while Archway Kim Wilde was serving two pints of lager. They were both neck and neck, which depressed me greatly; if Bald Bloke got his pints first, I decided, I was definitely going to be upset.

Plan A

1. *Weasel Man finishes first.*
2. *Pretend to tie shoelaces until he finds something else to occupy himself with.*
3. *Failing that, head for the Gents' and try again later.*

Plan B

1. *Archway Kim Wilde finishes first.*
2. *Ask what bitter she recommends and then order a pint of it.*
3. *Engage her in conversation at every opportunity but play it cool.*

Archway Kim Wilde finished her pints first. I nearly let out a whoop of joy, which would've been premature because Bomber Jacket Boy, obviously a student, was holding her back from the finish line by fishing about in his pocket for change. Bald Bloke had handed Weasel Man a crisp tenner and received his change before Bomber Jacket Boy had even finished counting out his coppers. I'd turned towards the toilets, already attempting to convince my bladder that it needed to go, when Bald Bloke turned back to the bar and said to Weasel Man, 'Oh, and a pack of ready salted crisps, please.'

I glanced hopefully at Archway Kim Wilde as Bomber Jacket Boy walked away from the bar with his two pints.

Hurrah!

Her: What can I get you?
Me: A pint of bitter, please.
Her: Which would you like?
Me: Which would you recommend?

Her: I don't know, I don't drink bitter. Most people like the Griddlingtones though.

Me: A pint of that then.

Her? Nothing. Not another word. Not even when I gave her the money. What a miserable cow. I wondered whether a tip would change her mind but as I'd only given her two pound coins I strongly doubted whether she would've been all that impressed. She didn't even look at me when she gave me my change because she was too busy smiling at a new bald bloke now standing at the bar smoking a thin cigar. Out of the corner of my eye I angrily looked him up and down. He was wearing a grey leather blouson jacket, the type which you only ever see in clothes catalogues, and a pair of grey trousers which were the epitome of the word 'slacks'. I wondered, if it came to violence, whether I stood a chance. As he moved his hand to his mouth to take a deep drag on his cigar, the tattoo across his knuckles which read 'ACAB', drained me of my entire stock of bravado. She chatted to him about football: goading him playfully about West Bromwich Albion's recent performance while he in turn cast aspersions on Spurs. I listened to him crack an abysmal 'joke' about a rabbit going into a bar, which had Archway Kim Wilde on the verge of wetting her knickers, before I decided to leave them to it.

I looked for a seat well away from the bar because I was scared I might 'say' something in a casual glance, offensive enough to get my head kicked in. I ended up sitting next to the fruit machine and the door to the Ladies'. I settled myself down and searched for my fags and then sighed as I realised I'd forgotten them. I stared at my solitary pint, the head of which was already beginning to go flat. For the first time in over a year I felt like crying. Not big, manly tears like the soldiers who had faced death, pain and man's inhumanity to man in Oliver Stone's *Platoon*, but small childish tears that didn't make sense and didn't need a reason; the kind mums have an incredible knack of wiping away so well that it almost seems like they never existed.

The table in front of me was bare. No cigarette butts, empty glasses or crisp packets. It would be obvious to everyone in the pub that I was here Alone. I didn't even have the energy to go into the pretence of being early for a date. It was written all over my face anyway: 'It's my birthday tomorrow. I have no friends. I hate my job. I can't get over my ex-girlfriend. Shun me. For I am a latter-day leper.'

This, I thought to myself, *I can safely say is the lowest point in my life.* As if to prove this proposition I began to search through my mental catalogue of disasters.

- Losing my Action Man at the age of six.
- Accidentally leaving my Maths homework at home when I was thirteen.
- Failing my O-level French at sixteen.
- Being dumped by Aggi at the age of twenty-three.

In five minutes that was all I could come up with. I felt something was wrong, they were all a bit obvious, really. None of them seemed depressing enough, even though I'd been devastated by them all at the time. I'd made myself immune to them by thinking about them so much that they had ceased to have any effect on me. There were other thoughts, however, thoughts floating around my head, locked away in boxes marked 'Do Not Open. Ever' and abandoned on the less-travelled byways of my mind. Things which I hadn't forgotten but had instead simply learned to ignore. I couldn't do it with large-scale events like Aggi's dumping me – only small things that were easily hidden. These tiny thoughts were like stagnant pools that would only smell if the horrors putrefying in their deeper waters were disturbed.

I took a sip of flat bitter and dived in.

Stagnant Pool No. 1 (Eau de Abandonment)

Dad left us when I was about nine. (About the same time that Action Man went MIA. Although I don't think the two events were connected.) And if I'm being honest he didn't just leave us, he 'went to live with another lady', which was how I put it to Simon the following Monday on my way to school. My parents had thought they'd protected me from potential psychological damage caused in the build-up to this event by cloaking their bitterest arguments in geniality, as if I was too stupid to work out what was going on. Then one Saturday morning Mum took me and Tom to Crestfield Park. On the way she bought me a brand new plastic football that had all the signatures of the England football team printed on it – I knew they hadn't really signed it but I was impressed nonetheless. Tom didn't get anything because at fourteen months old he wasn't capable of making her feel guilty.

When we got home all of Dad's things were gone. I asked Mum where Dad was and she said he'd gone to live with another lady and then began crying. As young as I was, I could see that she hadn't dealt with the situation very well at all. For the next three months I saw my dad every other weekend, when we'd go to the park or eat chips in a café in town, and then one day I arrived home to discover he'd moved all his stuff back in and everything returned to normal.

Then last year my mum announced that she wanted a divorce. She said she'd got tired of being somebody's wife and wanted to be herself. Dad said it was all for the best, then three days later moved out. They were really laid-back about it, as if it was something Tom and I should've been happy about.

Stagnant Pool No. 2 (Eau de Paternity)
A new entry.

This morning I was nearly a father. This evening I'm still just a loser.

I couldn't help but feel that I'd lost out on something. It was like I'd caught a glimpse of another place – a place that didn't look as depressing as the one I was in – a place that looked like heaven.

Stagnant Pool No. 3 (Eau de Fidelity)
Aggi's infidelity had completely thrown me. I didn't know what was real and what wasn't. Talking to Kate had taken my mind off it for a while but now this thought was back and refusing to be ignored, boxed away or submerged: *I had the best time of my life with her. Does her cheating on me mean I have to throw it all away? Kate's right. Is love really love if only one of you believes in it?*

I didn't much feel like finishing my pint now. I couldn't quite see the point. I was perilously close to crying in a public space. If I'd been a woman I would've had the right, culturally speaking, to nip into the Ladies', find a comfortable stall, pull off a few sheets of loo roll and have a good bawl. The best on offer in the masculine world was the smell of carbolic and stale urine as found in the Gents' – not really my idea of a comforting environment. I went in there anyway, just to get away from humanity for a while. To pass the time and give myself an excuse for being there, I took a leak, concentrating the contents of my bladder on a crushed fag packet in a valiant effort to make it move.

I returned to my table to see a young, trendy-looking couple hovering by it predatorially, their faces wildly exaggerating the effort it took to hold a pint glass and stand up at the same time. Ignoring them, I sat down and finished my pint. I considered lingering just to annoy them, but I still felt like crying, so instead I made ready to leave, casting a last glance in Archway Kim Wilde's direction that said: 'This is your last chance, babe. I'm walking out that door now and I ain't ever coming back.' My visual reprimand went unheeded – the delights of serving watery beer to the dead-beat regulars of the Angel were obviously more alluring. The trendy couple virtually threw themselves in my seat.

Walking back home through the debris of Henmarsh council estate, I kept my eyes glued to the pavement, scanning for dog crap. I didn't know anything about this estate, but the graffiti, up-turned dustbins, discarded armchairs and occasional syringes provided sufficient evidence that this one was as dangerous as any I had come across in Nottingham or Manchester. I was, of course, classic mugging material: four-eyed, weak-willed and middle-class with a cash-card. It was a wonder there weren't queues of long-limbed teen-age miscreants waiting to take a swing at me. Although I was feeling apathetic towards most aspects of my life at this moment (including personal safety), getting beaten-up, I reasoned, wouldn't exactly improve my frame of mind and so I speeded up my pace.

Just before I reached my road I spotted the pale light of an off-licence, tucked behind a row of shops that I had somehow managed to miss on my Get To Know Your Locale tour of Archway. On a whim I entered and purchased the following:

> 2 packets of salt and vinegar Hula Hoops.
> 1 packet of barbecue beef Hula Hoops.
> 1 box of Swan Vestas.
> 1 bottle of tequila.
> 1 small bottle of lemonade Panda Pop.
> 1 bottle Perrier (sparkling).

I paid for the booty on my credit card, because the man at the till didn't have one of those swipe machine things, so I figured that he wouldn't be able to tell that I'd reached my card limit. Anyway, save for the thirty-seven pence change

I'd received from Archway Kim Wilde, I didn't have any real cash on me.

Plastic bags in hand, I made my way to 64 Cumbria Avenue, where I was welcomed by the cheery glow of a naked electric bulb emanating through the net curtains of the front ground floor flat. Peering through the window as I walked along the front path, all I could distinguish were the vague outlines of a man and woman sitting at a table, possibly eating.

Inside my flat nothing had changed. The answering machine had no answers on it and the flat, with my clothing strewn everywhere, looked like the community centre jumble sale from hell. I turned off the lights and fell onto the bed, hoping beyond hope that the day had been sufficiently exhausting for me to fall asleep before my brain could kick into gear again. Meanwhile, some twelve feet underneath me, the man in the flat below whom I'd seen dining turned his quiet meal for two into a very loud meal for two. I listened as a record needle was dragged across side one of Led Zeppelin's *Houses of The Holy*. (I recognised it immediately. Once when Simon's parents kicked him out briefly after they'd caught him smoking dope in his bedroom, he'd slept on my bedroom floor for a month until they took him back. *Houses of The Holy* was the only record he listened to.) When the 'DJ' finally left the needle to rest, Jimmy Page's amazing guitar-smithery was immediately interrupted by a slow, steady knocking – the unmistakable sound of headboard against wall. With nowhere to run or hide, I resigned myself to depression once more. I felt around on the floor in the dark until I found a mug that at some point during the week had contained Vimto, and after locating my tequila poured some of it in. I took a sip, switched on the radio and turned up *The Barbara White Show* until it was loud enough to reduce Mr Doing-it Downstairs' sexual workout to no more than a gentle thud.

Barbara was as amusing as ever. Thanks to her, within five minutes of listening I felt considerably better. There were a lot of people out there (and I do mean 'out there') who were in a far worse state than I'd ever be. Her first caller, Mary, was undergoing a course of chemotherapy for breast cancer while coping with the recent loss of a husband from cancer of the throat. On top of that she was worried about her teenage daughter who she feared was agoraphobic. I had to give Barbara her dues, even the hardiest of agony aunts would've been fazed by a caller so obviously without hope, but not she. Without pausing for breath she set her empathy zap gun to ooze-factor ten and swamped Mary in a sea of sympathy. But that wasn't her job done, by any means. In a world where there are so few certainties, Barbara, unlike politicians, wasn't afraid to put her neck on the line and say she had the answer. She was definitely growing on me. She advised Mary not to feel guilty for worrying about her own problems and gave her the phone number of a bereavement counselling group. As for the depression, she advised her to see a doctor, extolled the virtues of Prozac, herbal tea and soap operas and finished off by telling her to give her daughter a jolly good talking to. I was impressed.

I switched off the radio.

Silence.

I switched it back on and listened to an advert about a new Eddie Murphy film.

I switched it back off.

Silence again.

The man downstairs must've finished.

I poured myself another tequila, turned on the light and reached for my phone book, scanning through the lists of numbers as if they were meals on the menu of a Chinese takeaway. I found the number I was looking for and dialled.

An answering machine clicked on, there was a crackle and high pitched squeal before a section of film dialogue played: 'Life moves fast. If you don't stop and look around once in a while you might miss it.' It was Matthew Broderick in *Ferris Bueller's Day Off*. Simon was so predictable. 'Hi, you're through to Simon and Tammy,' continued the tape. 'Leave a message after the beep!'

A deep breath and a swig of tequila and I was ready.

'Simon, you're not in right now but I'd like to leave a message,' I gurgled quite magnificently. 'I hope you're horribly maimed in a terrible car accident. What's more, I hope you catch a gruesome tropical disease that causes your genitals to dry up like the seaweed in a Chinese restaurant, and that what you're left with crumbles and blows away in the wind. I wish every kind of nastiness I can think of and while I'm at it give me back that twenty quid you borrowed from me last May.' Tears worked their way into my voice. 'Give me back that twenty quid you sodding sod and everything else I ever lent you. Give me back that twenty quid. Give it me back now!'

It wasn't until I'd finished my rant and wiped the tears from my eyes that I realised I'd been cut off. Most answering machines stop recording after thirty seconds. I knew this, because I once drunkenly tried to leave the lyrics to The Velvet Underground's 'She's My Best Friend' on Aggi's mum's answering machine. I hadn't even managed to finish the first verse.

I called back and finished the message.

'This is me again. What was I saying? Yes, that's it. Give me back my twenty quid you git. You've had my girlfriend and now you want my money? Give me back my twenty quid or I'll phone the police. I'm not joking, you know. Poking my girlfriend might not be illegal but theft is!'

I slammed the phone down and laughed. I'd stopped crying now and felt a little bit better.

The journey to the kitchen from the bed – once only a few jaunty steps away – had now become a long and dangerous expedition, requiring me to stumble drunkenly into the few pieces of furniture I had, banging my shins hard enough to make the left one bleed onto my jeans. Ignoring the pain I searched through all the cupboards until I found what I was looking for: the equipment I needed to make the mother of all tequila slammers – a Tupperware beaker and a salt cellar. Racing back to my bed I poured a quarter of my tequila into the beaker, added a generous dash of lemonade and shook the salt cellar near the rim. Drawing a deep breath I covered the beaker with my left hand, raised it to shoulder height and then, leaning over the edge of the bed, slammed it down onto the carpet. Tequila spilled all over my jeans. I laughed maniacally and took a huge gulp from what was left.

It was not long before I was well and truly on my way to not knowing what planet I was on. My next mission, I decided, was to open two of the packets of Hula Hoops and endeavour to throw their contents, hoop by hoop, directly into my mouth. I scored four direct hits and crushed the rest under my feet, forming a huge powdery desert of reconstituted potato. Still hungry, I opened the third pack, barbecued beef flavour, and consumed them in the conventional manner – but only after I'd worn every single one of them on my fingers, waving them in the air. This was good. I felt happy. I was Forgetting. Only one thing could make me happier. I turned on the TV and put *Star Wars* in the video. When Simon and I had first seen the film at the age of six we thought it was real. We used to talk about Darth Vader and Luke Skywalker as if they lived at the end of our road rather than in a galaxy, far,

far away. This strong belief in the film had lingered with me throughout my life, to the extent that I even involved it in my final year dissertation: *Star Wars – Better than Shakespeare?* Eight months' research, 15,000 words written in the six days prior to the deadline with only twenty-three hours' sleep, and all Joanne Hall, Head of the Film Studies faculty, gave me was a 2:2!

Fast-forwarding to the scene where the Imperial Guard are attempting to board Princess Leia's ship, I pressed pause just as she was about to put her hologram message for Obi-Wan Kenobi inside R2D2. Carrie Fisher looked gorgeous – she was vulnerable, trusting, desperate, lonely. All the things Aggi never was. *Princess Leia needs a hero but Aggi doesn't need me.*

The phone rang.

I ignored it, I was having a Princess Leia Moment. The picture was perfect – The Viceroy and First Chairman of Alderaan frozen in time and space. *Princess Leia*, I thought, *I love you.*

The phone continued to ring.

Grudgingly, I answered it.

'Hey, Will, it's me.'

I pressed play on the remote control without saying a word. My Princess Leia Moment was gone. Soon storm troopers would arrive and spoil everything.

'Will, I know you're there,' said Simon, 'I'm really sorry, man. It was a really stupid thing to do. It was really stupid. If I could have my time again I swear I wouldn't do it. I wouldn't go anywhere near her.'

I didn't know what to say.

'Will, come on, talk to me.'

'What do you want, Simon?' I yelled hysterically. He must've thought I was well and truly off my rocker. I calmed down.

'What could you possibly want from me now? You've had it all, haven't you? You've had my girlfriend, what else do you want?'

'Look, it wasn't like that,' he said, trying to be earnest.

'It wasn't like what?'

'It just happened,' he said, clearly uncomfortable that I wasn't making it easy for him. 'It only happened the once. And neither of us wanted it to happen again.'

At the back of my mind a question was lurking. Every second it loomed larger on the horizon, but I knew I had to resist it, because I didn't think I had the guts to gamble everything I believed in just so I could hear something as nebulous as The Truth.

'When did it happen?' I asked. My hands were shaking. I didn't want to hear his answer.

'When I came to stay with you at university.'

He was being vague on purpose. 'You came to stay a lot of times. Which time?'

'At the start of the second year when I came up to see U2.'

I should've listened to my instincts. My brain immediately flashed to that fantastic scene in *A Few Good Men* where Tom Cruise demands to hear The Truth from Jack Nicholson. Nicholson in full menacing mode looks Cruise straight in the eye and tells him he can't handle the truth. I was in the same boat as Mr Cruise. Aggi had got off with my best mate five months into our relationship. It hurt.

'How did it happen?' I asked, more to myself than to Simon, as I knew he'd never go into the details.

Surprisingly, he answered my question.

'Do you remember that night?'

I had to say that I did, but not all that much of it. I'd been drinking all night with my mate Succbinder (whom I haven't seen or heard from since I graduated) because we didn't really like the band, but we thought it might be a laugh anyway. Aggi and Simon were really into the music so they went off to the front of the stage while Succbinder and I propped up the bar at the back, sipping expensive watered down lager from plastic cups.

According to Simon's version of events they'd tried to find me and Suc at the end of the gig but we hadn't been where we'd arranged to meet, which was in front of the merchandise stall at the back of the hall. Bored of waiting, Aggi and Simon had decided to go to 42nd Street, a club in town, and it was there that they first kissed.

They'd got a taxi back to mine and Simon admitted that he'd tried to persuade Aggi to sleep with him but she'd said no. And then they started kissing so passionately that 'No' turned into 'Will used the last one yesterday' and when a team of wild horses couldn't have kept them apart, Simon had sprinted to the all-night garage up the road in three minutes, shaving a good thirty-two seconds off my own record for that desperate dash. They did it on the sofa downstairs. Twice. Afterwards, Aggi had crept upstairs and slept on the floor in my room, because I'd been sick on the bed and was lying across it fully clothed.

In the morning I woke up in my underwear and remembered the horrific journey home and the ten pound cleaning levy the taxi driver had charged before he threw me out. I looked around, the bed had clean sheets on it and Aggi had even tidied up my room. I felt so guilty for getting drunk and not meeting her after the gig that I tried to be especially nice to her all day. I bought her chocolates, took her to see *Metropolitan* at the Cornerhouse and cooked her dinner in the evening. She in turn didn't complain that there was sick in her make-up bag and bought lunch for the two of us. We must have been driving each other insane with guilt.

Simon finished unburdening himself by telling me that Aggi had told him the day after, that if he ever breathed a word of what had happened to anyone she would kill him. Not because she was scared I might be angry, but because she knew it would break my heart.

I could tell by the tone of Simon's voice, as though he were confessing his sins to a Catholic priest, that he thought I'd forgive him there and then, as if the pain of being so frank about his treachery was penance enough. He probably was genuinely sorry, but I couldn't help thinking that some part of him was enjoying this scene. Here he was getting to play the sterling role of the blackguard with a heart. I told him to write a song about it and slammed down the phone.

After five minutes swearing at the phone I ran out of expletives and tequila. I tried to call Alice again because now, more so than ever, I needed her. Her answering machine was still on. I left a completely incomprehensible message and searched for a diversion. An English exercise book belonging to Susie McDonnell which had fallen out of my school bag caught my attention. I picked it up off the floor and considered marking the whole of my year-eight's class work. Although I probably would've got through them a lot quicker than usual I knew I'd only have to do them again in the sober light of day. Flicking absent-mindedly through the back of Susie's book I noticed a couple of badly spelt messages to her friend Zelah Wilson, who sat next to her in class, and quite a good sketch of Terry Lane, the year-eight Lothario, underneath which were the words: 'Terry Lane! Give me one, please!' I laughed and turned over the page, and there written in green Biro in Susie McDonnell's unmistakable handwriting were the words, 'Mr Kelly is a twat.'

I marked Susie's essay and gave her three out of twenty and wrote 'See me' in very large letters.

Turning to the back of Susie's exercise book again, I found two blank pages and across the top of them in large sprawling capital letters I wrote the words, '**I WANT . . .**'

12.14 A.M.

I WANT . . .

1) I want to get over Aggi.

2) I want to move to a better flat.

3) I want to leave teaching.

4) I want adventure.

5) I want to be stronger (physically).

6) I want to like people more.

7) I want to talk to John Hughes over lunch.

8) I want more Hula Hoops.

9) I want to make a film better than *Good-fellas*.

10) I want to grow old gracefully.

227

11) I want to dump Martina without breaking her heart.

12) I want to live in Brazil at some point in my life.

13) I want world peace (please).

14) I want to know what was so wrong with me that Aggi could even consider getting-off with Simon.

15) I want to know why the sky really is blue.

16) I want my parents to get back together.

17) I want to stop smoking.

18) I want to get married.

19) I want Alice to be here.

20) I want a cat.

21) I want a film to be made about my life.

22) I want a clean towel.

23) I still want Simon to die a horrible death.

24) I want to never run out of fags.

25) I want to be somebody's dad (one day).

26) I want to believe in something that can't be explained.

27) I want Princess Leia.

28) I want to be able to play guitar better than Simon.

29) I want to be a hero.

30) I want to sleep.

SUNDAY

8.08 A.M.

My eyes cracked open and my head shuddered violently as the telephone yanked me into consciousness. Though still disorientated by sleep, I managed to reach down to the floor, locate the source of the noise by touch alone *and* flatulate silently, all before picking up the phone in the middle of its second ring. All the same, it took at least a minute or two of grunting and stretching before my brain, still some two laps behind my body, was able to catch up. Someone was talking to me, using words that I recognised to be English; now all I had to do was arrange them in some sort of order and I'd be able to have something roughly approximating a conversation.

'Sorry I didn't return your calls, Will. It's just that . . .'

I didn't recognise the voice.

'Don't be sorry,' I said weakly, scratching my groin. 'Just tell me who you are.'

'It's me, Alice.'

'Oh yeah. Nice one,' I said, confirming her statement. 'What time is it?'

'Ten past eight. Sunday morning.'

'I'd heard the rumours, but I didn't know such a time really existed, you know. Ten past eight: Sunday morning. Well I never.'

233

I finished my bout of primary school sarcasm and was about to go off on a surreal tangent about the various theories I'd been contemplating in recent weeks about time travel and the nature of reality, when Alice started to cry.

'Oh, Alice, I'm sorry,' I apologised. 'I'm a git. Just ignore me.'

'It's not you,' she said.

Holding the phone close to my ear, I slipped out of bed, opened the curtains and looked outside. It was raining. Next door's dog had just finished his morning dump and was haphazardly flicking soil over the steaming deposit with its hind legs.

'It's Bruce,' she said, between sobs. 'He's left me.'

I listened carefully as she explained what had happened. Bruce had arrived back at the flat on Saturday afternoon after supposedly being 'at work' and, cool as you like, announced that he was leaving Alice for another woman. After a lot of shouting and crying on Alice's part, he was decent enough to admit that the other woman was, in fact, Angela, his project supervisor. When she'd asked how long it had been going on, he'd refused to say anything more than that he was moving out immediately and would be back to get the rest of his things. And that, as they say, was that. Five years of relationship demolished in under half an hour.

Armed with all the information, there should've been nothing stopping me from taking up the role of best friend and stalwart, as Alice had when Aggi had dumped me. The job of making her feel better was entirely my responsibility, but much to my shame I didn't feel up to the task. Every sentence that came to my lips sounded either too stupid or insensitive – the sort of thing that would've worked wonders for someone like Martina but would be an insult to Alice. She deserved better than meaningless platitudes, but that was all

I had in stock. She was my best friend and she was hurting and there wasn't a word in the English language that could make it stop.

Still, clichés are clichés for a reason. They exist to fill in conversational gaps, to make the person who says them feel marginally less impotent than they are and most importantly of all, to cause as little further upset as possible. To this end I imagined what Barbara White would do in my situation. First off, I had to ask a great number of questions, no matter how obvious, to show that I cared.

'Are you okay?'

'No, I'm not okay, Will. I feel crushed. Completely crushed. I never thought this would happen to me. He said he loved me. He said he wanted to marry me. He said that he'd always love me. He lied. He lied.' She began to cry again.

My mind remained blank. The spirit of Barbara White took control once more. 'You must be pretty cut-up about it.'

'I can't believe he's gone,' said Alice oblivious to my inanity. 'He's gone. What am I going to do now? I haven't done a thing since he left but cry. The cat's crapped over the bathroom floor, I'm supposed to be preparing for a meeting with my senior manager tomorrow and I was going to paint the kitchen this afternoon too.' She laughed sardonically. 'I hate that sodding cat anyway. She always liked Bruce more than me.'

'Perhaps she'll like you more now he's gone,' I said sagely.

Alice began to cry again.

I abandoned Barbara White mode, as it wasn't doing me or Alice any good. Instead I did what I should have done from the start: relied on my natural ability to tell It the way It is. 'Y'see, Alice,' I said crawling back into bed, 'it's like this: life is a load of old arse. Always has been and always will be.' I felt cold. I pulled the duvet up to my neck. 'I know how you feel. I do, I really do. There you are living life safe in the knowledge that the only thing that keeps you sane, the only thing that makes it all worthwhile is the person you love and then *vroooooooom!*, he clears off faster than the Tasmanian Devil with a rocket up his bum. And all that's left to remind you he was ever part of your life is a pile of photos, a few letters and too many memories.'

Alice didn't say anything. I didn't know whose benefit my little speech was for, so I changed the subject.

'Did you manage to sleep at all last night?'

'No. I lay awake all night thinking and crying. I would've phoned you earlier but it was really late when I felt able to call.'

'Look,' I said gently, 'you can phone me whenever you like. Morning, noon or night. It's like Diana Ross once said, "Ain't No Mountain High Enough".' I cleared my throat and presented her with my best impression of that former Supreme's soul stirring hit.

'Cheers,' said Alice laughing. 'You're a mate.' She paused as if catching her breath and then started crying again. 'Why has he done this, Will? I met her, you know. We all went out for dinner when she gave him the promotion to her department. She was exceptionally nice to me too. All night she kept saying that we must go out together some time. She must be about forty-two but she's really beautiful. She's got her own personal trainer. I don't know . . . what's wrong with me? Why doesn't Bruce love me any more? He must really worship her to do this to me after all the time we've been together. This kind of thing doesn't happen overnight. How long has he felt things were wrong and not told me? How long has he been sleeping with her and then coming home to sleep with me?' She broke down, violently sobbing into the phone. This was my closest friend, the only person in the world I could actually rely on, and there was nothing I could do or say to heal the pain. So we sat not speaking, wrapped in our own thoughts for close to an hour. Our connection via the telephone representing the closest two people can be when separated by 120 miles' worth of fibre optic cable.

Next door's dog began barking violently, waking me up from my trance-like state. I shook my head, trying to remember what I'd been thinking about in the time that had elapsed. I couldn't remember. I thought perhaps I'd fallen asleep.

'Hello?' I called down the phone line. 'Hello? Alice?'

'Oh, Will!' said Alice sleepily. 'I just dreamt that Bruce was here with me. We were lying in bed, his arms wrapped tightly around my waist, and he kept kissing me gently on my neck and telling me that he loved me.' She began crying again.

'What time is he coming back?' I asked, once her tears had subsided to a gentle whimper.

'Some time this evening,' she said. 'He's at her house now . . . wherever that is.' I could tell it took all her strength to hold back another flood of tears, but she did it. 'What can I do? I can't take this any more. He's just walking all over me and I feel like I can't do anything to stop him. I feel so helpless.'

'What do you want to do?' I asked. 'Do you want me to beat him up?'

'Yes,' she said bitterly.

'Oh,' I said, swallowing hard as I pictured all six foot, four inches of Bruce. 'While it would give me the greatest pleasure to kick all kinds of crap out of Bruce on your behalf, I think you ought to take on board the fact that given my weak stature the letting of blood would be all mine.' Alice laughed. 'You're my best friend though, so I'm quite prepared to bleed over his Armani suit for you. Anything to make you feel better.'

Alice became serious again. 'I want him to hurt, Will. I want him to hurt as much as I do. He wouldn't care if I started seeing someone else. It'd probably make things easier for him. I just want him to hurt like I hurt. I want him to feel my pain.'

It was up to me to make things all right. I felt like Hannibal from *The A-Team*. 'So hit him where it hurts.'

'I'd never get near enough to get a kick in,' said Alice, only half joking.

Taking out my imaginary cigar, I shook my head and wondered if George Peppard had ever tried it on with Audrey Hepburn.

'No, I don't mean that,' I said. 'I mean destroy all that he holds dear. Exactly what time is he coming back?'

'I don't know. Around five maybe. I said I wouldn't be in and I won't. He'll probably have that bitch waiting for him outside.'

'Right,' I said. I searched around on the floor for a pair of socks for my cold feet. 'There you go, you've got plenty of time to have the locks changed and make him regret ever wanting to see his boss naked.' The duvet slid off the bed as I made myself comfortable. The flat was freezing. The plug-in electric radiator by the front door was at least three feet too far away for me to consider it worth the effort of getting out of bed. I pulled the duvet back onto the bed, covering myself right up to my neck, relaxed and checked the details of my plan. 'You've got a cordless phone, haven't you?'

'It's what I'm talking to you on.'

'Excellent,' I said – which would've been sufficient in itself – but I couldn't resist adding, 'Let's party.' I smiled involuntarily, my body's way of telling me that on my internal scale of attitude, I was much closer to corny than ironic. 'Which room are you in right now?'

'I'm in the sitting room.'

'What can you see?'

'The sitting room.'

'No, I mean what can you *really* see?'

I listened to the rustle of Alice's hair brushing against the receiver as she looked around the room. 'A sofa, a TV, a pack of B&H, a coffee table, some magazines: GQ, *Marie Claire*, *The Economist*, a fish tank, a hi-fi . . .'

'Stop right there,' I interrupted. 'Is it Bruce's hi-fi?'

'His pride and joy. One of those high tech jobs. Ludicrously expensive.' She sounded distant. 'It's Bruce's pride and joy.' More tears were right around the corner.

'Right. Pick it up!' I shouted, hoping I could generate enough mystery to stop her thinking about Bruce.

'Why?'

'Just pick it up!' I yelled. 'Have you got it?'

'Yes.'

'Take it to the bathroom.'

Alice made her journey to the bathroom in silence. All I could hear was a very faint buzz of static from the phone line.

'Don't walk!' I commanded. 'Run!'

'I'm in the bathroom,' said Alice breathlessly, after some moments. 'This thing's a bit bloody heavy. What shall I do now?'

Another involuntary smile spread across my face. 'Put the hi-fi in the bath, put the plug in and turn on the tap.'

Alice laughed nervously.

'You *are* joking?'

Yet another involuntary smile emerged because I desperately wanted to say, 'No, I'm deadly serious.'

Fits of shrieking and laughter filled my ear drums.

'Excellent,' said Alice giggling. 'Shall I add some Radox?'

The sound of running water and laughter seemed to be everywhere. As we waited for the bath to fill up, Alice reminded me that I'd promised to visit her this month. I said I'd love to but couldn't afford it. She offered to pay for my train ticket. I was genuinely moved.

'It's full,' shouted Alice excitedly.

'Right,' I said. 'Let's take a look at his clothes, shall we?'

'I'm heading into the bedroom now!' screamed Alice in full *Challenge Anneka* mode. 'I'm opening his wardrobe. I can see his favourite jumper that he bought from Duffer of St George, a couple of hand-painted silk ties, two Agnes B shirts and three Armani suits.'

'Anything else take your fancy?'

'Oh, there's a pair of black Katherine Hamnet trousers that he used to jokingly call his "pulling strides" and a limited edition Tommy Hilfiger T-shirt he adores that he got on a work trip to the States. Come to think of it, Angela was on that trip too. Bitch. What are we going to do to them?'

'Head for the kitchen.'

'I'm running through the hallway,' said Alice, unaware that this was the longest she'd gone without crying since our call began. 'Hang on, I've dropped the T-shirt. I'm going through the living room. I've just spotted his vinyl copy of the *Enter The Dragon* soundtrack. It cost him a fortune.'

'Good, bring that along too.' *Enter The Dragon* was Lalo Schifrin at his very best. A loser like Bruce didn't deserve it. 'Right, are you in the kitchen yet?'

'Yes.'

'Find the biggest pots and pans you can. Throw in some water and bring Bruce's stuff to the boil. Anything left over, toss it in the washing machine with some bleach.'

'Wonderful,' said Alice, genuinely elated.

'Feel any better?'

'I feel ecstatic!'

Next door's dog began barking again. A man's voice shouted, 'Will you be quiet, Sultan?' I laughed, because for a few seconds I thought he'd said Satan.

'What are you laughing at?' asked Alice.

It wasn't worth explaining, so I didn't. 'Take the rest of his belongings and chuck them in a black bin bag and leave them by the front door.'

'Front door? What about the rubbish chute?'

'Nice one. Oh, and if you've got any paint throw that in too.' Over the next hour we painted Bruce's black Patrick Cox shoes in the white emulsion meant for the kitchen walls (Alice's idea); cut the toes out of all his socks (Alice's idea again); cut his face out of every photo in the flat and burnt them while I played the soundtrack to *South Pacific* down the phone (my idea); rubbed his toothbrush in the cat crap in the kitchen (my idea, obviously); and threw his leather briefcase, including all of the work-related documents within, off the bedroom balcony (a joint effort).

Alice let out an exultant yell once she had frisbeed Bruce's briefcase out of the window. I listened to her fall to the floor and let out a heavy sigh of exhaustion and though I'd barely exerted myself I distinctly felt in need of rest and recuperation too.

'Do you ever wish you'd done this to Aggi?' said Alice, her voice muffled, as if she were lying face down on a sofa.

'No.' I immediately paused and reconsidered the question. 'Well, yes. I suppose sometimes I do but then I still kind of hope that one day we'll get back together. Thing is, Aggi always took her clothes very seriously. If I'd ever messed with them I guarantee she would've had a lobotomy rather than take me back.'

'Do you really think you'll still get back together?'

'I dunno,' I lied.

'That's it for me and Bruce. I never want to see him again.'

'Do you mean that?' I glanced over at Aggi's photo on the wall next to me, resisting the temptation to see if the marker pen would wipe off. 'Do you *really* mean that?'

'Yeah, I do.'

'Well, you're a braver man than me.'

There was an awkward silence in which neither of us knew what to say next. It was Alice who spoke first.

'Work. I'm fed up of it. I've been working so hard for so long and it's not worth it. I've made a decision. I'm booking a flight – one of those three month round the world things – as soon as possible. Bruce and I used to talk about it all the time . . .'

She started to cry again.

I imagined not being able to talk to her for a quarter of a year. I imagined trying to cope with life without her. I imagined telling my television how much I hated my job. It was really too depressing for words. I stopped imagining.

'You can't go,' I said only half joking. 'It's my birthday.'

'Oh yeah,' said Alice perking up. 'Happy birthday!'

I thanked her for the card and the presents and told her about the episode with the postman. She laughed and said that she didn't trust the Royal Mail either.

'I'm glad you liked the presents,' she said warmly. 'My favourite thing was the donkey. It reminds me of you.'

I laughed. 'Cheers.'

'I think it's important that you've got this donkey,' said

Alice thoughtfully. 'You've got a lot of love inside you, Will, and it's got nowhere to go. Maybe you can love and care for this donkey. You've both been neglected.'

I eyed Sandy's picture suspiciously. I was fond of my mange-ridden donkey but I wasn't about to fall in love with it, at least not quite yet, though I appreciated the thought. I told Alice that she'd given me the best birthday I'd had in a long time and that without her I would be lost. She accepted my thanks silently and then said: 'What are you going to do today? Anything special?'

'Well,' I said, wondering whether to tell the truth, construct a plausible lie or make a joke out of it. 'I thought I'd throw myself a surprise party, the surprise being the fact that I won't bother going.' Alice laughed. 'No, I think I'll just be staying at home enjoying the day with my favourite people: Mel and Choly. Ho ho.'

'Will, let me come to London,' said Alice seriously. 'Please. I can get the next train. We could go and celebrate your birthday in style, have a laugh and forget what a "load of old arse" life is.'

Of course I wanted to say yes, but we both knew it was a recipe for disaster: take two consenting adults, add a dash of vulnerability, a bottle of wine or two and a few 'just hold me's' and before we knew it Plato would take the night off and leave us to deal with the disastrous consequences of two friends settling for second best.

'Thanks for the offer but I'd rather not today,' I said, strongly believing that I'd probably live to regret this decision. 'Next weekend maybe, at least then we'd have more time together. If you came now and went Monday morning I'd be more depressed than if you hadn't shown up at all.'

'Okay,' she said, obviously disappointed, but probably nowhere near as disappointed as I was. 'Have a great day, won't you, Will?' Almost under her breath she added, 'I love you.'

'I love you, too,' I replied.

There was a world of difference between Alice's 'I love you' and Martina's. Alice had only wanted to say 'I love you' because when you had someone to say 'I love you' to, you miss saying it when they're gone. I knew that and Alice knew it too. It didn't mean that anything special was going on here. It was just the sound of two desperate people being desperate.

Alice made ready to say good-bye. 'Look, thanks for . . .'

'Yeah,' I said. 'No problem. What else are friends for?'

11.57 A.M.

As I sat flicking backwards and forwards between a gardening programme, a repeat of *Grange Hill* and *The Waltons*, a speckled grey and white pigeon momentarily sat on my window sill, spread its wings and cooed before disappearing into the late morning sky. It had stopped raining, and the sun was shining brightly off the hundreds of raindrops on the window pane, making them sparkle like stars. I opened the window and got back into bed.

This was quite possibly the worst and best birthday I'd ever had. On the one hand, if I actually cared about birthdays this could have been the depressing episode which broke this particular dromedary's back. After all, I was now twenty-six, still recovering from the fallout of a pregnancy scare, the focus of a mad woman's unrequited love, in an awful excuse for a flat, in a less than salubrious area of London and all alone on the anniversary of the date I was born and the day I was dumped. But it was this fact – the fact that I was on my own – which I considered the silver lining in my otherwise dismal dark cloud. I'd spent my twenty-fifth birthday with Simon and Tammy in the Royal Oak. It had been awful. There I was immersed in my own private tragedy, deeply lamenting the passing of youth and my failure in life, while my companions' sole topic of conversation was how Ray and

245

Sophie, the couple they shared a house with, hadn't bought a communal toilet roll for over a fortnight.

The phone rang.

My brain was alert to the call a split second after it had rung, but my body wasn't interested in speedy responses. The distance between myself and the phone, which had been abandoned under a pile of clothes near the wardrobe, seemed so utterly overwhelming that I never thought I'd make it. In fact, my movement was so sloth-like that the answering machine had turned on before I even got there.

'Hi, you're through to me,' said my machine, in its flat East Midlands accent. 'Leave whatever you want after the beep.'

It beeped accordingly.

'Hi, Will,' said Kate's voice. 'I was just phoning for a chat really. I'll probably try you later.'

I ceased all effort to get to the phone, and lay on my stomach on the carpet, my legs resting uncomfortably against the side of the bed. *Should I pick up the phone?* I wondered. *If I answer I'll have to talk to her and as much as I like her, I'm not sure I want to communicate with the world today. Today – my birthday. Today – the third anniversary of my being dumped. Today – today. I still like Kate, I just need a breather. I can always phone her later. Yeah, that's what I'll do, I'll call later.*

I picked up the phone and apologised. 'Sorry about that.'

'I thought you weren't in for a minute,' said Kate. 'That would have really spoilt my Sunday.'

'Well, we can't have your Sunday spoilt, can we?' I said, wondering if I'd ever learn to control my guilt. 'How are you?'

'I'm okay, I suppose,' she sighed. 'After I got off the phone with you last night I did my washing down at the launderette. I was going to stay in like I told you, but then Paula and a bunch of her mates persuaded me into town for a drink. I ended up going to a club and then we finished up the night back here with four bottles of Martini, watching the end of *An Officer and a Gentleman*. Richard Gere can whisk me away on his motorcycle any time he wants.'

I attempted to laugh, but it came out halfway between a snort of derision and a clearing of the throat – I was already regretting picking up the phone. Kate wasn't cheering me up, she was depressing me beyond belief. I should have listened to my instincts. I wasn't feeling very talkative, and recognising this mood from previous encounters, I soon realised that unless this conversation was brought to an end quickly, I'd become more obnoxious than usual, which could only lead to trouble.

'What did you do last night?' asked Kate.

'Oh nothing much.' I licked my lips and scratched my head. 'A couple of mates came over and we went for a drink in the West End. Bar Rumba. Do you know it?' She said she did. 'It was good. I ended up with some girl called Annabel.'

'I take it she's not with you now,' said Kate. 'What was she like?'

I tried to detect any trace of emotion – there wasn't even the palest shade of jealousy.

'How do you know she's not still here?' I asked.

'The flat's not really big enough for you to refer to a woman you've just slept with as "some girl called Annabel" is it?' said Kate. 'I used to live there, remember?'

I laughed. 'No, she went early this morning.'

I expected Kate to put the phone down.

'I said, what was she like?' repeated Kate not quite aggressively, but not all that far off either.

I answered her question. 'Not really my type. She was a

bit stupid. I asked her who was her favourite out of *Starsky and Hutch* and she said, Hutch, when everybody knows that Starsky was far cooler because he had a better car, better jumpers and, anyway, Hutch was a tosser.'

'I think you're the one being a tosser here, Will.'

'Possibly.'

'Unequivocally.'

'Maybe.'

'Incontrovertibly.'

'So what do we do now?' I asked.

'I put down the phone,' she replied resolutely. 'And we never speak again.'

'Good-bye then.'

'Have a nice life.'

She slammed the phone down.

I got out of bed and closed the window. The sun had stopped shining, and next door's dog was going berserk at a squirrel in a tree. I thought about getting dressed or eating breakfast, anything apart from the subject of Kate and what an idiot I'd been. I got back into bed and pulled the duvet over my head.

On the surface, the ambiguity of our peculiar relationship might have allowed my conscience to remain untroubled, but that wasn't to be. Just because what was happening between us didn't have a name it didn't mean that it could be ignored. My lies were bound to have hurt Kate, because I knew that had they been said to me I would have been devastated. So instead of nurturing our blossoming relationship, I'd simply rounded up all the worst clichés of my sex and thrown them in her face. I wanted Kate's forgiveness, but more than that, I wanted her back as a friend. I had her phone number. I'd scribbled it on the back cover of one of my students' exercise book, Liam Fennel's, to be exact, during our mammoth conversation on death. I remember feeling at the time that her offering it to me represented a turning point: she was letting me in, making me part of her life; showing she trusted me in the only way she could. It was an action as intimate as any kiss.

'Hello?'

'Hi, Kate, it's me,' I said quietly. 'I'm sorry. Look, I'm really sorry. Please don't put down the phone.'

'Why not?' said Kate angrily. 'You don't want to talk to me, do you? What do you want?'

'I want things to be like they were,' I said. 'Can we do that?'

'No.'

'Why?'

'Because.'

I understood her 'because' and she knew that I knew I understood it too. 'I know. I'm sorry. I lied. I lied about going to the West End last night. I lied about having friends to go to the West End with last night. And I lied about meeting a girl last night. I went to a local pub on my own. I got depressed and drunk (in that order), came home, made an abusive call to my former best mate and fell asleep.' I paused. 'I just wanted you to know.'

'And now I know,' said Kate as if she didn't care.

'I know it's no excuse . . .'

'Too right.'

'I give new depth and meaning to the word "arsehole".'

'And the phrase "self-deprecation",' added Kate.

The ice between us slowly melted and things eventually got back to their usual rhythm and energy. I told her about the previous evening in great detail – although skipping over any mention of Archway Kim Wilde – and she was highly entertained but, I think, more than a little disturbed.

'Will,' said Kate cautiously.

'Yes?' I responded.

'You do know your behaviour's pretty strange, don't you?'

'What do you mean?' I asked. 'I'm not *that* weird, am I?'

'Well . . .' she began.

'Well . . .?' I said expectantly.

'I don't mean to be insensitive, but somehow, I think that if I stopped one hundred members of the general public and told them that yesterday you smashed your best friend's demo tape and mailed it back to him, called him up and left abusive messages on his answering machine, sat depressed in pubs on your own . . .'

'Don't forget being obsessed with my ex-girlfriend three years after she's dumped me,' I interjected.

'Yes, that too. Added to the fact that you talk to strangers on the phone and give them fictional accounts of your evening's activities – you lied about going to Marx's grave with friends too. You went alone, didn't you?'

I said yes and added helpfully: 'Don't forget scribbling moustaches and thick eyebrows on a photograph of my ex-girlfriend and helping a friend destroy her cheating boyfriend's possessions this morning.'

'You helped a friend destroy her boyfriend's possessions?' asked Kate in genuine wonderment.

I told her everything that had happened, missing out the part about the frisson of sexual tension in the air between Alice and me. She was especially shocked by the episode with the toothbrush and the cat crap.

'You're mad!' exclaimed Kate. 'You really are mad!'

'Steady on,' I joked. 'I wouldn't go that far.'

'Will,' said Kate. 'Can't you see this isn't normal behaviour?

All one hundred members of my general public survey would've had you in a straitjacket quicker than you can say Mental Health Act.'

I scratched my head and decided it was time to get out of bed. *Kate*, I thought to myself, as I pulled on my jeans, *may have a point*.

'You know the Edge,' I explained to her.

'The what?'

'The *Edge*,' I repeated. 'As in "close to the . . .".'

'Yes.'

'Well, I think I'm about as close to it as it's possible to get without going over. You don't have to tell me about my behaviour, plenty of others have mentioned it, but none of them have told me a single thing I don't already know.' I stopped for a second, pulling a T-shirt on over my head. 'I know I must seem weird to you, but believe me, it all makes sense from where I'm standing. It all stems from Aggi. It really does. She told me that she'd love me forever. I took her at her word. And now she doesn't want to know.' I picked out a shirt from the wardrobe and started putting it on. 'Take Alice, for example. If she started bombarding Bruce and his new girlfriend with threatening phone calls he'd be able to get a court order to stop her. But where is her recourse? Society – I do hate that word – hasn't provided any form of protection for her. His behaviour is deemed okay by their standards but her behaviour will just get labelled obsessive. But isn't love obsessive? Isn't that what it's all about? It eats you up, controls your mind, takes you over and everybody says, "Oh, that's so beautiful, they're in love." But when it's over, and you start sending your ex-lover letters written in chicken blood, you're suddenly labelled "insane" because you're willing to do anything – absolutely anything you think will bring them back to you. Now tell me, is that fair?'

There was a long pause. Kate coughed nervously. 'You didn't really send Aggi letters written in chicken blood, did you?'

'What do you think I am?' I joked. 'A voodoo priest?'

'Good,' said Kate with a sigh of relief, '*that* would just be too weird.'

2.15 P.M.

I was about to confess to Kate how, at my most 'insane', I'd briefly entertained the thought of murdering Aggi, when the phone made a double beep, which broke my train of thought. I ignored it but it did it again seconds later. For a minute, my heart sank because I thought I'd broken the phone, until Kate pointed out that a double beep meant I had a call waiting. When I'd phoned BT to take over the line, the operator had asked me if I wanted the Call Waiting service. It was probably a bit decadent of me but as it cost nothing and was at a point in my life where I actually thought I might have more than one call at a time, I'd said yes. Following Kate's instructions, I pressed the star button.

'Hello? Is Will there?'

It was my brother.

'It's me here, Tom,' I replied, wondering what he wanted. 'Who were you expecting?'

'I don't know,' said Tom in his monotone voice, which hadn't just broken at fourteen, it had completely collapsed, losing all sense of expression along the way. 'I thought you were sharing with someone.'

I cast my mind back to the twenty-minute conversation I'd had with my brother where I'd told him I was getting a place on my own and he'd said, 'Nice one, I'm gonna get me a bachelor pad some day,' and I'd said the day he'd get a bachelor pad would be the day Mum and Dad died, and he'd moaned at me for making jokes about our parents' mortality and I'd told him that there was no point in sticking his head in the ground because it was the same end waiting for us all, and he'd raced upstairs to his bedroom and played his Bob Dylan albums loud enough to disturb the neighbours.

'I did tell you,' I said. I remembered Kate. 'Listen, I'm on another call at the moment. I'll phone you back.' I went to press the star button but changed my mind. I'd talked to Kate for a long time, and now I thought – especially after my earlier performance – was my chance to quit while ahead. 'Hang on a second,' I said to Tom. 'I'll be right with you.' I pressed the star button and got Kate back on the line. 'Hello, Kate? Sorry about that, it's my kid brother. Can I phone you back later?'

'No problemo, Mr Spaceman,' said Kate. It was the second time she'd called me this. I was about to ask her what she meant by it when it clicked, it was an obscure reference to *Gregory's Girl*. I felt like I'd just discovered the meaning of life.

'No problemo, Mrs Spacewoman,' I replied happily.

'I'll speak to you later.' She giggled and added: 'Oh, and Happy Birthday!'

Tom and I weren't exactly close. It was only in this last couple of years that I'd even considered him part of the human race. There were eight years separating us; what my parents had been thinking I don't know. Maybe he was a mistake. Even so, recently he'd turned into a reasonably personable mistake. Yes, he was nosy, lazy and prone to borrowing things without asking, but there was something about him that was incredibly likeable. We rarely fought because he was just too laid-back to get uptight about anything. When he was born, I was determined to let him know who was boss and spent the next few years trying to discover more and more ingenious ways to make him cry, like stealing his dummy, pulling faces at his cot, telling him he had an allergy to ice-cream which would make him choke to death, but everything I did simply washed over him. My theory was that he'd received from my parents a double helping – that's to say my helping – of the genes that control the ability to give a toss, which, I reasoned, explained without any loose ends, my complete inability to be carefree.

'So, what can I do for you?' I asked Tom.

'Just wishing you a happy birthday and all that,' he replied. 'What've you been up to?'

'Nothing much,' I said casually. 'I went out with a couple of people that I know down here. Nothing special. We just went up the pub, had a couple of pints, went back to a mate's house and watched some Hong Kong action flicks: *Drunken Master II*, *A Better Tomorrow II* and *Fist of Legend*.'

It wasn't that I hadn't learned the lesson that lying was neither big nor clever, I had. Very much so. But as Tom's big brother, and quite possibly the only stabilising influence in a family that was falling apart around his ears, I felt a responsibility to be someone he could look up to; possibly even aspire to be, just as Simon's older brother Trevor had been when Simon and I were growing up. For many years, even after Trevor had died in a car crash at the age of twenty-one, mine and Simon's only ambition was to grow a moustache, drive a decrepit Mini Cooper and 'score' with 'chicks' in tan tights. I remember Simon once captured the essence of our admiration succinctly, when years later he described his brother to Tammy as: 'Like the Fonz, only you could touch him.' Trevor was cool. He made the world sound easy.

'Where's my card?' I asked Tom.

'The same place as my seventeenth birthday card,' he retorted.

I ignored him and set about finding a topic of conversation that he wouldn't be quite so cheery about. 'How are your A levels?'

Tom tutted loudly. 'Oh them,' he said absent-mindedly. 'They're all right, I suppose.'

He'd had his heart set on going to Oxford, I think, because Amanda, his hippy chick best friend/potential love interest, had applied there. My mother had called me up at the start of the week and told me the results of his mocks, which to put it kindly, weren't exactly the kind of grades that got you into premier league educational establishments. I kind of felt sorry for him, and Mum said she thought he'd be really lost without Amanda.

'Have you decided about which universities you're applying to?' I asked, in full big brother mode.

'So Mum's told you then?' said Tom.

'What is it I'm supposed to know?'

'It doesn't look like I'm going to Oxford,' he said, not even revealing the slightest hint of emotion in his mono-tone voice.

'Not if you carry on getting grades like that,' I said. 'What did your teachers predict?'

'Three A's.'

'What did you get?'

'A B and two U's.'

On his behalf I tried to look on the bright side and told him the myth about Nottingham having the highest ratio of women to men in the country. He wasn't impressed. Instead he began to list the pros and cons of his five places of study. It was tedious to listen to, truly painful. I diverted his attention. 'Where's Mum?'

'She said that she'd call you this afternoon,' said Tom, now mumbling.

'Are you eating?'

'Yeah, Sunday dinner,' he explained, munching on another bite. Clearly I was boring him as much as he was boring me. 'Roast chicken and fried egg sandwich,' he added. Though I felt like throttling him for his lack of manners, I couldn't help but find him amusing. 'Mum's gone to Aunt Susan's,' Tom continued, 'and then she's picking up Gran from her day out.' I nodded pointlessly as I remembered the Kendal Mint Cake episode. 'She won't be back till about four or five.'

'Anything else to tell?' I was going to ask him how Dad was, but I didn't bother. Dad had apparently gone up the wall over Tom's exam results. It wasn't worth stirring.

'I saw that girl you used to go out with a while ago,' said Tom clearly. Either he'd put his sandwich down out of politeness – which wasn't likely – or he'd finished it. 'What was her name again . . .?'

'Aggi,' I said, feigning a lack of interest. 'She was called Aggi. She's probably still called Aggi.'

'Yeah, I saw her last Saturday in Broadmarsh Shopping Centre coming out of the Index catalogue shop.'

'Did she say anything about me?'

'No. She asked me how I was and what I was up to and then went off.'

'She didn't say anything else?'

'No.'

'Was she on her own?'

'Yeah. She's quite good looking, you know,' said Tom, as if he'd arrived at this fact using the latest scientific calibration techniques.

'Yeah, I know,' I said impatiently, thinking to myself that if he was mentally undressing my ex-girlfriend I'd give him the punching of a lifetime when I came home for Christmas.

I tried to resist the temptation, but I couldn't keep my

tongue still any longer. 'So, you're sure she didn't ask about me?'

'Yes, I'm sure,' he sighed theatrically. 'No messages, no secret handshakes and no mention of you.' I sighed in return, although not loud enough for Tom to hear.

'Well, that's all my news,' said Tom. 'Happy birthday. I'll see you next time you're home maybe.'

'Yeah,' I said. 'See you later.'

I thought about Aggi and birthdays. As an exercise in self-flagellation, I made a list of all the things she'd given me as presents in the past:

20th Birthday

Bottle of Polo after-shave.
Rebecca, Daphne du Maurier.
Monty Python and The Holy Grail.

21st Birthday

Best of Morecambe and Wise Vols. 1 and 2.
The Edible Woman, Margaret Attwood.
An Action Man.
An anthology of poetry by e. e. cummings.

22nd Birthday

Let It Bleed, The Rolling Stones.
The Greatest Hits of Burt Bacharach.
A packet of Liquorice Allsorts.
A pair of boxer shorts from M&S.

23rd Birthday

She dumped me.

I made another list of all of the things I'd bought her on her birthdays:

19th Birthday
Fame annual (1982).
England's Dreaming, Jon Savage.
It's a Wonderful Life.

20th Birthday
Star Wars.
A dress she wanted from a second-hand stall in Afflecks Palace in Manchester.
The Greatest Hits of The Smiths Vol. 2.

21st Birthday
A bottle of Bailey's Irish Cream.
The Empire Strikes Back.
Oliver Stone's *The Doors*.
A plain silver ring from Argos.

22nd Birthday
The Best of Scott Walker and The Walker Brothers.
Betty Blue.
The Best of Hancock Galton and Simpson.

I never gave her the twenty-second birthday presents. By then she'd already dumped me and wasn't returning my calls. I still had them at the bottom of my wardrobe under a pile of clothes that I didn't wear any more. They were still wrapped up in the gift paper designed by a female artist Aggi liked. Once, in a maniacally depressed mood, I considered cere-monially burning all the presents Aggi had given me, but I really would've been cutting off my nose to spite my face. The only thing I couldn't look at were the books, as she used to write messages in them; things about the book or how much she loved me. When it all ended I took them off my bookshelf and gave them to the Oxfam shop in West Bridgford.

Bizarrely, Aggi and I had never got around to doing The Exchange of the Carrier Bags – that curious post-splitting-up ceremony, where former lovers attempt to behave like mature adults as they return each other's belongings; records, hair brushes, books, etc., in a plastic carrier bag – it's always a plastic carrier bag – without falling apart. One of the parties, of course, always fouls up the genteel nature of proceedings by being totally devastated that the relationship is over. Aggi knew I would be that party. I tried to force her hand and arrange it through her mum, saying that I'd left some important stuff relating to a job I was after in her daughter's room, but after The Calling Round The House Drunk Episode her mum said she'd have to check with Aggi first and she, of course, said no. And so, in our great love war, these were the items belonging to me that went Missing In Action:

- A compilation tape of sixties music Simon had made for me.
- The spare key for the lock on my mountain bike.
- *Nevermind*, Nirvana.
- 1 black T-shirt.
- *The Beauty Myth*, Naomi Wolf.
- A pair of red baseball boots.
- An Action Man.
- A first-year essay from History module one, entitled: *Discuss the Origins of the Second World War* (52%. Well structured but would

have benefited from more original research.).
- Dad's watch.
- A videotape with four episodes of the third series of *Blackadder* and an episode of *The A Team* recorded on it.
- My copy of *Catcher in the Rye*.
- *Unreliable Memoirs*, Clive James.
- *The Unbearable Lightness of Being*, Milan Kundera.

On the other side of the coin, the following were my prisoners of war:

- *Star Wars*.
- *The Empire Strikes Back*.
- Three pairs of earrings.
- *Fame* annual (1982).
- *The Complete Works of Shakespeare*.
- *The Murder of Roger Ackroyd*, Agatha Christie.
- *Fear and Loathing in Las Vegas*, Hunter S. Thompson.
- *Riders*, Jilly Cooper.
- Her copy of *Catcher in the Rye*.
- *The Greatest Hits of The Pretenders*.
- New Order, *Technique*.
- Four editions of *Marie Claire*.
- A calculator.
- 25 A4 envelopes.
- A pair of Marks and Spencer 60 denier black tights (unworn).

2.42 P.M.

I wanted to call Kate back straight away. I missed her more than I'd missed anyone since Aggi. The more I thought about her the more relaxed I felt. If I concentrated, I could recreate the comforting nuances of her voice in my head as she talked to me about life, films, funerals, careers and love – it was almost too wonderful for words, which led me to think that perhaps the outer reaches of my brain were beginning to obsess. I had to stop my head from taking over my life and learn to take things one day at a time. As an exercise in willpower and something of a diversionary tactic, I promised myself that before calling Kate, I would sort out the mess in the flat once and for all. It was disheartening not being able to locate anything I needed. I had all but run out of clean crockery and the smell of festering food – melted ice-cream on the carpet, half eaten sandwiches curling before my eyes, spaghetti-hoop-encrusted plates simply crying out to be put out of their misery – was as low as I could go. I cleared the dirty crockery into the kitchen and got down on my hands and knees and tried to scrub the ice-cream out of the carpet – it wouldn't budge, it had bonded to the fibres. Moving on, I put all of the kids' exercise books in neat piles against the wall, and emptied the contents of my suitcase into the wardrobe, which required me to push the doors shut with both hands and lock them, as if the clothes inside were lunatic hordes trying to escape their asylum. The room was now beginning to resemble the flat that I had signed a six-month lease for only a fortnight ago. I filled the empty plastic Asda carrier bag that doubled as my bin with all manner of detritus: a half eaten Mars bar, crushed Hula Hoops, invitations from Barclays to receive a credit card and much more. I was about to add a letter from the TV licence people that had arrived on Wednesday when I thought the better of it. It was addressed to The Occupier. Instinctively I reached for my marker pen and wrote 'Not Known Here' and crammed it in my overcoat pocket ready to be posted back to them – the name in my passport did not say The Occupier, and I wasn't about to start responding to it now just to satisfy lazy TV Licensing Authority bureaucrats. It was a stroppy, mean-spirited and more than a little pathetic thing to do, but I must say, I really did enjoy it.

All week I had been freezing in bed because Mr F. Jamal had made the mistake of positioning the sofa-bed underneath the windows, which wasn't a good idea, particularly as the windows were in such a state of disrepair that the draughts coming through them could have filled the sails of a small yacht. To rectify this situation, I dragged the sofa-bed across the room and positioned it against the opposite wall, stopping every now and again whenever the carpet snagged itself under the bed's wheels. Although its new location meant that I couldn't open the bathroom door to its full extent – the only other alternative meant blocking the sole exit out of this tiny hell hole – I decided to leave it in its new home. Sweating profusely after this brief exertion, I considered it time for a fag break, but my conscience would have none of it. Instead, I continued my rearranging frenzy while my momentum was up. The room's two wardrobes, I decided, would look far more pleasing to the eye, on the wall opposite the kitchen door, as where they currently stood made them look too imposing. After a short debate as to whether it was worth emptying their contents first (it wasn't), I began struggling with the smaller of the two wardrobes.

At first I rocked it from side to side, but disturbing creaking noises emanating from the joints indicated that this wasn't the way forward. Instead, lowering my shoulder against one side, I pushed hard, as if in a rugby scrum. It took a great deal of exertion before it moved, but as it finally did so something fell, scraping against the wallpaper. Leaving the wardrobe where it was, my fertile imagination took hold, suggesting that it might be a rotting hand, which would of course have accounted in some part for the smell of my room. Although only half joking, at the back of my mind it had occurred to me that it would be typical of the kind of misfortune which had dogged me this last twenty-six years, that Kate, the Kate whom I was obsessed about to the point of possibly falling in love, would turn out to be a serial killer. I was relieved and yet a little disappointed to discover not one, but two objects, neither of which was a severed limb. Lying at the base of the wardrobe were an envelope of pictures from SupaSnaps and a hairbrush.

The object in my hand (the photos, not the hairbrush) took my breath away. I felt dizzy and nauseous and so sat down clutching them to my chest. I could feel the adrenaline caused by my excitement whizzing its way around my body. Somehow I knew that these photographs would contain pictures of Kate, my Kate, the Kate of my dreams – the Kate I'd never seen. A hand-delivered argument from my conscience lodged itself in my head.

'Looking through someone else's photographs,' it said, 'without their consent constitutes an infringement of a person's moral rights and is tantamount to the deplorable act of reading a diary, or private letters. I strongly recommend that you leave these photos well alone – especially as I know you're hoping she might be naked in some of them.'

'What a load of old arse,' said my brain, in an alarming show of bravado. 'We want to look. And we want to look now!'

I had neither the will nor the inclination to leave the photos unseen. These weren't just photos – they were photos of the person in the world I most wanted to see.

This must be what it's like when blind people have operations to give them sight, I thought . . . *For the first time in their lives, they can just see and believe.*

The photos were holiday snaps which, as far as I could tell, had been taken one summer in Paris. The majority of them featured either one of two girls in their late teens or early twenties, although there were a few bottom halves of the Eiffel Tower and shots of the Arc de Triomphe and the Louvre thrown in too. There were two good head shots of the girls, which I separated from the pile to study closer. One girl had long dark brown ringleted hair which, though tied back away from her face, still appeared unruly and untamed. She wore no make-up though her skin was quite pale. Her lips, however, were a healthy pinkish colour and she had small silver studs in her ears. In some of the other photos she was wearing a plain white T-shirt and jeans and it was clear that she was taller than the other girl. The only other detail I noted was that she had a nice smile.

The other girl, as far as I could tell, had naturally blonde hair (or a very good hairdresser) which was cut into a sharp bob. Despite the fact she was pushing out her tongue, which screwed up her face, it was obvious she was very attractive – more attractive, in fact, than her brown-haired companion. Her skin was tanned and her eyes were the bluey-green of tropical oceans. A white chiffon scarf adorned her neck and she too had small silver studs in her ears. She was wearing a yellow halter-neck top with a short royal blue checked skirt. The only other detail I noted was that she had legs to die for.

If I had to choose one of them just on looks, I said to myself, *then I'd like Kate to be the blonde.*

I phoned Kate.

'Hi, Kate? It's me, Will.'

'Hello,' said Kate cheerily. 'How was your brother?'

'Okay,' I replied, fingering the corner of the blonde girl's photograph. 'He's trying to work out which university to go to.'

I was impatient to find out which of the girls she was, but I didn't want to bring the subject up out of the blue. I don't know why. I suspect my conscience had a great deal to do with my unease.

'Tell him not to bother,' said Kate. 'Look at me.'

I did. Well, at least I looked at the photos of the two girls in my hands. Kate began talking about how a lot could be learned about life from just living but I tuned out, concentrating on the photos instead. I moved off the bed, over to the wall where Aggi's photo was. I positioned the two possible Kates on either side of Aggi and wondered if, one day, I'd be compelled to deface one of these photos too.

I couldn't wait any longer.

'What colour's your hair?'

'My hair?' said Kate quizzically. 'I don't get you. What's that got to do with Keynesian economics?'

'Nothing at all,' I replied sheepishly. 'But please, tell me what colour your hair is.'

'My hair?'

'Yes, your hair.'

'It's a reddish colour,' said Kate. 'Why do you ask?'

267

'It's not brown?'

'No.'

'And it's not blonde?'

'No.'

'It's not brown or blonde?'

'No.'

'Oh.'

Neither of the girls in the photo was Kate. As always I had let myself run headlong into disappointment. I tossed the photos into my carrier bag bin and made ready to cut this conversation short as I felt the black clouds of my sullen nature descending.

'It's not naturally red, of course,' announced Kate after some time. 'It's a dour brownish colour by nature. I inherited it from my dad.'

'I thought you said it wasn't brown,' I snapped.

'It's not brown,' said Kate, her voice revealing a distinct edge of worry that I should consider her hair colour to be so important. 'It was brown. But now it's red. It's quite simple, you know.'

Reaching into the carrier bag I plucked both photos from the rubbish and examined them closely. Instantly the scales fell from my eyes. The brown-haired girl was, to me, the most gorgeous creature that had ever existed. I returned the blonde girl to the bin and lay back on the bed, holding the real Kate's photo above my head, staring in wonderment.

'I have a confession to make.'

'Sounds juicy,' said Kate. 'Let's hear it.'

'I think I found some of your holiday snaps,' I announced, still gushing.

'The ones where I'm in Paris?'

'Yeah, I think so.'

'I wondered what happened to those,' said Kate pondering. 'Were they behind the wardrobe?'

'Wow.' For a nano-second I imagined hidden cameras. 'How did you guess?'

'It's not that big a flat,' replied Kate. 'I checked everywhere except there. I couldn't be bothered to move the wardrobes. You'll probably find my favourite hairbrush there too. Weird things backs of wardrobes, things always drop behind them.' She paused. 'So what do you think? Are you disappointed?'

'No. Not at all. Who's the blonde girl?' I asked, immediately regretting having opened my mouth.

'That's my flat mate, Paula. It's okay, most lads fancy her. She's very pretty.'

'She's all right, I suppose,' I said casually. 'Not really my type. To make things even, do you want to know what I look like?'

'No, thanks,' said Kate. 'I think you're nice whatever you look like. I'm trying to imagine that you look totally hideous. That way I can only be impressed.'

'I'll send the photos back to you, shall I?' I said, even though I was desperate to keep them.

'Nah. You keep them,' said Kate. 'It was a terrible holiday anyway. We spent two weeks getting chatted up by loads of really slimy blokes. One guy even told me that I looked like his mother. Now is that pervy or what?'

We spoke for at least an hour, in which time she told me all about the holiday to Paris which she'd actually taken this summer. In return I told her about the holiday to Tenerife I'd taken back in July with Simon and Tammy. We'd rented a one bedroom apartment on the agreement that the living room would be *my* bedroom. Instead, I ended up sharing it with Simon three nights in a row after Tammy had thrown him out simply for being a git. And when they weren't arguing, the living room, with its paper thin walls, wasn't nearly far enough away for me to be saved from hearing them thrashing about in the throes of passion. It was a very depressing holiday.

I was beginning to get hungry as I drew my holiday narrative to a close and on top of that a niggling worry about the cost of all these phone calls had wormed its way into my head. I'd been on the phone for hours. As it was, I already owed the bank millions, my dad £300 which I'd borrowed for the holiday and Tom £30, and he hadn't even got a job. I rounded things up and said good-bye, telling Kate that I'd give her a ring at the end of the day to tell her how the rest of my birthday had gone.

I plucked my beautiful lilies from the kettle and placed them on the bed as I was in need of hot water to make a Spicy Tomato Pot Noodle (discovered hidden behind the Honey Nut Loops). Brown water was still on the menu so I used my initiative and filled the kettle with the sparkling mineral water I'd purchased the previous night. While waiting for the water to boil, I flicked through the photos in the main room again, separating them into two piles: 'Kate' and 'Not Kate'. I took the pile of 'Kates' with me into the kitchen, which was now full of steam, and poured the hot water up to the marked level on the Pot Noodle and then added a touch more for good luck. Usually I hated the three minutes it took for the noodles to soften, but time flew, engrossed as I was in flicking through my 'Kate' pile again and again, studying each one for clues about her personality.

With half the Pot Noodle I made a sandwich, adding some of the soy sauce from the sachet and then wiping the Pot Noodle dust from my hands onto the seat of my jeans, I made my way to the bed but not before returning my flowers to their 'vase'. Between mouthfuls, it slowly occurred to me that there was a high probability that in spite of myself, I might actually be happy. In the last hour or so I hadn't thought a single negative thought. *Maybe this is what happiness is*, I wondered. Part of me reasoned that I should sit back and relax and enjoy this sensation, fleeting as it was bound to be. The rest of me – that part of me that tried to touch the grille on the front of the gas fire when I was three, despite the fact that I'd been burnt by it before – wanted to investigate this feeling. Would it, could it, stand the test?

I thought about school and Alec Healey in year-eleven, the most evil child I had come across so far.

I was still happy.

I thought about the worksheets that I had to do by third period on Monday morning.

And I was still happy.

I thought about Archway and all the dog crap therein.

And I was still happy.

I thought about my twenty-sixth birthday and how as of today I was officially nearer to thirty than twenty.

And I was still happy.

I thought about all the money I owed the bank and even added two years' worth of student loans plus an extra year for my teacher training.

And I was still happy.

Then I thought about Aggi.

Here's the scene: *I'm sitting on the sofa bed with the phone in my hand pointed at my temple as if it's a loaded weapon I'm about to use to blow my brains out.*

Before reaching this stage, I had spent a considerable amount of time – in between peaks and troughs of maudlin inactivity – agonising over what I was about to do. In the end, like most major decisions in my life, I made a list, hoping logic would throw up a reason to hold back.

Three reasons why I should phone Aggi

1. I think I'm feeling something for Kate. Something that's got an air of permanence about it. If I get involved with her now it's going in one direction. Forever. Kate could be everything I've ever wanted. I don't want to lose her now. I owe it to myself to put a full stop at the end of this thing between me and Aggi. No other kind of punctuation will do.

2. Deep down I'm not even 100 per cent sure I still love Aggi. This thing between Simon and her has only high-lighted what I would've known if I'd been paying attention – that maybe I don't actually love her any more. Maybe

I am over her. Maybe I've blown her importance out of proportion. In my head she's become this huge thing – My Legendary Girlfriend. If I don't find out what she really means to me, how am I ever going to be sure I'm over her?

3. I can't think of another reason. I don't think any more reasons exist.

Three reasons why I shouldn't phone Aggi

1. I may discover that the reality lives up to the legend and then I'll want her back more than ever but she still won't want me.

2. If I make a decision based on how she reacts to me, doesn't that mean that she wins again? I don't want to turn Kate into a runner-up prize. She deserves better than that.

3. It's just a bad idea. And if there's one thing that I've learned it's that bad ideas should just stay bad ideas.

The last in-depth news I'd heard about Aggi's whereabouts was from her oldest school friend, Sally. When Aggi and I had split up Sally, overcome with compassion, had informed me that even though I was no longer with Aggi, she really did want to remain friends. Seizing the opportunity to have a mole within Aggi's ranks, I took up the offer and went for a drink with her despite the fact that she was exceptionally dull. She worked as a computer systems analyst, but never spoke about computers, as her real passion was fell walking, a subject which she could, and indeed did, talk about for hours on end. In between discussions endured on the merits of various youth hostels in the Lake District, I would pump her mercilessly for information on Aggi, which was forthcoming, up to a point – she never spoke about Aggi's personal life. According to the last Sally update, given some time after Easter, Aggi had moved to London after securing a job as a junior press officer for Amnesty International and was living 'somewhere in Barnes' (Sally would be no more specific than that). There was no point in asking Sally for Aggi's number, although I'd endured more hiking talk than I'm sure my ex-girlfriend ever had, for Sally's loyalties lay with Aggi. Instead, I called Aggi's mum and asked her for the number. I could hear the worry in her voice when she heard my request. 'The Calling Round The House Drunk Episode' was probably still as fresh in her mind as ever. Whatever her misgivings, she gave me the number, although it saddened me greatly to hear the doubt in her voice. Before ending the call, she asked me what I was up to. The fact that I was a teacher not only impressed her but seemed to make her more relaxed. The last thing she said to me was, 'You will take care, won't you, dear?' She meant it too.

I am not feeling confident about this at all.

I dialled. The phone rang five or six times.

'Hello?'

It was a male voice that had all the authority of someone who earned three times as much as I do. I also noted traces of solicitor who spends his weekends playing rugby.

'Hello,' I said in a thinly disguised, well-spoken voice. 'I'd like to speak to Aggi if I may.'

'She's in the kitchen,' he gruffed. 'Who shall I say is calling?'

'Tell her it's Simon,' I said, reasoning that it would be

275

sheer folly to say, 'Tell her it's Will, her ex-boyfriend. She's probably told you about me. No, I'm not the one with the stupid Morrissey glasses. I'm the one who is completely off his rocker.'

'Hi, Simon,' said Aggi warmly. 'What a surprise!'

'Look, Aggi, it's not Simon, it's me,' I confessed.

She paused, briefly stunned, but bounced straight back totally unfazed. She was good at this.

'Hello, Will,' she said calmly. 'How are you? And why are you pretending to be Simon?'

'I'm fine.' I nervously twiddled the phone cord around my wrist. 'How are you? You all right?'

'Oh, not too bad,' she sighed. 'Work's really busy but that's the way I like it. What are you doing with yourself these days?'

'I've moved to London,' I said coldly. I didn't want her to think this was leading up to some sort of 'Why don't we meet up for a drink' type of proposal. This was strictly business.

'Oh really, where abouts?' she asked.

I was about to drive my mental removal van to somewhere more upmarket when I told the truth. 'I've got a place in Archway. It's only temporary. Flat 3, 64 Cumbria Avenue.' Saying it aloud made it sound less of a hovel than it was. If it hadn't been in Archway, the toilet of the universe, she might have been impressed.

'I know it,' said Aggi. 'A friend of mine used to live in Leyland Avenue, which runs parallel to your road. She was broken into thirteen times in four years.'

Defeated, I changed subjects. 'I teach English at a comprehensive over in Wood Green.' I lit up a cigarette. 'I doubt if you'd know it. It's pretty small. Five hundred kids tops.' I inhaled and coughed violently as if I'd never had one before. 'Sorry about that. I'm just recovering from the flu.' I coughed again, this time a little less abrasively. 'Where were we? Yeah. English teacher. That's me.'

'That's great.'

'Why?' I asked abruptly.

'Because you must be good at it. I always said you'd make a great teacher.'

I grew impatient. We were pretending to be old friends who spoke regularly on the phone. It was disturbing me greatly, because if there was one thing I was certain of, it was that I wasn't her sodding friend.

She was prepared to let the conversation drift along until I got to the point. I took control. 'I can't do this right now. Was that your boyfriend?'

'Yes.'

'Are you in love?'

She finally lost her cool. 'What's it to you, Will? Three years and you still know how to drive me up the wall. What do you want? You don't really honestly want to know, do you?'

'No,' I replied calmly, hoping that the serenity of my denial was needling her. 'I don't, but you want to tell me, don't you?'

She didn't say anything.

'Look,' I said, 'just tell me, okay?'

Playing me at my own game, she calmed down.

'Yeah, I suppose I do,' she said. 'We get on well. We have a lot in common . . .'

I interrupted. 'Like?'

'You want a list?' She was angry now. 'Well, we both like being part of the human race. We both like taking things as they come. Neither of us are obsessives. We both real-ise there's more to life than what's on TV. We both like to have a laugh. We both know where we're going. We're prepared to give each other space. We both want to do

277

what we can to fight injustice. Do you want me to carry on?'

The only thing I could think of to say was: 'A match made in heaven.' It was an empty, facile statement. It didn't make me feel better.

Aggi's tone changed. No longer fired by anger – instead it was powered by sympathy. Not sympathy for me, but for the man she had been in love with all that time ago. 'Will, are you drunk? I know it's your birthday. Why are you ringing me today of all days?'

'Because.'

'Because?'

'Yeah, because.'

Her patience finally ran out. 'I'm going to put the phone down. I'd really like it if you didn't phone me again.'

'No,' I said sulkily. I flicked a long stem of ash from my cigarette onto the carpet. '*I'm* going to put the phone down.'

'You're being childish.'

'I'll take that as a compliment coming from you.' I stubbed the cigarette out against the side of the bed. 'Don't worry, I won't phone you again. I've got what I wanted.'

'And what was that?'

'To topple you off that pedestal I put you on,' I said confidently, 'and baby you're gonna come crashing down!'

She put the phone down.

Looking back at the conversation I like to think that I won – use of the word 'baby' without the faintest degree of irony notwithstanding – I mean, I got quite a few blows in, I thought. But deep down, as always, it was Aggi who had won. She hadn't given me a second thought in the last three years. I didn't mean anything to her at all. And this was the first time I had really understood this. I'd spent nearly three years of my life with her and she'd binned them without a second thought. *I bet she can't even remember getting off with Simon,* I thought to myself. *Why hadn't I asked her about Simon? That would've scored me some points.*

I felt relieved. In a way I couldn't believe I'd carried a torch for her this far – I should have used it to set fire to her years ago. For three years it had been my constant hope that one day she would come back to me. I had even purposely chosen relationships that I knew would have a limited shelf-life because I wanted to be able to dump them at the drop of a hat – at the first sign from Aggi. I never wanted any of them. I just didn't want to be alone. I was a user. At school being called a 'user' was the third worst insult, only surpassed in grievousness by '. . . and your mum' and 'No mates'. It meant you didn't like people for who they were but what you could get from them. In a way I suppose I'd used Aggi. I got someone to listen to me moan about life, watch episodes of *Blackadder* with, someone to kiss when I needed warmth, someone to understand me and someone to make it All Right when everything was All Wrong. She got nothing. She was my Legendary Girlfriend but I wasn't her Legendary Boyfriend. And it was only now that it was too late that I realised this.

I called her back. Her boyfriend answered.

'Is Aggi there?' I asked, completely unsure of what it was I was going to say to her.

'She's in the bathroom. Look, who is this? Is this Will?'

There was little point in lying. 'Yes.'

'You've really upset her, you offensive piece of crap. I've a good mind to come round to your place and beat some politeness into you.'

I lost the plot. 'You don't know what an evil bitch she is. You don't know. But you will. You'll find out when she sleeps with your rugby playing mates. She's probably already started on the scrum half. Then it'll be the tight head prop, then the loose head, then the hooker, then the wingers, then the full back . . . what am I talking about? She's probably had 'em all by now, one after the other. Yeah, she'll be starting on the opposing team next . . .'

I didn't hear what he had to say in reply. I slammed down the phone. It was an evil, spiteful thing to do but I didn't care – just like she didn't care about me. My eyes locked on the scrap of paper where I'd written Aggi's number. I picked it up and moved to the kitchen, pulling her photo down off the wall as I passed. Turning on a cooker ring I simultaneously set fire to the photo and her phone number. As the flames licked their way up to my fingers I let the ash fall in the sink, watching the fragment embers until they burned out. I half expected the fire alarm to come on but it didn't. I turned on the tap. Soggy jet black ash blocked up the plughole.

To celebrate my freedom, I lit another Marlboro Light, opened the window and sat on the ledge even though it was drizzling outside. I wanted to feel like a huge weight had been lifted off my shoulders but I felt exactly the opposite. I'd always secretly credited myself with a little bit of intelligence. I thought I was smarter than the average bear. So it came as a bit of a shock to discover that I was as much of a mug as anyone else.

Ash fell onto my leg. I made a move to flick it off but didn't bother because it didn't hurt.

After a while it got too cold on the ledge, my jeans were soaked through to my underwear and I could barely see out of my glasses. Back inside and lying in bed under the duvet, I wondered what Aggi was thinking about this very second. She must have thought I was mad calling her out of the blue after three years. She was half right, I suppose, I did call because of my birthday. Maybe it was the symmetry of it all. A reunion three years after she dumped me would've fitted in well with my romantic view of her. What a gal, eh? Comes back to me on the anniversary that she chucked me away – now that's what I call stylish. I wanted to blame someone but the only person here was me. I sat down and did some calculations. Three years I'd spent wishing she'd come back to me – roughly 11.5 per cent of my life. I searched the room for a suitable metaphor and spied a half drunk can of Coke. It took a while but I calculated that 11.5 per cent of a 330ml can of Coke was – roughly speaking – three mouthfuls! *Sodding sod! I've wasted three mouthfuls of the only can of Coke I'm ever going to get!*

In the bathroom, the light on and the extractor fan in full swing, I gave myself a pep talk. Half talking to my Audrey Hepburn poster and half talking to the mirror above the toilet, I told myself that this was it. I wasn't going to take life lying down any more. Nothing was going to stop me from doing all the things I talked about doing but always found an excuse for never bringing to fruition. For the last three years I'd been living in a state of limbo. I'd been going to the same places, hanging out with the same people, listening to the same music – doing the same everything as a living monument to Aggi. I'd become chief curator in the National Museum of Ex-Girlfriends. I was stuck in the past unable to get on with the future because everything I ever wanted *was* in the past. No. Enough is definitely a-sodding-nough.

Back in the main room, I lit another cigarette, and stood on the bed to get as close as I could to the smoke alarm. Taking a deep drag, I blew right into the sensor and under the cover of the siren I yelled: 'Things are going to change!'

5.30 P.M.

My hands trembled as I picked up the phone. I didn't know why, really – there was nothing to be nervous about at all. I'd already envisioned what would happen: I'd say hello, she'd say hello, we'd talk about life, the universe and everything; I'd make some facetious comment that would make her laugh; we'd have a good time; I'd forget all about Aggi. I'd feel human again.

'Hello?'

'Er, hello, is that Kate?' I asked an unfamiliar voice.

'No, it's her flatmate. Who's this?'

'Oh, it's Will,' I said, taken aback. It hadn't occurred to me that Kate's flatmate ever answered the phone. 'Is she there?'

'Oh, you're the guy she's been talking to all weekend,' said Paula, lacing her voice with mock surprise. 'She's off her tree, is that one. She's been talking about you non-stop. I'm surprised she didn't pick up the phone herself, she's been hovering by it all afternoon. You said you'd phone her back straight away, you lying sod. Tell me, why *are* men so crap?'

If Kate's flatmate was trying to embarrass me she was doing a particularly good job of it. The thought of someone this shallow being conversant with the intimacies of mine and Kate's relationship annoyed me greatly; she was sullying the beautiful thing we'd created. I grew impatient. 'I don't know why men are so crap. I only know why I'm crap. Could you put her on, please?'

'You're keen,' said Paula, clearly pleased to discover she was capable of winding me up. 'That's a good quality in a man. Have you got any friends?' Not a single decent witty comeback or insult came to my lips, my wittiest barbed comment: 'Oh, just sod off, will you?' seemed rusty and dull in comparison.

'Paula!' yelled Kate. 'Get off the extension, will you?' Paula giggled maniacally. 'Stop teasing him.'

I let out a sigh of relief. 'Hi, Kate?'

'Yeah, it's me,' she replied. 'Sorry to have put you through all of that. Paula's in a bit of a mad mood today. Must be something to do with the moon.'

Kate's voice sounded magical, as if it had the power to do whatever she commanded, and right at this moment she had told it to provide me with comfort. I felt like I'd been rescued from the clutches of an evil dragon by a knightess in shining armour. If it had been possible for her to have lifted me up in her arms and carried me to safety, I honesty believe I couldn't have thought of anything I wanted more at this very moment. I took a deep breath.

'Kate, will you marry me?'

'You what?'

I cleared my throat needlessly, hoping that a simple cough would somehow steel my reserve.

'I said, will you marry me? I've been doing a lot of thinking and I've worked out two things: one is that I love you and the other is that I have to act on this new feeling as soon as possible.'

She laughed nervously. 'Are you joking? Because if you are, Will, it's not funny.'

'I am not joking.' My heart smiled as I paused. 'I've never

been more serious in my life. I decided this afternoon that I love you, it's as simple as that. You've changed my life, Kate, you've changed my life more than anyone I've ever met. I need you. I know it sounds melodramatic but it's true.' I bit my lip. I had a lot more to say but I was scared of overwhelming her like I'd done thirteen years ago with Vicki Hollingsworth. 'Look, you don't have to answer me right now if you don't want to . . .'

'How long have I got to think about it?' interrupted Kate, her voice barely audible.

'Three minutes.'

We both laughed.

'Okay,' said Kate still giggling. 'Synchronise watches . . . now!'

For the duration of the three minutes we were silent, lost in a world where only we existed. I listened intently each and every time she inhaled or exhaled. At one point I nearly broke out in laughter, when, for the second time this weekend, I thought about a Sting song, 'Every Breath You Take.' For once, a crucial moment in my life wasn't overwhelmed by thoughts of what might be or might not be. Nothing came in or out from the moment she'd said, 'Okay'. I was so without grounding, floating out of my body, out of this world's experience, that it wasn't until I was well into the second minute that I noticed I hadn't been breathing – listening to her respire seemed sufficient in itself – and it made me happy.

I looked at my watch. The three minutes were up.

'Okay,' said Kate

'Okay, what?' I asked hesitantly.

'Okay, I will marry you.'

'Are you joking?'

'No, I'm more serious than *you'll* ever know,' laughed Kate. 'You're the most important person in the world to me. I love you. Do you know how I want to die? I want to die saving your life.'

I was speechless.

'Don't worry, I was only joking,' she reassured. 'I do love you though. I spent the afternoon making you a birthday card. Can I read it to you? It's got a picture of Jimi Hendrix on the front that I cut out of *Q* magazine. I've put a speech bubble in his mouth that says, "I say a little prayer for you". Inside, it says "Dear Will, Happy Birthday. My prayer for you is that I hope you never have to spend another birthday without me. Ever yours, K."'

I was touched, the thought of her cutting things out and gluing them down solely for my benefit brought tears to my eyes.

'Thanks. It's a really nice thought.' I looked around my room despairingly. 'I'm just sorry I haven't got anything to give you.'

'I've got you,' said Kate. 'What else does a girl need?' She paused as if she'd run out of words. 'So what do we do now?'

'I don't know, I hadn't planned this far ahead.' I stood up and paced around the edge of the room as far as the telephone cord would allow. 'I suppose we should tell our parents.'

'My mum will be overjoyed,' said Kate. 'I spent the whole of my teens telling her I'd never get married and look what you've made me do. My dad will be impressed too. He's never liked any of my old boyfriends but I know he'll like you. I just know he will.'

I gazed out of the window. A thin covering of grey dirt coated the pane. The garden was overrun with tall yellow flowered weeds and stinging nettles. Next door's dog was nowhere to be seen. I could hear kids playing football but couldn't see where they were. 'Both my folks will be pretty stunned,' I said quietly. 'My mum will think that . . . well . . . you know . . .' I paused, embarrassed at the thought of being accused of getting someone pregnant for the second time this weekend. 'How's that for irony? I've got you in the club and we've never even shaken hands.'

'What do you think all this business on the phone has been about?' said Kate earnestly. 'I know more about you, and feel closer and more intimate with you, than any boyfriend I've ever had, even my ex. I've seen the real you, Will. You didn't bother putting on an act because you thought you'd never meet me! What kind of bloke on the pull starts off by talking about his ex-girlfriend?'

'I suppose you're right,' I said, wishing she hadn't mentioned Aggi. Just thinking about her made me feel sick. I changed the subject. 'We've still got to come up with a plan. Where are we going to live and all that?'

'It doesn't matter. I'll come to London . . .'

I stopped her there. I didn't fancy staying here at all.

Samuel Johnson said: 'When a man is tired of London he is tired of life . . .', I thought to myself. He was only half right. I was tired of This Life, and with Kate I'd have the chance of resurrection and redemption.

'No, I'll come to Brighton first thing in the morning,' I said. 'I've always fancied living by the sea. I'll hand in my notice. I'll say I've had a bit of a mental breakdown or something. It won't be too hard to convince them.'

'Okay, whatever makes you happy. Paula's going off on a course in Cheltenham for the week so we'll have the flat to ourselves. What do you like to eat?'

Her question took me by surprise. I was about to say anything with pasta in it but I held back because I didn't know if she liked Italian food. But deep down this was bigger than pasta dishes, this was about fate. I knew that if I said pasta and she didn't like it I'd interpret it as some sort of sign from above that we were completely and utterly incompatible.

'Anything,' I lied. 'I'm not fussed really.'

She paused, audibly mulling it over. 'Okay, I think I'll make you tagliatelli in a spicy tomato sauce. I love it.'

Before I had a chance to register my delight a flood of thoughts erupted from the ground, smashing through the mental dam I had erected. I needed to know she was as serious as I was. 'Look, are you sure you want to do this?'

'Of course I'm sure,' said Kate, so surely, so steadfastly, so assuredly, that I felt the kind of admiration for her normally reserved for pensioners reminiscing over Winston Churchill's 'Fight them on the beaches' speech. 'I'm even surer than you are,' she continued. 'Just because you've been with someone, say, ten years, doesn't mean that your marriage is any more likely to succeed than if you met and married someone ten minutes ago. There's no way that you can accurately predict the future, so why bother trying?'

'But you can reduce the odds of everything going a bit pear-shaped, can't you?' I said, nervously. Next door's dog barked wildly. The palms of my hands began to sweat at an alarming rate. I wiped them on my jeans but within seconds they were literally dripping with perspiration again.

'Everything about love is random,' said Kate calmly. 'So why try and bring order to it? It's not worth worrying about. I know we could just move in together and that would make everything much easier, but it works both ways. It's easier to walk out, it's easier to be unfaithful, it's easier for everything to just disappear. If I'm going to invest my emotions in another human being again then I'm going to make sure if it doesn't work out it'll be the messiest, most savage divorce ever.'

'Like *The War of the Roses*,' I joked. 'Kathleen Turner's finest performance.'

She ignored my aside. 'Splitting up shouldn't be amicable. Not if what you had was love. It's not the way love works; well, at least the kind of love I'm talking about.'

Kate really was Winston Churchill and I was the British Nation. I would fight the enemies of our love on beaches, street corners or supermarket car parks. In short, I was roused.

'I love you,' I said.

'I love you, too,' replied Kate. 'I can't bear to be away from you. I miss you. This is going to sound weird but even though we've only known each other a weekend, I feel like we've created a million memories together. I've gone over everything you've ever said to me again and again in my head. I love your voice. It makes me feel safe.'

'When did you realise?' I asked.

'That I loved you? When you told me the story about the worms dying and how you tried to save them. I thought to myself – that's the man for me!'

I could hardly believe what I was hearing. 'Really?'

'Yeah, really. I like the way you talk about your childhood. You seem incredibly fond of it. I like that. I can tell that you're special. You notice things differently to other people. You torture yourself for not being this go-getter kind of person, but you are what you are, so why change? Even though you don't think so, you *are* important and you *have* made a change. Look what you've done to my life in three days. Before I spoke to you the biggest thing on my horizon was trying to work out how I was going to afford to pay back my grant cheque. Now all I've got to worry about is you.'

Kate asked me when I'd realised that I was in love with her. I rolled the question around in my head, momentarily sitting down on the bed to aid my thinking processes. 'I didn't decide,' I said shakily. 'It just happened. When I picked up the phone I realised that out of the billions of people on the planet, you were the one I wanted to speak to the most. It was like the deepest part of me took control and said what it felt, unafraid of embarrassment or rejection or any of that other stuff that normally leaves me paralysed with fear. I didn't think. I just was. Normally I find it necessary to have a three hour debate with myself just to decide what flavour crisps to buy, and here I am making the decision of my life purely on instinct. I kind of feel like Stone Age Man. Quick, I feel the need to hunt and gather.'

Kate laughed. 'I know exactly what you mean. Y'know, I didn't need three minutes to think about my answer. The minute you asked me I knew the answer was yes. A mate of mine, Becky, does psychology at Cardiff and she told me this fact: apparently when you're asked a question, whether you want to or not most people answer straight away in their heads and then spend the time available to them trying to make sure they're right. The instant you asked me I knew the answer was yes.'

'So what do we do now?' I asked.

'You ask me properly,' replied Kate.

'What do you mean? Get down on my knees?'

'Yes. And be quick about it.'

'Okay. Kate . . .'

'Are you down on your knees?' enquired Kate doubtfully.

I was astonished at the depth of her insight into my personality. 'How did you know I wasn't down on my knees?'

'Well, were you?' countered Kate.

'No, but that's beside the point,' I laughed. 'You ought to trust me, you know. I'm your husband to be.'

'And I'm your wife to be so you'd better watch out. Hurry up.'

I got down on one knee.

290

'Look up as if you were gazing straight up at me,' said Kate.

'Okay, I'm looking up as if I was gazing up at you,' I said. My knee began to wobble. I focused my attention on the right-hand corner of the curtains. 'I've even got my hand outstretched as if I were holding your hand. "Would you do me the honour of becoming my wife?"'

'Yes,' said Kate matter-of-factly. 'Now it's my turn. I'm down on my knees and I'm holding out my hand as if I'm holding yours and gazing up at your beautiful face. I love you, Will. Will you marry me?'

'I, Will, will.'

We both laughed.

There was a long moment of silence when I felt neither of us really knew what to say or do next. Kate wasn't playing around, this was for real, which made me feel excited and exhilarated. I had so much adrenaline shooting through my veins that it wouldn't have been enough to simply pace around the flat trying to expend it, I wanted to run, to Brighton preferably. Over the moon? I was high jumping the Milky Way and sprinkling star dust in my hair!

'We've got a lot of things to sort out,' I said, drawing a deep breath in an attempt to steady my breathing. 'I've got to tell my parents about this and sort out how I'm going to tell the school that I'm leaving. I know this is going to be hard but I think we ought not to phone each other again today. Let's just wait until I come over to Brighton tomorrow morning. Then we can talk until we're blue in the face. I think we both need some time to get our heads around this; plus, I'm afraid the phone bill is going to end up so large we'll have to take our honeymoon in Skegness.'

'I like the sound of a week in Skegness with you,' said Kate joyfully. I closed my eyes and tried to encrypt that enchanting sound in my head. 'But I suppose you're right, we do need to calm down a bit. Okay, let's make a pact we won't call or speak to each other until you come to Brighton . . . unless there's an emergency.'

'What sort of emergency?' I asked.

'You know, deaths, births, fires, pestilence, irate parents.' There was a brief pause. 'I love you,' said Kate as a good-bye.

'I love you, too.'

I was so filled with *joie de vivre* that I wanted to tell the world that I – yes, me, William Kelly, cynic *par excellence* – had found love. In the end, however, I decided against informing the inhabitants of Archway of my newfound love. Instead, for some considerable period of time I lay very still on the bed, listening to the sound of my heart beating until hunger drove me into the kitchen. My evening meal consisted of two slices of dry toast as I didn't have the energy or inclination to 'cook' and I'd used the last of the Flora in the construction of my Pot Noodle sandwich.

The piles of exercise books propped against the wall which all required marking pricked my conscience, compelling me to propose the suggestion that even if I wasn't going to school tomorrow, I should at least fulfil this small requirement of my job description. I didn't mark them, of course, as in truth my motivation had less to do with professional pride or guilt than it had to do with avoiding calling my parents, my mother in particular. My newfound positive attitude to life, however, wouldn't let me kid myself – not any more. I was determined not to worry. I could tell my parents, my brother, my Gran, my friends – without fear of what they might say – because finally, I had something I could believe in.

My mother

'Mum, listen,' I said, employing the same tone of voice I'd used four years ago to tell her that Tom had broken his leg playing football.

'What is it?' she gasped, immediately recognising the gravity of the situation.

I cleared my throat to postpone the inevitable temporarily. 'I'm getting married.'

My mother was silent. She wanted desperately to believe I was joking. 'What for? Who to? Do I know her?'

Questions. Questions. Questions. This reaction was typical of my mother. When faced with a problem her natural instinct was to interrogate her subject until she was better informed than even they were. It was like *Mastermind* only in reverse: her chosen speciality was my love life, but it was she who got to ask the questions and I who had to answer them. This was very weird.

I told her the story from beginning to end. She listened attentively, but it was clear that the story made little sense to her. In her world, things like this just didn't happen.

My mother's first words were: 'Oh, Will, what is it? You haven't got her . . .' I knew she wouldn't finish the sentence. I contemplated finishing her sentence for her just for a laugh, but I feared the missing word's shock factor had the potential to put her heart in arrest, if not kill her on the spot.

I comforted her. 'No, you're not going to be a gran. You're going to be a mother-in-law.' She let out a sigh of relief. 'It's nothing like that. It's love. I love her more than I've ever loved anyone.'

'But what about your job?' she questioned. 'You've only just got going. Won't they have something to say about running off to Brighton?' Again, this was classic 'my mother'. Practical considerations were always top of her list; while all things spiritual were right at the bottom, just below embroidered toilet roll covers.

I explained to her what I was going to do about my job and even as I spoke it was plain to me how flimsy and ill conceived my 'plans' were, but it did nothing to shorten my stride towards making them happen. I told her more details about Kate: how her laugh sounded like summer; her breath like the breeze on a beautiful day; and most importantly of all, how I truly believed she thought the world of me. My mother remained unmoved.

'Don't go throwing your life away, Will,' she said losing control of her voice. She was close to the Edge. I decided to be more careful with my words. She had never thought it necessary to need much of an excuse to cry, and with a situation tailor-made for the shedding of tears on her doorstep, unless I could convince her what I was doing was the right thing, she would break down. I'd never made my mother cry before. And I didn't want to start now.

'I'm not throwing my life away, Mum,' I said warmly. I looked around my sad, messy little flat. This was my life. This was what I was giving up. Nothing. I became angry that she couldn't see for herself how unhappy I was here. 'I'm not throwing my life away,' I said acerbically, 'I'm getting married. There's a difference, you know.' Before I'd even come to the end of the sentence I regretted it. At first Mum didn't say anything in reply; I thought I'd managed to escape retribution, but then she started to cry.

I felt awful. 'I'm sorry.'

'It's a big step, you know,' she said sobbing. 'You shouldn't do things like this lightly. Look at what happened to me and your father.' I wanted to say I'd rather not look at them because it would've been a clever thing to say, but I didn't because I'd already hurt her more than I thought I could endure. Instead I kept quiet, dwelling upon my parents' marriage. As much as I loved them both, they weren't particularly good advertisements for holy matrimony, but neither were they particularly good advertisements for joining the human race. In the end, I decided, it made no odds.

'Yeah, I know it is,' I said. 'And I'm not doing it lightly, Mum. I won't be any more sure in ten years than I am right now, because I am 100 per cent sure.'

'What's her name?' she asked.

'Her name's Kate.' The words came out so quietly that I wasn't sure she'd heard them.

'Kate what?'

My mother wanted more details, they were the only things that made sense to her. Facts, figures, information – The Tangible.

'Er, I don't know,' I said faltering. I tried desperately to remember. 'It's Freemans. Like in the catalogue. Kate Freemans.'

My mother couldn't believe this. 'You're getting married to someone and you're not even sure about their surname?'

I looked at my watch. The second hand *was* moving, the watch's mechanism *was* ticking but time felt like it had stopped.

'Listen, Mum,' I said, deciding I'd had quite enough. 'I've told you now. You're obviously upset. We're not getting married right this second so there's plenty of time to get used to the idea.'

She didn't say anything.

'Look, Mum,' I added, 'before I go I've got something else

296

to confess. I think I've knackered that saucepan you told me not to take.'

She put down the phone.

My father

'I'm getting married.'

My dad remained silent. Unfazed, I continued talking, though it was like communicating with a brick wall. 'Look, Dad, there's nothing to worry about, okay? I'm twenty-six years old. When you were twenty-six you'd already been married two years and you had me to look after. I know you think I'm being rash but I'm not. Do I sound like I don't know what I'm doing?'

He remained silent. And from past experience I knew why. My dad never liked being put on the spot. He liked to consider things in his own time before passing judgement on them. Not that his considered reaction would have been any more promising than his unconsidered, but at least given his own time he would have known exactly what he wanted to say.

'Marriage?' he said, unsure of his words. 'Why? Why this way? Is it because of the divorce? The divorce had nothing to do with you. I thought you were okay about it.' It wasn't like my father to use pop psychology to come up with a causal link between the divorce and my getting married. He didn't believe in conditioning or the influence of environment. He once told me that everyone should be responsible for their own actions and not getting enough love or attention was no excuse for being a thug. 'You can't excuse Hitler everything he did just because his mother made him wear short trousers,' he announced one day, more to the television programme which had provoked this reaction than to us, his family.

'I don't know, it just is,' I said, focusing on why marriage was the answer to all my problems. 'I'm fed up with all the what-ifs life throws up, Dad. I'm fed up of them all. I'm fed up with waiting for life to happen before I can have a life. If I don't do this one thing the way I want to do it then I really will be a failure. She's everything I've ever wanted. I can't let go.'

'Can't it wait a while?' he said, bitterly. He was angry now and so was I, but not about what he was saying. I was angry because it had taken me so long to work out where I'd been going wrong all along. *All this wasted time that I'll never get back again.*

'Wait for what, Dad?' I retorted angrily. 'Wait for you to talk me out of it? Wait for me to talk me out of it? Haven't you ever felt the need to trust your own judgement? Just this once I need to listen to what *I'm* saying. It's like there's a voice inside me that I've always shouted down or ignored, but for once I'm going to listen to it. I have to listen to it because I think it's making sense.'

I laughed inwardly. This was *Pretty In Pink*, *East of Eden*, *St Elmo's Fire* and *The Breakfast Club* rolled into one. Be that as it may, I couldn't hold in what I had to say just because I was treading on the same hallowed ground as James Dean, Molly Ringwald, Emilio Estevez, Judd Nelson or thousands of other celluloid coming-of-agers trying to navigate their way through to adulthood. My life would resemble a teen movie until the day I died – I guarantee I'll be the only eighty-year-old man in the world suffering from teen angst.

After my speech, my dad refused to say anything for a while. I told him about all of the beautiful things I saw in Kate and how she made me feel, but I was fighting a battle that had been lost before the first bullet was even fired. His silence did nothing to hide his feelings, he was angry and disappointed (in that order). Still, I felt pleased that I'd had the guts to tell him – the old me would never had done that.

'It's a real shock,' said Dad, finally breaking his silence. 'But if you really do love this girl then what can I do? I just worry. That was the job I was given when you arrived twenty-six years ago. I suppose you're not the only one with an inner voice, son, I've got one too. And it's telling me I've raised a fine son. Happy birthday.'

My brother

'I'm getting married.'

'I know. Mum and Dad both went ballistic,' said Tom excitedly as if my life was a *Sun* exclusive. 'Mum started crying and Dad came around and said he thinks you're mad. Mum was straight on the phone to Aunt Susan to see if she could try and persuade you out of it.'

'Why hasn't she phoned then?' I enquired suspiciously.

'She told her that she wouldn't do it,' he said. 'Mum didn't say why, but I think Aunt Susan thinks Mum should mind her own business.'

It was good to know that someone was on my side. Aunt Susan was right, it wasn't anyone's business but my own. *I'm twenty-six*, I thought to myself, *I don't need anyone's approval*.

I asked Tom what he thought.

'I think it's a bit weird but it's cool,' he said absent-mindedly. 'To tell you the truth I never thought you'd ever get over that Aggi bird.'

'Are you playing that sodding computer game?' I asked threateningly.

I heard him put it down on the table next to the phone.

'No,' he said defensively. 'Well, what about Aggi?'

'It's over.'

'This girl, Kate, did you really meet her this weekend or are you just winding them up?' he asked. I retold the story adding a few details that I hadn't thought my parents would have been interested in. Tom was completely unmoved by it all but listened intently. When I finished all he said was: 'I don't get you.' He wasn't being thick on purpose, he'd inherited my mother's literal mentality. The concept of higher love eluded him too.

'I've only ever talked to her on the phone,' I told him.

He laughed, still unsure whether to believe me.

'It must've been an excellent conversation,' said Tom.

'It was,' I replied.

My Gran

'I'm getting married.'

'I know, dear,' said Gran. 'Your mother told me not ten minutes ago.' She sounded sad. I hated disappointing her.

'I'm sorry, Gran,' I said.

'What for, dear?'

'For doing this all wrong. Mum and Dad are furious . . .'

'Never mind them,' she interrupted. 'The important question is are *you* happy?'

Whereas my mother asked every question but the important ones, Gran asked the important questions and worried about the details later. Apart from her narcotics fixation, my Gran was all right.

'I am, Gran,' I said happily. 'Yes, I am.'

'Then that's all that matters. Your parents have got everything all muddled up. They don't know what's really important in life. At least it looks like you've got your priorities right, Will.'

'Kate's lovely, Gran,' I said. 'You'd really like her.'

'I like her already,' she said.

Those four words cheered me up immensely.

'Do you know what?' continued Gran. 'They've forgotten what it's like to be in love, your parents. No disrespect to them, I suppose it's their way. During the war with so many young men going off to fight, never sure if they'd ever come back, people got married as soon as they knew it was love. Straight to the church and no messing. When you don't know how long your next minute's going to be you soon learn to take time seriously.'

Alice

Before I had a chance to tell Alice about Kate and me, she told me she had some news of her own: she'd not only managed to book her three-month world trip, she'd booked on a flight to New York leaving on Monday afternoon at 4.00 p.m. too. I was shocked at the speed of her actions. I hadn't had the opportunity to give her leaving much thought, but in the split second available to me I gave it my fullest attention. It was a bad idea. The worst she'd ever had. Right up there with going platinum blonde (for three weeks when she was nineteen – I'd called her Andy Warhol for weeks afterwards) and going out with Simon. She thought she needed space but I knew she needed friends – me especially. That was my considered reaction. I took another split second to reconsider it. I was being selfish. It wasn't about her happiness, it was about mine. I didn't want her to go because I didn't want to miss her. I wanted her to be here for me. All I could think to myself was that I'd already lost one friend this weekend. I couldn't afford to lose another. My conscience was well aware of the fact that I wasn't considering for a second that she might need something different. She'd decided to deal with Bruce's leaving in a more constructive way than spending the next three years moping, moaning and miserable. I felt ashamed of myself and told her in an overwhelmingly enthusiastic manner just how happy I was for her. She gave a short, sharp but unsteady laugh and joked about sending me a postcard. I told her not to send it to London. She asked me why not and I told her the reason.

'I'm getting married.'

She didn't say anything.

'Alice, I'm getting married. It's true.'

She remained silent. Rather optimistically I hoped that she was simply lost for words so I began the story which by now had formed itself into a ten-minute after-dinner speech – all that was missing were the cigars and the ten-year-old brandy – but before I could tell her I was going to Brighton, however, she started to cry. I wondered whether I was being insensitive, what with Bruce leaving her earlier this morning.

'I'm sorry,' I began.

'What for?' said Alice.

'I don't know. Being happy. You've had a terrible day and the last thing you need is me being so bloody cheerful. It's enough to make anyone sick.'

'It's got nothing to do with you, okay? The whole world doesn't revolve around you, even though you might think it does. You're so self-centred sometimes . . .'

'I thought that's what you liked about me.'

'Yes, go on. Make a joke about it, why don't you?' Alice

was really angry now. 'You're such a bastard, Will, you really are.'

She started crying again. I was at a loss what to do next. This wasn't what I'd expected. I thought she'd be pleased. Three years I'd been moaning to her about Aggi, and now that I was happy Alice thought I was public enemy number one. I thought she'd be happy for me. After all, I was happy for her. We were both finally sorting out our lives and moving on – she had her trip of a lifetime while I had wedded bliss. It was like she'd thrown all the rules of logic out of the window and was making up new ones as she went along. This was very un-Alice. This was uncharted territory.

She stopped sobbing. 'You can't marry her. You just can't.'
She started sobbing again.
She stopped sobbing. 'Why can't you see how wrong this is?'
She started sobbing again.
She stopped sobbing. 'Please don't do this.'
She started sobbing again. This time her tears were even more heartfelt than they'd been this morning.

I patiently waited out her tears as if they were a passing storm and eventually she 'explained' all. She said that she didn't want to see me unhappy and that if I married this girl then I would be unhappy because I was doing it on the rebound. I said three years is a long time to be on the rebound and I was bound to bump into someone sooner or later, but she didn't laugh – she just cried even harder. When those tears passed she told me that Kate was probably after my money, which brought a moment of levity that we both enjoyed. I told her that Kate was as wonderful as a person could be, and that if she could only meet her she'd be bound to like her. Alice disagreed and said that I was just like every other man and that I only thought with the contents of my boxer shorts. I asked her why, when she'd been in support of so many of my ridiculous plans, was she so opposed to this one and she said because this one was the stupidest I'd ever had. I asked her why she was being so weird and she said she didn't know. And I asked her if it was Bruce and she said no. I asked her if she was having her period. Her reply was both physically impossible and potentially unrewarding.

'Listen,' I said, hoping what I was about to say would miraculously change her view of the situation, 'you will come to the wedding, won't you, because . . .'

'Over your dead body!' she hissed.

'That's a no then?'

She started to cry again.

'It's just that with me not talking to Simon and not being on particularly good terms with the rest of the human race, I was kind of hoping you'd be my best man. Your speech would be much funnier than his would anyway.'

'Cheers,' said Alice through her tears, 'but I won't be coming. Everything's going to change, Will! Everything's going to change!'

'Nothing's going to change,' I reassured, even though I wasn't entirely convinced I was telling her the truth. In a way she was right, we'd reached junctures in our lives that would take us in different directions. I couldn't quite see why my marriage should make such a difference to our relationship, when she'd been living with Bruce for five years, but for some reason I knew that it would. One day soon the circumstances that we now found ourselves in would take their toll. It was just a matter of time.

After a moment's silence she sighed wearily and said, 'You've got to do what you've got to do.'

I tried to think of something comforting to say but the only thing I could think of to say was: 'Ditto.'

Martina

'I'm getting married.'

Martina didn't say a word. I wondered whether she'd misheard me. 'Martina, I'm really sorry but I'm getting married.'

It was entirely in my imagination but I was certain I heard her heart break.

'Martina, I'm sorry,' I said. And I truly meant it. 'I'm really sorry. Are you all right?'

She put the phone down.

Simon

As Simon's phone rang for what seemed like years I thought deeply about how much I hated him. Granted, for best mates we had never been particularly close, but we were all each other had and he hadn't seen that. And that's what hurt. And so now I wanted him to die. I really did. But before his death I wanted him to know that I'd finally found happiness. Because now, more than ever, I could see that Simon – irrespective of whether success or failure lurked around the corner – would one day wake up to discover that he was Fat Elvis, bloated by excess, talent slashed up the wall, wearing totally ridiculous clothes and lonely as hell.

His answering machine clicked on. I didn't want to leave a message – I wanted him to hear it from me. Just as I was about to put the phone down he picked up.

'Will . . .' He started crying.

I didn't say anything. I was getting tired of people crying on me. I decided he was either having some sort of premeditated crisis to get back in my good books or was exploring new emotional avenues to inspire material for the album.

'Will, me and Tammy have split up.'

This was no big surprise and certainly nothing for Simon to get all weepy about. He didn't care about anyone but himself – these tears weren't for Tammy.

He stopped crying and told me what had happened. Simon had come home to find Tammy crying (yes, she was at it too) on the sofa. In her hand was a packet of three condoms which she'd found in the case of his acoustic guitar – there was only one condom in it. Tammy had been on the pill since she'd met Simon so she concluded that two missing condoms added to one boyfriend whose eye for the ladies was well documented, equalled infidelity. Despite Simon's uncanny ability to tell the most outrageous skin-saving lies convincingly, just like his previous confession to me, he'd felt compelled to tell Tammy the truth. Yes, he had cheated on her; yes, he had been sleeping with someone else and no he didn't love her any more. She'd packed her bags and left without saying another word.

'Why did you do it?' I asked.

'What, go off with someone else?'

'No. Why did you tell her the truth? What's the thing you've got with the truth? Why did you tell me about you and Aggi?'

Simon paused, but it wasn't theatrical. He seemed genuinely lost for words. 'I don't know.' His voice sounded croaky. He coughed. 'Hang on a sec. I need a fag.' He coughed again. 'The reason I told you and Tammy the truth is that I fell in love. It sounds stupid and I know you think I'm talking out of my arse but it's true. The band were playing at a university gig down in London. I met a girl there. At first it was just a bit of a laugh, just like it always is, but then suddenly it wasn't. I used to tell her the band were touring a lot so she never hassled me about being away so much. I saw her for about six months. And then one day I was flicking through "S" in the rock and pop section in HMV when I thought about this girl and I couldn't get her out of my head. That's when I knew I had to do it. I called her up and dumped her. And then I wrote her a letter in case she didn't get the message.'

In spite of my hatred I was hooked. The thought of Simon being in love was just too much to contemplate. I lit a cigarette and told him to continue.

'I realised I was falling in love and I didn't like it. I've only got to look at you to see what love can do. It's such a crap, pointless emotion. All that intensity, all that demanding, no one could voluntarily want to be in that sort of condition.'

I laughed. Simon had a heart? This was too weird. It was a given. One of those irrefutable laws of the universe. Energy cannot be created or destroyed. All barbers are mad men. Simon doesn't give a toss about anyone but himself.

I still didn't understand. 'But why did you tell me and Tammy the truth?'

'I told Tammy the truth because I'd never loved her. I'd never even told her I liked her. So the least I could do was tell her the truth. And I told you because this weekend I realised I'd made a huge mistake. The biggest mistake of my life. I'm still in love with the girl that I dumped and I don't know where she is or how to contact her. I've never felt like this before. I can't sleep. I can't eat. I can't listen to music. I even split up the band today. The record contract, the album, everything I've spent my life working towards is history. On Friday I realised that if I'm like this after three weeks without her then what you've been going through this last three years must have been torture – and so I owed you the truth. I'm sorry, I really am. Will, I love this girl so much I don't know what to do.'

Simon was being real. He meant every word. It was hard not to feel sympathy for him but I managed it. I was glad he was hurting. I was glad that he knew what it was like to be in pain. I silently whispered a prayer of thanks to the gods of malice who had obviously heard my pleas and come up trumps. I had to rub it in. I didn't even need to tell him about my forthcoming nuptials, Simon's life was falling apart, and that was all that mattered.

'What's her name,' I asked, wondering what kind of girl could bring the mighty, magnificent Simon to his knees.

He took a long drag on his cigarette. 'Kate,' he said. 'Her name's Kate.'

The world's not that small. Of course it was her. I checked all the details. Where did she go to university? The University of North London. What was her surname? Freemans – like in the catalogue. What colour was her hair? Reddy brown. What was her favourite film? *Gregory's Girl*. Where did she live? If I had any hope at all that our Kate Freemans were similar but separate Kate Freemans, cast into the public arena by the gods of fate just to pull my plonker more than was necessary or indeed, healthy, Simon's answers crushed it instantly. Kate had lived in my flat. When Simon had dumped her she'd told him that she was going to leave London. As I was in need of a flat Simon, callous bastard that he was, had passed this information on to me but lied about his source. He asked me why I was asking all these questions so I lied, and said it was because I thought it was really funny. I put the phone down and fell into a deep shock.

> *Kate and Simon.*
> *Kate and Simon.*
> *Kate and Simon.*
> *Kate and sodding Simon.*

The whole concept was too much to bear. It was impossible

even to begin to comprehend the sheer scale of devastation Simon's revelation was wreaking inside me. I just couldn't face it. So I didn't. I locked 'Kate and sodding Simon' in a box marked 'Just don't – all right?' and tossed it into the darkest corner of my mind, promising myself on pain of death that I would never go there. Some might call it denial but the only word I had for it was survival.

I needed a diversion and I needed one quick. I turned on the radio. *The Barbara White Show* had just started. She was telling the listeners (aka 'you gorgeous people') they were the most important part of the show: 'You can have the best experts in the world,' she said drooling over each word, 'the best Agony Aunt money can buy, but without you and your problems, it doesn't mean a thing.'

'. . . and thank you, Patricia. I hope everything works out okay for you and the children. Okay, next on the line is Will, from Archway, North London. Hi, Will, or is it William? You're through to *The Barbara White Show*. What can I do to help you?'

'Hi,' I said nervously. I looked around the room for something to drink. There was a tiny splash of yesterday's tequila in a Tupperware cup that hadn't been cleared away. I took a swig. 'You can call me Will, Barbara.'

'I know you feel nervous,' gushed Barbara. 'I am too. Just tell your story in your own time.'

It was an utterly inane thought, but it suddenly occurred to me that she really did sound like she did on the radio. I took another sip of tequila, coughed and wondered what the thousands of listeners 'out there' thought I sounded like. When I was a kid I used to cup hands behind my ears and try and imagine what I sounded like to other people. It never worked, not unless of course I actually did sound hollow and echoey.

Barbara mechanically peppered my narrative with reassuring 'uh-huhs' and the odd 'hmmm yes' – the same as she did with every caller – but as soon as I said the word 'marriage' she abandoned auto-Barbara.

'Will, let me stop you there!' exclaimed Barbara. 'I need a recap!' She let out a sigh of mock exasperation. 'So let me get this straight! You got a call from the girl who used to live in your flat and after a couple of hours of conversation you've decided to get married?'

'That's right,' I said, pleased at having got her attention.

'Will, let me tell you, this is a wonderful story!' She clapped her hands and let out a little whoop of joy, the kind only Americans could get away with. 'So let me guess, you're worried that you might not be doing the right thing, huh?'

'Yeah, that's right,' I said, considerably less smugly than before, because I was now feeling more than a little bit stupid and exposed.

'Can I ask you when you first realised that you liked this girl?' asked Barbara.

I considered her question. It was hard to believe it was only a few hours ago. *This morning I was me and now I'm someone else*, I thought to myself. *Or is it this morning I was someone else and now I'm me?*

'Some time this afternoon,' I said staring around the room until I located what I was looking for. 'It wasn't anything in particular that she said.' I put Kate's photo up on the wall next to my bed with Blu-tac. 'Something clicked in my head and I knew she was the one.' The Kate in my photo smiled down at me radiantly.

'Can I ask you how old you are?' enquired Barbara.

Barbara, I felt, was suddenly beginning to get on my nerves. Her fake politeness, accent and probing, grated against me immensely. 'Yeah,' I said, almost spitting. 'I'm twenty-six. Today's my birthday.'

'Many happy returns for the day,' said Barbara paying no heed at all to my annoyance. 'Have you ever been in a long-term relationship before?'

My anger subsided. 'I went out with a girl for three years from roughly when I was twenty to when I was twenty-three,' I said, hoping she wouldn't ask for Aggi's name.

'Was it a mutual break-up?'

I wanted to lie. I needed to lie.

'No,' I said remorsefully. 'She wanted out of the relationship. I think she wanted more freedom. Maybe I was boring her, I don't know. I loved her a lot. I thought she was the one, but I could never get her to think long-term. She got over me straight away, which really hurt. She got on with her life as if I was a minor interruption.'

I'm pleased I've told the truth, I thought. *It's another sign that I have changed. The old me is dead. Long live the new me!*

'Is there anything else I should know?' asked Barbara.

I paused before answering and wondered what kind of details she required. Simon and Kate's box rattled in its secret hideaway. I ignored it.

'She also got off with my best mate while she was going out with me,' I confessed, picturing Aggi and Simon in an embrace. I wondered, too, if I ought to have explained the phrase 'get off' but decided against it. 'I only found this out yesterday.' I paused again. 'Oh, and she also dumped me three years ago today.'

'She dumped you on your birthday? That must've been terrible,' sympathised Barbara.

'It was,' I replied.

'Have you dated other people since?'

'I didn't for the first year,' I confessed. 'I couldn't face even thinking about other girls. In the last two years I've been out with a few, some of them I quite liked too.'

'Can I ask you what went wrong with these relationships?'

'I don't know.' A montage of ex-girlfriends' faces swirled inside my mind. What a question! It would have been easier to tell Barbara the meaning of life than to work out what had gone wrong with them all. I knew the problem was always me, but what it was *about* me I didn't know. 'They fizzled out, or they had to move away,' I told Barbara while still trying to figure it out. 'I thought I was cursed for a while.' I conjured up a reason. 'I think it all went wrong because at the back of my mind I always thought to myself, what would I do if the girl I loved came back and I was going out with someone else? I suppose that's why they all failed.'

'Will, can I stop you there? We're just due for a commercial break. You hang on the line and we'll talk to you just after this . . .'

I was forced to listen to four adverts: Double glazing, a specialist bed company, an athlete's foot cream and an agency that you pay to pay your bills for you. This was hell. I was in hell. I had sunk this low. I wanted to put the phone down but couldn't. This was the first time I'd told anyone the full story. The director's cut of My Life with all the scenes my parents didn't want to know about, and the scenes my friends wouldn't have understood.

'Before the break,' announced Barbara, 'we were talking to Will, from North London, who has asked a girl he's never met to marry him after speaking to her on the phone on Friday. Will, can you continue your story?'

'What else do you want to know?' I asked.

'Why do you think that this relationship will work when all the others failed because of how you felt about your ex?'

'I wasn't sure about that either,' I admitted. 'Which is why I phoned her up this afternoon.'

Barbara could barely contain her excitement. 'What did you say to her? Did you tell her that you were getting married?'

'No. I called her . . .' I paused, searching for the right way to say it. 'I called her to give her one last chance. I didn't tell her that, but that's what the call was about.'

'How did she respond?'

'Well, I hadn't spoken to her for three years. She's living in London with her boyfriend.' I added absent-mindedly: 'She was surprised to hear from me.'

'But how did she respond?' repeated Barbara eagerly.

I stared vacantly into the bottom of the empty Tupperware beaker in my hand. 'I don't know. I think I managed to get her back up. I was fed up that the fact that I'd been a major part of her life for three years didn't mean a thing. I ended up being a bit sarcastic, I suppose.'

'And she didn't stand for it? How did you feel after the call?'

'Devastated. All this time I'd been thinking that there might be a chance that we would get back together . . .'

Barbara interrupted. She couldn't wait to get stuck into that one. 'What made you think that? Did she tell you that?'

'Well . . . no, not really,' I replied. 'She'd told me it was over and that there was no chance that we'd ever get back together,' I said blankly, realising how stupid it all sounded.

'So why did you think that you'd get back together?'

Barbara, in her own 'subtle' way was trying to imply that I was stupid for living a lie, and she was right. I helped her out.

'I don't know,' I said. 'I'm stupid. Perhaps I'm an optimist. I don't know. It's three years today that we split up. I suppose she was on my mind.'

'So, Will, this girl you're going to marry, does she know about all this?'

'She knows about my ex,' I said. 'But she doesn't know that I called her today.'

'Why didn't you tell her?' asked Barbara.

'Because . . . because . . . because,' I paused and examined the empty Tupperware beaker again. 'I . . . er . . . don't know . . . okay . . . er . . . I do know.' I gave up. 'I didn't tell her because then she'd think that I only asked her to marry me because my ex didn't want me back.'

'But isn't that the case?' asked Barbara accusingly, sounding for all the world like a hot-shot lawyer in a court room drama.

'No,' I stumbled. 'Well, yes. But it isn't as simple as that. I had to know one way or the other about my ex in order to get on with my life. I must have had the idea of marrying my new girl in my head all the time. I knew that it wouldn't work if there was a chance I could get back with my ex. I needed to know that my ex didn't want me so I could get on with my life, otherwise I'd just keep thinking about her.'

'Round and round,' said Barbara wearily. 'Just like a roundabout in a children's playground. So what would've happened if your ex had said that she'd take you back?'

'I probably would've gone back to her,' I confessed dejectedly.

'And what about this girl that you were going to marry forever and ever, forsaking all others 'til death do you part?'

'I suppose I wouldn't have married her.'

'How can you consider marriage to someone if there's another partner who looms so large in your past, Will?' asked Barbara.

She had hit the nail on the head. I got out of bed to take a look out of the window because my room felt like it was shrinking. My knees started to buckle before I could reach my destination and so, instead of continuing my journey, I opted to sit on the floor under my own steam before gravity came into force.

'After all that time I'd invested worshipping that woman,' I told Barbara, 'don't you think I owed it to myself to try and get her back? I'm glad she doesn't want me. I want to move on. And now I can.'

'Will, do you want to know what I think?' offered Barbara. 'I think that your ex has confused you so much you don't know whether you're coming or going. Sometimes when you're the partner that has been left, you find it hard to get on with life. You ask yourself the question "Why aren't they hurting as much as I am?" It's not unusual for people in this situation to see hope in the relationship when there is none. I did it myself with my ex-husband. After we divorced I felt that if I was there for him one day he'd realise that he needed me like I needed him. Do you know what happened? He married a girl half my age and invited me to the wedding because he thought I was over him! Can you believe the nerve of that guy? I understand how you're feeling, Will, more than you know. But you've got to ask yourself, why do you want to marry this girl?'

I surveyed my tiny room. I had my answer. 'Because she's made me realise that I can move on. I can finally live my life and think about the future.'

'Marriage is a big step,' said Barbara. 'I know that this girl sounds like the answer to your problems, and she may well be. But I think you've got to ask yourself why this girl you've never seen is so important to you. This kind of thing happens all the time, Will. I had a caller last week who thought she'd fallen in love with the man she ordered office stationery from. When you're on the phone you can be someone different. You can flirt and have fun, secure in the knowledge that you don't have to meet this person face to face.'

'It's not like that,' I protested.

'I'm not saying it is, Will. But what I am saying is that you have to check that it's not. Can I give you some advice? Try and work out whether you've really been *you* on the phone or whether you've been the *you* you wish you were. The girl at the end of the phone is in love with the person she spoke to. But will she be in love with you?'

A gust of wind blew a heavy sheet of rain against the window. Kate and Simon were making another attempt to escape from their box. I shivered. I placed the receiver on the floor and cradled my head in my hands. In less than half an hour Barbara had managed to crumble my rock solid faith into dust.

'Right, that's all we've got time for, Will,' said a tinny sounding Barbara from the floor. 'Thanks for calling. Please, please, call me, Barbara White on *The Barbara White Show*, in the next couple of weeks and tell me and the listeners at home what happened. We found your story riveting.'

1.13 A.M.

The doorbell awoke me from a nightmare in which I was a US Marine being held prisoner in a bamboo hut by a combination of the Vietcong and Aggi. At least I thought it was the doorbell. As no one had rung it during my week's residency it was hard to know exactly what the noise could be. I attempted to ignore it, assuming it was just some dipsomaniac Archway dropout playing funny buggers, and hoped that they'd get bored before I'd be forced to go downstairs and throw water over them. It continued, long, shrill, angry bursts of doorbell for minutes at a time. I stared at the television and wondered if the TV licence people had the technology to monitor TV sets even when they were off. What can I say? It was 1.15 a.m. and I wasn't really thinking straight. I turned over and pulled the duvet over my head. The TV licence people could just sod off too.

Consciousness was once again slipping from me, taking with it the worries of the day, when there was a knock at the door. I checked my watch again. It was now 1.23 a.m. Someone had either let the dipsomaniac dropout in or I was about to get fined £600 for having a TV in my room that was switched off. I pulled the duvet up a bit higher, determined to ditch reality as soon as possible before it all got too much. This time, the rain of blows that smashed against the door nearly took it off its hinges. I crawled out of bed, not even bothering to put on any sort of proper clothing, pulled the door slightly ajar and peered through the gap. The woman from downstairs (she of the Garfield slippers) peered back at me angrily. She wasn't wearing her usual towelling dressing gown. Instead she had on these fluffy sky blue pyjamas with elasticated ankles that made her look like she was wearing a romper suit. Her face was all red and blotchy and her hair was flying off in all directions. Honestly, it would have been impossible for anyone, even the angriest man in Angryland, to have looked more thoroughly enraged.

Peppering the rather short question, 'Do you know what time it is?', with an unfeasibly large number of expletives, Garfield woman began tearing strips off me. Bewildered as I was at being woken up in the middle of the night, I couldn't resist the opportunity to indulge in a spot of neighbour baiting. 'You're banging on my door because you haven't got a watch, you mad cow? Away with you before I call the police!'

She didn't laugh. In fact I was sure that if the door had been open any wider, I would've received a swift Garfield in the crotch.

'It's not enough that you never take your turn with the fire alarm, now you want me to be your personal man-servant! Next time, pal, answer the bloody doorbell when it's for you!'

I attempted to look suitably chastised but in reality I think I probably just looked puzzled. 'I take my turn with the fire alarm! If it's fire alarms you're moaning about, ask the bloke over there,' I pointed across the landing, 'that bugger's never done it.' The expression on her face was one of purest anger. I attempted to calm her down. 'Look, I don't know what you're on about, okay? There was some mad person ringing my bell too, but as I don't know any mad people I reasoned that it couldn't have been for me.'

'I think I can explain,' said a voice just to the side of Garfield woman. 'I thought I'd got the wrong number. I rang this woman's doorbell by accident after you didn't answer yours.'

I opened the door a little wider to take a look at the mystery woman. It was Aggi.

I looked her up and down, not believing my eyes. She was wearing black leggings and a purple kind of smock thing. Her hair was messy. While she wore an expression as uncompromising as Garfield woman's she was still as beautiful as ever.

'I think you'd better come in,' I said warily. I threw a stern look in Garfield woman's direction in case she thought the invitation included her.

Aggi came in, closing the door behind her, but remained standing. I sat down on the bed and felt ludicrously self-conscious. Not only was I wearing nothing but boxer shorts and odd socks, but they happened to be a green pair with Subutteo sized golfers all over them, a farewell gift from my mother. What's more, there was nowhere for the flab around my midriff to hide, so instead it just hung there dejectedly, waiting for me to get The Message. This was the way that the love of my life saw me for the first time in three years – looking like a bucket of lard in novelty underwear. While I pulled on a T-shirt, Aggi averted her eyes, content to gaze despondently around the room, admiring the decor and saying nothing.

I finished dressing, looked up and smiled. 'Hello.'

Aggi's face suddenly contorted with anger as if she'd just turned on a switch marked 'Screaming Mad Banshee

Woman from Hell'. I was scared. The kind of woman that could get angry at a slightly overweight but cuddly bloke in silly boxer shorts, was the kind of woman that would get a six month discharge after pleading temporary insanity.

'I am sooooo angry,' she screamed.

I winced, assuming that she was still smarting from the comments made in regard to her popularity with sportsmen. I considered reminding her that I was wearing glasses but thought better of it.

'Toby wanted to kill you, you know. He wants to smash your face in, and he would, you know. He knows how weird you are. He's waiting in the car outside so don't get any ideas into that warped head of yours.'

'Is he a solicitor?' I asked timidly.

'Yes,' she spat.

'Does he play rugby?'

'Every weekend.'

'Oh,' I said.

I felt about this small, which is to say just a bit smaller than a gnat's knackers. It was like being scolded by my mum, only worse because I didn't have any trousers on and well, my mum would never threaten to get her boyfriend to beat me up, even if she had one. The only good thing was that as far as I could gather, Aggi's boyfriend hadn't told her exactly what I'd said, although I was sure she'd heard enough to get the general impression. It was totally embarrassing. Aggi was unrelenting in her attack – she paced the room saying all kind of nasty and venomous things about me all of which, unfortunately, were true. Every sentence she said began with 'How dare you . . .' I didn't have a leg to stand on. I'd phoned her out of the blue three years after I had any right to and assassinated her character in front of her boyfriend, who could clearly beat me to a pulp with both arms tied behind his back. It was ridiculous. I sat there, head bowed, and took it, if not like a man, then the nearest approximation I could conjure up – a creature half adolescent and half sheep.

When I thought she'd finished I looked up. But I was disappointed to discover that she was far from finished. 'If you ever try and contact me by phone, letter or even try and send me bad vibes, I will go to the police, you bastard. Don't think I won't!'

She turned and opened the door without even looking at me. *This is it, this is her hello and good-bye. Surely I deserve more than this*? It was better to have her shouting at me in my flat than living in the knowledge that the second she walked out all memory of me would be wiped clean – she'd ditch the lot. The good and the bad. It was too terrible to contemplate because if I didn't exist in her head then I didn't exist at all.

'What about you and Simon?' I said, in a manner ranking lower than mumbling.

She turned around, her hand still on the door handle, the expression on her face puzzled. 'What?'

I coughed and studied the soles of my feet. I had a verruca the size of a five pence piece on my heel that I'd never seen before. Without looking up I repeated the question. 'I said, what about you and Simon?'

Slowly she came back in and closed the door carefully with both hands, crossed the room and sat down next to me on the bed.

'He told you, then?'

I nodded.

'When did he tell you?'

'Yesterday.'

'Why did he tell you?'

'Because he's in love.'

Aggi's eyes filled slowly with reluctant tears. I watched them roll down her perfect nose, along the edge of her perfect upper lip and onto her perfect chin. I didn't want her to cry. Everyone was crying this weekend.

'I never meant to hurt you, Will.'

'But you did.'

'It just happened. I was angry that you weren't there.'

I swallowed hard. 'So you got off with my best mate.'

'It was just sex. I didn't love him. It didn't happen again.'

'Does that make a difference?'

She was staring into her lap now, but she met my eyes briefly and said: 'No. I suppose not. At least not to you.'

I edged away from her and began to shake, as if just being in her proximity would cause irrevocable damage. Here she was sitting in my room reminding me of a betrayal that, though it had happened years ago, was as fresh in my mind as if it had happened yesterday – which in a way it had. 'I worshipped you from the moment we met. I adored you. You were all that I wanted. What did I do wrong?'

She started crying. I put my arms around her shoulders. Holding her felt exactly the same. Nothing had changed. It was like travelling to the past in the present – none of it seemed real. I tried to brush away her tears but she just cried even more into my neck, making the collar of my T-shirt damp. She lifted up her head and stared right into my eyes.

'I'm sorry, Will. I'm so sorry.'

I didn't say anything. I wasn't trying to be the martyr, I just didn't have anything to say. She looked so pitiful, her eyes were red and puffy. All I wanted to do was make everything all right.

'You know me. I've never regretted anything,' she said, 'and don't think for a minute that I regret ending our relationship. I don't. We were dead. Going nowhere. But if I could have my time again I would never have done that to you. You don't need to tell me that you loved me. I always knew it. You were my best friend for those three years, Will. I can never repay you for all the wonderful things you did for me. I don't know . . .'

Her words trailed off as she buried her face into my shoulder. I looked down at the top of her head, studying her crown sadly. In a perverse sort of way it was almost worth letting Simon sleep with her just to know that after all this time she really did care – albeit in an abstract fashion. She hadn't forgotten – there was some small part of her that cared enough about me to believe in the concept of regret. I was locked in her head – the one thing she could never get over. This was beautiful. This was more than I could ever have hoped for.

Aggi gradually lifted her head up until her eyes were directly in line with mine, her lips parted, her nose barely an inch away from mine and her head tilted in that magical manner that only ever means one thing. I cast a glance at the door, I couldn't help myself, my thoughts had already raced downstairs in fear that fifteen stone of rugby playing brute was about to burst in and beat me to a pulp. Aggi, seeing my distress, pressed her index finger up to my lips. 'I lied,' she said. 'I just didn't want you to get the wrong idea.'

And then she kissed me.

All at once the universe seemed to make sense. The weight of the world was no longer on my shoulders. This was the feeling that I'd been pining for all this time, and yes it was worth the wait. I couldn't kiss her fast enough. I kissed her face, her hands, her neck – everywhere that was available – but within seconds I was overwhelmed by feelings twice as powerful, twice as destructive and twice as painful as those I'd just experienced.

I pulled away from her in shock. 'I can't do this.'

'I told you Toby isn't here.'

I shook my head. 'It's got nothing to do with him. It's to do with me. *I* can't do this. *I* can't cheat on Kate.'

Aggi's face changed immediately. All the sadness seeped away leaving an expression of quiet defiance. 'Is Kate your girlfriend?' she asked with a touch of sarcasm clearly evident in her voice.

'No,' I replied. 'She's my fiancée.'

I explained the whole story to her even though it hardly made sense to me any more. She nodded at the appropriate moments and laughed at a few inappropriate ones. When I finished I could see that she still didn't believe me. *Seven days ago I wouldn't have either.* I weighed up the situation:

Aggi	Kate
Aggi was here in my room.	Kate was in Brighton.
I'd known Aggi six years.	I'd known Kate two days.
I knew every detail of Aggi's body.	
	I knew every detail of Kate's photo.
I loved Aggi.	But I loved Kate even more.

There was no explanation or rationalisation except to say

that it wasn't guilt talking, it was me. It wasn't that I was over Aggi – three years of intense high-level obsession does not disappear overnight – but it was like this: I'd thought Aggi was the ceiling of my love but Kate had shown me there was something even higher. Overwrought? Yes. Melodramatic? Possibly. The brain-addled words of a troubled soul in love with love itself? No.

'So that's the way it is,' I said after some moments of very uncomfortable silence.

Aggi laughed. 'I can't believe you're doing this, Will. I really can't. But don't insult my intelligence with your pathetic stories. I knew you were bitter but I didn't know it ran this deep.' She stood up, straightening her top and wiping the stray mascara from her cheeks. 'I suppose it's what I deserve. Well, the score's even now. I'll never have to feel guilty about sleeping with Simon again and you get your imaginary girlfriend.'

I looked up at her dejectedly from the bed. 'Yeah, whatever.'

MONDAY

5.45 A.M.

For a few seconds the end of the world was no longer nigh – it had arrived. I, as fully expected, had gone to hell and besides not being quite as warm as I expected, the most notable thing about Hades was that it was very noisy and looked like my flat. I glanced at my watch, it was 5.45. Monday morning. Thanks to Mr F. Jamal's dodgy smoke alarm, The Rest of My Life had begun an hour earlier than anticipated. In less than five hours I'd be in Brighton with Kate, and the smoke alarm, flat, Archway, Wood Green Comprehensive, Italian newsagent's, Simon, Aggi and everything else that sought to rain on my parade would be nothing more than a bad dream.

The fire alarm stopped ringing.

The front door belonging to one of my downstairs neighbours slammed loudly, the vibrations causing my windows to rattle. Peace was restored. I bathed in the silence.

Today is going to be the adventure of my life.

This was the kind of thrill I'd been looking for all my life, a book with an ending you couldn't guess – a Rolf Harris sketch that you couldn't work out until he'd scribbled in the last details with his squeaky marker pen.

Last week I could have predicted my every movement down to the very last detail weeks in advance. 10.00 a.m. Tuesday – English with my year eights. 8.15 a.m.

331

Wednesday – running up to the school gates attempting to finish early morning cigarette. 11.00 p.m. Friday – in bed asleep dreaming about ex-girlfriend. Now thanks to Kate I don't have a clue what's about to happen to me, but at least I know who it will happen with. Security and adventure – the best of both worlds.

The duvet, which had slipped off the bed during the night, was lying perilously close to the ice-cream stain in the carpet that had refused to die. I pulled it back on the bed, tucking the edges underneath my bum to form a misshapen cocoon, with my head poking out from the top. The draught coming through the windows, seemingly unhindered by the curtains, indicated that the day of my emancipation was a cold one. Straining intensely, I listened out for any other meteorological news. There was no mistaking the gentle yet unrelenting tapping of drizzle against window pane.

My thoughts automatically turned to breakfast but excitement caused by the day's forthcoming events constricted my stomach to a tight ball of muscle – no Sugar Puffs or Honey Nut Flakes, frozen bread or toast without margarine would make it in there today.

In the bathroom, Audrey Hepburn, hand aloft, cigarette-holder drooping daintily from her fingers, greeted me with her usual wistful smile. As I closed the door behind me I turned on the light, positively encouraging the extractor fan to lurch back into life. While in the shower I occupied my mind trying to imagine the Kate in the photo on my wall in three dimensions. Post-shower, I dried myself off using the Towel, wandered into the kitchen and dropped it into the bin. For some, redemption was out of the question.

Cold and naked I stood on the bed to prevent dust, dirt and carpet fibres clinging to my damp feet and meditated on what to wear. First impressions, I reasoned, counted for an awful lot, in spite of what Kate had said. I wanted her to be attracted to me the moment she saw me so that there could be no doubt in her mind that she had made the right decision. Following several changes of clothes I went with a pair of navy blue trousers that I'd bought from Jigsaw's summer sale – a minor blip in my strictly second-hand policy – and an ancient chalk blue Marks and Spencer shirt with huge collars purchased from Aggi's Oxfam. I examined my ensemble in the largest shard of broken Elvis mirror I could find: I looked good enough to eat.

Checking my watch, I began hurriedly packing my rucksack, throwing in the remainder of clean underwear – roughly three pairs of pants. I say roughly, because I had included a black pair that my mum had purchased when I was younger than some of the kids I teach now. It had been my intention to go to the launderette over the weekend – it had been one of the things To Do – which, sadly, I never even got around to thinking about let alone doing. I threw in an assortment of T-shirts and jumpers, and cursed my lack of clean socks, throwing in a couple of dirty ones instead, swiftly followed by my duty free cigarettes and picture of Sandy the donkey. My eyes scanned the room in search of things I might have forgotten, while in my head I ticked off a mental list of things I usually forgot: toothbrushes, soap, shampoo – stuff that Kate would be bound to have in her flat. Thinking about Kate reminded me of her cheque. I slipped it into the side pocket of the rucksack.

Sitting on the edge of the bed, staring at the ceiling, I attempted to prepare myself mentally for the day ahead. A radio alarm clock in the next door flat went off and Thin Lizzy's 'Waiting For An Alibi' broke my concentration. A random thought entered my head: I wondered whether I ought to take a present for Kate. Within five minutes this thought had taken precedence over all others and turned itself into a national emergency. I scrambled around the flat searching for something that might constitute a present. My eyes fell on my *Star Wars* video. If she liked *Gregory's Girl*, I said to myself – my reasoning faculties had all but disappeared by now – then she'd probably like *Star Wars*. Genuinely at a loss for a better present, I dropped it into the rucksack and made a mental note to look out for a florist's at Victoria Station.

Ready to brave the elements and with my essentials on my shoulders I took a final look at what I was leaving behind. This flat which had been my worst enemy for over a week now felt like a close friend. We'd shared good times, bad times and mad times. But somehow I was grateful to it.

I was halfway down the stairs before I got the feeling I'd forgotten something important. I tried to fight it – after all, Lot's wife had been turned into a pillar of salt – but the feeling would not subside. I returned to the flat. I checked that the lights were off. They were. I checked the cooker was off. It was. I checked the toaster was unplugged. It wasn't. As I unplugged it I laughed to myself. I had finally become my mother. Every family holiday as far back as I could remember always commenced with the ritual of my mum running around the house maniacally unplugging household electrical items. 'If the house gets struck by lightning,' she used to say, 'anything plugged in will go up in flames and burn the house down.'

Before closing the door I glanced down at the phone. The answering machine wasn't switched on. After rectifying the situation I closed the door, walked out of the flat and stepped into a brand new day.

1.48 P.M.

'Right,' I said, addressing my year eights as they shuffled into the classroom, knocking over chairs, tables and anything else that stood in their paths, 'get out your copies of *Wuthering Heights*, please, and turn to where we left off on Friday.' This simple request resulted in a flurry of fruitless activity: Kitty Wyatt, a tiny mousy-haired girl whose diminutive stature and continually flushed cheeks gave her a remarkable similarity to a garden gnome, ran out of the room crying, swiftly followed by her friend Roxanne Bright-Thomas, who informed me that Kitty was having 'women's problems'. Colin Christie, a thug whose reputation preceded him all the way to the staff room, and the child most likely to have spat on my back, hadn't got his book and was locked in a struggle with Liam Fennel who, quite rightly, wasn't pleased that his own copy was being forcefully commandeered. I ignored them all.

'Lawrence,' I said, pointing to an overweight boy sitting next to the radiator by the window, 'I do believe it's your turn to read today.'

'But, sir,' he complained, 'I read last week!'

'And you did such a good job of it that I'm going to get you to do it again this week,' I replied tersely.

He was right, of course, he had read last week but given the mood I was in since returning from Victoria Station, I

335

didn't really care about being fair, nor was I ever likely to.

As Lawrence commenced reading and the class settled down into some semblance of peace, I sat down at my desk and took the opportunity to gaze out of the window and study the afternoon sky. In spite of earlier meteorological activities, the day had in fact turned out very pleasantly indeed: the sun shone brightly through the oaks, ashes and silver birches lining the playing fields, cottonwool clouds were dotted about the heavens, even the oases of grass amongst the sea of mud that constituted the football pitch appeared to have an added lustre to them. I opened the window to let a little air in. *Today*, I thought, as the dark clouds of depression slowly lifted from me, *is a day possibly worth living.*

I'd actually been sitting on my freedom train. Not at the ticket office or even the platform – on the sodding train – rucksack in the rack above my head; in my right hand, the latest issue of the *New Statesman* (working that 'I give a toss about politics' look to the max), a Marlboro Light in the other and both feet resting on the seat opposite. I was literally five minutes from leaving Victoria Station and fifty-five minutes from becoming the happiest man alive. But it had felt all wrong. Not right. Just All Wrong.

I tried not to think about it. I looked out of the window, speed-read an article on European federalism, counted the change in my pocket but nothing could shake this feeling. Within minutes I was back on the platform watching the last carriage of the 8.55 to Brighton disappear into the hazy distance.

I called Kate. Dialling her number felt as natural and as necessary as breathing. I almost forgot why I was calling her – I just wanted to hear her voice. It was some time before she answered. She was just on her way to meet me – too excited to wait any longer – and she'd heard the phone ring just as she closed the door. She'd rushed back thinking the worst – that I'd had an accident and was calling her from hospital, or even worse, that the police had found her number on the body of an unidentified corpse in the Thames. I was sorry to disappoint her.

Straight to the point was what the situation called for, any side-stepping of issues was only going to cause more pain in the long run. I took a long, slow breath and patted all over my body trying to locate my cigarettes. 'Kate . . . Listen, Kate. You know that I love you, don't you? I love you more than anything, but I've got to ask you something. I need to know this: if your ex-boyfriend wanted you back would you want to be with him and not me?'

She was honest enough to mull over the question, which many, myself included, would never have dared. It was strange, she had become so used to the more bizarre aspects of my personality that the question and its abruptness didn't faze her for a second. I was odd but she loved me. I was bordering on being unhinged and she didn't care.

She took her time, which was nice of her. She really was weighing up her answer, in spite of the fact that I was so obviously the low fat option. She'd loved Simon so fervently that it would be impossible for her to lie without my knowing. Her love for him hadn't fermented into bitterness. Neither had she stopped loving him. She'd simply filed her love away in a box similar to the one I'd put her and Simon in, and now it was open there could be no stopping it.

'Will, I don't know why you're putting yourself through this. I love you. Nothing's changed since yesterday. My ex isn't going to come back to me. I haven't got a clue where he is. He could be anywhere. And he certainly hasn't got any way of contacting me. There's no point in discussing it, Will. Don't you see? We've been let down by other people but finally we've got someone that we trust. We've got each other.'

I was silent. I was right. I lit a cigarette and slipped another fifty pence piece into the pay-phone. Over the station Tannoy a nasally voiced BR employee announced: 'This is a reminder: Victoria Station is a no-smoking zone.' I returned my mind to the call. I could think of nothing more to say.

'Will, don't go all moody on me now,' said Kate anxiously. 'We're nearly there. You'll be getting on the train. I'll meet you and everything will be all right.'

I wanted to believe her. 'All right?'

She sighed lightly. 'All right.'

I checked my timetable for the next departure. There was another train at 9.35. I slipped the timetable back into my pocket, then took it out, screwed it up and tossed it on the floor. I wouldn't be on the 9.35 or any other train.

'No, it won't,' I said in response to her efforts to comfort me. 'Everything will not be all right. It's not happening, Kate. It's over.'

'Will, don't do this,' she said, trying to stop herself from crying. 'Don't do this. It's not fair. It's not fair. If Aggi told you she wanted you back you'd be there in a shot, wouldn't you? You can't deny it!'

'No. I can't,' I lied. 'And neither can you. But at least you've got hope.'

Kate didn't understand. 'Will, what's this all about?'

Leaning against the back of the telephone booth I slipped gradually to the floor as the will to remain upright left me. The person in the booth next to me, a middle-aged balding man with a sad, pathetic boyishness about his face looked at me with a puzzled expression. I met his eyes – not defiantly, not even passively – I just met them. He removed his gaze straight away and turned his back on me. I returned my attention to the phone.

'Your ex-boyfriend,' I began lifelessly. 'His name's Simon Ashmore. He's in a band – Left Bank. He used to be my best friend. He's not now. He wants you back. He says he's sorry. He says he loves you.'

Kate began to cry. I stood up. I wanted to run after the train just so I could be there to make everything okay.

'But he said he hated me. He said he never wanted to see me again. Why's he come back into my life?'

'Because he loves you.'

'But I love you,' she said.

'And I love you and will always love you. But this isn't meant to be. It's not just about love. You said that love's a random act. It's true, it can happen anywhere at any time with anyone. But this, this is about being in love with the right person – the right person doesn't come along twice in a lifetime. You've found yours, and it's Simon, and that makes me happy.'

She cried her heart out. I told her his number but she wasn't in a state to listen. When she finally regained her composure I had to wait listening to the sound of telephone static in one ear and London commuters in the other while she searched for a pencil. I gave it to her again. She cried some more. I was determined not to make a scene – I didn't want there to be any guilt, but neither did I want to belittle the selflessness of this act – so I held back my tears as best I could, which was right up to the moment when she said: 'I'll miss you forever.'

And then I broke down.

The balding man was so intrigued by my sobbing that he chanced another glance in my direction. Our eyes met but

I saw through him, through the telephone booth, through Victoria Station and through London – out into the world at large and the everyday activities that make up people's lives. This was the end. Through my tears and sobs I heard the pips. I searched maniacally for coins but found none and so resigned myself to saying good-bye in the seven seconds that remained.

'Sir, I've finished the chapter. Shall I start the next one?'

Six.
Five.

'Er, Mr Kelly?'

Four.

'Sir! Mr Kelly!'

Three.
Two.
One.

'Mr Kelly! I've finished!'

End of call.

'Sir! Sir! Mr Kelly!'

Lawrence had stopped reading and was now trying to get my attention by waving his arms.

'What do you want?' I barked, annoyed that he'd disturbed my train of thought.

'I've finished the chapter, sir,' he said hesitantly. 'Shall I carry on?'

I stood up and approached the blackboard at the front of the classroom. A brief gust of wind caught the letter of resignation I'd been working on and sent it spiralling to the floor. I hastily put it back on the desk and commanded my pupils' attention.

'You've just heard Lawrence read one of the most famous passages in English Literature on the subject of love,' I said, carefully examining their expressions to see whether Ms Brontë had managed to penetrate their stony hearts. 'Catherine Earnshaw has just explained to her servant, Nelly, the difference between her love for Linton and her love for Heathcliff. What, if anything, has this made any of you feel?'

A wall of thirty-two pairs of eyes returned my gaze blankly. I was alone on this one.

'Okay, so that probably *is* asking a little too much of you,' I said, surprised that my sense of humour was still functioning. 'Cathy's talking about two types of love here: the first is her love for Linton which she says is "like the foliage in the woods. Time will change it. I'm well aware. As winter changes the trees."' I paused, studying the activities of my students: Kevin Rossiter was scraping the inside of his ear with a plastic pen lid, Sonya Pritchard and Emma Anderson (now quite ordinary girls in their school clothing) were passing notes to each other and Colin Christie was attempting to suck back a carefully manufactured thread of spittle all the way from his chin to his mouth. 'But,' I continued wearily, 'her love for Heathcliff was like "the eternal rocks beneath. A source of little delight but essential." Now here's the good bit; she says, "Nelly, I am Heathcliff!" My question to you, 8B, is this: which kind of love would you prefer?'

Although I hadn't intended it as a rhetorical question I hadn't expected anyone to answer either. In fact I was halfway to writing some suggestions on the board when a solitary arm waved diffidently in the air – it belonged to Julie Whitcomb, the girl who'd been so cruelly spurned by Clive O'Rourke on Friday. Her fellow students shuffled their chairs in order to stare at her in amazement. I smiled at her, giving her the nod to answer.

'I'd like the kind of love that lasts, sir,' she said, avoiding all eye contact. 'I'd like the kind of love that lasts forever. It doesn't matter if it's plain, it doesn't matter if it's ugly. It just has to be there.' She stopped and fixed her eyes on the novel in her hands, her face glowing redder than Kitty Wyatt's on a cold day. 'I'd have Heathcliff's love over Linton's any day, sir.'

I thanked Julie for her contribution. 'That was an excellent observation. But I have another question, 8B: what about Heathcliff in all this? I don't want to spoil the book's ending for you – but let me tell you, if you're a tall, brooding, gypsy boy made good, it isn't a happy one. The thing I'd like to ask you – a question I'll admit I don't know the answer to – is this: was he right to love her so much when he knew she'd never love him the way she loved Linton?'

'What do you mean, sir?' asked Julie.

'I mean it's all very well Cathy loving Heathcliff "like the eternal rocks beneath", but isn't he being just the teensy weensiest bit naive to think that the "higher" nature of the love they shared was in any way a substitute for having her there in his arms? Heathcliff let her marry the man who brutalised him!'

Julie Whitcomb put her hand up again, shouting, 'Sir! Sir! Sir!'

I looked around the room, there were no other signs of life.

'The thing is, sir,' began Julie, quite obviously speaking from the top of her head, 'I think that love's more complicated than we think it is. Sometimes you fall in love with someone that's just no good for you. It's not your fault and in a way it's not their fault either – it just is. And I think that's what happened here. Heathcliff fell in love with the wrong person. I . . .' She looked down at her desk sheepishly. 'Sorry, sir, I finished the whole book over the weekend, sir. It's just that once I started I couldn't stop.' I smiled at her reassuringly. 'Anyway, I like to think that Heathcliff would've found the right person if he'd only looked. I think the right person's out there for everyone, but you can only see them if you want to see them. The thing is, Heathcliff couldn't see anybody but Cathy.'

She buried her head in her book, overcome by self-consciousness. Most of the class were dumbfounded by the depth of her perception, although out of the corner of my eye I observed Kevin Rossiter sucking on the very pen lid he'd been using to clean his ears, Colin Christie eating a packet of crisps and Susie McDonnell and Zelah Wilson leaning back on their chairs whispering to each other – probably remarking how much of a twat I was.

I looked at Julie Whitcomb, so small, so helpless and yet so wise beyond her years and was moved. Here was someone who wanted to learn, someone who was reading a text and responding to it. This was why I'd become a teacher. I felt a flush of pride and wondered if I was responsible for inspiring her or whether she was merely a freak of nature.

I agreed with everything she said. It wasn't just about being in love, it was about being in love with . . .

'The right person!' I yelled aloud, thinking back to my conversation with Kate. 'You're right, Julie. It's not just about being in love. It's about being in love with the right person! The right person was there all the time! She was there all the time!'

The entire class thought I'd taken leave of my senses but as it meant that they didn't have to listen to me witter on about a book bearing as much relevance to their lives as a Latvian bus timetable, they didn't care. Smiling enthusiastically at Julie Whitcomb as I approached the classroom door I shouted, 'Carry on reading by yourselves,' and ran into the corridor in search of the nearest phone.

'I need the phone,' I said. 'It's an emergency.'

Margaret the ancient school secretary examined me with an air of studied uninterest. When I was introduced to her at the start of term the first thing she'd said to me, after looking me up and down disapprovingly, was, 'Don't think you can use the photocopier willy-nilly, young man.' Later in the week she'd point blank refused to give access to the stationery cupboard without her being there, and on Thursday she'd told me off for slouching in the corridor. She was pure evil in a tweed two-piece. There was no way she'd let me use the telephone to make a private call, even one that might change the entire course of my life.

'Is it concerning school business?' she bellowed. 'The headmaster doesn't allow private calls, you know.'

'It's a matter of life and death,' I said patiently.

'Whose life?' she replied tersely.

I studied her face: her thick grey hair in a tight bun; her mean, snaky eyes; her sallow cheeks, thin, tight lips and saggy liver spotted neck. She would've looked more compassionate if she'd been carved out of stone. Lacking the energy to even make an attempt to change her mind I ran out of the door and across the playground to the school gates. It took five minutes racing around Wood Green High Street before I finally found a telephone box that hadn't been violated by Wood Green Comprehensive kids.

I checked my watch. It was 2.24 p.m. I dialled the number and waited. It rang three times before the answering machine picked up:

Hello, you're through to Bruce and Alice . . .

I checked my watch again. Her flight wasn't until 4.00 p.m. I still had a chance. I fumbled through my phone book and found her mobile number. It rang six times before directing me to her voice mail.

I was too late.

I had no more tears left to cry. I'd finally become immune to life and was comforted by the lack of emotion. It wasn't that I didn't care – I did – I just ceased to see hope where there was none. It was a lesson I was learning three years too late, but it was necessary all the same. As I walked back into school, up the stairs and towards my classroom, I promised myself that I'd never let this happen again. Never.

As I approached the classroom door, my hand about to press down on the door handle, I noted that the rabble inside were strangely quiet. 8B were never this quiet voluntarily. I decided they were either dead or being babysat by the headmaster. For my own sake I hoped they were dead, because the only other option was that the school secretary had told the Head I'd gone mad and abandoned the class. This, I decided, was the end of the line for me and teaching.

345

I was going to get sacked for sure, which scared me even though I'd made up my mind to resign. I was half tempted to carry on walking down the corridor and go home, but cowardice, I reasoned, was just another form of denial and I'd had about as much as I could take of not facing the facts.

I opened the door and there in front of the class was Alice.

She was wearing black jeans and a dark blue fleece-lined jacket, the kind that people who participate in outdoor pursuits wear. Her hair was out of place, as if she'd been running, and her cheeks managed to look flushed in spite of her perpetual tan. She had a rucksack on her left shoulder which she was keeping in place with her right hand. She released her grip, allowing the bag to slide off her shoulder and hit the floor. She didn't look down, she just stared at me.

As I took my first step towards her my breathing started to deepen. I looked down at my hands, they were shaking. She took a step towards me, her lips tightly pursed. She put her hand to her mouth and took another step. Every second it took until we were face to face, close enough to touch, seemed too long. It was a magical moment, but for once not one that was a product of my imagination.

She wrapped her arms around me. And slowly, very slowly all the pain and worry locked within my frame flowed away. My senses were filled by her perfume, her body. We fitted together perfectly. Her face was buried into my shirt, next to my lunchtime tomato ketchup stain, the existence of which she was thankfully oblivious to. I took her hands and squeezed them gently. My hands still wouldn't stop shaking. I was terrified. Absolutely bloody terrified. And she seemed terrified too. We stood there motionless, staring at each other, hoping beyond hope that what was happening was as real as what we were feeling.

'What are you doing here?' I asked stupidly.

'I've come to save you,' she replied.

'Save me from what? Kate?'

'Lung cancer, eating biscuits in bed, growing fat and old and lonely without me.'

We both laughed.

'It's a long story but Kate is history,' I explained guiltily. 'She's history but happy.'

'And Aggi?' asked Alice, her smiling face converting to a stony seriousness.

'Aggi?' I repeated, as if I wasn't entirely sure who she was talking about.

'Yes, Aggi.'

I smiled. 'She's ancient history.'

Alice didn't laugh or for that matter return my smile.

'How can you be so sure? I've heard you say a thousand times that she was your perfect woman. You've always had such high standards when it comes to love. You were telling me only a few weeks ago that your perfect woman had to be this, had to be that – it was just short-hand for she had to be Aggi.'

'Sometimes, you're as divorced from sanity as I am,' I began, mock chastising her. 'You've got it all wrong. You are the standard. Before Aggi there was you. She had to fit *your* standard. I know I thought Aggi was The One but I was wrong. You were The Original One. She was The Wrong One. And now you're here.'

'And now I'm here,' she smiled, relaxing.

'But you know it'll never work,' I said softly.

'It's doomed from the start,' she laughed, tears gently rolling down her cheeks.

'We might as well give up now,' I said, shrugging my shoulders.

'We'd be fools not to,' she nodded.

I wiped away a tear and kissed her eyebrow. 'Friends should never be lovers.'

Standing on tiptoes she reached up and lightly pressed her lips against my ear. 'Or lovers friends.'

Colin Christie made puking noises. Sonya Pritchard and Emma Anderson shouted, 'Give her one, sir.' Kevin Rossiter flicked the pen lid he'd been cleaning his ears with at my head and Julie Whitcomb, star that she was, stood up and gave us a round of applause.

EPILOGUE

In a world where the accumulated wisdom of thousands of centuries still exists – everyone from Socrates to Saint Paul through to Freud and Stephen Hawking – it might seem crass to quote Oprah Winfrey in order to explain where I'd been going wrong in life all this time, but that's the thing about common sense, it appears in the oddest places.

I came across the nugget of wisdom in question one afternoon a couple of years ago, while I was on the dole and living at my mum's. Having just watched *Escape From The Planet of The Apes* on video for the third time that week, I happened across an episode of *Oprah*. Too lazy to change channels and, dare I say it, intrigued by the show's title: '*Men who love too much; Women who love too little*', I opened a packet of milk chocolate Hobnobs to share with my faithful hound, and settled down to enjoy the programme. As I bit into my biscuit Oprah said something so profound that I inhaled a large fragment of Hobnob, resulting in such a violent fit of coughing that I was nearly sick over poor Beveridge. This is what she said:

'Love ain't supposed to feel bad.'

Of course, like most profound statements (including the biblical 'Love your neighbour', Marshall McLuhan's 'The medium is the message' and Morecambe and Wise's 'More tea, Ern?', it made an impact on my life for approximately three seconds before it was consigned to the dustbin of history. Until now.

You see, sometimes I'll catch Alice looking at me while I'm watching TV and she'll have a huge inane grin on her face that really doesn't become her. I'll ask her what she's doing and she'll take her time before answering my question with silence. Then she'll ask me if I love her. I'll pretend to take *my* time thinking over the question and then she'll throw a cushion at me. This is my cue to tell her that I love her with all my heart (which I do), then she'll tell me that she loves me more than anything (which she does). Then it will be my turn to joke that because we're 'friends' and 'more than friends' it kind of makes her my best girlfriend. And then she'll laugh, look me in the eye in a manner which still makes me go weak at the knees and say, 'No, I'm your Legendary Girlfriend.' Whenever she makes this statement I always nod and smile in agreement – but the truth is I'm not so sure one way or the other. The one thing I am sure of is this: our love doesn't feel bad.

And that is all that matters.